Covert Ops: Shadows of Retribution

Steve Barker

Steve Barker

FIRST EDITION

Published in 2025 by

GREEN CAT BOOKS

19 St Christopher's Way

Pride Park

Derby DE24 8JY

www.greencatbooks.com

ISBN: 978-1-918028-05-8

ACKNOWLEDGEMENTS

Thank you to
George James
Simon Munnery
Derek Barker
Cody McColl

My Editor, Lisa

for their help with this book

Contents

Steve Barker

Chapter One — Meetup

Sun breaks over the Isle of Wight, slicing through mist with blades of light. A warning, not a welcome. Every shadow looks wrong. Every shape on the horizon carries weight. Peace never lasts, not for men like me.

Months have passed since I pulled my girls from the bastards on St Kitts, but vigilance holds. I've crossed to the mainland multiple times, eyes sharp, instincts sharper. No one touches my daughters again. Not without a war. Simon and George stay hidden, watching the edges. Lucy watches me. Always waiting for the next fight.

On the surface, things appear quiet. But I know better. In the world we operate in, peace isn't real—it's the pause before everything explodes again. Which reminds me, I must call Simon today. He mentioned a possible mission sometime after the last one to retrieve my kids, and I haven't heard anything since. Sure, the sunshine and time with Lucy are great, but nothing beats the adrenaline rush of a successful mission.

Finish my mid-morning coffee as Lucy comes through the front door. She's been to town to buy new clothes for next week's girls' night out with Abbie and Bethanie.

After setting down bags in the bedroom, Lucy glances at me. "You contacted Simon yet?"

"About to," I say, reaching for my mobile to prove my point. It takes several rings before Simon answers.

"Hi, Steve. What's up?"

"Nothing much. Everything's quiet on my end. I wanted to follow up on the mission you mentioned a while back. Is it still happening? Lucy's set on moving, and some extra cash will help."

"Are you a mind reader, Steve. I planned on calling you today. The contact reached out again yesterday, probing our interest. Emphasising urgency—the operation he wants us to do must happen soon. Dave, our contact warned that delays could lead to casualties."

"Any idea what the mission involves?"

"From what I can gather, this one's straightforward — an artefact pick-up, I think. He's asking to meet in the next 24 hours. Can you make it, or should I shut it down?"

"Yeah, I'm interested, and tomorrow shouldn't be a problem. Let me confirm with Lucy first, I don't want to get on her bad side. If I have any problems, I'll phone you back. In the meantime, send me any info you have on the mission and the contact."

"Will do. Give me a few minutes."

"Thanks, Simon. See you in Southampton tomorrow, if the boss gives the OK."

The call ends, and I head straight for the laptop, waiting for details from Simon to come through. While I wait, Lucy's movements catch my ear in the kitchen.

"Fancy a trip to the mainland? Meeting tomorrow with a possible client," I shout across the room.

Lucy raises a thumb, mouth too full of food to speak. Turning back to the computer, I refresh the page, and Simon's email appears at the top.

Subject: Mission Brief: Recovery of WWII Artefact

Simon,

This message comes with urgency. A critical task needs your team's sharp precision and expertise.

Objective: Extract Dr Petrov and recover a WWII artefact — failure will put dangerous power in the wrong hands.

Details: The artefact's whereabouts have stayed concealed until now. Dr Ivan Petrov, a historian of considerable repute, claims to have uncovered its location after extensive investigation. Bringing Petrov to us takes precedence at this point.

Mission Requirements:

- Assemble a covert team capable of handling high-risk operations.

- Secure Petrov and the artefact and ensure their safe transport to our facility near Basingstoke.

- Maintain operational secrecy to prevent any leaks or interference. This communication will automatically delete itself in 24 hours.

Your team's experience in this kind of mission will be crucial for success. I have confidence in your ability to oversee this operation without a hitch.

Please confirm receipt of this email and provide an estimated timeline for the mission planning phase at a meeting on Friday at 14:00 at my office. The place is easy to find. Type the firm's name into Google Maps.

Best regards,

Dave Bate

CEO, Guardian Security Solutions

South.

So we still have the info at a later date; the email hits the printer. The paper is still damp when I pass it to Lucy, who takes a few minutes, eyes scanning the page, absorbing the information.

"From this, it appears like a straightforward search and rescue. It shouldn't take much time. Make sure we secure enough dosh for the new place," Lucy remarks, after reviewing the printed copy.

While on the computer, I fire off an email to Derek. 'Get your arse over here ASAP. We've got a green light for a possible mission. You know the drill, arrange your flights and let me know the details.'

With emails sent, switch off the laptop and stare at the clock on the wall as the big hand edges toward the twelve, making the time 14:00.

Turning to Lucy, "It's another sunny day. Fancy a drink at the boozer?"

"Sounds like some sort of plan, Steve. Give me a few minutes,"

Time slips away, and soon enough, the pub stands before us, its lights flickering like a promise of good times. With a firm push, the door creaks open, unleashing the familiar aroma of worn wood and beer, a scent that clings to memories tethered to recollections best left in the shadows.

Bathed in golden light from a nearby window, the bar's polished surface glimmers, reflecting years of weary patrons and shared confessions.

An open fire snaps and pops, embers swirling around the remnants of burnt charcoal, illuminating two brown leather sofas that face each other in front of the flames. Scanning the room towards the fire, I spot our usual seats, which remain unoccupied — a welcome sight.

A couple of people are sitting at the bar, deep in conversation with Gary, the barman we've come to see. On a raised platform to the left, a cluster of tables buzz with animated laughter and chatter of energetic young men and women out for a good time.

"Gary is over there," Lucy whispers, nudging me as we approach the bar.

The moment we draw near, Gary's attention shifts, lifting his head. "Steve, Lucy. As always, it's a pleasure to see you both."

"Hey, Gary," I reply, "Got a couple of minutes?"

"For you two? Anytime," wrapping up with the last customer before coming over to us. "What's on your mind?"

Lucy smiles before glancing around to ensure she can't be overheard. "We might be going away on another mission. You did a fantastic job with Hadley on our previous time away in taking down the son of the Acosta. Need you to keep our daughters, Abbie and Bethanie, under surveillance in case someone tries to take revenge. It's been quiet since we returned, but you never know."

"Consider it done," Gary replies, stepping away to serve a woman waiting further along the bar.

With drinks, we walk over to the sofas and slump into the soft cushions. The rise and fall of voices interweave with the sharp chime of clinking glasses, creating a backdrop that evokes familiarity. At one end, the fire crackles, casting flickering shadows on the walls. The room is already warm from the sun's rays penetrating through the extensive windows, making the fire's presence more for show than necessity.

Without lifting her gaze, Lucy says, "So, what's the plan from here?"

After sipping my drink, "Might as well settle in for a bit, grab a meal and a few beers. We can head to the mainland early in the morning to see the kids before our rendezvous with Simon and George in Southampton. Where it goes from there depends on how the talk unfolds."

"Smart move. I'm hungry, and you get out of washing up," says Lucy, a grin tugging at her lips as I reach for the menu.

"You are so kind," I reply.

After a few hours at the pub, fuelled by the buzz of drinks and a steady flow of conversation, we head back home. Thirty minutes later, we arrive at the lodge. The moment we step through the door,

Lucy drops onto the sofa, laying out the 9 mms on the coffee table. I'd pulled them from the hide outside before entering the lodge. Each is a silent reminder of past missions and the possible job ahead.

Noise from the television hums in the corner, a meaningless backdrop to the task at hand as Lucy breaks down the pistols, hands moving with practised efficiency. Parts line up with care, their sequence ingrained in muscle memory. Metallic clicks echo across the room as parts snap into place. Each motion tells its own story — decisive, purposeful, unhurried. Wiping, inspecting, reassembling — it's not just maintenance. It's preparation for what might be coming.

While Lucy concentrates on the weapons, I turn my attention to the rest of our equipment. Head off to grab my Bergen from under the bed in the spare bedroom.

Contents are dumped onto the kitchen table in one fluid motion. Gear arranged like an arsenal, ready for deployment. Apart from the occasional maintenance, the stuff remains untouched since the last mission.

In the Bergen, every item sits where it belongs, primed for action, ready to deploy at a moment's notice, including a plastic case, its compartments lined with components for making improvised explosive devices (IEDS).

Several splash maps, veterans of past missions, are always on hand and stacked. The tactical kit follows, layered and ready, with camo netting on top — an ingrained sequence, a ritual of readiness.

With the maps sorted, I concentrate on the spare combat clothing and GORE-TEX waterproofs, ensuring they're in good condition before replacing them in the Bergen, then turning my attention to the hammock and bivvy bag, examining every fibre for any sign of weakness lingering over the mesh where a tear could mean trouble. There is nothing worse than hearing the infernal buzzing from the tiny bloodsucking bastards from inside your net.

With my gear squared away, I move to Lucy's hammock and bivvy. A quick check for damage is all that is required. Handling her kit beyond that is not going to happen. Each soldier develops their way, and she's no different.

With the day's tasks wrapped up, the rest of the night slips by. The TV's glow washes over us as an animated flick plays out a colourful distraction. Sometimes, it's nice to escape the real world, away from the death and mayhem that follow us. We hit the sack around 22:00.

A sudden jolt snaps me awake, and my breath catches in my throat. The clock blinks 02:00, but it's not the time that matters. It's the memory, the same one that haunts me every night.

In my mind, the image of the terrorist burns deep, lifeless eyes locked on me, yet alive with hate. The barrel of his 9mm digs into the skin of my forehead, ice-cold and unyielding as blood hammers in my skull; a relentless beat that blocks out everything else.

The sound comes again—a click, hollow and menacing. Lying still and staring up at the ceiling, my body is drenched in sweat, muscles tense, bracing for a shot that never comes. My pulse pounds in my ears, a fierce rhythm that almost drowns the raw rasp of my breaths as the air drags through my chest, thick and stubborn, resisting like I'm drowning. By all rights, I should be dead, but instead, I live with the guilt of surviving.

The solid bedframe under my hands serves as an anchor, dragging me out of the past and back to where I need to be. I may be awake, but I'm still there, on the edge of life and death, staring into the eyes of a man who wanted to end me. The night remains quiet, but in my mind, the echoes of that click, that cold steel, stay as I try to get at least one more hour of sleep.

Two hours later, I'm awake again. This time, the memory of the vehicle checkpoint in Northern Ireland hits. Hidden beneath layers of dirt and silence, the pull toward the enemy's post feels like a heartbeat inside a coffin. Sweat once more slides down my back. Uncertainty gnaws at me, not knowing if I will see another day.

By 05:00, I give up. The memories are unrelenting, and slumber is now a distant dream. So, I clamber out of bed, careful not to wake Lucy, and head to the kitchen. The promise of a steaming cup of caffeine is keeping me from surrendering to the haunting images replaying in my mind.

Shadows stretch across the walls in the kitchen's dim light as I switch the kettle on. It's not long before the hiss of boiling water cuts through the early morning. The scent of coffee, sharp and bitter, fills the air. Steam curls up from the mug as I take a long sip. The bite of hot liquid claws at me, tearing through the haze, bringing everything into brutal, vivid focus as it slips down my throat. The burn is what I need right now, steadying the chaos in my head.

I approach the laptop and switch it on. My fingers find their rhythm over the keys, pulling up the search bar — one name: Guardian Security Solutions. A single press of the enter key ignites the sequence, and GSS flashes up on the screen.

It appears Dave Bate holds the reins, and I'll be sitting across from him soon. Digging into his background and the organisation is essential. The results show his company's profile and a string of articles.

GSS is a private security firm that supplies bodyguards and retrievals to those who can afford them. The 'about' section states that the company comprises former military personnel from around the world, most of whom are former special forces personnel. A sparse collection of photos appears on the site, identified only by first names, careful to reveal nothing more.

Faces flash across the screen. One familiar face stands out from the lineup, cutting through like a ghost from my past. Billy. His presence rips open old wounds, memories clawing their way to the surface.

Our paths crossed in the heat of that first mission, Billy moving with the precision of a combat medic and special forces soldier. He had a way about him, something that made him stand out. From the moment we were forged together by black ops, our connection sealed fast after that. Billy's dry wit was sharp as a blade, slicing through the darkness of our missions.

One particular operation remains etched in my memory. Deep behind enemy lines, the mission focused on extracting a high-value target locked in a secure site. Our team slipped through the darkness, blending into every shadow. Then, without warning, the silence broke as the inevitable unfolded—a blast shuddered through the compound, and screams followed, raw and piercing.

Billy zoned in on the wounded's distant cries, absorbing the surroundings as if they were laid out in front of him. His voice tore through the chaos.

"Light, now!" he yelled.

A quick flick of the torch sent a red beam over the wounded man, the injury more evident with each passing second.

Shrapnel tore through the trooper's leg. Blood flowed out in a dark, unbroken stream. Billy worked fast, hands moving with practised ease that only comes from experience. A tourniquet was applied, the wound cleaned, and an IV was inserted while reassuring the injured.

"Stay with me, mate. You're going to be fine."

The man's eyes reflected a fragile hope, gripping Billy's steady words like a lifeline. In that moment, Billy stood as more than a medic—the man was the thin wall between the trooper and the creeping blackness.

Mission complete and the team withdrawing, the trooper's heartbeat stayed even, a testament to Billy's calm skill amid the confusion. I've seen him pull off the impossible before, and I know this won't be the final time. In the thick of the firestorm, with disarray erupting around us, Billy kept pulling men back from the edge—an unwavering force amid all-consuming disorder.

The battlefield shapes warriors, but with Billy, it's different. When the bullets flew and the chaos hit, the man never wavered, right there with me. He's more than a teammate; he's the kind of brother only war can create. Built under combat, our loyalty runs deeper than blood. We would always have each other's backs, no matter how grim things got.

Every joke Billy told struck at the perfect beat, underscored by a tenacity as unyielding as it is contagious. I remember one night, sitting around a fire, the exhaustion setting in, Billy smirked and shook his head.

"You know, there'll come a time when we see this for what it is—fucking utter insanity." Classic Billy, cutting through the tension with humour.

"Speak for yourself," I shot back, unable to hold back a chuckle.

The past slips back into the shadows, a reminder that not everything fades with time. I turn my attention back to the computer and scan the details on the screen. The company's portfolio reads like a who's who of high-risk clients, their expertise keeping influential people alive in the most hostile environments.

The brief sent to Simon suggests a clean operation, but the gaps tell a different story, revealing threads of something far beyond a straightforward extraction.

A hit of caffeine punches through the distraction—this task requires my total concentration. I need to be alert and prepared for whatever comes next. The clock on the wall ticks one second at a time as I lean into the chair's back, eyes fixed on the screen.

It must have been about 45 minutes later when the unmistakable sound of water striking the tiles in the bathroom drags me from the depths of my thoughts, pulling me back into the present. Lucy is up, getting ready. Daylight starts to slice in through the window as the door to the bathroom clicks and opens, releasing a brief waft of mist. A second later, Lucy moves across the room, towel-clad, with damp hair plastered against her bare shoulders.

Coffee in hand, she leans down, placing a soft kiss on the top of my head.

"What's occupying your mind?" her tone is laced with curiosity.

"I'm looking up GSS," I reply, tapping the keyboard. "I'm trying to find information on Dave Bate and GSS. Due diligence, and all that malarky."

Still with a brew in hand, her attention shifts to the display. "Spot anything that stands out?"

"They are a private security company with many ex-special forces people on the payroll. Dave's got a solid reputation, but I want to be sure."

Lucy nods, sensing the tension. "Instead of making breakfast, why don't we grab something on the boat?"

"Good idea. Let's get a move on." A brief grin flickers, recognising the practicality of her actions.

With our gear stowed, the drive to East Cowes unfolds in no time. The ferry terminal comes into view, where the Red Falcon looms, its gangway alive with early commuters. Once onboard, travellers shuffle into place, their movements a backdrop to the rhythmic hum of the engine and the sharp tang of salt carried on the breeze.

On the top deck, Lucy leans against the railing, eyes on the horizon. "There's something about the ocean... it's both calming and dangerous. The surface only hints at what dangers might hide below."

"Like our world, full of twists you don't see coming," I mutter, feeling the sea's pull as I stand beside her.

As the ferry moves away from the dock, the coastline of the Isle of Wight begins to shrink, replaced by the open expanse of the Solent. The dark and choppy water matches my unease as other passengers go about their business.

"Expect the unexpected. This mission goes beyond the artefact. Something bigger is lurking, something we've missed," I say, still looking out across the sea.

Without breaking focus, "We'll make it work. We always do," Lucy replies, radiating confidence.

But the holes in our intel keep me on edge. Time drags as it always does, as the ferry ploughs through the waves. Minutes crawl by like hours as the vessel makes its way toward Southampton.

At last, we dock and disembark, blending into the crowd of commuters. The city's streets are already busy, the town is already awake and bustling. With Lucy at the wheel, I take out my phone and dial Abbie's number. The call connects after a few rings, her voice bursting through the line, upbeat and welcoming.

"Morning, princess. Are you at home? Lucy and I are on our way to see you all."

"Hi, Dad, I'm at Bethanie's with the kids. Hadley's also here," Abbie replies.

"Great. We'll be over soon."

After a short drive, we arrive. As the car eases to a halt, I hear laughter from the grandkids drifting from the garden. A firm rap on the door draws a quick response. Abbie opens it, her face lit with excitement.

"Dad, Lucy! Come in," she beams, stepping aside with an inviting gesture.

We step into the front room where Bethanie and Hadley are sitting. "Morning, everyone."

"Morning, Dad," Bethanie says, standing to hug me.

"Hi, Dad," Hadley remarks, hand clasping mine with warmth and strength.

"Good to see you all," I say, looking around the room.

We spend the next 60 minutes or so catching up. The conversation is light and filled with laughter. The grandkids run in and out of the garden, their energy infectious. It's a welcome break from the looming mission, a reminder of why we do what we do. I check my wristwatch. The hour ticked by far too fast.

"Sorry, folks, but we need to make a move. We have a meeting with Simon and George soon."

Bethanie nods, understanding. "Be careful, Dad."

"Always am," the words are laced with certainty as a smile crosses my face.

After saying our goodbyes, we head to the car. With Lucy in the driver's seat, the engine kicks over, and we head toward Southampton. In the city, traffic flows while pedestrians weave between cars and buses. The high street is alive with motion. We clamber out of the car after finding a parking spot near the military careers office at the bottom of High Street.

Across the road is a small café. Pushing the door open, the tiny bell overhead rings with a faint, metallic chime that cuts through hushed voices. Inside, the air is thick with the scent of fresh coffee and frying bacon, blending into an inviting warmth that contrasts with the cool air outside. A few patrons glance up as we enter, but most are absorbed in their plates, each forkful given silent priority.

Sunlight pours through the vast, panoramic window stretching across the front, casting a soft glow over the nearby tables. Beyond the street, life bustles, but inside, time moves at a more sedate pace. Individual ticks of the clock are drawn out as if reluctant to move forward, as if the place has carved out a sanctuary from the hurried world outdoors. Beneath the window, a small table with two empty seats stands ready, bathed in sunlight, almost as if it's calling out for company.

As you enter, the serving area stretches along the wall to the right, displaying laminated menus, a stack of canned drinks, and a card terminal stand next to a cash register. A glass dome showcases a selection of cakes—sponge, carrot, and chocolate—sliced thick and tempting. But we're not here to indulge.

Beyond, two rows of tables run parallel against the walls, where two groups of older couples sit, age traced across their features as they exchange quiet words while nursing steaming mugs of some type of beverage, their heads bent in hushed, intimate conversation. Each glance toward the window meets the rush of the outside world.

At the far end, Simon and George wait at a table close to the open-planned kitchen with a casual air but eyes sharp, taking in the room. Simon spots us first, lifting a hand in greeting, gaze flicking over our shoulders, checking if anyone is following us. Past them behind the counter, a man leans into the heat of the grill, turning eggs and pressing bacon flat—the sound of frying cutting through the kitchen's atmosphere.

"Morning," I say, as we reach the table.

"Steve, Lucy," Simon says, offering a firm, confident handshake. George follows suit, his grip a reassuring affirmation of solidarity.

Chairs scrape across the floor as we settle in beside George and Simon. We've been there for a few minutes when the waitress arrives, notepad in hand, ready to take our order.

"What can I get you, folks?"

"Four full English breakfasts, please," I say, glancing at the others to ensure they're on board.

"No problem. Any more drinks?"

"Three coffees and one tea," Lucy says, sparking instant agreement.

Simon shifts forward as the young lady departs. "Dave's briefing starts at 14:00. He'll want a clear picture of our availability, numbers, and how fast we can mobilise. If the roles were reversed, any commander worth respect would want this kind of actionable intelligence."

George lifts his drink to his lips, scanning the room. "Whatever challenge lies ahead, there is a good chance we've managed tougher situations."

At that moment, the waitress approaches, steaming beverages in hand, and sets them down with a gentle thud. I pick up the closest mug, the heat from the beverage radiating through my fingers. In front of me, Lucy sips her brew while her gaze locks on mine.

As we discuss the details of the possible upcoming mission, the scent of bacon, eggs, and coffee swirls around me, each breath stoking my hunger as I wait for the food to arrive. Simon and George are focused, their expressions mirroring my thoughts.

With the team's eyes on me, "The email is concise, but we lack crucial intel. Maybe on purpose. The gaps in the info leave too much exposed." My calm voice masks the unanswered questions at the back of my mind. "We can't lock anything down yet until Derek shows up. His input on radio and communications is essential; without it, we're making educated guesses."

After taking a sip of his coffee and standing up, "Time to get Derek's update on tomorrow's ETA," says Simon, with a phone in hand before walking towards the door and leaving the building.

George's attention remains fixed on me, a spoon circling in his cup in controlled movements. "As for myself, I'm ready to spring into action once we receive the go-ahead. The intel is limited to Dave's email to Simon, but we'll tackle whatever the mission throws our way."

"True enough, George. Adapting is what's kept us alive this long. Stay alert during the meeting, grab the key details, and then we will solidify the plan," Lucy comments.

A sound in front of me attracts my attention; it's the waitress approaching, her arms laden with our full English breakfasts. She places the plates on the table, piled high with sausages, bacon, eggs, beans, and fried bread.

"If you need anything else, please ask," she says before walking away.

Simon steps back, tucking the phone away and sitting down. "Managed to reach Derek. He's en route and will arrive sometime tomorrow. Updates coming via text."

"Good," I say. "Can everyone confirm their commitment and ensure they can depart at a moment's notice once we get the green light after Derek arrives?" A chorus of affirmations answer my question. We've done this dance many times, and the team's readiness is one of our greatest strengths.

"Based on the direction of the conversation, we'll bring up questions tied to everyone's expertise during the session with Dave. Lucy, you focus on intel and tactical support; Simon, transportation and logistics; George, weapons and sniper overwatch. Leave the overall strategy to me. Also, ask about Derek's usual radio protocol and communications enquiries," I say.

Everyone nods, understanding their roles. The waitress comes to clear our plates, and I signal for the bill. Our minds are already moving to the next phase of the operation.

"Let's RV in the car park of Guardian Security Solutions," I say, standing up. "We'll regroup there and head in together."

Chapter Two — The Meeting

For 20 minutes, the two cars move in sync, weaving through the outskirts of Southampton, bound for Basingstoke. The cityscape gives way to a built-up area close to Popham Airfield. Lucy drives the lead vehicle with me sitting in the passenger seat. My attention drifts to my notebook, flipping through the pages as we speed toward our destination. Simon and George follow behind.

Entering the industrial zone, my gaze sweeps across the site, where a faint drone of machinery hums from distant metal structures. Bold, black letters spell "Guardian Security Solutions (GSS)" along the top of one building set back from the rest, a stark contrast to the building's washed-out hues. The first thing that hits me is that no vehicles are parked outside, which strikes me as odd, as this is a business park, and I would expect the cars to be outside all premises, adding to the mystery and intrigue.

Lucy slows the vehicle, as I take in more details. One of the roller doors is open, revealing three imposing, military-looking armoured trucks lined up against the far wall. Inside, several people move around, their desert camouflaged fatigues standing out against the industrial setting. Each person moves with a purpose, carrying an unbroken discipline. Tactical gear moulds to their bodies, weapons secured with meticulous care.

Lucy parks the car close to the entrance, and we clamber out, signalling Simon and George to do the same.

"Looks like this place is geared up for confrontation," George says, pointing inside.

"Yeah," I reply. "Stay sharp. We don't know what we're walking into."

Stepping into the metal-clad building of Guardian Security Services, I sense the buzz of disciplined activity. The expansive interior's ceiling stretches above, amplifying the muffled exchanges of conversation that drift through the space, tight and controlled.

No one's here to chat; it's all business. Their movements are smooth and calculated, the result of operations where even the slightest error invites chaos. Tasks would have been carried out with assuredness by those who've earned their place here.

Against the back wall, the three armoured vehicles we saw from outside become more prominent, their matte black surfaces absorbing the fluorescent light. These behemoths are built for protection, and their presence underscores the seriousness of the work conducted here.

Halfway along the left wall is a storage area that is a testament to military precision. Through the open doors, I spot shelves stocked with tactical vests, helmets, firearms, and other supplies, all arranged to suggest it's ready for immediate deployment. Each item sits right where it belongs, and everything is positioned with military precision.

The deep roar of a heavy vehicle catches my attention as an armoured car rolls out from a ramp, I'm guessing, leading to an underground parking garage. From its look, the expansive entrance was built for more than standard cars—armoured units could navigate through it without any issue, which explains why there were no vehicles outside.

Guardian Security Services isn't just a company; it's a fortress of elite protection. Every aspect of the building, from the reinforced walls to the methodical storage, reflects the unwavering commitment to excellence and readiness. From the look of things, the mission is always paramount, and the operatives are always well-prepared.

By my side, the team moves in silence, dissecting the scene as if danger waits behind the next breath. An invitation doesn't make this place safe — complacency isn't an option.

"It's evident that these individuals are organised and trained to a high level, capable of handling any situation with exacting precision. They're well equipped," I remark to George, observing a man approaching us; a tall figure, draped in black jeans and a green T-shirt. His close-cropped hairstyle reveals a scar that snakes down his cheek, hinting at past conflicts.

"Sure have. Unlike us on a mission who have to scrape around for kit," replies George.

Seconds pass before the man appears in front of me. "Morning. Guess you're Steve and the team, right?" a brief acknowledgement in his eyes. "I'm James. Dave's expecting you. follow me"

Following James, we are guided to the far corner, where we approach a separate structure within the unit. Inside is the operational control room, shielded by a reinforced steel door, thick and heavy, engineered to withstand the force of a missile strike. Its surface gleams under the overhead lights, a silent barrier protecting the heart of operations.

Monitors dominate the walls, their sharp glow piercing through the dimly lit space. These screens are not only displays but the lifeline of the operation, with data streams flickering across them — satellite feeds, decrypted communications, threat patterns — all contributing to a pulsating flow of information. I've seen this before. This isn't a room; it's the nerve centre of the operation, where intelligence transforms into strategy and precision drives every choice.

Rows of consoles blink with layered intel, their displays updating the moment data pours in from across the globe. Operators sit rigid, backs straight, their hands gliding over keyboards, pulling threads of information and weaving them into actionable plans.

Crossing the floor, more operatives are locked in. From my experience, they appear to be scanning reports, rerouting communications, and identifying vulnerabilities in enemy networks. This is more than technology or skill; it's discipline forged in the relentless drive to stay ahead, an unwavering determination. For a brief second, the room's energy envelops me —

a world bound by control, clarity, and the unyielding pursuit of dominance in the chaos we navigate.

After knocking, James opens the door to a separate office, and we enter. The room is spacious and well-lit, with recessed lighting casting a soft glow. The rich aroma of coffee mingles with the scent of paper, a sharp contrast to the control room. The walls are lined with bookshelves filled with manuals on tactics, espionage, and history. A whiteboard hangs from the wall, covered in diagrams and notes, remnants of past briefings and strategy sessions. Every detail is organised, reflecting the high stakes and precision required in our line of work.

A man in his mid-50s, well-dressed, is sitting behind a teak desk; I recognised him from his photo on the company website. Glancing up from the laptop as we enter, Dave greets us,

"Happy you could join us," pushing himself up and offering a hand.

Not being a man of many words when a few will do, "Nice to meet you, Dave. Let's dive into the mission specifics you need us to tackle," I state, my grip firm as I shake his hand.

Sitting back down, Dave gestures for us to take seats around the large desk cluttered with papers, a high-end laptop, and several secure communication devices. A one-way glass window stretches along one side of the office, revealing a sweeping view of the command epicentre while concealing our presence.

Dave cuts straight to the point, following my lead, wasting no time on the preamble. "First, welcome to the nerve centre. From this vantage point, all operations are coordinated, live feeds are monitored, and real-time intel is processed. We have plenty to discuss. Should you accept the mission, I need a rough timeline for deployment. Then we can break down the intel."

"Understood. Our approach is clear: infiltrate, survive, and take the objective. No compromise," I reply.

Lucy, Simon, and George nod in agreement, their expressions mirroring mine.

"Before we say yes, I have a few questions, the first and most important being: Any reason you're employing our team when you have all the operatives and equipment within your organisation?"

Dave's expression doesn't change, prepared for the line of enquiry. "Smart question, Steve. The truth is, we're overstretched. Multiple high-priority operations are ongoing, and I need a team with a proven track record. Our world relies on tight coordination, and your team's success is recognised throughout the security sector. This mission demands the best."

"A fair assessment," Simon states, pride radiating from flushed cheeks.

"Just as important is the next question. What payment are you willing to offer for our services for this task you want us to carry out?" I say, my gaze fixed on Dave.

Reaching into the depths of his desk drawer, Dave retrieves a plain beige envelope, sets it on the table, and slides it towards me.

"All the payment details are in here. All I need is your bank account number and a signature committing you to the operation, and then everything we discussed past this point is confidential."

Flipping the folder open, I scan the contents, and a figure leaps out—£1.5m. This amount carries weight beyond the cash; it says volumes about the task ahead. No one throws down that kind of money for something insignificant.

A look around at the team tells me all I need to know. Dave leans back, arms crossed, eyes focused, analysing my expression. Simon punctuates the silence with his pen, awaiting the cue to act. Lucy maintains her poised stance, yet the sharpness in her gaze speaks of careful calculations. George remains quiet but vigilant. However, the final decision rests with me.

After taking a deep breath and closing the folder with a silent snap, "Alright, we're in," I say.

In front of Dave, angled at me, a laptop hums, the display lights up, primed for the order that shifts everything into play. With a swift motion, I pull the computer towards me. Moments later, our account numbers are typed on the keyboard, repeating themselves on the screen. Each digit is locked in clean and official, at least on the surface. Payment is secured with a click.

To my left, Lucy is confirming the funds have been transferred to our account on her mobile phone. With a raised thumb, she indicates the money has been received. So, my hand moves over the line on Dave's document, a signature locking us into this operation.

"Now," I say, looking Dave in the eyes. "Tell us what we're walking into."

"Good news, Steve. The mission is split into two halves, tied together by Dr Ivan Petrov, a researcher focused on military technology of the past. At this moment, Viktor Readle's criminal organisation is holding him captive in a small village called Heinrichsberg in former East Germany. Extracting him is our first objective. The information the target possesses is vital for the next phase of your task."

"OK, what links it all, and what's the objective?" I ask.

"Petrov might be the sole individual aware of the location of a long-forgotten device from the end of the Second World War. The destructive force packed into this weapon could tear apart cities and leave nothing but devastation behind, endangering countless lives. As expected, criminal enterprises would go to great lengths to seize the relic. A benefactor is paying my company to ensure its recovery before it ends up in the wrong hands."

"Alright," I say, meeting his gaze. "What's the clock on this?"

A glimmer of relief dances in Dave's expression. "You need to extract Petrov in the next seven days. Information from one of my guys inside the village and deep undercover in Readle's organisation reveals they plan to relocate him in 10 days."

"Who's Readle?" I ask.

"Head of a Russian crime syndicate." Dave reaches behind him and produces a thick folder. "Here's the full mission briefing, including every piece of intel we've gathered."

Taking the documents from Dave, "The timeline shouldn't be an issue. The team should be ready to move soon. I'm just waiting for the fifth teammate to join us, before I can give precise timings."

"What's the assessment of the target area? How secure are the defences?" Lucy asks.

Dave's fingers move over the keyboard. The laptop monitor illuminates the target area in vivid detail, with every angle accounted for in the captured frame.

"The target is in a farm complex, built like a fortress, reinforced with walls meant to hold back more than curiosity. Multiple layers of security — armed guards and surveillance around the yard and its approaches. But there are weaknesses we can exploit."

"What's the approach for insertion and extraction? We should avoid alarms and keep casualties to a minimum," Simon asks, always focused on logistics.

Dave gestures to the highlighted paths on the screen. "Infiltration via stealth helicopter is confirmed. Extfil is the challenge. Several routes are in place to handle any on-the-ground shifts."

With a slight cough, George speaks up. "What's the topography like around the target? Need the most strategic positions for sniper overwatch."

The paper rustles as the map is laid flat, its edges creased from wear. "Elevated positions surround the site. Scout the area first. Use the buildings to secure your vantage for when you move in," replies Dave.

Lucy turns to me, then back to Dave. "And what about enemy forces? Numbers, equipment?"

"You're looking at 10 to 20 armed guards. Intel suggests ex-military, well-equipped. Automatic rifles and heavy ordnance are in play. Expect serious resistance."

"Two quick ones, Dave. First, how are weapons and gear handled? Are you supplying them, or are we sourcing our own from the payout?" I ask.

Without hesitation, Dave replies, "All company assets are at your disposal—firearms, ammunition, surveillance tech, everything you need. What's your second, Steve?"

"Can we use the briefing room?" The answer might be obvious, but I want confirmation.

"As I said, you have full access to the whole facility."

With clarity on the mission locked in, we say goodbye to Dave, promising to return tomorrow with an operational strategy for Dr Ivan Petrov's extraction from Heinrichsberg. Back at the vehicles, everyone clambers aboard the two cars, and we drive to a local pub 15 minutes away from the Guardian Security Solutions on the outskirts of the small village of North Waltham.

The convoy pulls into the car park of The Green Man, a countryside inn with stone walls draped in ivy and crowned by a weathered thatched roof that speaks of a long history. It's not far from GSS, but it's like we've entered another world.

Above the door, the sign creaks in the gentle early evening breeze. It is an old wooden board painted with a jovial figure clad in a traditional outfit, raising a tankard. Simon and George, in the second vehicle, park beside us.

With everyone out of the cars, we enter the pub. Inside, dim lights hang from the ceiling, and the warm scent of burning wood from the stone fireplace blends with the ale's rich, comforting aroma. The walls are adorned with old photographs and hunting trophies, giving the place a rustic charm. Old wooden beams overhead form a sturdy grid. Situated at the bar, locals hold their drinks close, their sidelong glances betraying curiosity.

Behind the bar, the bartender, an older guy with a welcoming face, handles our order without a hitch. Beers in hand, we walk out to the garden, lit by strings of miniature lights hanging from the trees. The evening is cool, the sky tinged with the last hues of sunset. A seat tucked along the perimeter keeps conversations safe from wandering ears.

Glasses settle down onto the weathered wooden table. Lucy sits, her gaze sweeping the pub as if mapping the exits.

"OK," she says, her voice carving through the faint chatter from other customers in the garden. "Forget Simon's rare generosity for a second — let's talk about what matters. The meeting."

A smirk crosses Simon's face. "Keep whining, and next round's on you," a sly grin cuts across his face.

The light banter slips away, replaced by the hard edge of reality, leaving only the sharp focus demanded by the moment. After a slow sip of beer, the bitter ale hitting the back of my throat, I lean forward.

"Dave laid it out, two objectives, both tied to Petrov. First, we get him out. Then, we lock down that relic before anyone else does."

"Three hundred grand per head — but cash won't mean a damn thing if we don't make it out," Simon says, leaning in closer.

George, silent until now, leans into the table. "The money's tempting, but as Simon said, it won't do us any good if we're not breathing at the end of this."

Silence falls for a few seconds, the mission hanging between us like a live grenade waiting to go off: two missions ahead, big money, and even bigger risks. Whatever we're after has already drawn the worst kind of attention.

"If the intel on the compound checks out, the enemy forces are a concern. Ex-military, armed with an assortment of weapons. We'd better be at our best," Lucy says, holding the briefing folder.

"No question about it, we've got the experience, the skills, and Dave's equipment in our corner. That's all the advantage we need," I say, looking around the team.

"No denying the challenge," Simon cuts in, voice firm. "But George is right. We've faced tougher situations, and this is no exception. Petrov and that relic are ours to take."

After another round of beers, my eyes lock with Lucy's. "No point going back home. Gear's sorted — let's find somewhere close to sleep for the night." With several nods of agreement, the rest also agree to stay.

"We wait for Derek. Be ready to move the second he's here," Lucy says, placing her glass down with a soft thud.

As The Green Man pub doesn't offer accommodation, Simon stands, stretching, tapping on his phone. After a quick conversation with the person on the other end,

"Hotel's booked," glancing up from his phone. "Sent Derek a text, telling him to meet us there."

After a short drive, the Fox and Hounds stands ahead. A haven for the night, its walls bathed in a warm glow from the streetlamps.

Roses climb the brick façade, their tangled vines framing the weathered stone. The cobbled path stretches out, leading toward the entrance.

Inside, the lobby exudes an understated elegance. Aged but sturdy armchairs flank antique tables that bear the patina of countless stories. A fire crackles in the stone hearth, sending light dancing across the room. Shadows flicker against the walls like fleeting memories. The receptionist handles the check-in, their quiet focus leaving no room for small talk.

The second floor beckons with the groan of wooden steps, the staircase creaking underfoot like a whisper from the inn itself. The rooms, each a sanctuary of comfort, await beyond the landing, their doors marked with brass numbers dulled by time. Here, comfort is not just a luxury but a necessity, offering a fleeting moment of rest in a place that carries echoes of countless travellers.

Simon chuckles, leaning against the banister. "George, those stairs squeak more than Steve and Lucy's bed during ops. Payback's a bitch," shooting a glance my way.

"Better put your earplugs in tonight, then, Simon. I'll be wailing like a banshee on heat," comes Lucy's instant reply.

We agreed to meet back in the bar in one and a half hours for a few pre-mission drinks, part of the routine we never skip before stepping into the field. As Derek isn't here, I am sure there will be another one before George and Simon head for their room further along the corridor.

The room offers a clean simplicity that hides its practicality — an unassuming mattress, a writing desk against the far wall, and a window that frames the garden bathed in pale moonlight. Modern conveniences blend into the corners without drawing attention; a flat-screen TV integrates with the muted decor, and a coffee maker stands ready for use.

My kit lands on the floor with a thud. Tomorrow, Derek will rejoin the team, and the plan will solidify. But for now, the mission brief is the key to our success and demands my full attention.

A few minutes later, Lucy steps into the bathroom, leaving me to start planning. I grab the documents from my Bergen, spreading the contents across the desk—a detailed map, reconnaissance photos, potential routes marked with precision, and team placements noted in clean lines. Every element is examined and re-examined, possible weak points turn over in my mind, their solutions already forming.

After 20 minutes, I pack everything up and put the folder in the safe. The door clicks shut, locking away the folder and its contents. A safeguard, but no system is flawless. A forgotten code, a misplaced key, or a determined person could still breach it. Locks delay, but they never guarantee security. Only vigilance and constant watchfulness fill in the gaps.

The clock above the desk ticks in a muted rhythm—40 minutes until the team rendezvous. Once the bathroom is free, there is plenty of time for a quick shower.

When I look up, Lucy has re-entered the room and is lying naked on the quilt, her body stretches across the mattress like an unspoken challenge. Her eyes burn into me, igniting something primal. The message in her body language ignites a raw surge within me, undeniable and direct.

A slow smile forms as she speaks, her voice dripping with suggestion. "Feel like giving this bed a workout?"

The room's chill brushes my skin, and discarded clothes are left in a trail behind me. Her scent—a mix of jasmine and that distinct, impossible-to-define something—pulls me in, each step erasing the space between us. I slide onto the bed next to her, hands moving over the lines of her form, sensing the throbbing of energy beneath my fingertips. Her body responds with a force beyond control, each breath drawing us deeper into this shared pulse.

Lucy's fingers explore my chest, trailing downwards, the sensation sending sparks of electricity through my veins. A single glance and the gap narrows, seconds brimming with words neither of us needs to say. Our mouths collide, her lips answering with a heat that holds back nothing, the tenderness that promises more.

My hands move to her breasts, cupping and creasing, nipples hardening under my caress. Lucy's body presses against mine, a quiet gasp slipping from her lips, her breath hot on my skin. My mouth finds her neck, tasting the salt and jasmine that lingers there. Every shift, every sound from her sparks something primal, each touch pulling us deeper.

Fingertips dig into my back, nails biting deep, drawing me closer with undeniable urgency. Heat radiates from her as a subtle tremor passes between us. My lips glide down, teasing the surface, pausing at the hollow of her navel. My hand pauses, and a small shiver ripples through her, impossible to hide.

Then, she forces me down onto the bed, a glint of mischief in her eyes. She positions herself above me, thighs tight against my hips, her body pressing into mine in a way that leaves no space between us. Her hands trace deliberate paths over my skin, each motion slow, exact, hiding the calm intensity.

My fingers are holding her waist. The steady push and pull fuels rising friction, raw and unrelenting. Sweat beads across her skin, catching the dim light, while her hair clings to her face in tangled strands. Every move she makes radiates pleasure that pulls me in.

Movement becomes more urgent, the tempo building, a crescendo of ecstasy that is almost overwhelming. Sensing muscles tightening around me, her breath coming in short, ragged gasps. Sensations sharpen, every nerve alive, the pressure mounting with a fierce intensity.

Our movements align, pulses synchronised, drowning out anything beyond this moment. Shadows shift along the walls, moving in rhythm, caught in the pulse of our entwined forms. The room is filled with the sounds of our lovemaking: soft moans and the whisper of skin against skin.

As we reach the peak, the world fades away, and time stays motionless in a rush of sheer pleasure. Our bodies shudder, a wave of ecstasy that leaves us breathless and trembling. Her body drapes over mine, muscles twitching with the last echoes of our shared passion. The heat from her breath lands on my chest, her heart pounding in time with my rhythm.

Locked together, the raw intensity lingers, our closeness refusing to ease. The heat of our lovemaking is slowly fading. Her fingers trace patterns on my chest, and a contented sigh escapes her lips. I pull her close, and our hearts beat in unison, a silent promise of love and desire that will never fade.

After my shower, Lucy and I make our way down from our room to meet up with Simon and George. Our footsteps down the staircase echo against the wood, the creak of old floorboards marking the descent. Inside the bar, several lanterns send pools of light across the tavern's walls, casting shifting shadows that dance with the murmurs of conversation. Laughter fills the space, accompanied by the crisp clink of glasses, lending the room a rare warmth.

Simon and George, hands cradling their pints, sit tucked in a corner, their eyes scanning the room. Simon's hand flicks in a small, deliberate gesture, a silent command that draws us over without exchanging words. The table sits near the fire, its crackling flames drawing the eye.

The bar is a sensory feast. Hunting trophies and sepia photographs adorn the walls, remnants of stories too old to tell. The subtle mix of wood smoke and hops lingers in the air, grounding the space with an earthy aroma that evokes simpler times. Exposed beams stretch across the ceiling, grounding the space in a sense of age and history.

"About time you made an appearance," Simon jokes, the hint of a challenge in his voice as we slide into our seats.

"We needed to make ourselves presentable," Lucy fires back, settling into the chair beside mine.

"Did that happen before you two couldn't keep your hands off each other? In case you're curious, yes, we caught every sound from your room," George says, grinning like he's won some inside joke.

"Glad you heard it. Something for you and your right hand to think about in the bathroom later!" Lucy replies.

As Lucy is absorbed in conversation, I head for the bar and return with a tray of beers, placing them on the table. George's face eases, a smile breaking the lines of a long-held smirk.

"Well, here's to a rare moment of calm," he says, a hint of warmth slipping into his tone.

A slight nod acknowledges the shift as the day's tension starts to ease. "Agreed. We've more than earned this." With a raised glass, "To the fallen and the road we're about to take. Here's to all of us coming back intact," I reply.

Glasses rise and meet mine in a soft clink, the weight of the mission unspoken but understood — a silent pact among soldiers bound by a common goal.

Casual comments replace strategy, our focus shifting away from the intensity of what lies ahead. Simon regales us with tales of misadventures with transportation logistics, exaggerated to the point of hilarity. George makes witty remarks about his time as a dog handler with the Ministry of Defence that have us all laughing.

Ale flows, and the laughter follows. We swap stories—past missions, mishaps, and odd spots we've been to. The emphasis shifts to Derek; the urge to give him a bit of stick is impossible to resist.

"Bet Derek's going to show up tomorrow with some wild story about why he's late," I say, grinning.

Without missing a beat, George chimes in. "Flight from St Bethanie's will be the excuse this time, no doubt."

"That man could saunter into his own funeral, 10 minutes behind everyone else and act like it's all part of the plan," Simon says, smiling.

A smile spreads across Lucy's face as she raises her drink. "To Derek's flawless timing—let's hope he shows up before the bullets start flying."

"To Derek." My comment resonates, glasses meeting with knowing grins.

The night unfolds with a rhythm of stories and brief laughter, cutting through the tension that clings from the days behind us. Conversation flows as easily as that exchanged between people who've faced fire together, the kind of camaraderie forged in combat and tempered by survival. The room carries the unspoken significance of our history, a bond that doesn't require words to confirm its presence. Tested through chaos, the unity built over countless missions forms an unbreakable core.

At the end of the evening, there's a pause, fleeting, a moment to exhale before stepping back into the storm. Without speaking, we rise as one, the unbroken rhythm of shared purpose guiding our steps. Leaving the bar, the hallway stretches quiet and dim, and with each stride, the coming operation looms larger in thought, pulling focus toward the tasks ahead.

Outside Lucy and my room, we gather in a loose group. Exhaustion lingering in our postures, but our resolve cuts through the weariness like steel.

Scanning faces, "Get your heads down. We've got a busy few days ahead of us tomorrow. Breakfast at 07:00. We move forward together, with no exceptions," I say.

"Together," the response lands with the finality of a pledge, the kind of statement that doesn't fade under pressure.

It carries more than agreement — it's survival itself. The unbreakable bond holds us as a team, a bond that makes us more than just a team, a unified force.

The bed offers an anchor in the shifting tides of thought. Lucy's arm drapes over me, a grounding touch in the fleeting calm. The hum of the bar fades into the distance, replaced by the steady cadence of her breathing. Thoughts of the mission push forward, the stakes tangible, the risks inevitable. With this team, readiness isn't a question — it's the foundation. Whatever comes next, we'll meet it head-on, as always.

Chapter Three — Briefing

With first light around 04:30, I'm already awake, reviewing the briefing again via the light filtering through the gap in the curtains—no need to disturb Lucy. Because I'm up at daft o'clock, doesn't mean she should be.

We overlooked something earlier. Once on target, we rendezvous with Dave's asset in Heinrichsberg. This will be an unknown, which I hate. Whatever experience the man brings, the years the team has worked together determine how we approach each mission. Make a note on the paper to get more intel on the man later today.

By the time I'd finished planning, Lucy stirs under the quilt, "What's the time, honey?" she calls out.

I glance at the alarm clock beside the bed, "It's 05:30; we've got 90 minutes until breakfast."

Now that Lucy's up, I might as well let more light in. So I fling open the curtains, allowing the entire early morning sunlight to flood the room, before walking to the beverage-making station and turning on the kettle to make a fresh brew for us both. At the same time, Lucy heads for the shower.

Steam still lingers in the bathroom as Lucy settles beside me at the table, mug in hand. "Derek checked in yet, Steve?" she asks.

"A message came through last night — he's on his way. First flight out, landing at Heathrow in 16 hours. That puts Derek here by midday. Told him we would be waiting at the airport. So there's no need to worry about transport—we're close enough."

"Makes sense, as we are only an hour away. Once you shower, we can head down for breakfast," says Lucy, after sipping on her coffee.

The lobby hums with quiet activity as we cross toward the hotel restaurant. The aroma of fresh coffee and sizzling bacon draws us into the restaurant. Warm light spills through the windows, catching the edges of rustic tables and chairs and casting a golden glow that softens the sharp edges of the morning.

The waiter, a young man of sharp appearance, greets us at the entrance with a tone that is professional yet not mechanical. He gestures toward a familiar corner near the fireplace, where the same table from last night waits for us. White tablecloths drape across the surfaces, their crisp folds broken only by small vases holding fresh-cut flowers, their vibrant colours contrasting with the muted hues of the room. The subdued hum of conversations and the clink of tableware fill the space with an unhurried calm, a distinct shift from the lively energy of last night.

A pot of steaming coffee arrives at the table, the deep aroma mingling with the distinct scent of breakfast drifting in from the kitchen. The first sip anchors the moment, sharp and grounding, its warmth cutting through the lingering fatigue. The sounds of the room—the occasional scrape of cutlery, murmured exchanges, the faint rhythm of work from behind the kitchen doors—blend into a muffled symphony of routine.

Moments later, George and Simon step through the doorway, their movements precise and unhurried. George takes the seat to my right, scanning the room and settling into quiet focus. Simon slides into the chair opposite, attention dissecting the space with the sharpness of a blade, always calculating, always ready.

The silence between us isn't uncomfortable—it's a testament to our focus, born from years of knowing when words aren't needed. The mission ahead looms, but for now, the coffee anchors us to this fleeting moment of stillness, a brief respite before we dive into the serious task of getting Petrov.

After a short time, "Morning, folks," says George, glancing at the menu.

"Morning," Simon adds, "What's the plan for today?"

The same guy who brought my coffee earlier takes our order. Simon points to something on the card. The man peers over Simon's shoulder and makes a note on a notepad.

"Three full English breakfasts and whatever Simon's having," I say, gesturing toward him.

As the server vanishes, the conversation remains light; even though words are exchanged, tension simmers beneath. Minds are elsewhere, locked on the intel, mapping out every move.

Minutes later, the same person reappears with our food. The plates are stacked high with eggs, bacon, sausages, and grilled tomatoes—a proper meal for the mission ahead. Simon's plate is only half-filled, sticking to his usual controlled intake—always measured, never indulgent.

"Still on the kiddie servings, Simon?" I say, eying his modest meal, far from what the day demands. But that's him through and through—light eater, even on days like this.

The corner of Simon's mouth lifts, his eyes holding a rebellious glint. "Just don't have the stomach for a big breakfast. Besides, someone's got to stay light on their feet, and it's not like I require a ballooning waistline like you fat bastards."

George snorts, stabbing a piece of sausage with a fork. "At this rate, donkey walloper, a strong wind might carry you off. Might need a sandbag to keep you from blowing away."

A teasing tone slips from Lucy as she cuts in. "No worries, Simon. Once this mission is over, we'll provide you with something more substantial. Maybe a teenager meal."

After a slow sip, Simon sets his mug down before replying, "The second word is off. You fuckers try to guess the first one."

Breakfast fades into background noise as Lucy leans forward, eyes focused. Derek's arrival is at 11:30.

"We hit the airport on schedule, so there is no room for delays. Intel and getting him up to speed waits until we're back in the vehicles, away from prying ears."

"Thought the hotel was supposed to be the meeting point... or did the green numpty change the plans?" Simon asks.

"Yes, and I agree, as we are only an hour away," replies Lucy.

George lifts his head from the plate, fork pausing mid-movement, "Anything new on the mission?"

"Nothing since last night," I say, glancing around the room as more people enter the restaurant, their conversations blending into the background noise.

"Once Derek's here, we'll go through the details. Everyone must understand the plan before returning to Guardian Security Solutions."

With breakfast out of the way and the time only 08:30, we head back to our room until checkout time at 10:00. This gives me more time to start formulating a strategy, something I need to get straight in my head, as lives depend on me getting this right.

At 10:00 sharp, the keys land on the receptionist's desk, exchanged for a polite acknowledgement. The air outside carries the crisp edge of an impending storm, its chill cutting through the morning stillness. Lucy slides into the driver's seat of the lead car beside me while Simon and George settle into the second car behind us.

The motorway stretches ahead, a muted ribbon of grey slicing through the dull light of the overcast sky. Raindrops streak the windshield, blurring the flashes of blue and white from road signs that whip past. The hum of the engine merges with the steady pulse of tyres on wet tarmac, creating a soundscape as mechanical as the operation ahead.

While Lucy drives, I take the time for mission prep, which is more than strategy; it's mental discipline, rehearsing every step, running contingencies, and holding the tension until the moment of action. The plan unfolds in my mind, layer by layer, each phase building toward the payoff. Stakes don't come down to money — they're about lives, choices, and the unknown variables waiting to throw everything off course. This mission is not just another task; it's a matter of life and death.

The rearview mirror reflects the steady presence of the second car. Unwavering headlights cut through the drizzle, their rhythm matching ours like an unspoken signal of unity. The countryside dissolves into the grey horizon as Heathrow emerges — a looming structure, industrial and alive, its presence a reminder of the controlled chaos within.

Following the signs for parking, Lucy turns into the short-stay parking. After finding two available spaces the engine is shut off, a welcome silence after the motorway's ceaseless drone.

The terminal looms ahead, bustling with activity and a sea of people moving with intent. The arrival hall is a vast expanse of polished floors and high ceilings, filled with the hum of conversation and the occasional announcement over the PA system. People mill about, their eyes fixed on the sliding doors where weary passengers emerge from customs.

Finding a spot near the rear that gives us a clear view of people arriving and control over our surroundings, Lucy is at my side, eyes sharp on the crowd. George and Simon are off to the right.

"Any sign of Derek?" Simon asks, eyes scanning the hall.

"Not yet," George snaps, frustration creeping into his voice.

Minutes feel like an eternity, ticking away until Derek comes into sight, steady in presence despite the fatigue clinging to him.

With a stupid grin, George advances, the faint trace of amusement flickering across his expression.

"About time you showed up, you green numpty. Aren't you taking this first in, last out a little too far? You're getting real good at this," George says with a smirk. "Might as well call you an American — always late to the fight."

With a chuckle, Derek meets George's gaze. "Good to see you too, George, you fat bastard. Shouldn't you be doing the royal guard routine in a sentry box?"

"Excuses, excuses," Simon quips, slapping Derek on the back of the head.

It's time to get moving. We've got work to do," I say, leading the way to the door.

The urgency of our mission is now taking effect, as we have the entire team together, except for the contact in Heinrichsberg. The drive gives me time to brief Derek on everything before we reach Guardian Security Solutions.

With Lucy driving, I spin around to face Derek. "Here's the situation: Dr Ivan Petrov has been researching old military weapons from World War Two. The artefact's whereabouts were lost to history until he uncovered critical intel, which is now sealed in his head. From our intel, no one else knows the location. A criminal organisation in Heinrichsberg, East Germany, is holding Petrov. We remove him first, grab Petrov, then lock down the relic."

Information slots into place as Derek processes the data. "Understood. What's the deadline?"

"The clock's ticking — one week to extract Petrov. Intel says they're shifting him in 10 days. Stealth insertion's locked in, but extraction's where it gets messy. We need to be ready to adjust as things evolve."

From the front, Lucy lays it out, her voice steady. "Their security has cracks, and we'll exploit every single one. This won't be a walk in the park."

Derek nods, absorbing the info. "And enemy forces?"

"Ex-military, packing automatic rifles, possible drones in the sky, maybe some heavier firepower. The odds are stacked against us, but we've got the element of surprise," I reply.

"What about our weapons and kit? Brought some of my high-tech stuff," Derek says, making mental notes of the conversation.

"Good news on that. Since we're working for a security company, we've got all the gear and transport we need."

After an hour and 20 minutes on the road, we arrive at Guardian Security Solutions, park, and walk in.

Inside, close to two parked armoured vehicles, Dave stands waiting, expression stern and focused. As we approach, "You must be Derek. Glad you're here."

We follow Dave into the store. Aisles are stocked with weapons, ammunition, and tactical gear. The team disperses, each demonstrating their expertise as they scan shelves and test equipment with the precision of seasoned professionals.

Dave catches my attention with a quick gesture, "Steve, let's go to the briefing room."

Trailing him through the narrow corridors, the atmosphere shifts. Walls lined with framed commendations and mission posters speak of history and success measured in blood and sacrifice. The din from the store fades with every step, giving way to the quiet focus of the path ahead. The briefing room door comes into view, and its purposeful design is a stark reminder of the gravity of our mission. Dave swings it open without hesitation, stepping inside.

Muted light from overhead fixtures casts an even glow, leaving no shadow unchecked. The table in the centre dominates, broad enough to hold mission plans and gear, yet unobtrusive. Tablets rest at each seat, their sleek screens reflecting faint illumination from the projector humming above—the room hums with readiness, each element in place.

"Grab a seat, Steve," Dave says, turning to his laptop. "Got all the intel here on Petrov's extraction. Let's go over it."

Settling into the chair, my attention locks onto the screen on the wall while Dave advances through the slide pack. The first image locks into place — a detailed map of Heinrichsberg. Roads snake through the place, their concrete and cobbled roads converging near the Elbe River, 200 metres south, its waters marked by faint contours and shaded currents. The layout shows a grid of long buildings skirting the village's edges, their placements deliberate and practical.

Dave begins. "This is Heinrichsberg. Petrov is being held in a farm complex on the outskirts. The place is fortified, with multiple layers of security."

Key landmarks stand out, marked with annotations. A fire station sits on one side of the central square, a blocky structure facing what could only be the heart of the village. Nearby, a cobbled street twists toward a bar and flats labelled Kuhstall. The name is scrawled in the map's corner like an afterthought but carries weight in the context of what's ahead. Each element on the map isn't just a location — it's a piece of a larger strategy waiting to take shape.

Dave clicks to the next slide, revealing a detailed blueprint of the house where Petrov is being held. The structure spans two floors. The ground level features a kitchen, a living room, and a third room with no designated use, leaving its purpose unclear. Three bedrooms occupy the space upstairs, their placements distributed along the narrow hallway.

"Petrov is confined to a fortified room on the second floor. Intel confirms his location, verified by our contact embedded within the village. The same source has mapped the guard rotations and pinpointed most of the surveillance camera positions," Dave states.

The diagram glows on the wall, stark and methodical. The layout isn't only a map — it's angles of approach, choke points, blind spots, exit routes, each piece fitting into the larger strategy.

"What's the plan for getting in and out?"

Dave clicks through to the next image, highlighting insertion and extraction points — a finger landing on a clearing beyond a dense stretch of woods. "Insertion is via helicopter. The bird sets down here," marking the location with his finger. "From there, advance on foot to the compound. Our contact will meet you at the landing zone to guide you through the approach."

The following slide shifts to the exfil, a network of routes displayed across the map like veins. "With Petrov secured, exit through this corridor," a finger traces a line to the designated exfiltration point. "Multiple fallback routes are ready if the situation shifts. Flexibility has been built in. Use it."

Dave's focus locks in on mine, razor-sharp, before continuing. "This operation is pivotal, Steve. Petrov's knowledge ties straight to the WWII relic. Failure isn't on the table." Dave slides a document over the table. "Inside, you will find information on all the key figures in Viktor's organisation that our intel has uncovered so far, including Natasha Belova; she is Viktor's cyber warfare expert. She is one mean bitch. If you get into a cyber war, she will be the one pulling the wires. Plus, there is info on Sergei Ivanov, Viktor's muscle and enforcer. Will kill without asking questions. If you get into a firefight with Viktor, you can bet Sergei is leading the attack. Plus, everything you need to know about Viktor.

"Go through this with your team. Make sure everyone understands their role and is prepared for anything."

"Understood. This is as good as done," I say, opening the documents.

Dave sighs with relief, "I know you will, Steve. You and your team are the best at what you do."

The team filters into the briefing room, their readiness evident. The projector hums overhead, its beam cutting through the dim light as murmured conversations fade. Chairs scrape against the floor as they settle into place around the table.

"Eyes front," my words cut through the silence, the gravity of the mission hanging in the air. The map flickers to life on the screen mounted on the wall, its contours tracing the eastern border of Germany. "Mission is a high-value extraction. Target zone: a farm complex outside Heinrichsberg."

Simon leans forward, "What's the insertion and exfil route?"

"Hold that question for the moment." The remote clicks, shifting the image. A photo fills the screen—a grey-haired man with eyes like flint. "Meet Dr Ivan Petrov, expert and researcher in military-grade weapons development. He's our asset, and the mission is to extract and deliver him to this secure facility for debriefing."

Derek taps a pen against the table. "Enemy presence confirmed, Steve?"

"Yes, ex-military. Armed and organised. The village is locked down tight, and Petrov's transfer is set in nine days." My glance shifts to George, "Overwatch is yours for both infill and exfil."

The response is nonverbal, a subtle change in posture that speaks volumes. A thousand-yard shot from George isn't a question; it's a guarantee.

The next slide clicks into place, revealing the town's grid. Roads, structures, and key points light up the framework of our operation.

"Each of you, with your unique skills and roles, is integral to this mission. Simon, transportation's yours as always." The pointer taps the map, highlighting a cluster of trees behind the settlement. "The Osprey touches down here. Terrain keeps it hidden, minimising exposure. Once boots hit the ground, transport becomes mission-critical. If conditions shift, rapid exfil is non-negotiable. Dave's lined up local support to back us up."

Dave steps in, his voice steady and precise. "Contact will meet you at the LZ. His Name is Billy James. He's an ex-British Special Forces combat medic, fluent in German, who understands the terrain and the risks. He'll get you to the complex. You might know him."

The room draws silent, as the name lands—memories surface, sharp and clear. Billy wasn't just another operator—his visits to the Isle of Wight bridged camaraderie into kinship. For a beat, the mission fades into the shared weight of that connection before snapping back into focus.

Simon doesn't miss a beat. "Good to hear Billy's on board. Wonder where he went. Send his mission contact details over. By morning, I'll have options lined up for transport."

"Derek, lock down comms. Maintain a clear line to base and us, and close down any interference before it starts."

"I'm already running the frequencies, Steve," Derek replies, his hands moving across his laptop. Encryption protocols light up the screen.

"Lucy, dive into the militia intel: their movements, patterns, all of it. The data in the pack needs to be cross-referenced with that of Dave's team. Updates. If there's a ghost route, find it. Coordinate with Simon and loop Billy into the analysis."

Lucy's focus sharpens, and the faintest flicker of understanding crosses her face as she absorbs the directive. Without hesitation, Lucy begins scanning through the material, the gears of strategy already turning.

"Any questions?" The silence holds weight, an unspoken confidence passing between us. "Good. We're wheels up at 04:00."

As the team scatters to their tasks, the image of Petrov stares back from the briefing screen. The man's presence isn't just a mission target, it's a keystone in a structure that's only beginning to reveal itself.

The corridor vibrates as the team digs into the mission. The air carries the weight of calculated urgency. All movements are precise and deliberate. Conversations are clipped and technical, every word driving toward the objective. Hours stretch as screens flicker with data, maps, and intel. Connections with Dave's team solidify, and a steady flow of information shapes the plan's framework. Critical points align, forming a strategy that leaves no space for errors or gaps.

Monitors display real-time overlays of the target zone while keyboards clatter in unison with Derek's encrypted frequencies. Lucy pieces together movement patterns, focusing through the noise like a scalpel. Simon's strategies for transport logistics and notes are concise and ready for execution. Every one of us commits the data to memory, knowing the tangible traces will be wiped before the first step is taken.

The rhythm of preparation builds, each second tightening the net around the objective. Questions are asked, answered, and catalogued. Scenarios are crafted, then countered, layers designed to anticipate chaos and convert it into control. The team's anticipation of turmoil is a testament to their strategic thinking and preparedness.

Two hours later, we leave the building, stepping into the night. The darkness shrouds the building, the cold biting against the intensity left inside.

"Everything's aligned, Time to move out," my words cut through the dark like an order already in motion.

For security reasons, we won't be returning to last night's location. Too predictable. This time, it's a local bed and breakfast tucked away in another village, a short drive from Guardian Security Solutions. With Lucy at the wheel, guiding the vehicle through corners with precision. Behind us, Simon, George, and Derek trail in the second car, their headlights carving through the night, casting flickering shadows across the deserted streets.

The B&B rises ahead, ivy creeping over the brick façade, its windows spilling a warm glow into the fading dusk. Lights trace the edges of the structure, blending old-world charm with clean, modern touches. The interior reveals a glimpse of calm—muted colours, worn furniture, and a quiet atmosphere that contrasts with the mission on our minds.

Check-in wraps up fast. The receptionist's polite curiosity is almost masking an instinctive wariness. The key cards pass hands, exchanged with a few words, and then the moment is gone. Up in the accommodation, our bags hit the floor, gear stacked within easy reach, all arranged for rapid access.

Twenty minutes later, we reconvene at the rear of the hotel. A wooden deck spreads across the rear, bordered by trees swaying a little under a cool breeze. Lanterns throw circles of light onto the planks, casting long shadows that flicker and shift. Tables sit weathered by time, their surfaces marked by countless moments like this, where plans are mulled over and decisions are cemented.

At the furthest table, beers land with a dull thud, condensation slipping down the glass as tension mixes with quiet camaraderie. The team settles, bodies relaxed but minds alert, ready for the next move.

"Alright," I begin, breaking the silence. "Let's go over everything one last time. Simon, you're handling the transport. Any updates?"

Simon keeps it direct. "A vehicle is lined up. Fast, quiet, and discreet. Billy's on board to help with the extraction. We'll be ready for whatever comes."

"Good," I say, turning to Derek. "Comms?"

With one quick tap on the tablet, Derek activates the communications. "Locked. HQ and the team are on a secure line. Enemy frequencies tracked; our digital signature sealed down."

"Perfect. Lucy, intel on the militia?"

Leaning closer, Lucy's voice hardens. "The militia's well-armed and trained. Their patrols are frequent, but their timing is predictable. Same route, same intervals."

After taking a swig of my beer, "George, did you spot any possible position for a sniper overwatch?" I ask.

"Spotted a few tall buildings; one of the tallest is a pub called the Kuhstall, which may give me a good view over the target area, but I need to scout the terrain as soon as we're on target. Then, we can ensure we have visual coverage from all directions," George replies, his focus razor-sharp.

"This is the moment. Plan for every outcome. Petrov will be extracted, and the relic secured," I say, after taking a deep breath.

A heavy silence settles over the table, the kind that speaks volumes without a word exchanged. Faces around me carry the burden of the mission ahead. The next 24 hours demand clarity, a clarity that will be our guiding light in the darkness, precision, and resolve.

"Zulu time tomorrow is 02:00. As Derek couldn't be bothered to show up for yesterday's customary piss up, let's have a few beverages and toast to the success of the first phase, but keep it measured. Remember, we need clear heads in the morning, so let's get some rest," I emphasise, knowing that the rest we take now may impact our performance tomorrow.

Drinks clink together, breaking the tension, and the camaraderie reminds us of the trust that has been forged between us. This trust is our anchor, our reassurance that we are not alone in this. Conversations remain light, skimming over the gravity of what lies ahead. Two rounds of beers consumed, and the group rises, movement deliberate but not rushed. The deck empties, leaving behind only the sound of the trees whispering in the breeze.

Inside, the hotel's atmosphere shifts, calm and understated. Carpets absorb the sound of footsteps. Framed photographs on the walls convey a sense of history and endurance. The faint scent of wood polish lingers in the air, blending with the sharp undertone of fresh linens.

The bed offers a rare respite, a momentary truce before chaos resumes. The room's simplicity blends comfort with functionality, its warm hues almost at odds with the cold precision of what occupies my mind. Through the window, the garden reflects the moon's light, shadows stretching and shifting like players in the game to come. Petrov's face and the Heinrichsberg map dominate my thoughts, the pieces aligning as preparation gives way to execution.

A measured exhale steadies the rhythm within; my focus narrows on the distant line, demanding nothing less than precision.

Chapter Four — Extraction

The chill cuts deep as we exit the building at 2:00. Darkness drapes over everything, a seamless cover that hides us. The mission is set, and each step counts down. There's no turning back from this point.

"Let's move," my words slice through the stillness.

Lucy climbs into the driver's seat, turns the key, and the vehicle growls to life as I clamber into the passenger side. Next to us, another engine roars into action—Simon, George, and Derek fall into formation.

The streets unfold under a cloak of shadow, stretching over the asphalt like a predator stalking prey. Streetlights flicker, casting fleeting glimpses of the unknown ahead. Blackened windows and skeletal trees whisper warnings we're in too deep to heed. Shadows devour the path forward, a silent promise of what waits beyond.

As we drive the plan cycles through my mind, every detail is calibrated. In no time, the Guardian Security Solutions facility emerges, lights breaking the darkness like a sudden flare. Over at the airfield, a Bell V-22 Osprey dominates the horizon, a sentinel waiting to deliver us into the fray. The imposing rotors cut through the floodlights, throwing jagged shapes across the tarmac—steel and readiness wrapped in shadow.

"Ride's ready to roll," Lucy murmurs, eyes fixed on the Osprey.

"Let's gear up," I reply, pointing towards the building.

With our vehicles parked, we head inside, navigating the corridors that have become familiar over the last few days. The facility is buzzing with activity. When we arrive at the store, our kit is already laid out for us.

"Grab your stuff," I say, pushing the pace. "Time's short."

The pungent smell of rifle oil lingers as the team collects their gear, checking and rechecking everything. Combat vests are donned, weapons holstered, and packs fastened. Once ready, we head toward the aircraft. The dark sky illuminates the Osprey under the floodlights. Dave stands beside the plane, his posture taut, expression complex, anticipating our arrival.

"Morning, is everything set?" Dave says, eyes scanning each of us.

"Ready as we'll ever be," I reply, our eyes locked in silent understanding.

"Fantastic. Remember, the clock's ticking. Move in fast. Extract Petrov alive. My team will monitor the situation from here."

"Understood," I say, glancing at the team. "Let's make a move."

The roar of the engines vibrates through the metal floor, a constant reminder of the power at our disposal as we step aboard. Inside, the interior is stark and functional. The aircraft is designed for versatility and speed, with rows of jump seats lining the walls leading to the cockpit.

Lucy settles in beside me. "This is it." The words fight through the mechanical roar, carried more by purpose than volume.

"Yeah," I respond, my eyes fixed ahead. "No turning back now."

A red light filters through the cabin, stretching shadows over faces. Simon, George, and Derek lock in on the opposite side of the aircraft. The bitter aroma of fuel melds with adrenaline's bite, pushing the anticipation into a tangible force. Each of us is lost in our thoughts, running through every aspect of the mission.

The ramp closes with a heavy thud, sealing us inside. The pilot's voice crackles over the intercom. "All set in the back?"

"Ready when you are," I reply.

"Roger that. Lifting off in five."

A deep rumble fills the cabin as the Osprey shakes, surging upward 300 metres into the air. The transition from vertical to horizontal flight is smooth, the landscape slipping out of view beneath us. The world outside becomes a blur, the landscape rushing past as we soar through the night sky towards our objective.

Once more, I glance around at the team, seeing the same determination and anticipation mirrored in their eyes as mine. This is the lull before the chaos breaks loose. We've prepared for every eventuality.

"The time to the LZ is 1 hour and 10 minutes, so we'll be on the ground soon. Remember the plan, and we will come through this," my voice cuts through the engine noise. Nods of agreement meet my words.

To keep everyone focused and prevent minds from drifting off the mission and to places you would rather not go, I say over the intercom, "Alright, let's run through the extraction again."

Simon leans in. voice steady. "Landing points in the clearing past the trees. From LZ, Billy will lead us to the compound — I'll handle the transport, out fast if required."

"Derek, you have the comms?" I say, turning to our communications expert.

"Link's secure. HQ and the team will stay connected throughout. I've got this covered," Derek says, fingers moving over the radio's surface, checking the frequencies.

I continue. "Lucy, what's the latest on the militia?"

"Nothing fresh since last night. Automatic weapons confirmed. Surveillance drones are possible. Deployment? Minimal probability of use before first light," Lucy says. Red illumination carves through the dark, the light casting a sharp glint in her eyes.

"George, you'll be our eyes on the ground. Locate the best vantage points for sniper overwatch," I say, looking straight at him.

George's face is set with focus. "After touchdown, and we come close to the village, I'll sweep the area, pick a high point, secure my position, and cover you. Not a single tango slips past."

"Perfect," I reply, locking eyes with the team. "We strike fast and vanish before anybody realises what's happening."

As the plan is refreshed in our minds, the pilot's voice crackles over the intercom, "Ten minutes to drop zone."

Everyone begins to give their equipment a final check gear and cock weapons. The clicks and snaps echo through the space, the rhythm sharpening our edge.

Lucy's hands work over the rifle with fluid motions. "Let's hope we're not walking into a hot LZ."

"Expect everything to go against the plan. If we encounter a challenging landing zone, we push through and finish what we start. Always," my words clipped, deliberate.

A strap yanks tight, webbing creaking under strain. "Transport's set." Simon's words land flat, unwavering. "Clean entry and exit."

Shifting an earpiece into place, a slight smile breaks through. "Our communications are locked in and running," Derek says.

George removes a round from the magazine before snapping the brass casing back into place, pressing down to check the feed, expression cold and steady. The pressure in my chest builds, every heartbeat counting the seconds until we land.

Outside, the night stretches on in complete darkness, with the aircraft's lights off to keep us hidden and allow our vision to adjust. The tension in the cabin is profound, the team lost in thought as we brace for what is to come.

The pilot's voice crackles over the intercom, "Approaching drop zone. Prepare for landing."

For the last few kilometres, the Osprey skims the terrain, hugging the contours like a predator stalking prey. The ride bucks and sways, the aircraft adjusting to every rise and dip of the ground. Turbulence surges through the cabin, jarring bones and tightening grips on gear. Below, the terrain stretches into a shadowed expanse, broken by the faint glint of moonlight off the treetops. A clearing looms ahead, the darkness both a refuge and a threat.

"Gear check!" The command slices through the hum of engines, demanding immediate action. Fingers move across straps and latches, securing weapons and equipment. The rifle rests steady in my grip, the cold steel a steadying anchor in the chaos.

The Osprey rotors shift for a sudden, vertical descent. The momentum pulls hard against muscles. The abrupt change is jarring but familiar — adrenaline courses through the body, pushing aside the churn in the gut.

The pilot's voice crackles through comms. "Ten seconds to touchdown."

The rear ramp grinds open, hydraulics groaning against the urgency. A blast of air rushes in, sharp and raw, bringing the scent of churned earth and the promise of violence. The clearing rushes closer, details sharpening as the ground rises to meet the aircraft.

"Go!" I yell, the shout cutting through the noise as the ramp slams down on the deck with a metallic thud. In an instant, boots hit the ground, bodies moving with the precision of a well-oiled machine. Movements synchronised, weapons trained outward as the team dissolve into the treeline.

Darkness blankets the terrain, swallowing forms and erasing outlines. The Osprey's rotors churn the air one last time before lifting away, leaving only the hum of the aircraft's retreat to fade into the distance. All around, shadows stretch and twist beneath the canopy, merging with the undergrowth.

The rifle steadies against my shoulder, the barrel tracing the edges of the unfamiliar. The absence of the aircraft noise amplifies the world around us — branches creak under unseen weight, and the occasional snap of a twig cuts through the near silence. The forest starts to swell with sound — insects drone; leaves shift against the night's breath; an unknown animal moves through the brush somewhere in the distance.

The team's weapons are trained outward, scanning for any sign of movement. Anticipation ripples through the air, like a predator waiting to strike, poised for imminent action.

"Simon, any sign of Billy?" I ask, my focus tracking the dark shapes for anything out of place.

"Not yet, he's supposed to be here," comes the reply.

Moments pass like hours until a figure peels away from the black, moving in our direction.

"Billy," I murmur, recognising the familiar gait.

A steady and sure voice cuts through the silence. "Steve, great to see you," the figure steps forward, emerging from the gloom, presence unwavering. "Timing's tight. Let's move."

"And you, mate, let's move out," I reply, my words leaving no room for hesitation.

Steps fall into a disciplined rhythm as the team advances, movements calculated, blending into the forest's cover. From this point forward, we will have no second chance, no retreat. The team's discipline ensures that every action is executed with order and control.

Shadows become allies, wrapping around us as we navigate the undergrowth. Billy takes the point with me, each step trying to avoid dry leaves and exposed twigs. The team stays tight, fluid in their spacing, and ready for any eventuality. George secures our six, a watchful presence. Lucy, Derek, and Simon hold their positions in between, their silence speaking volumes of their focus.

The morning chill rakes across exposed skin. Damp earth saturates the air, thick with the scent of pine resin and decay. The wind moves in a restless current, shifting between silence and something out of reach. Familiar sounds ripple through the stillness — branches creak under boots, and nocturnal creatures stir nearby.

Each disturbance sends a pulse of awareness through the body, sharpening instincts to a razor's edge. The village of Heinrichsberg huddles in the gloom, its buildings stacked tight, whispering secrets behind closed doors. Structures huddle in the darkness, shapes broken by jagged rooftops and half-lit alleys. Empty windows stare outward, vacant and unblinking, as if something lingers beyond reach.

The undergrowth rustles with sharp and unexpected movement. A deer bolts from cover, cutting through the trees, freezing us in place, before the forest swallows the moment, returning to an eerie calm as the animal vanishes. The silence stretches, punctuated by faint murmurs of wildlife that linger in the background.

"Clear," Billy's calm and controlled voice breaks through, eyes sweeping the terrain.

The formation resumes, weaving between the towering trees and dense shrubs. The natural cover shields our advance, obscuring the outlines of our movements. The shapes of rooftops pierce the treeline, signalling our proximity to the target.

Minutes stretch into 20 as we close in on Heinrichsberg's perimeter. The farm complex emerges at the far edge of the village, silhouettes cutting into the horizon. The pre-dawn light etches the structures in contrast against the surroundings.

The radio crackles as I direct the team, "Approach from the western side. Maintain cover and avoid unnecessary exposure."

"Roger that. You take point," comes the reply from Simon.

The terrain shifts, leaving patches of darkness that cloak our approach from the waking world.

"Monitor those windows for movement, Lucy," I whisper, eyes sweeping the nearby houses.

The route weaves through narrow lanes and neglected gardens, every step measured to keep us within the shadows. The air clings with an oppressive stillness, broken only by the faint scuff of gear and the occasional rustle of leaves. Every sound drills into the silence, amplifying the tension as we press on.

Ahead, the farm complex begins to take shape, a stark outline etched against the horizon. The dim light reveals structures weathered by time, their silhouettes projecting a foreboding stillness. Moonlight stretches over the horizon, revealing fractured light that dances over the terrain, hinting at safe pathways hidden in plain sight.

"Stick to the plan," I say, keeping my voice quiet and firm.

The team comes to a halt, taking up covering arcs of fire. A quick hand signal sends Lucy and George toward a faded grey barn on the left.

"Overwatch," I say, cutting through the quiet. "Find a line of sight on the target and cover our approach."

"Copy," Lucy confirms as the duo integrates with the environment, forming a protective barrier for the operation's critical entry phase.

Boots press firm into the earth, bodies ready to advance. Simon's rifle shifts, fingers coiled around the grip, tension crackling through each knuckle. A slow sweep of the perimeter locks in the unseen, waiting for something to break.

"Advance on my signal," I whisper, shifting focus to the route ahead. The open space between us and the target building stretches like an exposed nerve. Shadows from the nearby treeline offer a potential refuge.

The plan clicks into place, every detail running through my mind like a well-rehearsed script. Timing and precision will dictate the outcome. Nothing less than absolute coordination will suffice.

Lucy and George remain focused from their rooftop vantage point, sights locked in place. The stillness stays undisturbed until Lucy's calm voice filters through over the radio,

"LK, in position."

"Roger, keep us covered," my command cuts clean over the radio.

Shadows shroud the rest of the team as the farm draws closer; the ground beneath our boots is alive with definition. We find a cluster of trees 50 metres out, providing ample cover as we assess the scene. The quiet is unsettling, the type of stillness that suggests lurking danger.

Billy's voice cracks through the comms, "Two tangos by the gate. No movement. Need to neutralise without making a sound or raising an alarm."

A quick sweep takes in the guards and the path ahead. A silent signal brings Derek and Billy into position. Simon and I advance, primed to strike before the sentries have a chance of reacting.

Like a shadow, Simon closes in on one of the guards, knife flickering once in the pale light; moments later, the man's body sinks to the ground without a sound. Already on the move, I close in on the second. My blade finds its mark—below the rear of the neck, severing the spinal cord in one clean motion. An instant later, the body drops to the deck. A faint gasp is the only sound of a dying man before everything goes silent again.

No blood, no mess—just two bodies in the dark. We slip back into the cover of the trees, the guards dispatched, and the path ahead clear.

"Entrance secured," I say over the radio.

Crouched behind a brick gatepost, the rough texture digs into my shoulder as the rifle stays steady against my grip. Ahead of me, the courtyard stretches in uneven patterns. Cobblestones slick from recent rain reflect fractured light from dim lights hanging off the walls. Walls press tight on either side, closing the world into a confined space of stone and shadow, a funnel ready to trap anything that dares enter the kill zone.

A barn looms at the far end opposite the farmhouse, the black wooden door sealed tight, an imposing barricade against prying eyes. The aged timber stands out in stark contrast to the damp stone, exuding a foreboding presence that defies the stillness of the scene. Whatever lies within isn't innocent. The danger is unmistakable.

The farmhouse stands at the other side of the courtyard, weathered by years of neglect. Brickwork buckles under years of decay, fractures splitting through the surface like veins on dry skin. Timber splinters under its weight, edges curling, rotted from within. The structure refuses to fall, standing rigid, defiant, waiting for something to finish what time started.

Greystone steps climb to a shadowed doorway, the windows embedded in the building empty yet brimming with unseen menace. Instinct and experience suggests unseen threats behind the glass. The lack of activity warns of imminent chaos.

A flickering bulb above the door casts fractured light across the stairs, dragging shadows into a restless, twitching rhythm. The hum of electricity vibrates, making it the only sound breaking the unnatural quiet. The charged air mirrors the team's discipline, exact movements and breaths held in control. The rifle stays locked against my shoulder. My senses stretch to catch the slightest disturbance.

On my signal we advance into the courtyard, every step precise, each movement blending with the muted shadows. Near the barn, a flash of movement stirs at the edges of my vision—a detail too fluid for the inanimate. The figures emerge as if conjured from the dark, a patrol moving close by. Four men spread in formation, weapons held ready.

"Incoming," I whisper into the comms. "Four tangos. Prepare to engage."

Behind the fractured stone wall, Simon blends into the ruins, rifle following the shifting shadows. Billy locks into position by a stack of crates, weapon raised and aimed toward the darkened barn. Derek stays beside me, both of us motionless as the other two move closer. Their boots scuff the cobblestones, an irregular rhythm that betrays their relaxed yet alert state.

A sharp flick of my hand directs Simon, the signal passing between us with practised efficiency. Rifle barrel angled toward the nearest target, Billy adjusts, covering the rear. The world narrows to the sound of my pulse, steady and deliberate.

The crack of suppressed fire from the team's weapons breaks the stillness. Each shot is precise. Guards drop in sync, bodies folding into the shadows without resistance. No echoes, no warnings, only the quiet reclaiming ground as if nothing had ever disturbed it.

Simon's voice cuts through the comms. "Clear."

Billy and Simon hold the perimeter, shielding against more unexpected interference. Derek shifts beside me as we approach the farmhouse door, the surface scarred and reinforced with an electronic lock glowing in the dark. My hand presses against the cold metal of the door handle, testing the resistance. It's locked.

Derek retrieves his tablet, connecting it to the lock, the screen casting a faint blue hue as fingers move with practised skill. Seconds later, layers of security are bypassed and the lock releases with a sharp metallic click. The door swings inward, revealing the unknown depths of the farmhouse. The silence outside fades as we enter.

The timber beams above press down into the confined space, transforming the corridor into an oppressive tunnel. Dust hangs in the air while shadows choke the corners, merging into one another and reducing visibility to a narrow stretch ahead. Every step is taken with precision, yet even the softest creak echoes through the corridor like a warning waiting to spring.

A red flickering light at head height halts me mid-step. A raised hand stops the team, the unspoken signal spreading like a ripple through water. The sheen against the concrete walls speaks of a problem not mentioned in the intel — a motion detector.

In a hushed voice, I relay the info, "Motion sensor."

No need for words, a tool slides free from Derek's jacket, compact and efficient, shaped for moments like this. Derek moves forward, shoulders compressing against rough stone, edging beneath the detector, hugging the wall and remaining in the sensor's blind spot, slipping beneath the sensor's arc. A wire yields without protest. Just the faintest click, then silence. Seconds stretch. One heartbeat. Another. Then darkness. Sensor down.

"We're clear, but assume more ahead," Derek whispers, focus already shifting to the path forward.

The corridor extends deeper into the unknown, the end marked by a heavy door with no sound escaping from beyond. The intel suggests Petrov's location, but the dead silence wrapping the air screams of a trap lying in wait.

A signal sends Simon forward, closing the gap to the door. An outstretched hand grips the handle. The metal is cold and unyielding under Simon's touch. The turn is controlled, inch by inch, keeping the action smooth and soundless. A faint creak escapes as the door eases open, the noise no louder than the shuffle of a shadow.

The gap reveals a flickering light, casting shifting shadows that stretch and twist across the stained concrete floor. A sickly hue pervades the cramped room, revealing its raw, unvarnished state. The air carries the bitter tang of sweat and damp stone, a suffocating mix that clings to the walls. In this room, danger might lurk in every corner, unseen but real.

Petrov sits in the centre, bound to a chair, wrists lashed to the metal arms. Head slumped forward, chin brushing his chest. Layers of grime and dried blood streak tattered clothing, the body carrying the weight of exhaustion and torment. Once a figure of intellect and defiance, now cuts a broken silhouette in the harsh light. The scene radiates vulnerability, but experience warns against assumptions; still waters conceal the deadliest currents.

The team holds steady, our breaths slow and measured, blending with the faint hum of the flickering bulb above. The oppressive quiet presses inward, an ominous calm that hints at traps waiting to pounce.

A hand gesture sends Billy into the room, weapon sweeping the space. The rest of us, ready and alert, follow close, stepping into the unknown, where any move might ignite the chaos beneath the surface.

Kneeling beside Petrov, his tattered clothes reek of desperation and the violence he's endured.

"Petrov."

The name lands like a trigger. Shoulders jerk, a flicker of recognition flashing in a bloodshot stare. His head inches upward. The movement is laborious, fighting the invisible chains of exhaustion. For a fleeting moment, comprehension pierces through the haze in Petrov's gaze.

"Time to move."

As my blade slices clean through the ropes, the tension in the bindings releases in a whisper of worn fibres. Reddened wrists emerge, raw and swollen from relentless friction. My eyes scan his movements, reading the limits of endurance and gauging whether the next stretch will break him or if the fire inside burns strong enough to carry through.

Petrov's fingers jerk, spasming as sensation fights its way back. Joints stiffen, rebellion surging through limbs unaccustomed to movement. A shudder ripples upward, shoulders bracing, breath clamped between clenched teeth. Knees threaten collapse, muscle and willpower wrestling for control, neither willing to give ground.

"Can you walk?" I ask, ready to assist.

"Yes, I can walk," comes the reply from Petrov.

My hand locks around Petrov's strained arm muscles, bracing against the unsteady rhythm of motion. A lurch, then another, each step a battle between willpower and collapse. Silence swallows hesitation, urgency grinding down hesitation. The clock bleeds seconds, the gap between survival and failure shrinking with every breath.

From beyond the room, the piercing wail of an alarm erupts, cutting through the building and scattering any chance of extraction without detection. The tranquil silence shatters, replaced by the thrum of urgency pounding in my chest. This mission just took a violent turn.

Yelling at the top of my voice, "We've been compromised! Move, move!"

With Petrov between us, we hurry back down the corridor. Thundering footsteps race across the floorboards, the clash of shouted commands in English and German reverberating like artillery fire in a language war. Figures rush past doorways, shadows stretching as guards scramble in every direction, jolted by the alarm.

Chapter Five — Escape and Evasion

The instant we break from the farmhouse, the night explodes with gunfire. Muzzle flashes burst from the barn, cutting through the darkness.

The sharp crack of Simon's rifle answers first, followed by Billy's. Each shot is precise and controlled, but the enemy's return fire is fierce, bullets tearing the air around us.

The sound of rounds striking the stone walls echoes like a death knell, fragments of cobblestone spraying up like shrapnel.

"Sprint to the vehicle!"

My order cuts through the chaos as I grab Petrov's arm, dragging him toward the rusted shell of an old tractor. Inches away, rounds ricochet off the metal, the sharp clangs reverberating into the shadows.

Simon, Derek and Billy keep up a relentless barrage, their weapons barking in unison. Every squeeze of the trigger is a heartbeat — steady, unwavering. Each bullet strikes true, dropping targets with perfect execution. We dash across the courtyard, boots pounding against the cobblestones.

More armed people flood from the barn, expressions twisted with rage, rifles raised. The staccato bursts of gunfire ring out. For a second, time slows. The people ahead are targets, shapes to be neutralised. Nothing more.

"Kill the bastards!" my command hits hard.

We unleash hell. Muzzle flashes light our faces as the attackers drop, crumpling like discarded ragdolls, their screams swallowed by the night. The gate looms ahead, and we push through one at a time. Derek's boots hammer the ground close behind me, a reassuring rhythm that seals our escape. Beyond the boundary, the village stretches out in silence. Every shadow becomes a potential threat.

Speed carries us through the narrow lanes, the pounding of boots syncing with the thrum of adrenaline. The echoes of combat start to recede, leaving only the rhythm of our escape. An old barn rises ahead, its silhouette jagged and looming. Dropping inside, we take positions, weapons ready. Breaths come deep and fast but controlled.

"Contact! Multiple tangos incoming!" Derek's yells.

"GD, suppressing fire—now!" I yell into the radio.

"S3, Roger that," comes George's cold reply.

A nano-second later, the crack of a sniper rifle cuts through the air—every shot like a whispered death sentence. A blink and the shift begins as Lucy's shots rip through the air, resonating with a decisive finality. Armed men falter, their return fire stalling as they take in the sudden shift in control.

Chest hammering with a relentless rhythm, my back presses hard against the rough wall. George and Lucy anchor our retreat as the enemy assault begins to falter. Their indecision buys us fragments of time, the kind you can't afford to waste.

The narrow alleys stretch ahead as we continue to the vehicle, each stride sinking us deeper into exhaustion, but we can't afford to slow down. At last, the footsteps behind start to fade, a false reprieve before the next wave descends. The enemy will be regrouping, and their assault is likely to be more intense than before.

"Keep moving!" I shout, the command cutting through the chaos, slicing clean through the rush of adrenaline and sweat. Boots pound into the dirt, bodies surging forward. The team is united in purpose. Every motion intertwines with the next, a machine engineered for one outcome—survival.

The shadows pulse with menace, crouched in corners, daring us to take a wrong step. My focus sharpens as I scan the darkness for any movement. The twists and turns of the backstreets compress into a labyrinth meant to disorient. Each corner tightens the noose, the maze threatening to funnel us into an ambush. Boots strike the slick pavement, distant echoes chasing us like phantoms.

A distant shout rises, garbled and sinister, brushing against my senses like a forewarning of danger that lies in wait.

Billy's voice cuts through the haze, strained yet resolute. "We're close." The words carry a grit that pulls the team forward, past the drag of exhaustion and the weight of the unknown.

The alley spills open, revealing a garage just ahead. Billy had excelled in his prep, and the vehicle inside idles with a steady hum cutting through the night like salvation.

"Inside the vehicle, now!" I yell, my voice cutting through the chaos.

Petrov stumbles, my grip yanking him forward, a dead weight, but moving. Limbs tangle, no fight left—a hard impact against the seat. The door slams shut just as Billy's foot crushes the accelerator. The engine roars to life, tyres clawing at the ground, spitting dirt and gravel into a chaotic spray that disappears into the night behind us.

It's not long before bullets tear into the van, hammering the reinforced frame, each impact a sharp reminder of the enemy's focus. Sparks flare in the rearview mirror, fleeting bursts of orange against the consuming darkness. The farmhouse dissolves into a shrinking silhouette; the barking muzzle flashes grow faint as the distance swallows up movement. Speed is our ally now, momentum pulling us out of their reach.

Inside, the air brims with unspoken urgency. Petrov sits stiff, wedged between Derek and Simon. Trembling hands clutch knees, breathing erratic like he's still bracing for the bullets that have already fallen behind. The momentary silence is deceptive—a thin veil stretched over the unknown that waits ahead.

The van screeches to a halt at the pre-arranged point in the woods to pick up the two snipers. The doors burst open, and George and Lucy pile in, faces unreadable in the dim light. Once more, the vehicle lurches forward before the doors even slam shut, Billy's threading through the twisting lanes heading for the safe house.

Above, the moonlight streaks through the trees, flashing across our faces like strobe lights as the tyres bounce over ruts and unseen obstacles. The cabin rattles with every jolt, but no one flinches. It's a rhythm burned into us from years of operations, the dance of chaos and control that defines combat.

"Movement on our six. They're regrouping!" Derek yells.

The van's interior shifts. Fresh magazines click into place. Straps tighten, bodies brace. George's rifle rises, barrel angling towards the rear doors. Shoulders roll, posture locked, breath controlled. The precision of his movements conveys an unspoken truth: readiness is a matter of survival.

Through the windscreen, the road twists into an endless ribbon of uncertainty. Shadows blur with the terrain, the lines between friend and foe swallowed in the fog of war. My grip tightens around my weapon.

"Keep the vehicle steady!" I bark.

The words come out crisp, slicing through the pounding of tyres and the distant hum of pursuit. Billy nods once, knuckles white on the wheel as the van threads another tight corner, the rear skidding but never breaking out of control. The road stretches ahead, a black ribbon twisting through the emptiness, disappearing into the horizon. Fatigue circles like a predator, waiting for the slightest lapse.

Hand resting on the van's door handle, I pause, anticipation coiling like a spring. One checkpoint cleared, but the mission breathes on, the weight pressing harder with each step. We are ready for any threat. Senses heightened, ready for what might come next. They say the most challenging moments are always out of reach, waiting for their turn to strike.

The van grinds to an abrupt halt, tyres scattering gravel into the stillness. To our front, the safe house emerges, a silhouette blending into the barren fields. For now, a relic of a forgotten purpose stands obscured by isolation—a fortress born of neglect and necessity, the perfect refuge.

"Everyone out, now," I command, scanning the perimeter for threats. Shadows cling to the building under the creeping light of dawn, painting the scene with a deceptive calm that doesn't fool me for a second.

"Eyes sharp. Possible movement is inbound." The directive cuts through the quiet. "George, find a vantage point. Keep tabs on the horizon."

My focus shifts as Petrov exits the vehicle, pace unsteady but improving. Simon conceals the van by driving into the cover of overgrown brush, staying close for rapid extraction if needed.

As we move toward the safe house, the team fans out, our movements a dance of synchronised precision. Lucy holds the left flank, rifle steady, gaze sweeping over potential ambush points. Billy mirrors Lucy on the right, the barrel tracing an invisible arc of readiness. Derek trails behind, fingers gliding over his radio, hunting for electronic signatures that might betray Viktor's men closing in.

A hand gesture halts the advance. The door's lock remains untouched—a slight relief, though trust in appearances is a luxury we can't afford.

"Lucy, secure the rear. Billy, on the door!" I shout.

Every sound sharpens, from the crunch of boots to the faint rustle of wind through dry grass. Billy steps forward, hands steady, entering the unlock code.

The lock clicks open, the door swings inward, and the team slips into the waiting darkness like shadows. A solid thud echoes as the entry seals behind us, isolating the space from the chaos beyond.

The room is stark, the simplicity striking — bare concrete walls enclosing a space stripped of anything unnecessary. A skylight overhead casts weak light, enough to penetrate the gloom. A steel table commands the centre, with maps spread across its surface, some crumpled and marked with streaks of red ink, while others are pristine but ominous in detail. Communication equipment, such as radios, encrypted laptops, and a satellite phone, is assembled with military precision and serves as a lifeline to the outside world.

Along one wall, metal chairs rest, their edges scuffed and worn down to dull silver. Reinforced windows stand near impenetrable, blinds drawn so tight they turn the outside world into a forgotten memory. This is a stopgap, a tool, nothing more. Every feature screams function over comfort, designed to keep us moving forward without pause.

Petrov stumbles, steps unsteady, a hollow shell held together by instinct alone. A silent order directs him to the chair, a sharp drop sealing the command. The crash echoes as steel bites into the ground, a body slumped and drained. Whatever held him up before no longer does.

The lines across Petrov's face map the struggle, endurance etched into every crevice, though something new kindles behind the exhaustion — a spark daring to believe survival is within reach.

Billy circles the room's perimeter, weapon ready, scanning every angle like a hawk. The tension presses in, heavy and oppressive, the kind that never leaves even when the immediate danger recedes. This room is a hold, not a haven, a reminder that survival hinges on the seconds we don't waste.

"Secure the exits and keep your eyes on the perimeter," I order, voice sharp as steel. Billy disappears into the shadows of the room, steps measured and deliberate.

"Dr Petrov." I crouch to meet his gaze. "We've bought you some time, but the window is closing fast. Extraction comes soon, but you need to be ready to move."

"OK, I'll be ready," comes the faint reply from Petrov.

The room pulses with purpose, a machine of necessity set in motion. Complacency has no place here. Petrov's stare burns into mine, desperation clawing through ragged breaths.

"You can't imagine what they—" The plea shatters with the crackle of comms.

George's voice from the roof slams into the room. "Multiple contacts. Fast movers. Closing in."

The pulse in my neck thunders as I snap to action. "Positions! Threat inbound!"

Billy vaults to the window, now ajar enough to watch any approach, weapon raised, gaze slicing through the disturbed dust. Lucy anchors at the opposite side, rifle tracking every twitch in the shadows. Derek's hands blur across the comms console, scanning channels, hunting for intel that might tip the balance. The room contracts with tension, coiling tighter with each breath.

The door crashes open as Simon storms in, words cutting through the rising tide of chaos, "They're coming hard and have us surrounded."

The first crack of gunfire erupts, shattering the stillness. Glass from the window rains down in jagged shards, sharp as daggers bursting through the blinds, as glass shatters under a storm of lead. Dust swirls thick in the air, mingling with the acrid tang of gunpowder. The assault is relentless, impacting like a hammer blow, echoing off the walls.

"Take the arseholes down!" my voice tearing through the chaos, rifle spitting lead through shattered glass.

George's rifle erupts on the rooftop, delivering precision with every shot. The muted thuds of bodies hitting the dirt punctuate the cacophony. From Lucy's position, fire rakes through the advancing line, bullets finding their targets with surgical accuracy. Simon and Derek sweep the rear, movements sharp and seamless, fire-controlled and deliberate.

Rounds slam into the metal frames and ricochet, sparking like angry fireflies in the haze. The room pulses with raw energy, the battle unfolding in a dance of survival, each of us moving to the grim rhythm of combat.

"We need the exfil, now!" The command snaps from my mouth as I pull Petrov closer, his face etched with panic.

"Got the signal through—extraction in 10!" Derek yells over the sound of the onslaught.

Every second drags as rounds crash into the walls, sending tremors through the floor. My finger squeezes the trigger. The bullet finds the target, and the silhouette in the distance drops into shadow.

"If this keeps going, we'll be done in five minutes! " Simon growls, urgency pushing each word.

"Maintain your position!" I snap, teeth gritted. "Do not let anyone through."

"More hostiles, closing in fast," Lucy shouts over the chaos, "they've got heavier firepower. RPG inbound!"

The warning lands, and I drop to the deck, pulling Petrov with me. Seconds later, the explosion hits, the shockwave slamming into the reinforced walls. The air turns into a maelstrom of shattered glass, splintered wood, and choking dust. My ears ring, and my vision blurs from the force for a few seconds.

"Sitrep, now!" I yell; each word rasps, each syllable fighting through the haze.

"Holding firm!" George yells, "but they're gaining ground!"

Derek cuts through the noise over the comms. "Extraction inbound. Two minutes out."

The seconds drag like an eternity, every moment stretching thin under the weight of incoming fire. A new mag locks into place with a sharp click, muscle memory guiding my hands while my attention stays fixed on the chaos outside.

Simon's weapon tears through the early morning light, shots precise and unyielding. The team holds the line, keeping the enemy pinned, but the noose around us starts to tighten.

I scan the horizon, which reveals nothing but a void. Options are starting to dwindle, and the fight compresses into a crucible of survival. Another volley slams into the building, sending shards of concrete and splinters raining down. Close to the splintered frame, my barrel aligns with a target. The crack of the shot echoes in the room's confines, and a silhouette collapses lifeless.

"Hold positions," my voice cuts through the comms, sharp as a blade. "Two minutes—that's all we need."

The rifle settles firmly into my grip. Each squeeze of the trigger is precise, each round a counter to the attackers closing in. The team moves in harmony, the beat of fire syncing into a single rhythm that starts to push back the tide.

Smoke chokes the room, a swirling mass of dust and burnt powder that grips the lungs. Spent brass clatters like hollow rain, a grim punctuation to the ferocity around us. My rifle bucks, the recoil a familiar jolt. Cover is life; every motion is a negotiation, and the relentless assault is tearing apart our surroundings.

The heat of the fight consumes the thick and oppressive air. Bodies move with urgency, not thought. Survival transforms into instinct. Concrete chips away under merciless fire, the space narrowing with each strike. Voices mix with the percussion of weapons, commands cutting through the cacophony like lifelines.

Through the storm of battle, a new sound emerges, steady and mechanical—the unmistakable pulse of rotor blades slicing through the noise of the 50mm opening fire on the enemy from the aircraft. The unmistakable hum intensifies, each rotation pushing the Osprey toward us. It's the thread of hope we've fought to hold onto, the chance to escape this hell, and it's closing fast.

"Stand by!" I bark into the comms. This is the moment where survival meets execution.

"Extraction within sight," Derek's tone cuts through, sharp and urgent, driving the next move.

"Time to move—go, go!" The urgency in my voice cuts above the battle, driving Petrov toward the back door.

A fresh volley hammers the ground, forcing a sharp turn. Breaths burn as muscles push harder, every step carrying us closer to the Osprey. Its silhouette looms in the distance, the ramp open like a beacon in the storm. The roar of the engines drown out the cacophony, promising salvation beyond the fight.

Petrov stumbles, foot slipping on the ramp's edge. My hand clamps around an arm, hauling him upright without breaking stride. Simon moves in behind us, a living barrier against the chaos closing in. Shots erupt from George and Lucy's positions, sharp and unrelenting, carving a path through the onslaught.

With everyone onboard the ramp lifts, engines screaming as the ground falls away beneath us. Dust and shrapnel fade into the void, the battlefield shrinking as the Osprey rises. The hiss of the sealing door cuts off the last echoes of the fight, enclosing us in a tense, vibrating cocoon.

Sweat clings to skin, the hammer of adrenaline refusing to ease. Every breath drags sharp, the cabin closing around the bruised weight of survival. Each scar is earned, whether flesh remembers or not.

Petrov drops into a seat, shoulders slumped, a flash of hope sparking beneath a haze of exhaustion. Not victory—just distance.

The Osprey banks hard, engines clawing at the black. "Mission secure," I say, more command than comfort. Focus must hold. The chase may still come.

Metal vibrates beneath boots, rotor blades shredding the dark. The silence that follows a firefight cuts deeper than noise. I lean back, spine biting against steel, forcing the mind to stay sharp. Survival, for now, holds.

My voice rasps over the thunder of the rotor blades. "Everyone accounted for?"

"Everyone except—" Lucy starts to say, tension lacing words, hinting at something unsettling beneath the surface.

Cutting Lucy short, "Where's Billy?" A surge of adrenaline hits. Glances flicker around the team—Simon, Derek, George, Lucy—all here, but one.

"From the building, Billy's steps echoed my own, " Lucy replied, tone quaking, uncertainty and dread flickering across her face.

Staring out of the window below, I can see the terrain vanishing, like a frost that snakes through my core, locking every muscle. "Take us back!" I yell, the demand cuts the air, spilling out with pure instinct.

The pilot remains steady, voice piercing through the deafening noise of the Osprey. "Negative. The LZ's too hot. We're pulling out."

The thought of forcing the pilot back into the chaos like a demand etched in blood, raises in my head for a moment. The split-second tension between restraint and execution grips tight. But the weight of reality hits hard — backtracking isn't an option.

My fists curl, knuckles grinding against the cold steel of the fuselage. "Bollocks," I curse, as I slam my hand into the bulkhead. The dull thud shoots pain up my arm, but it's nothing; nothing compared to the knot twisting in my gut.

The Osprey climbs, the rotors drowning out the world, but I'm locked in the moment. Helpless. Powerless to change what happened.

George positions himself next to me, a steady presence amidst the chaos, silence stretching between us, resting a hand on my shoulder, solid but unsettling in the lack of solace.

"Turning back isn't an option, Steve. Sprinting towards the Osprey, I turned to witnessed Billy running behind me, boots pounding the ground. The safe house was shrinking in the distance. We were pushing hard, towards the Osprey, safety almost within reach. A shot pierced the chaos, and before I could register what was happening, Billy collapsed. One clean strike — straight through him, " George says.

Traversing exposed terrain always carried a price, something we all accepted. Billy stayed behind, guarding our six, never letting anyone become stranded. This time, the man who always protected our backs didn't survive.

Inside every part of me screams to charge through the streets, ignoring the gunfire, and haul Billy's body to the Osprey. But we all understand that's not going to happen. The extraction's long gone, and Billy... Billy's not coming back.

George's grip tightens on my shoulder. "Billy embraced the risks, just like the rest of us. A brother who understood the price. What happens next...it's beyond our influence."

Air fills my lungs, grounding me. Time to focus. The mission — always the mission. As my gaze sweeps across the team, the expression on their faces tells the tale: pallid and taut with agony. No conversation is necessary. Even Petrov is cornered and still registers the impact of what hit us.

Grief doesn't have space in any fight. Mourning won't serve the mission. It has no place for weakness, not now. Billy's gone, the reality cutting deep, but now's not the time to slow us down. Pain gets buried, and my mind shifts to the only thing that counts — strategy.

The Osprey vibrates beneath us, rotors carving through the darkness. Fields and roads merge as the ground rushes past below, the wreckage of our last encounter fading behind us.

"Objectives are completed," I mutter, not for the team but for Billy and me.

This doesn't alter the mission. The goal stands firm. Loss shadows every step we take, woven into the work. Some fight for the uniform. Billy fought for those beside him. Time erodes most connections, but not this one.

The moment Billy reappeared, the line reformed, seamless. Brotherhood isn't spoken — it's forged, held together by blood and war. Now, he's another mark on the roll of fallen heroes. Teeth clenched, my focus stays on the horizon. The mission continues. Grief is for another time.

The Osprey levels out. The cabin is swallowed in silence, save for the hum of the engines. Within seconds, the wheels hit the ground at Guardian Security, and Dr Petrov is ushered inside, yet my attention remains elsewhere. The man never wavered while covering our exit, ready to confront any threat for the sake of the team.

The team converges in the debriefing room, silence wrapping around us like a shroud. Words escape my lips, carrying a sour aftertaste like charred remnants.

"Today, we lost more than a soldier," I begin, my voice strained.

"Most stand beside you. Billy stood in front, taking the hit before danger reached the unit. Not just another trigger in the fight. The backbone, the one who carried more than orders, more than gear. Some fight because they must. Others because no one else will. The difference decides who walks out and who doesn't."

Simon's focus remains downward, "Billy saved so many, far beyond what anyone realises. Civilians, soldiers — Billy gave everything. Deserved far more than this end."

"Nobody walked in blind. We all understood things might go this way," Derek says, pushing through the silence, steady but cracked around the edges. Every mission carries a price. Billy understood that cost better than anyone. And he paid first.

With a steady gaze, Lucy's words fall like a command. "We finish this. For Billy. His sacrifice can't be for nothing."

Stillness locks in, sharpening the task ahead. "Right. Billy gets what's owed. This ends now." A cold certainty settles, pushing out everything else. The next move determines everything.

Chapter Six — Viktor Readle

Shadows from the building's perimeter cut across the view as Viktor steadies himself beside the window, focusing on an intense line to the horizon. Data streams hum around him, red indicators sparking with each new target, a lethal constellation flickering in the dim glow of the screens.

Outside the office, operatives move with purpose, adjusting to Viktor's rhythm. Orders are redundant now; the machine is already in motion. Every step of the operation unfolds on cue, momentum building like a loaded weapon. My gaze shifts to the map on the largest screen, where a single red dot blinks brighter than the rest. The ground speaks of purpose, shaping tactics into a singular direction, holding the weight of what comes next.

The air tightens as I emerge from the shadows into the control room, every movement measured and deliberate. Authority radiates, a force felt more than seen. The tailored suit isn't a disguise but a statement—control over chaos, dominance beneath refinement.

The hum of equipment fills the room, underscoring the murmur of operatives exchanging tense words, heads forward, movements sharp, each knowing this space's unspoken rules.

An aide approaches me, tablet extended. "The Petrov situation," the man announces, voice edged with caution. Placing the device in my hand before retreating a few feet, without waiting for an acknowledgement.

The screen flickers to life, spilling data like a wound bleeding failure. Lines of text lash out, harsh and unforgiving. Petrov escaped custody. 'One mission, one objective, and they failed'. The edges press against my palm, the plastic groaning under the strain.

The tablet slams against the desk, the echo slicing through the room. Heavy and charged silence floods in its wake. My hand remains on the edge of the desk, fingers pressing into the cold surface as if to anchor the storm brewing inside. Operatives glance toward the sound, but no one dares hold a gaze.

"Get Sergei and Natasha, in front of me. Now," I order the command, cutting through like a blade.

The aide vanishes, boots marking urgency across the polished floor. The room settles into tense anticipation, and operatives resume tasks, their actions a testament to the immediate need for resolution.

The failure of Petrov's capture demands more than reprimands — the incident requires resolution. I step to the window; the city stretches beneath the night like a predator waiting to strike. The rules of engagement have changed, and a shift in power dynamics has occurred. And those who cross me will soon regret.

A few minutes later, Sergei Ivanov enters the room, Natasha Belova following a pace behind. Sergei Ivanov's hulking frame appears, casting a shadow over the doorway. Muscles tense beneath the faint lines across the skin, carved into the flesh, silent testaments to every battle faced and trial endured. A hardened look anchors a stare, sweat carving tracks along a brow.

Natasha stands beside Sergei, an attractive woman with strong features and a commanding presence. Long, dark hair is pulled back in perfect order. Authority flows from Natasha's stance. Gaze razor-sharp, each movement under scrutiny, a thought already assessing the next move.

"Report," I demand, my eyes boring into Sergei.

With a quick cough, Sergei steadies himself. "The protection team met serious opposition. Many casualties on our side. Petrov's been captured."

My stare sharpens with anger, filled with rage. "Details, Sergei. What fucking allowed this to unfold while you were in control?"

Sergei's voice falters a split-second before speaking, "Overpowered and outflanked. And caught by surprise."

I turn to Natasha, "Your analysis on this fuck up?"

Natasha taps on the table's edge. "No accident here. Their movements aligned with precision, as though Steve's team were following a script we didn't know existed. Sergei's men got caught napping."

"Someone sold us out. I want whoever it is found. If they're breathing, I want you to send a clear message." My rage simmers beneath the surface, inches from an eruption.

Sergei and Natasha exchange a glance, Viktor's words sinking in.

"Yes, sir," both respond in unison.

"And our response? To this fuck up?" I yell.

"Our net is tight. Surveillance is in place. One wrong move on their part, and it's over," replies Sergei.

Getting up from my chair, I walk to the wall map. My finger traces the lines and paths of power and influence.

"Focus here," I say, pointing to the Broome, Western Australia area.

Unknown to GSS, Petrov cracked, revealing important intel under interrogation, laying down a possible path to the artefact before vanishing from our grasp. Steve's team thinks they're lost in the wind, but safety's a myth in their rearview.

"Copy that. Status on our operatives?" Sergei's words come out crisp, chilling in precision.

A chill fills my tone as I lay down the line. "Make sure everyone understands — there's no room for mistakes. Those who fall short will face the consequences."

A subtle realignment in Sergei's stance confirms he understood the command. "The orders will be relayed," a clear warning embedded in every word.

"Good. And Sergei... ensure all understand the consequences of defiance. And both of you, clean up your fucking mess. Get Petrov back or find the location of the relic," I add.

"Understood, sir." Their response cuts through the air, disciplined and exact.

Sergei and Natasha vanish through the heavy oak door, the faint echo of their footsteps fading down the hall. A cool breeze threads through the open window, carrying the scent of rain-soaked asphalt from the streets below. The city sprawls outward, an intricate labyrinth of light and shadow, a stage for every ambition and betrayal that fuels my empire. Neon signs flicker in defiance of the darkness, but my attention sharpens inward, tracing the contours of an unfolding plan.

Oblivious to the gathering storm, cloaked in shadows, invisible hands pull unseen strings, tightening around the throats of those too blind to recognise the noose. The pieces move, not by chance but by my design. Their failures are predictable, choices inevitable, and the weight of these decisions is unmistakable. The point at which retreat remains an option has long since disappeared.

My informant embedded within GSS has delivered a gift, wrapped in their arrogance — a whisper that Steve's team, long-time adversaries of mine, were tasked with recovering Petrov. Considering the tangled history Steve and I share, it's a delicious irony. That unfinished chapter now invites closure.

A storm brews beneath the surface of calm calculation. Their belief in victory is nothing but a mirage, a fleeting illusion soon to dissolve under the weight of their missteps. Their interference fuels my fire, sharpening the edge of vengeance rather than dulling it. The setback gnaws, but not as a wound — instead, it serves as a whetstone, grinding away weakness and leaving only the cold steel of resolve.

Rain glistens on the windowpane, a translucent map overlaying the city below. Ghosts of the past stir in the dim glow, reminding me of what forged this path. Power demands a price, and the currency is often paid in blood. Lessons from another life, hardened in the crucible of necessity, remain etched in the foundation of my actions.

No longer a chessboard of simple strategy but an arena where only one side emerges intact. Beneath the surface of calm, the reckoning builds. Steve's team will break, their destruction, orchestrated from the shadows I control.

My mind drifts back to Moscow, those frigid streets in 1991. As the Soviet Union fell apart, I saw everything crumble, but I rose. Quick, dangerous, and already recruited into the KGB before I knew the depth of the world I was entering.

The cold from those Moscow nights still lingers in my memory — the sting of the wind biting at my skin as I moved through the narrow alleyways. Ice slick beneath my boots. That first operation turned the tide, altering my path. Reshaping everything and laying the groundwork for the man I've become. The meeting is etched in my mind. The contact stepped into the dim glow of a flickering lamp, eyes uneasy. The man didn't belong in the shadows, but I thrived there.

'Do you think you're ready?'. A hint of dread coloured each syllable. The strain in the man's voice was unmistakable.

A single glance was enough. The mission stood for the Motherland, and failure wasn't an option. The briefcase slipped into my hand, filled with what I needed. The darkness swallowed me as I moved with the purpose of a man who understood duty.

That night, my hands became stained in a way that I would never wash clean—the targets, clueless about the fate waiting in the shadows. Nobody saw me approach, I left no trace, and no one would ever remember me. But I would. Every action taken for the cause was pushed far down because guilt had no place—only survival mattered.

When the Soviet Union collapsed, unravelling everything I once swore to defend, those who stood beside me now tear at each other, hunting for scraps of influence, while the streets spiral into disorder. Connection erodes, cutting me adrift from the ideals I fought for.

Adaptation was the only way. Utilising KGB training, critical contacts, and harsh realities, I built an empire from scratch. Arms deals, narcotics, top-tier heists—the jobs everyone else feared to touch. Each flawless job brought me closer to power, a steady ascent marked by cold efficiency. Yet, behind the triumph, a quiet void grows, gnawing away at any sense of fulfilment. The beliefs of my younger days were gone, consumed by a darker force and replaced by a shadow that cared nothing for pride, only staying alive.

Now, as I stand here, a man shaped in the crucible of a nation's ruin, I know there's no turning back. I am Viktor Readle, and the world will bend to my will or burn in my path.

My thoughts are cut short by the vibration of my phone. The screen lights up, and the name flashes across enough to tell me there's trouble.

Picking up the telephone, I answer, "Yes?" The edge in my tone speaks volumes.

The line hisses, and a strained voice breaks through. "Issue on our side. Shipment's been intercepted."

My jaw clenches. "Where?"

"Dock 42."

"OK, I'll deal with this myself." My words roll out smooth as steel.

The mobile slips into my pocket. My thoughts shift to the next course of action. Moving through the dim lights of the office, I blend into the shadows like I've done many times. Patriot to criminal — it's a line I crossed long ago. But the instincts never left.

With a swift motion, the drawer opens, and my fingers grip the 9mm. The cold metal presses against my palm, sharpening everything and focusing my attention. I tuck the pistol into the holster beneath my jacket before I leave without a word.

The path to the underground car park is quiet. My footsteps are the only echo in the corridor. The elevator doors open, revealing the black Mercedes poised and waiting. As I approach, a button press on the remote opens the boot, and the hidden panel lifts to reveal the secret compartment where rifles remain locked tight. Right where weapons should be. I shut the trunk and slide into the driver's seat, the engine rumbling as I turn the key.

Driving through the streets, the buildings blur past in a rush of shadow and fleeting neon, their lights retreating as the car cuts deeper into the labyrinth of streets near the docks. The engine's hum merges with the distant crash of waves, a constant rhythm against the stillness of the night. The path ahead narrows, wrapping itself around the edges of the city's underworld, steering toward a confrontation that sharpens with every turn.

Darkness stretches across the road, broken by faint patches of dim light. Even though silence fills the vehicle, my mind churns, dissecting possibilities and recalibrating contingencies. Precision defines survival here; anything less invites failure.

The car eases to a halt. The door opens, and the cold grip of my pistol aligns with the intent coursing through me. Dock 42 rises from the gloom, a silhouette of metal and shadow, secrets guarded by men too careless to notice the inevitable.

Steel crates loom in organised chaos, casting angular shadows over the tight passageways. Guards linger, weapons slung with the false confidence of men who believe no one dares to challenge their presence. Misjudgements like that write obituaries. The first target falls without sound, the silencer whispering lethal purpose. A body crumples into the black, consumed by the night as though the man never existed.

Each step carries precision, a predator's instinct coursing beneath the surface. The pistol fires, another shot slipping into the stillness, removing another piece from the board. There's no flinch or hesitation, only the unerring momentum of purpose. The path ahead becomes clear.

I find my container, which stands untouched, the rusted exterior masking the value concealed within. Fingers grip the padlock, the cold surface yielding to the turn of a key. The door groans in protest, metal grinding against itself as the hidden cache reveals secrets held within. Crates stacked with deliberate care reflect discipline that doesn't match the incompetence of the men hired to protect the contents. Markings line the boxes, codes known only to a select few.

Plastic-wrapped kilos of crystal meth and gleaming weapons fill the space, unspoiled by interference. Inventory undisturbed. A success marked by the silence of a flawless operation.

The stillness fractures. A faint groan emerges from the darkness. Out of instinct, my pistol moves, trained on a bloodied figure crumpled near the container's base. Uniformed, stained, chest rising and falling in shallow defiance of death. Recognition sparks in both eyes, eclipsed by fear. The arrogance of moments ago dissolves, leaving only the raw acceptance of an ending he cannot escape.

"Who sent you?" My tone shows contempt for the person on the floor.

Fear slips into a frightened gaze, voice cracking mid-sentence. "I... I don't know, I don't know. Please... don't—"

That's the wrong answer. My grip tightens around the 9mm's trigger. The pistol doesn't waver. Hesitation doesn't belong here. One squeeze and the plea vanishes. Darkness swallows another life, one more problem eliminated. Silence resumes undisturbed reign as the dock and its ghosts sink back into the depths of night.

As I disappear into the night, I reflect again on the path that brought me here. The KGB moulded me into a weapon, but the fall of the Soviet Union and the betrayal of a nation forged me into something else. In this ruleless world, survival means adapting and never backing down. There's no cause behind anything—just the fight to stay alive.

As I retreat to the sanctuary of my office, the door closes, shutting out the outside world. The drink cabinet beckons, offering a moment of respite—a bottle of Southern Comfort. The amber liquid swirls into the glass, and the sound of gentle splashes echoes in the silence. A brief, sharp burn travels down my throat, calming the chaos. Sitting at my desk, my focus shifts to the screens, casting a soft glow in the dim room.

Through the office window, I watch the door to the command centre open as Natasha steps inside. Her movements are deliberate and controlled, exuding an unspoken authority that fills the room. Monitors flicker with streams of information—maps, dossiers, intercepted transmissions. Natasha scans the data, dissecting and assimilating it in an instant, posture betraying nothing but focus.

Her presence alone transforms the room into a state of compliance. Voice remains unused, not absent, reserved for moments that require fire. Approval serves no purpose here. Those who wait trail far behind.

Without a word, attention moves to the screen, which displays the intel Natasha understands I rely on. After studying the information, Natasha enters my office.

"Viktor, latest intelligence on Steve's and GSS movements," Natasha remarks, the dossier hitting my desk, meaning as clear as the evidence inside.

Faces leap from the file: Steve, Lucy, Simon, George, and Derek. Everyone is a scar from the past.

"Do you realise what today is, Natasha?" The question slips out, steady, though a bitter edge undercuts the question.

"No, Viktor," Natasha answers.

"Today, of all days, Steve's team tore my life apart on St Kitts."

Old memories pressing in like walls refusing to let go. The mission unfolds in my mind, sharp, each step burns in like a chessboard gone wrong.

"One slip cost me everything. A brother-in-law who was closer than any brother could be. Killed by Steve and the other fuckers who work with him, the body was left to rot in the streets. They act as though loss is a casual term," I growl, words clipped and hard. "They've never seen their legacy reduced to nothing but whispers in the dark."

The sentence hangs unfinished, our eyes connecting. Natasha stands unflinching, ready, absorbing the tension like it's part of the plan.

"This war stretches past Petrov. Past the relic, this spills for my brother — blood for blood," I say.

Ash scorches the back of my throat. Retribution carves a place deeper than grief. That debt won't remain unpaid.

Natasha's expression mirrors my resolve, hatred flickering like a shared secret. Voice dropping, fierce and confident, "One name per strike, Viktor. Cripple one, then another. Make survival a myth, not a hope."

Standing up, I cross to the wall, a map of Australia in front of me, crisscrossed with red lines showing my influence across the country. My finger traces a path to Broome. Everything converges here.

"The World War Two relic isn't only a weapon—it's a raw authority that reshapes entire nations. It's the key to reclaiming what slipped through our fingers."

Natasha steps closer, "Steve's team could be moving Petrov soon. They're blind to the fact that Petrov informed us of the possible location. Our units can get ahead."

"Excellent," I say, my eyes fixed on Natasha. The next question drops without hesitation. "Now, what about Sergei?"

"He's preparing the operatives. Making sure everyone understands the stakes."

Anger courses under the surface, tempered by a dark satisfaction. "Strike fast. Leave nothing or nobody standing."

Natasha's eyes gleam with a lethal glint. "And when we have the relic?"

"We use it to our advantage." The plan's sharpening in my mind, each phase falling into place. "Let them witness that Viktor Readle doesn't yield. We take back what's owed."

A smile tugs at the corner of Natasha's mouth, sharp and dangerous. "Consider things done."

On the screen, Steve's image stares at mine. That look—a challenge, a memory, a spark to reignite the blaze buried deep. The fracture lines of the past claw their way forward, pulling me back to the Caribbean island the day everything unravelled. From all accounts, the explosion ripped through the humid air, smoke thick with the acrid scent of betrayal. A firefight erupted, the crack of rounds slicing through shouts and chaos. Amid the wreckage, my brother-in-law fell, the lifeless form crumpling into the dust.

"Steve." The word escapes as a promise, sharp and cold. Leaning into the screen, I let the venom thread through my voice.

"No escape this time. You'll taste the pain you delivered. You'll crumble as he did. And when it's done, I'll be the one standing among the bodies."

Returning to the present, the framework of the plan locks tighter, gears turning with unyielding precision. Every element snaps into place, driving forward with the certainty of a predator closing in on prey. This isn't about retribution alone. The relic isn't just a trophy; it's the keystone of the future I will forge. Viktor Readle becomes more than a name. Power reshapes itself in my image.

Back at the desk, the monitors flicker, static crawls over the glass like a virus. Shadows creep across steel, fractured remnants of past choices. Let them clutch their trivial victories. Nothing escapes my grasp. The endgame breathes through the wires, and I already hold the final move.

Like ominous sentinels, shadows stretch across the desk, their jagged edges shifting with the light from the monitors. Streams of data pulse across the screens, painting fragmented images of what has passed and what lies ahead. Their fleeting victories hold no significance here.

The control centre hums with tension, every move calculated, every operation thread in my grasp. Passing through the corridors, faces tighten at my approach. A subtle glance acknowledges my presence, a wordless deference that speaks louder than orders. Here, silence carries authority, and discipline permeates the air, binding to the singular focus of the mission's brutal inevitability.

After leaving the office, I drive down the streets towards home, and the streetlights flicker through the car windows, their rhythm echoing the precision of my thoughts. The engine's hum drowns the city's distant chaos, becoming a muted backdrop. In my mind, routes unfold like a choreographed dance, the geometry of escape patterns and fallback positions dissected and reassembled. Every move has a counter, every contingency a safeguard, a testament to the meticulous planning that underpins my control.

The fleeting thought of respite flickers but never takes hold. Peace offers nothing but vulnerability, a momentary illusion in a life built on unyielding vigilance. The familiar embrace of home looms closer, not as a retreat but as a controlled reprieve—a rare pause in the storm. The warmth is measured and temporary. Yet, even now, my mind is already anticipating the next strike.

When I arrive, the heavy wooden door swings open, welcoming me with a sense of stability that appears foreign these days. The warmth hits me first, then the sound of laughter, innocent and pure, unlike the darkness I navigate.

My beautiful wife, Anya, is there, waiting for me. Her smile is warm and gentle. Still, there's an edge—a hint of something vigilant, always calculating, always aware, observing, absorbing everything in the room with a subtlety that's become second nature. Anya's expression blends compassion with a hardened resolve, a gaze that speaks of loyalty and an ever-present readiness, never shifting.

Few possess this blend: fierce affection underpinned by a quiet strength that never falters. Awareness flickers in Anya's eyes, revealing the fractures beneath the calm façade, the consequence of battles and choices I can't share and don't want to. Anya says nothing, letting me shoulder the storm alone. Anya's presence is a tether, grounding me even as I spiral into the chaos of my own making.

Bright voices and quick footsteps bring life into the room as my daughters, Olga and Stefania, rush forward, joy breaking through the stillness. Both fling their arms around my neck. The warmth against my neck keeps me steady, every second in that embrace pushing back the relentless pull of the world outside.

For a rare, precious moment, I let myself drift into their embrace, feeling the warmth of innocence that maintains me in a reprieve from the relentless noise outside these walls. Their laughter is untouched by the weight I carry, a testament to freedom from the shadows that haunt me. In their eyes, I am their father — the man who chases them around the garden and spins them in the air until they squeal with joy. Not the man who keeps a reckoning ledger, preparing for the day the account must be balanced.

From the corner of the room, Andrie, my teenage son, stands motionless yet alive with an intensity that cuts through the air. That gaze — unyielding, dissecting layers of my composure, stripping away the carefully constructed façade I present to others. Andrie's stillness carries weight, contrasting the unrestrained energy of Olga and Stefania, who whirl through life with ease.

Beneath Andrie's surface, sharpness burns, revealing glimpses of a mind far older than the years would suggest. Silence here is not passive but a tool that searches, questions, and judges without needing words. Nothing moves without drawing Andrie's scrutiny, sharp instincts capturing what others overlook, dissecting intent from even the faintest gesture.

The space between us carries unspoken truths. Stillness isn't idleness — it's strategy. Every moment serves a purpose, each second a step closer to understanding forces he knows exist but cannot yet name. The hidden storm within me, a tempest of unresolved emotions and unspoken truths, brushes against Andrie, not too much, but enough to signal the shadows closing in.

The family embrace draws me in, crafting a tenuous sanctuary against the storms within me and beyond these walls. Their love, innocence, and quiet understanding form a cocoon, a fleeting sanctuary. My family reminds me of what I fight for and stand to lose. And in their presence, I'm reminded of my humanity — a truth I often bury beneath the weight of my chosen path.

Anya's touch draws me out of the fog, a hand firm yet unintrusive on my shoulder.

"Dinner is ready," Anya says, the curve of a smile accompanying the words. The warmth of her presence holds a quiet authority that demands acknowledgement.

At the table, conversation weaves through fragments of the day — school, errands, and inconsequential moments. Words flow around me like a distant current, their importance lost in the depths of my mind. Anya speaks with ease, questions delivered with precision, coaxing responses that fit the room's rhythm. Each reply from me lands, controlled and detached, the façade unbroken, the mask intact, my inner turmoil carefully hidden.

Anya's hand brushes against mine, a quiet anchor amid the noise. In that touch, something shifts, tethering me to this fleeting reality. A strength that radiates, unspoken but undeniable, a force that roots me while chaos brews in the recesses of my thoughts. Even as the mission looms, edges sharp and intrusive, threatening to consume me, Anya's presence carves a space where the shadows lose their grip.

The weight of duty presses against the walls of the moment, never absent. Shadows linger over the room, creeping at the edges, but Anya's resolve keeps them from consuming everything for now. Anya's steadiness reminds me of the life beyond the storm, even if only for a breath.

The living room becomes our haven as the children slip into the embrace of sleep. The air between us is thick with unspoken truths, a silent understanding that binds us. Anya's gaze meets mine, breaching the barriers I've erected. Anya doesn't need to speak. Tireless trust in me resonates in the silence, a solid and unwavering force, unburdened by expectations.

In the shadows, my empire waits, coiled and ready, a beast in hibernation. The machinery grinds forward, precise and relentless, prepared for the next move. But here, with my family in reach, the storm stills for a moment. The force driving me recedes just enough to grant a brief reprieve.

By 22:00, the house is engulfed in silence. Anya lies beside me, her soft breath against the dark. Sleep hovers just out of reach, a ghost that won't settle. I gaze into the emptiness above.

My mind races through variables, cold and mechanical. There is no emotion, only pathways etched in blood and steel. Each outcome is assessed, and each error is recorded for its cost.

Hours meld into each other. The first light of dawn slips under the door like a thief. A restless sleep brings no solace—only the sharpening of thoughts in preparation for what lies ahead.

I awaken at 5:00. The kitchen feels cold and uninviting. I arrange black bread, butter, boiled eggs, and kasha. My movements are deliberate and tidy. Ritual connects the mind to the body.

The children murmur above, their voices hushed. Anya stands by the door, her hand grounding me in silence. It's a weight offered without expectation, a reminder to safeguard our roots while navigating a world of wolves. There's no need for vows—just a mutual comprehension of survival's requirements. A decisive nod exchanges between us.

The door closes behind me, the house's stillness replaced by the weight of purpose. The mission wraps itself around me like a second skin. Every step forward tightens the grip of certainty, the world outside waiting for the predator to strike again.

The city stirs awake as I drive. My thoughts are already in motion, a rigorous march toward what must be done. The roads blur into patterns of movement and noise, nothing more than obstacles between me and the next step. When I arrive at the office, the time is 08:00. The building hums with life—operatives moving with quiet purpose, the gears of the machine turning.

In my office, the morning light filters through the blinds, casting a pale hue over the room. My focus locks onto the streams of intel on the monitors — maps, satellite images, mission briefings. The hum of machines surrounds me, and each face on the screen is a marked target. Everything is in place. The pieces move, the plan advances, and soon, the reckoning will begin.

The door swings wide, and Sergei strides in. Natasha follows behind, gaze cutting straight to mine, always assessing, never idle.

"Viktor," Sergei's tone cuts through the room, "We've got fresh intelligence indicating a possible site for the relic."

"Show me," I gesture for Natasha and Sergei to come closer.

On the desk, creased files overlap, with maps pinned down by bullet casings and blood-smeared reports. Natasha's finger hovers just long enough to demand action. Orders arrive with the silence of a closing grave.

"Attention shifts to an area near Broome, Australia. Recent activity around the bunker suggests someone's searching for clues," Natasha says, pointing to the map.

"We wait until verification comes through," I say, looking up.

"Surveillance is escalating. Drones are sweeping the zone. Ground and air assets are doubling. We'll have confirmation soon," Sergei says.

My mind races with the possibilities, piecing together the final stages of the plan. "And Steve's team?"

"According to the operative we have embedded in Guardian Security Solutions, they're moving," Natasha answers. "Focused on Petrov, unaware of the relic's true importance. For now, intel suggests they're blind."

The edge of a smile forms on my face, controlled and ruthless. "Perfect. Maintain that. But don't drop your guard. Steve's team adapt fast." Routes and symbols draw me in, outlining each critical path by hand.

"We're on the verge," I mutter, hand stopping at the line leading to the relic's site. "We can't afford any mistakes now."

Sergei steps forward, eager for orders. "What do you need from us, Viktor?"

"Double down on all routes. Lock down each area and squeeze our contacts until no scrap of information is left hidden. I want anything buried, pulled up, and on the table."

Every contour takes on purpose. Routes transform into lines of assault. The landscape surrenders, and every feature is fused with our strategy. "We've set the scene. Options vanish fast, and the snare surrounds Steve's team, closing in. Advancing with arrogance, unaware of what's been lying in wait, walking into our trap," I say.

My finger lands on the choke point, pausing for a moment. "With each inch of advance, they'll feel the net closing. No one gets through without our say."

Natasha nods, already calculating the next steps. "And Steve's team?"

"Containment collapses if they enter the perimeter," I snap. "Eliminate them, clean and final."

The room chills as my words settle over us like a storm cloud. Sergei and Natasha exchange glances, understanding the weight of what lies ahead.

"Understood," Sergei responds. "The moves will be made."

At my desk, eyes locked on the monitors, data streams lighting up the screen. "We're on the verge of something massive. Failure is not an option," I say, staring at the pair of people in front of me.

Unfazed, Natasha leans closer. "This isn't a game, Viktor. The relic is ours, and Steve's crew will be erased."

Moments later, the door closes behind Sergei and Natasha, leaving the room steeped in the tension of unfinished business. The silence carries weight, not of calm but of a storm gathering momentum—unwavering resolve courses through me. Steve's team has been a nuisance for far too long, evading traps and surviving when they shouldn't. That ends here. No escape, no reprieve, no more second chances.

Leaning back in the chair, the leather creaks. The moment offers clarity, a narrowing of focus, sharpening determination into something razor-edged. The relic, a weapon from the past that can shift power, lies so close its energy hums in the air, a force waiting to be claimed. Everything rests on this—power, control, the future drawn in a straight, unbreakable line.

Steve's self-assurance anchors the team's movements, yet the danger creeping closer thrives on unchecked certainty. Confidence breeds complacency, and in that lies their undoing. Steve's team and GSS march toward a reckoning nobody, apart from me, can anticipate, the walls of their safety closing in with every step. Unseen hands tighten the noose and the strike. When the time comes, I will leave no room for counteraction. The reckoning is inevitable, and the tension is palpable.

Dust clings to the object, ancient lines etched with blood-debt and intent. Power flickers beneath that worn casing, more than a symbol—proof of control reasserted. The close arrives cloaked in stillness. They expect to triumph. A miscalculation invites the cut they never prepared for.

Chapter Seven — Debrief

The team gathers in the debriefing room. Petrov's extraction took a toll, and Billy's absence hangs over us, overshadowing what we achieved. The room is bathed in a sombre light, the overhead projector casting a glow on the wall as we prepare to revisit the mission, each of us bracing for the challenges ahead.

"Alright, let's break this down," the words cut through the silence. My eyes sweeping across the team, their focus unshaken despite the exhaustion. "Derek, give us the rundown on comms."

Derek brings up the schematic on the screen. "Clear comms all the way in. The perimeter is where we first encountered interference. That's when we caught encrypted communications on militia channels. The unease in their movements shows they're aware of us nearby, though our exact location eluded them."

"Right," the mission replaying in my head. "Lucy, you tracked the guard rotations. How accurate did the intel appear?"

Lucy leans in. "Intel synced up. The guard changed every four hours, more fortified at night. We timed the breach with precision, slipping past unseen. Hostiles flanked tight before boots cleared the threshold. That ambush didn't guess. Someone traced our axis and relayed the information. This op's burnt from the inside."

Simon chips in, "Transport held up as planned to the extraction point. Billy's wheels were parked where they were meant to be. Hostiles advanced harder than expected."

"Every piece of Billy's intelligence held up under pressure. We slipped through the compound, meeting little resistance — until the militia hit back with a swiftness we didn't foresee," I say, my words cut through, calm and controlled.

"Spotters tucked in along the treeline. That's where we fucked up. Handed Viktor's people the advantage," George adds.

"Someone fed intel out before first contact. Time to drag that rat from the wire before another op burns under our boots. One more delay, and more names will be carved on a wall. This ends now — fast, brutal, and without another breath wasted," I continue.

Derek glances up from the laptop. "I've been analysing the intercepted communications. The trace leads to a server in Eastern Europe. GSS bleeds from the inside — someone deep in GSS fed Viktor live data, before we moved. This intel doesn't just leak. It's delivered. Deliberate. Tracked too well to come from outside contact or interception. Someone is undermining our every move.

"Locate the breach, identify who's responsible, and eliminate the threat," Lucy says, gaze sharp and focused.

"You're right, Lucy," I say, a firm sense of purpose locking into place. "Billy deserves the truth. First, we find Petrov, make sure the intel on the relic's location hasn't been compromised."

Simon stops pacing and turns to me. "What's the status on Petrov, Steve? Is the man cooperating?"

"According to Dave, Petrov is nervous yet willing to cooperate. Grasping the gravity of the situation. The man's expertise on World War Two relics is unmatched, and Guardian Security Solutions is handling protection until relocation."

George sits forward, "What's our play? We can't sit idle with a traitor loose in GSS. It's suicide. Plus, we're short on details for the mission's next stage."

"That won't happen. Derek, keep monitoring the comms. Lucy, go deeper into the data. Simon, ensure Dave's team is ready with transportation. Petrov's info is pointing to Broome, Western Australia, for the artefact," I say, looking around the team.

Everyone's thoughts fix on the task at hand — tracking down the mole, securing what we need, and honouring the friend whose sacrifice now fuels our every step.

With the team off to sort out equipment, I sit alone in the room. The hum of equipment in the command centre reaches my ears as I stare at the map on the table, my thoughts far away.

Billy's death is a fresh wound. A flood of memories crashes in — celebrating in dark corners, drinks lifted in hard-earned victories, laughter resonant and unbreakable. Billy stood beyond rank. Fire forged us — blood sealed what time never breaks. Brothers by bond, made in blood and battle.

Flashbacks hit me hard. Billy's grin in the rare quiet moments, the way he cut through the tension, casting light into even the darkest hours. Billy's firm resolve became a silent reassurance to the team in the heat of action. One memory cuts through the rest — a lethal stretch behind enemy lines, both of us running on adrenaline and impulse. Billy's actions, pure instinct, dragging me back from death's reach without a pause.

Regret hits like a hammer, cold and merciless. 'Billy never got back up. Responsibility for Billy's life fell to me, and I fucked up.'

After about 30 minutes, Dave arrives. "Fantastic work today, Steve." The cadence of his voice delivers the praise, calculated and deliberate, rooted in unshaken command. "The mission's next stage, crucial to the operation, kicks off tomorrow. Use these hours to decompress and refocus. It's essential for what lies ahead."

"Understood, Dave."

With the briefing wrapped up, we head for the equipment store, everyone lost in thoughts of what's waiting for us. Missions like this carry a price that everyone accepts. Determination threads through the room, tempered by scars and silent experience from a hundred past battles.

The equipment store holds a charged stillness, as if bracing itself, attuned to the importance of the moment. Shadows pooling over racks lined with tactical vests, high-calibre rifles, and the essential tools of the trade. Hands move in unison, setting the gear back into its lotted location, each lock and latch a familiar ritual. Each metallic snap reverberates and settles, fusing into the silence, reminding us of the line between preparation and execution.

The usual hum of machinery and the faint buzz of the lights fade, leaving only the occasional sound of equipment being stowed. The sound of weapons locking fills the air, precise and controlled, matching the tension rippling through the team. My hands wrap around the familiar heft of the weapons and gear, the snap of metal aligning my concentration. The rifle finds its place in the cradle with a muted thump, a constant that speaks to what we're trained for.

With gear stored, we leave GSS behind. A short drive later, the vehicles glide to a halt, the quiet hum of the engines fading as we pull up in the car park. No words are exchanged; each of us is absorbed in the next steps, the plan unfurling in our minds. Old memories blend with new calculations, layering steel into the focus required for what's to come.

The hotel looms in front of us, a hulking structure that blends into the dim, washed-out landscape. As dusk settles, thin shadows creep over the aged surface, the building twisting from a refuge to a location of silent preparation.

Inside, the reception is as lifeless as a graveyard. The lights cast a pasty yellow over chipped walls and faded carpets. A young man, just out of his teens, sits behind the counter, face bathed in the bluish glow of the computer screen. The tinny sounds of a game trickle out, faint explosions and crackling static filling the air. He's too wrapped up in the digital world; eyes locked on the monitor, fingers moving in steady taps, oblivious to our presence. The type of distraction we're counting on.

"Reservation for four rooms, name's Barker," I say, leaning on the counter.

Our normal setup is tight on foreign ground, with zero room for gaps, with Simon, George, and Derek sharing quarters. However, on home turf, the option allows for more flexibility — each person will have a separate room, and Lucy and I will stay together in the same room.

The man glances up, taking the confirmation Derek printed earlier, eyes scanning the document. "Your rooms are in our annexe across the car park. Here are your keys. Breakfast is served in the bar from 07:00 to 10:00."

With the keys in hand, I take point as we exit the lobby. In the car park, we pass several cars and approach a small, nondescript structure behind the hotel, the form just about visible in the darkness.

A shove on the door releases a mix of stale air and a faint metallic tang. Inside, a narrow staircase winds upward, each step creaking in protest, the sound carrying in the silence as we make our way to the second floor. Above, a flickering bulb illuminates the corridor with a shaky light, casting restless shadows across the walls.

At the door to my room with Lucy, I take a moment to breathe and slide the key into the slot, hearing the lock click open. I step inside, tossing the bags onto the bed with a thud. As I scan the space, the weight shifts off my shoulders, and a breath slips out, steady and controlled. The single window offers a glimpse of the street below, empty and still in the night.

"Coming to the bar, Lucy?" I ask, pulling off my gear and heading toward the shower.

"Try to stop me. And don't trash the bathroom," Lucy snaps, stripping down without a second thought. Clothes land on the floor by the side of the bed.

Showered and dressed in tracksuit bottoms and a T-shirt, I call out, "Meet you in the pub," and head for the door without looking back.

"OK, honey, won't be long."

The door swings open, cold wind cutting at my back. Outside, the weather is brutal, rain pounding the car park, turning the area into a lake. Inside, the bar offers a stark contrast — warm and filled with the murmur of conversation. A corner by the window catches my eye, set apart from the flow of the room. I couldn't ask for a better setup.

The chair grinds against the floor as I pull back from the table, hands firm on the wooden frame. Outside, rain trails down the window in broken lines, each streak reflecting the chaos stirring beneath.

A young waitress moves toward me, projecting a balance of warmth and professionalism. "Evening," she greets, offering a rehearsed smile. "Will you be dining tonight?"

"Not sure at the moment. Expecting a few people to join. When everyone arrives, I'll call you over."

"Can I fetch you something to drink while you wait?"

The menu gets a glance, though I've already decided on what I want, which is the usual: "Five Stellas. Start with that."

"No problem," she replies, jotting down a note on the notepad. "Be right back."

My focus locks onto the window, drawn in by the relentless tapping. The sound doesn't soothe. It scratches — at the same tempo as rotor blades slicing through smoke over a bad extraction.

At the other end of the room, the door swings open, letting Simon and Derek into the room, water dripping from their clothes. With a quick gesture from me, they cut through the tables, finding several chairs, and sitting down at the table.

"Hell of a night outside," Simon mutters, dragging a hand through soaked hair. "This weather is relentless."

"Right, but a drink's in order tonight. It's been that kind of day," Derek replies, leaving no room for debate.

Moments later, the waitress places the beers on the table, catching my eyes with a brief smile. "All set. Give me a shout if you need anything else."

"Thanks, I will," I reply, picking up my beer.

Before long, George and Lucy arrive. Rising to my feet, I call out Lucy's name. Her gaze locks onto us before walking over, with George a step behind.

"What a day," Lucy says, sitting beside me.

"Yeah," I say, motioning to the server for another round. "If nothing else, we've earned this break."

Raising my drink, I say, "To Billy." The team echoes my move, the sound of glass-on-glass clinking in unison—a haunting reminder, a quiet honour to the brother now gone. "Catch you in the FRV." The words come out steady.

For a moment, no one utters a word. The bar's chatter creates a backdrop, letting us forget about the mission for a while. A deep sip of the beer brings the cold, contrasting with the warmth around us. Outside, the rain continues to beat down—a constant reminder of the storm we're facing.

Lucy speaks with a gentler rhythm. "You remember when Billy told us about that mission in Mogadishu? Outnumbered, surrounded... nothing to do with glory. Steve and Billy held their ground because no other choice became available. And no room for failure."

Lucy's words hang, pressing down on the moment.

"Billy fought like a man with nothing left to lose that day," I say, voice steady but carrying an edge, raw with memory. "Glory meant nothing. Recognition held no value. Billy threw himself forward for a single purpose—to pull people out alive. Billy measured worth by survival, not praise."

Lucy leans back in the chair, a faint smile brushing across her lips, "Billy said you never cracked when the mission turned dirty, Steve. Your partnership meant more than faith. Response matched reaction. One blink, and the other took the hit instead."

My voice softens, brushing against something almost fragile. "Yeah, Billy's laugh still lingers, reserved and genuine, as if sharing that story meant more to Billy than anyone listening. Pride in the reason. The why. That always mattered more to Billy."

Simon's chuckle cuts through the moment, "Yeah, Billy never let Steve live that one down. Would bring it up every time we met. Telling the tale about pulling Steve out of some burning wreck and saving the day single-handedly. Every time Billy spoke, the edge behind a grin suggested a debt signed in fire and carried forward. Like breathing beside someone who pulled you from the grave once before."

Simon's laugh trails off, but the bond in the tone lingers. For a moment, it's like Billy's in the room, laughter threading through the stillness.

"Classic Billy," Derek adds, leaning forward, voice thick with nostalgia. "Chaos didn't chase him—he dragged it along like spare kit." Derek doesn't blink. "Steve shared something none of us touched. Not a command. Not blood. Something forged."

"Billy gave more than any of us can ever repay. Finishing this mission is how we balance that debt," George says, tone unwavering.

"We will finish this," I say, keeping my voice firm. "Tomorrow, we press on. But tonight... tonight is for Billy. For remembering why and who we fight for."

Beer in hand, I lean back, watching the rain still hammering against the glass. The bar is warm and inviting, a brief respite before the storm of our next mission. Around me, the team is unwinding, the tension easing with each sip of our drinks.

For a moment, the weight of our mission lifts, replaced by the camaraderie we've built over years of shared danger and triumph. Our laughter mingles with the hum of our surroundings.

Simon leans in, grin spreading, that familiar spark of mischief. "So, any second thoughts about being a green numpty back in your army days, Steve?"

My lips twitch into a smirk. "Not a chance. Somebody needed to make sure the rest of you stayed in line."

Derek's glass meets mine with a firm clatter. "Someone needed to give you donkey wallopers a lesson in hitting the damn target. Let's face facts without us riflemen. You would all be driving blind, taking shots at phantoms."

Lucy reclines with a glint of humour, voice laced with sarcasm. "So, I suppose my role in the Intelligence Corps revolved around cleaning up after you blundering idiots. You boys charge in, and I'm left sorting out the mess."

George joins in, unfazed. "None of you needed to wrangle a pack of hounds in a firefight. Holding that line with rounds going off? Different kind of skill, one you idiots never obtained."

After taking a gulp, my beer hits the table with a dull thump. "Managing dogs, huh? Surprised, though your motto is, 'If it doesn't move, polish it'."

Simon can't resist jumping in. "Nah, Steve, he's too busy looking for a guard box to stand in. You understand how the guardsmen are—always after that perfect parade stance."

Lucy lifts a glass before George says a word, a sharp grin cutting through. "To the green numpties, the donkey wallopers, the spooks, and the dog handlers. We may be a strange bunch, but we're the best at what we do."

The glasses go up, and camaraderie thickens in the air. For that moment, the weight of the mission ahead fades, and we're a group of soldiers bound together by the scars we've earned and the bonds we've forged.

For the rest of the night, laughter and banter flow with ease, but each of us understands what lies beneath. This short respite isn't just comfort; it's fuel, a necessary pause before stepping back into the fray. As the night wears on, we share more stories and laughs, enjoying the company, the beer, and the brief escape from the harsh realities of our world.

Exhaustion catches up after a few hours, prompting a retreat to our rooms. I linger outside Lucy's and my door and turn to the team, heading to their rooms.

"Breakfast at 07:00?" Three quick confirmations, and I close the door behind me.

Exhausted, Lucy and I strip down and slide into bed, weariness pulling at us. Lucy drifts off fast, arm resting over my chest, her presence grounding me.

Rest never comes easy the night before a job. Nothing suggests tonight will be any different. So I stare at the ceiling, my mind running through the day's events and those yet to come, wondering how we would find and extract the artefact. That's assuming Petrov's intel and research hold up.

The wristwatch flashes midnight. The eyes close, reaching for sleep. When open again, the time reads 02:30 — two hours straight, a rare feat and a new personal best.

The rest of the night continues in the same fashion: go to sleep before waking again. This went on until 05:00, when I give up, clamber out of bed, and wander over to the window, peering out across the car park. 'At least it's stopped raining,' I think to myself.

Careful not to disturb Lucy, I settle into the chair by the small table, coffee in hand, and stare out the window, watching as the minutes drift by.

The clock reads 06:00, dawn's light slipping through the curtains, spreading shadows over the room. Lucy sleeps on, expression softened, almost peaceful. But now is the time to wake from slumber. So I step up to the bed, place a hand on Lucy's shoulder, and give a gentle shake before backing off. Lucy doesn't hesitate to lash out if woken too fast; reactions are automatic and swift.

"Lucy, time to start a brand-new day," my voice soft but firm.

Looking up through half-closed eyes, "Already?" Lucy replies, the presence of sleep still visible in her eyes.

"Yeah, we've got a long day ahead. After your shower, we'll head down for breakfast."

"OK," Lucy says, stretching for a moment before slipping out of bed and making for the bathroom. The sound of the water running creates a steady beat, a small anchor in the storm we live in.

Clock digits shift. Mind snaps toward breach plans and extraction routes. Lucy steps out of the shower, alert, movements precise. Steam rising from damp hair. Beauty sharpened to a fatal edge, impossible yet undeniable. I wonder again how someone so captivating can also be so lethal.

"Ready?" I ask.

"Ready," Lucy replies.

Lucy and I step into the restaurant, and the rich, unmistakable scent of fresh coffee and sizzling bacon fills the air, surrounding us like a warm welcome. The aroma is a blend of toasted bread and a hint of sweetness.

The rest of the team is already settled at a worn wooden table, voices a hum against the background chatter and the clinking of cutlery. Plates are piled high with scrambled eggs, sausages, bacon and beans — the kind of hearty meal we seldom enjoy on the job.

Derek is busy cutting through a mountain of food while George shovels in mouthfuls like it's someone's last meal before going on compo rations. All except Simon, whose plate stands out, holding a modest helping that belongs to a child — a couple of eggs, a single slice of toast, and half a sausage cut down the middle.

Same old Simon, disciplined to the core, even when surrounded by indulgence. Catching my eye, a smirk playing at the corner of his mouth as if daring anyone to comment.

"Morning," Simon says, lifting a cup in greeting.

"Morning," I reply, pulling out a chair for Lucy before sitting down.

Lucy and I order breakfast: a full English spread with bacon, eggs, sausages, beans, and toast. The familiar meal takes the edge off, and the conversation follows, relaxed and easy.

Derek's smirk grows, pausing mid-bite. "Steve, you've skipped the black pudding. Didn't think you would pass up something this decent."

A short laugh escapes. "If you say so, Derek."

Coffee in hand, Lucy's gaze moves around the team. "So, what's today's agenda, Steve?"

"Finish scran, pack up, and return to Guardian Security Solutions. We need to be ready for the next mission briefing. If we're lucky, Dave will have the intel we require," I reply, swallowing the last bite of dead pig.

With tea in hand, George takes one sip and sets the mug down. "Fine by me. Time to move."

With the food finished and the cups empty, I push my chair back. "Let's make a move," the bacon flavour still in my mouth.

The group disperses to the rooms, gathering equipment. Gear packed and everything checked, we head for the cars. In the car park, gear gets loaded with the sound of zippers and metal clinking in the air. "Ready?" I ask, breaking the rhythm of preparation.

"Ready," comes the reply from the team, voices aligned like a steady beat.

Doors shut, engines ignite, and we pull away. Upon arriving at Guardian Security Solutions, we file into the building. The interior is bustling with activity, a stark contrast to the quiet of the early morning drive. The hum of computers and the murmur of conversations create a backdrop of efficiency and urgency.

Heading straight into the store, "Grab your gear. I'll check in with Dave for any updates," I say.

The team acknowledges each other and splits up, with each member handling a different assignment. My steps lead me toward Dave's office, and my mind turns to the mission ahead.

Dave is waiting for me, a tablet in hand. "Glad you all made it, Steve. How are the team holding up? Get any rest last night?"

"Making do and focused on the task at hand," I reply. "What's the current status?"

Dave taps the tablet, and the screen bursts into life, casting a glow across the room. Maps, documents, and satellite images layer themselves, a digital web of information waiting to be unravelled.

Dave's finger traces the rough western coastline of Australia, marking an unremarkable, isolated spot.

"Broome," Dave says, tone carrying a sharp edge. Looking up, eyes glinting with a new intensity, "Dr Petrov gave us more than we expected."

The tablet's glow casts shadows over the table, flickering across our faces as we lean in to take in the details. Broome sprawls in isolation, a harsh landscape where the coastline meets bushland, surrounded by endless rainforest and rugged scrub in every direction. Remote enough to keep secrets buried and forgotten. The type of place where something as valuable and dangerous as a relic can be hidden. The relic didn't vanish. It got placed—buried deep where eyes never reach.

Dave zooms in, Broome's outlines sharpening on the screen. "Under Viktor's imprisonment, Petrov witnessed the cracks in discipline. Observing information to the last detail. Petrov picked up on subtle shifts—supplies and personnel moving beneath the radar, all heading here," Dave says.

An index finger taps a point on the map, narrowing down the location with a precision born of hours spent analysing fragments and pieces of intelligence.

"Petrov picked up on every hushed conversation, each covert move Viktor made in this region," Dave says, marking a boundary on the screen. "Bit by bit, stitched together with our intel, and with Petrov's research, we've got a rough idea of where this artefact might be hidden."

The screen reveals a stretch of wilderness, marked with the faint gridlines of satellite coordinates. Broome's secrets lie somewhere in that shadowed expanse, waiting.

I angle closer to the map, arms crossed, hearing Dave out. From what we know about Viktor he doesn't act on instinct alone. Men and resources moving? He's bearing down. Far too close for comfort.

"How the hell did Viktor catch wind of the artefact's location in Broome?"

The question tumbles out, unchecked. It's been haunting me all along. We've covered every track, but Viktor somehow stays a step ahead.

Dave's stare cuts across the table, unblinking. "Either Petrov talked, or files got breached. Viktor's primed and ready." Documents scatter on polished oak—ink and photos sharp under sterile lamplight.

"Remember, a traitor sits inside GSS, feeding Viktor intel. Petrov's extraction leaked—likely this too," I reply, spreading relevant documents across the table.

A moment of silence follows before Dave replies. "We have a couple of individuals under surveillance, with keyloggers on computers, monitoring phones and other communications. We'll identify the leak. Only a select few have clearance on Petrov and his notes. Viktor's information on the relic's whereabouts must have been pulled from interrogating Petrov."

"OK, that makes sense. Keep us informed when you catch the informant," I say, returning my focus to the screen.

"Petrov picked up on something else," Dave says, rifling through the files. "Viktor's team is preparing to move something substantial within 72 hours. We have a small window with a specific timing. Something about a convoy. I don't have details."

The strategy crystallises, every detail coming into sharp focus as my mind shifts into overdrive. This isn't about securing a relic. Viktor's staging a larger play. Plans are lining up, and if we're going to intercept, we can't afford a single misstep. Time's already slipping through our fingers, and any delay means the relic might vanish, placing Viktor one step ahead and leaving us scrambling.

Pursuing the relic is Viktor's next move, but the endgame reaches far beyond — an elaborate setup designed to alter the entire playing field, and the clock's ticking. And the window is tight.

The objective isn't to outrun Viktor but to undermine operational momentum before the strike hits hard. Every second counts now, and our next move must be swift and precise, slicing clean through hostile intentions, stopping plans cold before damage ignites.

"That's our opportunity," I say, studying the map. "We strike before Viktor can consolidate. Should Petrov's intel prove reliable, we will ambush the convoy, gathering what we need on their movements. Ground confirmation with the team will be critical.

With the documents spread out, eyes scan the pages for marked locations. "We cannot afford to waste time. Waiting too long shifts the balance, giving Viktor more room to adapt and dismantle our strategy.

"Agreed," Dave confirms. "Intercepted communications show that Viktor's men are in motion."

"Fantastic, keeping one step ahead is crucial."

"Briefing's set for 10:00. We'll go over the details then," Dave replies.

After parting with Dave, I return to the team at the equipment store. "Briefing in 10," I announce.

The team assembles their gear, mood tense but determined. We walk to the briefing room, where Dave is already organised. The projector brightens the room, casting an image of Broome and the surrounding area onto the wall.

"Take a seat," Dave says, and we settle into the chairs around the table.

Chapter Eight — Danger in The Shadows

The sun hammers down, relentless and unforgiving, as Viktor stands at the centre of the temporary base in the Australian Outback—a fortress carved from the bones of an old mining facility, now transformed into something more formidable.

Dust from the Outback clings to everything outside, turning metal to rust and coating the ground in a blood-red haze. Craggy cliffs stand tall in the distance, shadows stretching over the land in dark, blade-like slashes.

The walls carry a quiet vigilance, holding something beyond the worth of mere steel and stone. Reinforced fences stand firm, silent guardians against the encroaching wilderness. Razor wire crowns the barricades, glinting under the harsh light. A network of sensors and thermal optics guards the perimeter, ready to detect even the slightest movement that indicates an intruder, creating an unspoken assurance of security.

The control room holds steady, sharp energy, and every motion is purposeful, reinforcing the focus that defines this team. At the core, I track the data stream on the screens, each mapping movements, intelligence, and the lifeblood of my operation. This is more than four walls; it's the heart of the operation, reinforced by layers of steel and circuitry, built to repel any external force, holding the world at arm's length.

Men and women sit at their stations, their focus unbroken. Fingers glide over keyboards, each tap feeding the vast network that keeps my syndicate one step ahead. The wall is filled with monitors, streaming live footage from cameras stationed around the compound; every angle covered, with no gaps left unchecked.

The glow from the screens bathes the room in a cold light, a constant reminder of the vigilance required. The hum from the servers pulses through the walls, channelling the data that fuels the heart of this operation. Technicians handle their role with practised accuracy, smooth and exact motions, and an unspoken awareness of the cost of failure beneath every move.

Moving through the room, my presence speaks for itself; no words are needed. Screens reflect a part of my empire, controlled and executed. Outside, chaos may reign, but within these walls, order prevails.

Sergei Ivanov commands the space near the central console, cold, green eyes betraying nothing but calculated malice.

Walking over to join him, my attention is drawn to the live map of the digital table, which covers the compound and adjacent areas. Red and green dots track drones and patrols, adding another layer of security to the perimeter.

"Sergei, update me," I say, breaking the stillness between us.

Sergei moves closer, words calm but laced with warning. "Viktor, movement near Broome escalates. We may not be the only ones hunting this artefact. Our informant inside GSS says Steve's team is getting ready to depart from the UK."

"Nobody gets ahead of us—double the patrols. Increase intelligence efforts. The moment Steve lands in Australia, I want to be alerted, and every move tracked," I say, staring at Sergei.

"Natasha's already analysing the latest intel and will have a report soon," Sergei replies.

My gaze shifts to the window, where the vast emptiness outside contrasts with the controlled chaos here. The solitude offers a quiet assurance that what's created in the dark remains unseen.

The door creaks open, and Natasha enters, razor-focused, tablet in hand, fingers moving across the screen, marking Broome on the tablet with a single tap, sending the data to the map display.

"Intercepted multiple comms from Steve's unit. Guardian's confidence in their security is misplaced. Our field contact just handed over a full log of their communications," Natasha says, voice piercing the shadows, steady and precise.

"What about equipment?" I ask.

"GSS have been working with local assets—fishermen and small-time transport operators. Locals smuggle gear under the radar using hidden roads, vanishing into the scenery, confident they're unseen. But they're wrong. We keep everyone leashed, recording every last metre of their route. Every silent step taken echoes back to us," replies Natasha.

My gaze sweeps over the map, tracking the routes and running the time and distance in my head. From past dealings, we have come to understand how Steve's team operates. He's too meticulous to leave loose ends. Whoever's manipulating intel from the dark believes they're untouchable. That's about to change—time to push loyalties and find out who's prepared to switch sides.

"These villagers aren't soldiers, yet they understand the terrain better than any satellite. Slipping in supplies as if it's routine. Updates flow in from our asset planted inside Guardian. Some locals play their parts without seeing the full scope, but others hold the entire picture. Knowing who's calling the shots and siding with Dave at GSS, no doubts," Natasha says, edging closer, fingers tracing the map towards a scatter of villages near Broome.

After a brief pause and a shift in Natasha's tone, "It's not only Steve's team we're following. Sergei's intel checks out. Another player stirs in the region, pushing boundaries with each pass. Their approach lacks the finesse of a professional unit like GSS, yet they're combing through familiar grounds. Ground intelligence locks on their position—desperate, armed, and sniffing around for the relic. They're after the relic, camped out beyond Broome—a distraction at best, a complication at worst."

My eyes flick over the intel before I say anything. "Too many threats moving into play, but all manageable. Steve's got locals, true, but our line of sight catches every angle. As for that third party... they won't last. Keep a close eye on these villagers. If need be, erase any issues."

Natasha's eyes narrow, an unspoken resolve anchoring in the gravity of what's to come.

My expression hardens. "We cannot allow any disruptions. Sergei, mobilise your team. Natasha, track their communication channels."

"Already in motion," Sergei mutters, hand resting on the 9mm pistol's grip. Intent coils in the silence between words.

Maps light up on the screen as Natasha examines each route. "Primary routes are locked in. Sergei will receive updates without delay."

"This is where it ends. The relic is ours, and anyone who stands in our way—in particular, Steve—will be eliminated." My gaze fixes on Natasha and Sergei. I step back from the table.

Sergei's gaze locks with Natasha's, an unspoken message passing between each other before saying in unison, "You've got our word. This mission succeeds."

My lips pull into a hard, fleeting smile. "Let's make everyone understand the consequences of stepping into our path."

The rivalry between Sergei and Natasha is undeniable. Their feud is ripe for exploitation—something I'll use to my advantage.

"Sergei, Natasha," I say, my tone firm. "Remember, I expect results, not excuses. The relic is within reach, and I require both of you at your best."

A lethal focus settles in Sergei's eyes, voice blunt. "No time for subtleties. The second Steve's boots hit the soil, we storm their camp, eliminate all, and secure the relic."

Natasha raises an eyebrow before saying, "Brute force won't solve this. We need to be more innovative. We need to access their communications, monitor their actions, and predict their plans. Let Steve take us straight to the relic's precise location."

Sergei's face tightens, frustration slipping through. "Time's not a luxury we've got. No room for games while they're closing in."

Natasha's eyes flash. "My 'games' have kept us ahead so far. Dismiss all you want, but my intel keeps us alive. Without intel, you're blind."

Catching the intensity building between Natasha and Sergei—the perfect catalyst, the friction is an asset ripe for manipulation, and I'll harness the rivalry to shape their next moves.

"Enough," I say, my voice cutting through their argument. "Both approaches have a place. Sergei, your strength lies in action. Natasha, your intelligence and strategy are crucial."

Sergei squares up, voice like ice. "Fine. But a single mistake, and we're doing this my way."

Natasha smirks. "And if brute force gets us nowhere, we follow my lead."

Speaking together, but with an undertone of disagreement, "Agreed."

With my eyes on Sergei, I give the order: "Keep your squad primed. Alert to everything."

Moving my attention to Natasha. "Secure our cyber perimeter. No data leaks. Track Steve's every move—details, whispers, and the slightest mistake."

Orders in hand, both exit my office without a glance back. The chessboard materialises in my mind, moves falling into place with careful definition, every step already in motion.

As the door clicks shut behind Natasha and Sergei, I pause, savouring the silence that cloaks the room. Shadows stretch and dance along the walls, mirroring my dark reflections. The relic might be close, its power within my grasp, yet Steve's team still linger like ghosts on the battlefield, unpredictable and dangerous.

Sergei is formidable; brute force is a tool I've wielded with cold precision on many occasions. Natasha's razor-sharp intelligence navigated us through peril before, yet both remain double-edged blades — loyalty, after all, is never absolute, only borrowed until the scales tip.

With the relic almost secured, Steve is a little more than a final obstacle, skilled and ruthless, as were others who challenged my resolve. Everyone fell, each underestimating the darkness within me and the depths to which I will descend. Calculated manoeuvre brings Steve's team closer to the noose tightening, constricted by an iron-clad chain of command I've crafted myself. Their fate is already sealed. Victory isn't just inevitable — it's already mine, a certainty I carry with unwavering confidence.

The friction between Sergei and Natasha is a strong motivator, and I'll channel that energy. It crackles in the air like static before a storm — volatile but useful. Still, it gnaws at the edges of my focus. I can't let it. I've seen what happens when personal tensions spill into operational space — one hesitation, one misplaced bullet, and it's not just the mission that crumbles.

My focus must remain indestructible. No room for grudges. No indulgence in emotion. I've buried those luxuries under years of discipline and blood-soaked choices. This isn't about them — it never was. The mission comes first. Always. Personal vendettas are a liability and a failure? That's not in our vocabulary.

Beyond the glass, the stark terrain grabs my focus, laying out the high-stakes game ahead. Each challenge fuels the fire within; in my world, failure isn't part of the equation.

Maps sprawl out before me, strategy taking shape. Lines converge at points where blood will follow. Sergei and Natasha's focus will sharpen under the strain. They will secure the relic, and if loyalty wavers, final breaths will be taken as lungs fill with dirt. The same fate awaits Steve's team.

The game is already in motion, and I have no intention of losing. Possession of the relic grants me the control I need, a power strong enough to redefine everything around me. A quiet utterance of their names, a smile twisting at the edge of my mouth. 'Sergei, Natasha... let the chase begin.'

Stacks of paperwork crowd the desk under the faint glow of the lamp, casting shadows across scattered intel reports, financial leads, and operational notes. Each page fits into the broader scheme unfolding before me. This isn't just about the relic. This is about the entire empire I've built, the influence spread across every corner of the globe. Pages come into focus with sharp, meticulous attention to detail. Every bit is crucial to my operation.

A knock interrupts my concentration. My hand freezes over a classified file, eyes shifting toward the door.

"Enter," I say, my voice hard, leaving no room for delay.

The door swings open, and Vad appears in the doorway carrying a silver tray. The man's bulk fills the frame, a tattoo peeking from behind a white collar, as he sets the tray down with the assurance of someone who understands the gravity of our mission.

"Lunch, sir." The warm aroma of seasoned meat cuts through the sterile air, a fleeting reminder of life beyond strategy and concrete.

Vad stands before me, one of the rare few with my trust, built on years of unwavering loyalty. "What's on the menu?" The words leave my mouth as cold as the air around us.

"Steak, medium-rare, with a red wine reduction. Roasted Yukon Gold potatoes, mashed with garlic and butter. Fresh vegetables on the side," lifting the cloche.

A hint of approval crosses my face. "That'll do. Thanks."

"If you need anything else, I'll be in the kitchen," stepping back, giving a slight nod.

The door clicks shut as Vad leaves, and I reach for the fork and knife. The first bite of steak is perfect, but my thoughts stay locked on the documents spread across the desk. Each report and intercepted message is a puzzle piece coming together.

As I eat, my mind churns through the layers of the operation — the compound's security, my men's loyalty, and Steve's unpredictability. With the tray out of the way, I lean in, hands forming a steady base under my chin. Vad's meal, a fleeting intermission, gives way to the task demanding my entire focus.

With the chase for the relic reaching a peak, pressure pushes everything to the edge, and instincts are ready to strike. A smirk pulls at my lips as the plan crystallises, the strategy falls into place, and every possible turn is already dissected.

With the meal finished I stand at the window, the view beyond the glass is empty, unyielding. A fitting reflection of what's on the line — pure power, unbreakable control, and an undeniable force. These are the elements under my command. I return to the desk a few minutes later, ready to dive deeper into the plans. Shadows align with purpose, and my path is a steady climb to more power and dominance.

After clearing the desk, my attention pivots to leaders across borders. Each manages a critical segment of the network, and everyone is a pivotal asset in the origination I've assembled; updates are overdue.

Leaving my office, I enter the makeshift conference room. The table is covered with cutting-edge tech. Screens flash with maps, surveillance feeds, and strategies. The hum of the machinery pulses through the room.

Sergei and Natasha stand across from me, trusted and sharp. Both understand the stakes, just as I do. The endgame is in sight. None of us will let the relic slip through our fingers. Everything is falling into place. Now, it's time to set the final pieces in motion.

My gaze sweeps the room, landing first on Sergei—frame tense as iron, fists tightening and releasing, braced for orders, before shifting to Natasha, eyes lit with anticipation, fingers hovering over the tablet, ready to act.

"Sergei, Natasha. The relic we hunt is no ordinary artefact." I pace toward the map pinned on the far wall; the image of the Australian outback dotted with our strategic points of interest. "This is a weapon—a remnant from the last war that should have remained buried," my steady, unyielding voice cuts through the air.

Turning to face them, my hand hovers over the marked point. "Under my control, the relic tips the scales, reshapes influence, shifts the entire game. In our possession, the device guarantees supremacy and resets power," I add.

"Additional orders, Viktor?" says Sergei, gaze locked and unyielding. The words linger for a moment.

"Sergei, increase the pressure on our informants." The edge in my tone leaves no room for uncertainty. "Use whatever methods are required. Reinforce where their loyalties lie. Let all understand the cost of slipping up. Kill a few if you have to."

A flicker twitches beneath Sergei's cheek—quick, buried, violent.

"Consider it done." The voice carries iron and ash.

Tension fuels movement, and the scent of pursuit thickens a grin. Borders vanish, and Defences dissolve.

Natasha's gaze stays locked on me, unflinching, calculating my tone, dropping but carrying unyielding authority. "Natasha, I want deeper access to GSS databases, private channels, and military logs. More information is needed on the other party involved. If they're out in the outback, their operations are mine to uncover and control.

A subtle smile touches Natasha's face. "Count on me for what we need, Viktor. No network is beyond my reach," her voice is unwavering.

Natasha misses nothing. Codes yield. Networks fracture beneath fingertips, slicing through silence absent remorse. Holes in security beckon demise, eliminated in a swift movement. Precision dictates identity — risk exiled by flawless commands.

Back at the map, urgency drives my tone. "Double our effort. This relic comes to us first, no matter what they're planning." My finger traces the route of our next operation, slicing through the outback and leading to the suspected site.

"Having the relic expert in enemy hands is not perfect, yet insights obtained during Petrov's captivity are critical. Progress is vital. Each setback strengthens our enemies. The relic belongs here, and GSS will be brought to its knees. Failure collapses everything we've built," I say, throat tight. The words cut hard against the rhythm of the room.

Distance collapses between the map and Sergei; authority sharpens words to razors. "I reinforce my earlier command. Informants must understand that betrayal offers no sanctuary. Should anyone waver, they will be regarded as liabilities and marked for swift and absolute elimination."

A familiar, lethal grin spreads across Sergei's face. "I'll ensure everyone grasps the situation."

"Go now. We're too close to falter; every move counts. The relic is rumoured to be near Broome, not far from here. The area's vast and remote, perfect for hiding something like this. Steve's team are the most significant threat. Their resilience demands attention and must be taken out. We cannot afford another St Kitts disaster," I say, my voice carrying the significance of urgency.

Sergei's stare sharpens to ice; words slice like razors. "Consider Steve's unit already erased from existence."

Natasha delivers her verdict like a sniper's bullet—cold, precise, and lethal. Words carved from steel, every syllable a blade. "Crippled communications ensure Steve's unit remains blind, deaf... helpless." Her voice is devoid of emotion.

Natasha steps forward, eyes locked on the map like a surgeon about to make the first cut. "Trapped," she continues, the word hanging in the air like a death sentence. "And awaiting slaughter." No inflexion. No remorse. Just cold, tactical truth delivered with the finality of a carved gravestone.

A brief smile surfaces across my face, "Strike with force, no leniency."

A simple gesture clears the room, leaving me with the map. Routes lock into place, tactics intertwine, and each decision is a calculated link toward reclaiming the relic. The flickering screens reflect the data flow, maps shifting beneath my fingertips. Targets lock into place, every change revealing a potential path forward.

Power, unbound and far-reaching; the potential is staggering. A future shaped by my hand, paving the way, reshaping everything. With my syndicate sculpting a future of absolute authority. Governments kneel, rivals crumble, and I rise above it all. But first, I need to secure the relic and crush anyone foolish enough to stand in my way.

"Steve, you've been in my way too long. This ends now," I mutter to myself, the name bitter on my tongue.

Peering out the window, I witness light slashing across the outback, carving jagged lines in the dust and rock, transforming the terrain into stark contrasts of shadow and brightness. The brutal landscape stretches on, every step a reminder of the merciless expanse, where control thrives, and chaos can be bent to my will. Sergei's raw power and Natasha's surgical precision are the tools that will tear through any obstacle between us and the relic.

My attention returns to the room where streams of intel flood each screen, threads of strategy tightening into place. No detail slips through; every action belongs to an answer, waiting.

Steve's group is led by false confidence across the terrain, but I've already claimed it. The board is set, and the pieces are in motion. Ruthless, precise, and relentless—that's how this will end.

Leaving the conference room, I move through the corridors of the mine. Walls thick with steel, security tight enough to stop an army. This isn't just about protection—it's a declaration, a mark of dominance. People stand ready, each knowing their role. They're part of a system already in action, flawless, and every piece is locked into place.

The hunt is what drives us. Every choice carries tension. A single miscalculation might cost us everything. Steve's team will not escape. They're walking into a trap. As for the relic, it's close, almost within my grasp. This moves beyond any single objective, casting a shadow over everything that follows.

Footsteps echo down the hall, a steady rhythm bringing a sense of calm. This is where I belong—on the edge of conflict—the rush of seeing opponents scramble as the noose pulls tight. Watching the opposition unravel before comprehension takes root—a few moments deliver such satisfaction.

A whisper escapes my lips, audible but thick with finality. "Let the hunt begin."

My hands curl into fists, not from tension but from certainty. The game is mine. And this? This is the chapter that defines everything — my legacy.

Chapter Nine — Team Briefing.

The quiet buzz of the servers fills the briefing room. At the centre, the team assembles, their silence echoing the gravity of what's to come. Each face tells a story of operations that never made the news—missions in the shadows, decisions created under fire. The air is charged with collective anticipation, an unspoken pact binding us to the mission's dark promise.

Simon leans against the wall, arms folded, jaw clenched as if bracing for what's coming. Already engrossed in the info on the tablet, Derek's hands move over the screen, extracting details that might mean the difference between survival and disaster.

Across the table, George and Lucy face each other, scanning the room with the same unyielding focus they've maintained since the beginning. Lucy's stare catches mine, unspoken understanding. We've faced situations like this before and will navigate them again.

Dave commands the front of the room as satellite visuals rotate, setting the scene. A hardened gaze holds steady on the intel. The remote triggers a change of slides, revealing the compound's satellite image, still bearing the marks of our strike.

"Listen up, everyone. First, we'll review the debrief from the last mission and then discuss our upcoming objective. Dr Ivan Petrov's extraction succeeded but came at a price. Billy's death means we need answers," Dave says, voice slicing through the faint chatter.

A knot tightens in my stomach. The memory of yesterday, the chaos and gunfire, the moment Billy fell - it's all too fresh.

Dave continues. "The data reveals that Readle's network consisted of more advanced surveillance than we predicted. Their response came swift, with far more firepower than we projected. We underestimated their strength."

Lucy edges closer, "Understanding how Viktor's organisation gathered classified intel is critical. What or who warned them of our presence?"

"That's a valid point, and evidence suggests a mole is embedded in our origination. Their identity remains hidden, but we have identified a few suspects. Until we drag the source into the light, operate like we're already compromised," Dave says, leaving no room for doubt.

The frustration flares in Simon's eyes, jaw locked. "So, what's our next move?"

The screen flickers, shifting to a barren stretch in the Australian Outback. "This is where Viktor's dug in. Repurposed mining grounds, fortified with a layer of defences," Dave announces.

Several images rotate on the screen. High fences, razor wire, automated protection—it's a fortress. Dave outlines the perimeter, pointing to critical areas.

"The task is twofold. Step one is to locate and retrieve the World War Two-era relic weapon that Viktor's team is hunting. Step two, neutralise Viktor's organisation. Everything flows through this base. Striking here dismantles the core of the organisation," Dave says, pointing to the screen.

Derek studies the screen, mind already working through the technical challenges. "What's the plan for insertion?"

"Once you have landed at Darwin airport, you will insert via helicopter under the cover of darkness. For security reasons, the LZ is away from your first RV. It's a five-mile tab to a small compound close to the edge of a forest..."

George interrupts, "Don't even think about fucking pushing me out again, Simon."

"I'll think about not kicking your fat arse out, George, as you bounced last time, you fat bastard," Simon replies, laughing out loud.

Continuing, "From here, it's a short hike to the area where, according to Dr Petrov, you might find the relic. As soon as it's secured, proceed to the next objective," Dave says, looking around the room.

"Keep the entry tight. No sound or fuck ups. The last operation left too many loose ends. This is more than a mission; it's personal," comes my reply.

"One last thing," Dave mutters, "Intel shows Viktor's gearing up for something huge tied to the relic. Full details aren't clear, but we can't wait for Viktor to act."

Every piece of intel paints Viktor as relentless and calculated. The objective won't be disruption. Viktor's steps are measured and cruel. The unit stands ready to strike clean, eliminate the source, and dismantle the network. Light from the display illuminates faded text as Dave loads the latest intel, revealing an ancient document scarred with an emblem from a long-buried past.

The screen shifts again, displaying stark images of scientists amid their bleak, antiquated machinery. "Alright, everyone," Dave begins, "here's the latest intel on our next objective. We're dealing with a World War Two relic, a weapon with the potential for catastrophic destruction. This artefact came from an Axis power project shrouded in such secrecy that it was almost invisible in records. The device never witnessed the battlefield, never left the shadows."

Dave scans the faces, gauging our reactions and letting the info sink in before continuing. "In the war's final months, every shred of evidence vanished, swallowed up in the chaos and confusion. Erasure down to the last detail — labs gutted, files incinerated, and those involved either silenced or made to disappear. The blueprints, the plans... all gone, like it never existed."

Shifting to the map on the table, Dave's fingers run across an invisible line. "Forgotten in the rubble of history, until now," Dave continues, as if invoking something dormant.

A noticeable intensity fills the briefing room. Lucy's eyes drill into each frame, scrutinising the images. Derek checks and rechecks the incoming intel, fingers tapping in perfect rhythm. Simon and George lean in, minds attuned to every unfolding detail.

A press of the remote and a new map fills the screen, red dots and thick lines plotting a course from Europe's cities straight to the rugged heart of the Australian Outback.

"Reports suggest Viktor's been accumulating critical information for years, "Dave says, unwavering. "Petrov's files in Viktor's hands put the target within reach." Dave's silence, coupled with a stern expression, reveals the stakes. From what we understand, drama isn't Dave's style. If Dave's unsettled, the storm ahead will be lethal.

"We're not dealing with another routine gun run," Dave asserts. "The relic, in Viktor's hands, turns it back into a weapon. A threat no one's prepared to handle."

"From the shadows, Viktor controls the game. Billy's position in Heinrichsberg cracked open intel that Viktor thought hidden. It's that information that's brought us all here, planning our counteroffensive," says Dave, looking at us.

My thoughts drift to Billy's discovery before everything collapsed. The map glows under a red light. Viktor—keeper of the device or courier for destruction?

Dave's eyes shift, the brief flicker betraying a tension we have not seen before. "Billy found out he's tapping into connections in the Russian GRU. Not just poking around but aiming to hand the relic over—or worse, deliver to somebody who's both resourceful and merciless enough to use the device." The words drop like a hammer, and a chill settles over the room.

"Whoever the potential buyer is, they will not be the type to play games; they're the kind to tilt the balance, to take this thing and turn the world into a twisted version of itself. If any exchange goes through, it won't be whispers and threats anymore. We're talking about someone with the will and power to bring entire nations to their knees. And this... it's the key," Dave continues.

George leans forward, voice steady. "What kind of weapon are we up against, Dave? Biological? Chemical? Nuclear?"

"A hybrid," Dave replies. "Something that incorporates elements of all three. The details are sketchy, but the destructive potential is clear."

Lucy tracks each option, mind shifting into gear—a mirror to mine. If the relic falls into Viktor's grasp, this isn't just about power. It's a match to global instability, with Viktor holding the torch.

"Allowing that to happen is not an option," I mutter, more to myself than anyone else. The room falls silent again, everyone absorbing the implications. The mission's priority hasn't changed, but the scale of what we're facing now is far more dangerous.

"Viktor is close," Dave states, "according to the intel from my team, he's already deployed units to the Australian Outback. Should Viktor obtain the relic, nothing we do will matter. We must take action now, or everything Billy gave will amount to nothing."

My thoughts focus on Billy's sacrifice, which paved the way for the path we tread now. Paying the price for the intelligence we hold. Either Viktor breathes borrowed time, empire burning, or we don't return.

"So what's the plan?" Simon asks.

"Intercept any unit en route to the target," I reply, the intel unfolding before me like a battlefield waiting to be claimed. "If the GRU is involved, we're against more than a tactical unit. Their eyes will be everywhere. Armed with Billy's intel, we hold the advantage. A strong push now prevents this from escalating any further."

"Steve's right, you've got the green light. Grab the relic, and make sure Viktor never gets close," Dave adds.

The rest of the slide shows detailed schematics of the relic, along with notes in German and a translation overlay. The weapon goes beyond raw impact—designed to fracture thought, bend allegiance, and engineer silence through fear. Firepower stands secondary. Control drives the blueprint—a psychological siege delivered at scale.

Lucy speaks up, voice steady. "What's our window? How long do we have before Viktor locates and activates the device?"

"Intel from monitoring Viktor's comms indicates the operation hits within two weeks. That's the window we're working with," Dave asserts, advancing to the next slide.

The screen displays aerial photos of a compound with several abandoned bunkers in the Outback, surrounded by desolate land. "This is where we believe search efforts are concentrated."

My gaze sharpens, thoughts spinning fast. "What's the strategy? How are we playing this?"

Dave's briefing gains momentum as the compound's blueprint illuminates the screen. Finger-tracing primary infiltration routes, marking potential choke points, and each detail exposing where Viktor might have forces dug in.

Every detail matters in this type of operation. "The extraction route alone will require threading through a gauntlet of hidden patrols. Dense thickets and sharp rocks, offering little cover, but at the same time, give us those extra seconds if we're compromised."

"Is that rainforest on the map, Dave?" I ask.

"Yes, Steve, several rainforests are scattered around the place, but most are not dense. The bunkers are perhaps located deep in the undergrowth."

"Thanks, that is useful," I reply.

"Expect pushback at these positions," Dave indicates, pointing to the mine and bunker locations. "Once the relic's exact location is confirmed, breach this zone," zooming into the heart of the compound. "The window's narrow to grab the relic and extract before Viktor's reinforcements breathe down your necks. The bunkers are positioned an hour from the mine, giving Viktor a tactical advantage."

Routes align. Each detail is etched into place. Every exposed angle and critical junction is checked, with no allowance for mistakes. A missed element here risks everything. Anything unseen might be an ambush. Standard dangers line the route, expected and mapped. But something breathes beneath the mission — silent, patient, waiting to strike unseen.

Bathed in the screen's cold glow, Dave scans the room, locking eyes with each of us, tone holding steady. "This isn't about us. Viktor's success will have global repercussions." Dave's words settle in the room, sharp like a knife blade.

Photographs flicker across the screen, Viktor's target clear in the grainy details — the truth buried in every worn corner of the images. What lies before us isn't an object. It's the blueprint for twisted ideals, a symbol of control ready to seize without hesitation.

"Our mission cuts deeper than stopping Viktor's ascent. We sever the hand trying to rewrite history and bury the ambition behind it," Dave adds, his words fading, yet the plan remains vivid. Orders are in place. Our survival once we leave that compound now depends on our actions.

As the door closes behind Dave, the team dives into briefing notes, each line etched into memory, while I map out the precise steps needed to secure both of Dave's objectives. As always, this type of mission must be broken down into parts, refining each task to its core as my pen scratches vital points. I sense someone standing next to me. It's Lucy.

"Thought this might keep you going, Steve." The familiar scent of coffee fills the air as the cup is set beside me.

"Thanks, honey, almost got the preliminary details nailed down," glancing up from the paperwork as I speak.

Forty minutes pass, and a basic plan for the mission takes shape. Yet, as always, circumstances on the ground can alter plans in an instant. Adjustments will be made as needed.

Everyone is back sitting around the table, each sifting through the stacks of intelligence reports, satellite images, and maps on the table. The screen hums with shifting visuals at the front of the room behind me.

"Alright, team," I begin, "We've got a lot to cover, and time is against us."

A press of the remote pulls up the following image, a high-definition spread of the Outback, dotted with red marks highlighting every threat, target, and obstacle scattered across that ruthless stretch of Australian wilderness.

"The objective is straightforward," I say, pointing to various spots on the map where Ivan Petrov suggests the relic might be hidden. "Locating and securing the World War Two relic before Viktor is essential. The landscape is both vast and unforgiving. Prepare for extreme temperatures, rugged terrain, and possible encounters with hostile wildlife. Experience gained from our mission in Australia, where we rescued Ana and others from a similar cartel, provides us with crucial insights into the region."

Simon studies the map. "What's the infill plan, Steve?"

"Dave's brief sets us up for a helicopter insertion, fast and below the radar," I say, tracing the planned route on the screen. "Landing zone's marked here in a tight clearing. Be prepared to fast rope down. We'll navigate to the RV site on foot from the infill site. Isolation keeps us concealed yet leaves us vulnerable, an edge that cuts both ways."

Derek leans forward, "What about local threats? Any intel on Viktor's presence in the area of the RV, or other interested parties?"

I switch the screen back to a series of intelligence reports. "From what Dave told us, Viktor maintains a formidable foothold here, complete with a fortified base inside an old mine sending out numerous patrols. Gathering comprehensive intelligence on Viktor's operations is essential. Disrupting activities is a secondary objective but crucial to our overall mission, which will be in four parts: insertion and patrol to the RV where we will set up camp — patrols to find the relic. Then, destroy the organisation, followed by exfil."

"Any updates on the third-party Dave flagged?" Lucy asks, looking at notes.

"Intel is lacking. Lucy, it's your responsibility to retrieve what's necessary."

"Understood. I'll start once we wrap up here," says Lucy, anticipating the next move.

I continue, "Phase one begins when we touch down in the clearing. If the Osprey can't land, we fast rope down — no hesitation, no screw-ups. The second your boots hit the ground, we're moving."

The map zooms onto our insertion point — a desolate section encased by rugged cliffs and dense brush. "This is our LZ," I say. "The terrain's unforgiving but works in our favour. It's isolated, Outback territory. No lights or sound unless necessary and a last resort."

Data flows onto the screen, sketching the course from the infill site to the RV, pinpointing each tactical marker. My finger skims the plotted course, charting a line over rough terrain, every contour a reminder of the ground we're set to tackle.

"From the LZ, we head straight for the RV. It's a few clicks, and the terrain's a beast."

The team understand the protocol. They're seasoned, but mastery lies in relentless drill, sharp repetition, and honed instincts.

"This is where you peel off," I say, pointing at George.

With another tap of the remote, the screen shifts and zooms in on the ridge that covers the RV. This will give you full coverage of the RV site.

"Set up overwatch from this elevated position. Monitoring the entire perimeter. Should anything appear suspicious, alert me know right away. No movement will occur without your clearance."

A subtle tilt of George's head tells me he's already calculating every angle. No need for further instruction; George understands the role.

"Simon, Derek, Lucy and I will be the ones to infiltrate the RV." The map zeroes in on the RV, with critical points marked. "Execute with stealth. Clear and secure every square foot. Sweep tight, no corner overlooked — we can't afford even a slight oversight here."

I glance around the room before continuing. "Once we've secured the RV, we will move into phase two: patrols, recces, and ambushes if needed. The relic's location is still a question mark, but thanks to Petrov, we have areas to search, and it's our job to find the device. We're in crowded territory. Viktor's crew, militia and unknown parties might be watching. Each one is competing for the same outcome."

With one tap on the remote, I shift the map again, zeroing in on the RV's boundary and marking the paths leading to the spots we've identified. "Here's what we're looking at. The terrain is rough and thick with vegetation; visibility will be our biggest challenge. Patrols will occur beneath the cover of darkness. That's when we gain the advantage against local forces. Realities on the ground might shift things. Adjustments will be needed if the undergrowth is too dense or movement draws attention. Daylight patrols may become unavoidable."

The map zooms to the dense undergrowth, showing a thick barrier of twisted trees, tangled brush, and shifting ground that'll be hell to navigate. "The outback's unforgiving, slowing our pace but working in our favour. Viktor hurls bodies at the task, but numbers won't subdue ground that punishes both sides. The Outback shows no respect for uniforms. Stay silent and sharp. The landscape becomes both an ally and a hurdle, hindering our moves but also shielding us from view."

The screen changes again, highlighting critical areas of interest—where the relic might be hidden and where Viktor's people are likely to focus their efforts.

"Keep an eye out for signs of something wrong—altered terrain, strange activity, or anything that contradicts the natural environment. Call in any sighting. Heroics have no place here."

My gaze sweeps across the room, taking a moment to assess each person, driving home the importance of what's coming—an unspoken understanding passing between us.

"Finding the relic is only part of the equation. The priority is to beat everyone else. Time is limited, and mistakes are not an option. If we face hostiles, a quick assessment will determine our response; if needed, we will eliminate the threat."

With everyone taking mental notes of the brief so far, I continue to the central objective of recovering the relic. "To start with, our priority is intel collection. Every point of data builds the roadmap, allowing us to execute a flawless recovery."

"Makes sense, Steve. The relic might be anywhere, even down an old mine shaft," Derek points out a few old-looking buildings scattered around the area.

"Excellent point, Derek. Now, let's discuss overall responsibilities. George, your role is essential. Lock down the area with continuous overwatch. Track every movement and neutralise potential threats without delay," I reply.

"Understood," George replies, expression determined and focused.

"Station yourselves along these high points," tapping the ridges on the map, "They're perfect for monitoring the entry and keeping eyes on the target location. Use your rangefinder to mark distances and note any obstacles. Wipe out anything unusual – an unexpected silhouette, a sudden movement, even an animal that might give us away. Remember, Viktor's men are trained to disappear into the surroundings. Keep focused."

A grin pulls at George's face. "Roger that. By first contact, they'll already be bleeding out."

"No doubt about it, George," I say. "Your secondary role, along with Lucy, is to cover our retreat if things go south. Once we secure the relic, you'll move to a position where you can monitor our exfil route. If we encounter resistance on the way out, your fire will keep heads pinned down while we make a tactical withdrawal."

George's gaze is unwavering. "Isn't a tactical withdrawal a fancy word for run away?"

"Yes, but without the court-martial," I continue. "We're counting on you," I say, my voice firm. "Your vigilance and precision are our first line of defence and our best chance at survival. The transport and logistics are in your hands, Simon, and your role is vital, as always. Maintain smooth transport and secure all routes. Provide the team, where possible, a clear, safe path."

"Copy that, Steve. Where's our primary insertion point?" says Simon, expression mirroring the gravity of the moment.

My hand points to the map projected on the screen. "Our route takes us through this series of dirt tracks. They're remote and less likely to be monitored by Viktor's men, but also rough and unpredictable. Conduct a thorough reconnaissance of these paths, utilising the most recent satellite imagery to assess their condition. And don't forget about the extraction point. Once we have the relic, we need a fast, efficient way out. Align with air support to ensure the LZ is tight and the timing is perfect. Coordinate with Derek — any lapse, and we lose control of the entire operation."

A flicker of resolve crosses Simon's face. "Everything will be aligned. Air support will engage the instant we give the green light."

Continuing, "Logistics extends beyond just transportation, involving more than just moving from point A to point B. It's about having the right equipment and supplies for any scenario. Review our inventory — make sure we're stocked with food, water, medical equipment, and ammunition."

"Done," Simon answers, voice clipped. "Dave's pushed locals into motion. Gear's inbound to the RV. I'll confirm all."

"Thanks, Simon. Ensure each piece moves as planned; our safety and exfil depend on your flawless coordination."

After drinking water, I moved on to comms. "Derek, you'll handle communications. Your role is critical. The team's relying on you to catch every whisper, every shadow. Engage all intel streams — satellite feeds and decrypted comms. Study Viktor's organisation from the inside out. Predict their next steps before they even move. I want ears on each decision. Viktor's men don't set foot anywhere without us knowing."

"Guardian link established, channels locked down with encryption. Intel feeds will be transmitted in real-time, and backup will be prepared to act on the signal. Emergency support will remain on standby," Derek answers, hands moving over the tablet, data streaming. "By intercepting their local comms, we'll detect anything Viktor's people say."

"Appreciate it, Derek. Track anything Viktor and his team throw — data spikes, frequency shifts, planted signals. Neutralise fast. Kill any breach on contact," I say, voice flat, final.

"Countermeasures are in place to block any interference," Derek affirms. "Secure lines will remain operational from start to finish."

"One more thing," my voice drops with gravity. "If we become compromised, you're the one who will call in the extraction. The evac plan demands perfection. Any setback means the difference between extraction and a body count. Also, assist Lucy in sifting through Viktor's data. Burn through the layers. Force the truth out piece by piece. Every exposed thread draws the relic nearer."

"Done. A clear escape route will be locked in, " Derek says, promising swift exfil.

After turning to face Lucy, "You're handling interrogations and all intelligence. Stay sharp, help steer us, and make sure we keep Viktor scrambling."

"Will dig deep into Viktor's channels, revealing any plans," Lucy says, eyes scanning the data on a tablet computer.

"Analyse every shred of information down to the core. Activate your connections to identify key players, uncover secrets, and anticipate Viktor's next moves. Your findings will shape our approach." My voice leaves no room for hesitation.

Lucy responds with conviction. "Our system catches every break in their rhythm. Nothing will slip through unseen."

"Extracting intel means going through interrogation, if necessary," I state. "A captured operative's value lies in what we can uncover. Your skills will obtain what we need to push forward."

"Copy that. Give me the right tools, and no stone goes unturned. What's hidden won't stay that way for long," Lucy responds with solid conviction.

"Stay tight with Derek's intel. Filter analysis into any tactical approach, keeping Viktor's path clear. If anything shifts in the intel, bring the intel to me straight away."

"Expect nothing less than precision. Derek and I will ensure seamless coordination on the intelligence front," Lucy states.

"Also, operational shifts are inevitable. Relying on your insight to pivot when required — every quick decision matters," I add.

Lucy doesn't hesitate. "Right behind you, Steve. Viktor won't have a clue what's coming."

"One final point," I say, lowering my voice. "Preparation for the unexpected is essential. Viktor is both cunning and resourceful. If things go awry, rapid adaptation will be crucial. Your ability to think on your feet and deliver immediate intelligence will serve as our lifeline."

Wrapping up the briefing, I address the team. "Oversight of the tactical aspects will be my responsibility. As always, leadership remains with me. Expect swift movements, hard strikes, and no traces left behind." The room falls silent, the weight of my words hanging in the air.

"We have encountered challenging missions in the past, yet this one is different. Stakes are raised, and risks are amplified. Precision is necessary in every move, and calculations must be exact. A formidable and ruthless adversary lies ahead. Viktor Readle won't hesitate to exploit any weaknesses," I say, my voice firm.

As I move through the room, the intensity of the mission begins to resonate. The Australian Outback presents a harsh and unforgiving landscape. Trust in our training and each other is paramount. Communication will be key. Derek will inform us of any developments, but we must always maintain situational awareness.

To summarise, I first focus on Simon. "Your logistics and transport plans are vital. Getting stranded or facing unexpected obstacles isn't an option. Preparedness for anything is key: a quick extraction, evasive manoeuvres, or a prolonged engagement. Make sure all our vehicles are ready and stocked with essential supplies."

Moving my gaze to George. "Overwatch is yours. Ensure a clean line on approach, covering every sector, and eliminate any risk."

"Our advantage lies in anticipating Viktor's next move. Track movement before they commit. Intercept. Break the pace. Strip away momentum and dismantle before any impact occurs. Derek cut off all possible leaks — complete lockdown on comms. Any weakness here risks the whole operation," I say, scanning faces.

After taking another swig of water, I continue, "Our primary objective is non-negotiable: locate and secure that World War Two relic weapon. Viktor must not reach the device. We need leads on networks — track the syndicate's patterns, identify who's pulling the strings, and neutralise any imminent threats. The mission is more than survival. It's about preventing a catastrophe on a scale we can't let take shape. The second objective is explicit — Viktor's network goes down with him. Let's go to work."

Focus fills the space, and each person is committed — a quiet force that ties us to the goal. "Let's clarify to Viktor Readle that they've underestimated us. We will hit fast and hard, leaving nothing behind. Always remember why we're doing this — for our fallen brother, Billy, for our loved ones, and the safety of many.

Victory is essential. Take an hour to pull intel on your tasks, then regroup here for a debrief. After that, we'll grab food," I say, taking another drink of water.

Each of us grabs our briefing packs and settles into the task. The room is filled with the rustle of paper and the murmur of focused conversation. The team absorbs every detail, eyes flicking over maps and reports.

After 10 minutes, everyone disperses, each on a mission. Lucy's up first, and heading to the control centre, where Dave's intel crew awaits. A precise objective drives movement. The mission is already taking shape in Lucy's head.

George shifts, shoulders loose, then angles toward the armoury to confirm that our arsenal is up to the mission. Derek ambles toward the equipment store, eyes set on finding radios that'll withstand the Outback.

Simon passes through, refining transport protocols. Without wasting a moment, Simon veers off to integrate with Dave's men and adjust their timing.

The team fades into shadows, the silence broken only by machines pulsing with data. Before me, screens bleed satellite feeds and threat grids — battlefields mapped in brutal precision. The relic waits. Viktor's cold ambition and the threat of destruction loom ahead, an unspoken gathering force of danger.

Execution must cut clean — no stumbles, no mercy. Lives hang from every choice made in silence. With Readle, no quarter is given. The man is ruthless, and fucking up isn't an option if we intend to finish this mission.

Clarity takes hold, fusing all the moving parts into perfect alignment with razor-like accuracy. Like a tuned machine, every action aligns in harmony, gears meshing in perfect rhythm. Actions click together with practised ease, forming a tight chain of execution designed with a precision that leaves no margin for error.

As I make my rounds, I'm reassured by the team members' efficiency and focus. Their dedication and expertise remind me why we're the best at what we do. Critical elements are examined in fine detail, refining the approach into a lethal, seamless plan. A battle that will test our skills is in progress, and our certainty in our capacity to prevail is absolute.

In the control room, light from the monitors outlines Lucy's face as she analyses the intel, exchanging updates with Dave's team without missing a beat. The rhythmic hum of equipment fills the air, echoing a sense of focus. The screens flicker with real-time data — satellite feeds, movement trackers, and surveillance from our drones.

Lucy's fingers tap over the keys. Outback maps appear on the screen, layered with Viktor's suspected coordinates. Eyes narrow, dissecting the landscape, each icon a breadcrumb leading to our objective. One misstep or sound out of place, and figures cut through the dark faster than thought.

Down in the armoury, George moves with the same meticulous care. Every weapon is stripped, cleaned, and reassembled with a precision that borders on obsession. Scopes align under an expert touch, fine-tuning, ready to combat the desert's unforgiving light. Magazines slide in and out without a hitch, hands moving with a practised rhythm honed from countless missions.

A rehearsed grip runs down the length of the barrel, methodical and sure. "A final check before we go," George remarks before grabbing another rifle, inspections unrelenting.

George's discipline leaves nothing unchecked; a jammed weapon in a firefight means one thing — a fatal miscalculation.

Embedded in the task, various radios are lined up for testing. Derek switches through channels. The air crackles with static, still hunting for the frequency that'll cut through the Outback's isolation. Australian conditions are punishing on the equipment, but Derek pushes the radios to maximum capacity, reinforcing range and stability, ensuring every unit stands ready for the demanding environment.

"Comms are solid,' Derek says, gaze fixed on a stubborn radio. "These units can take anything the Outback dishes out."

In another part of the room, Simon is in deep conversation with Dave's transport team. A map across the table shows the locations of Viktor's men already on the ground. Vehicle specs are laid out. Paths crisscross on the map, a tactical guide designed to keep us one step ahead, each turn calculated against Australia's rugged terrain.

Under Simon's gaze, routes, tracks, and shortcuts turn to tactics. A fast retreat is outlined and prepped, with vehicles armed to rip through any blockade.

All parts aligned, every detail sharpened, and on cue, the operation primed to unfold with exacting precision, ready to move as a single, unbreakable unit. Yet, anticipation permeates the environment. Intel, weapons, and gear are secured, but in our line of work, guarantees do not exist."

Back in the briefing room an hour later, Lucy takes the floor. Military intelligence instincts are razor-sharp, diving into Viktor's recent moves and laying out patterns we need to understand.

"Viktor's syndicate is on the move," Lucy announces, gesturing to the map on the screen. "Intel confirms Viktor relocated base of operations to a repurposed mining facility in the heart of the Australian Outback. The location is isolated, surrounded by harsh terrain, and equipped with advanced security measures. The stakes are high, and we must be prepared for anything. Local intel confirms these as active sites. Surveillance picked up increased activity—personnel shifts, equipment drops, coded messages. Viktor's reach is formidable, resources vast."

Simon takes charge, addressing the logistics. "Transportation is essential, as the Outback offers no mercy. The terrain calls for vehicles that can handle any ground, every path selected for discretion and rapid retrieval, ensuring our movements stay covert and controlled." Red dots scatter across the map, marking potential extraction zones with solid cover and straightforward access. "Set secondary routes for each, and secure fallback points. Without these contingencies, the plan is compromised."

"Keeping channels open in this environment is no small task," Derek says, marking the comms diagram. "Long-range, high-frequency units are our best shot at holding the lines. Signal interference is a significant threat. Viktor's tech team can jam our signals, so readiness to adapt is crucial. Regular check-ins and contingency plans for signal loss are non-negotiable."

Every eye is glued to the screens while the team absorbs the intel. "Let's evaluate potential challenges," I declare, meeting stares. "The environment stands as our primary obstacle. The Outback's brutal heat, limited water sources, and hazardous wildlife might threaten the mission.'"

Lucy interjects, voice sharp. "Mercenaries under Viktor, don't hesitate. Some wear pro kits. Others might be street scum with rusty triggers and twitchy nerves."

Simon adds, "The terrain will be challenging to navigate. Sandstorms, jagged paths, and hidden ravines can impede us and increase our exposure to danger. Staying vigilant and adaptable is crucial."

Derek cuts straight to the point. "Our edge comes from remaining one step ahead, predicting their next move. Without perfect communication and preparation, we're walking into danger."

The room falls silent as the magnitude of our mission sinks in. Each of us understands the stakes.

My gaze sweeps over the team, setting the tone. "Strike without hesitation, eliminate every target, and disappear."

As we finalise our plans, a sense of foreboding lingers. The vast and unforgiving Outback awaits. But so do we, armed with determination and a relentless drive to succeed.

While others prepare to leave, I pause as Viktor's face dominates the screen. The mission holds meaning for each of us, yet for me, it is more profound than a simple operation. It's a quest for vengeance for Billy. Stopping Viktor now means halting a firestorm before it swallows something worse.

Chapter Ten — Departure to Australia

We opt to stay at Guardian Security Solutions, a place with a presence that can't be ignored. When we step into the canteen, the aroma of food surrounds us.

The room is arranged with military precision—clinical, deliberate. Rows of tables and chairs stand at attention like soldiers on parade, each squared off to the exact degree. The surfaces gleam under the harsh fluorescent lights, sterile and cold, and the air is thick with the scent of disinfectant.

It's the kind of order that speaks louder than chaos—a silent reminder that control is everything. Even here, in this mundane space. This isn't a break. It's a battlefield dressed in clean lines and polished floors.

"Let's eat," I say, walking toward the serving area.

The team moves in silence, trays in hand. The food is simple—grilled chicken, vegetables, rice—enough to fill our bellies but insufficient to make anyone comfortable.

We settle at a secluded table, distancing ourselves from the others who are sat at tables eating. Across from me, Lucy's gaze sweeps the room, trained eyes picking apart faces, hunting for the traitor blending into the background. Sitting on either side, George and Simon are silent, a language in itself. Derek stares past us, fingers drumming the table as if the rhythm alone might bring clarity to thoughts.

Each mouthful is swallowed, the act mechanical and lifeless, fuelled only by the need to keep going. A sense of déjà vu pervades the moment, poised on the brink of significance, yet the stakes are elevated this time."

Fork in hand, George tears into the meal, grinning. "This beats the hell out of combat rations," muttering between bites.

Simon's plate, as usual, holds a kid-sized portion, almost laughable. But no one says a word; the jokes about tiny meals are losing their edge.

With a slow sip, Lucy lets the drink settle before adding, "Might as well enjoy this—calm like this doesn't last."

Savouring the bite, the rich flavour of roast chicken holds me steady, "True enough. *Quiet* like this rarely lasts," I note, allowing the stillness to sink in before shattering.

With a dinner plate like a mountain of food, "Prepared and primed," Derek remarks. "We've tackled more demanding challenges," before starting to eat.

The rest of the meal concludes in silence, a familiarity that speaks volumes more than words. It is not a silence of awkwardness but one of shared understanding forged in countless missions together.

Shadows of what's to come hang thick in the air, clinging to the skin like the damp residue of a jungle downpour.

For now, it's just us and the scran. Forks scrape across metal trays with slow, deliberate movements, each grating sound loud in the stillness- a tinny rhythm that fills the void where a conversation might thrive. The plates are empty, but no one's in a rush. It's not about the food—never is. This is the last calm before the chaos.

Around us, the canteen begins to thin out. Boots shuffle. Trays clatter. Crockery stacks with dull thuds behind the serving line. Operators file out one by one, heading back to gear checks, comms tests, and the unspoken countdown ticking in all our heads.

But we linger. Not out of laziness. Not out of comfort. We're absorbing—the quiet, the stillness, the thin veneer of normality that will be stripped away the second we roll out. We're seasoned enough to understand what's coming and smart enough to respect the silence before the storm.

The next destination is the rest area. A few chairs are scattered around, old paperbacks fill the shelves, and a TV flickers in the corner. Although designed for downtime, the room seldom offers true respite.

Dropping into a chair, the cushion adjusts beneath me. For a moment, the pressure of the job fades, if only for a second, just enough to let me breathe.

Lucy snatches a few magazines from the coffee table — military history and some half-torn survival rag — then drops into the chair beside me with a graceful thud. Lucy flips one open with a casual flick, then glances in my direction.

"A little light reading before we dive back in?" Lucy asks.

I allow a chuckle to slip out, dry and unexpected. "Why not? A distraction sounds perfect right now. Even if it's a five-year-old article on a cold-weather kit, I'll never wear it."

Lucy smirks, settling in, legs crossed, eyes skimming the pages but not reading. We're all just pretending to be somewhere else.

Simon sprawls on the battered couch like he owns the place, arms folded behind his head. Voice floating across the room, laced with fatigue, "Taking a nap. Wake me if something blows up or Lucy starts quoting from the mag."

"I'm not above taking the piss, reading a feature on surviving wild pig attacks. Might be useful if I come across one with your appearance," Lucy calls back, mocking.

A soft chuckle escapes from Derek, near the TV. Flipping through channels with George, the pair are locked in a silent battle to avoid the news and find something mindless, before settling on a grainy war film — one of those black-and-white epics where everything explodes in slow motion and no one runs out of ammo.

The broadcast drone settles over us like a worn blanket—familiar, strange and comforting. The kind of noise that reminds you you're still alive.

I shift in my chair, toss the mag onto the table, and fix my eyes on the screen. But my mind won't stay put. Instead, it slips past the reel of old cinema and into the actual film playing behind my eyes—the mission, the layout of Viktor's compound, the hard glint of weaponry under floodlights, and the faces of the team.

Then Billy's face punches through the fog. Silence in the final moment. I clench my jaw, try to blink the image away and focus on the film. But it's just noise now, a background to the war inside my head.

Around me, no one speaks. Everyone is caught in their loop. Lucy flips a page but doesn't read. Simon breathes deeply, already halfway to sleep. Derek and George sit like statues, eyes on the screen, but at a guess, their minds are elsewhere—rehearsing breaches, scanning fire zones, reliving near misses.

This is our version of peace. Not laughter. Not comfort. Just a few stolen hours where no one's bleeding, no alarms are screaming, and no one's telling us to move.

As the clock approaches our departure time, I glance at the team. They're relaxed but ready, each finding a way to prepare for what's coming. A surge of pride and determination flows through my body.

"Alright," I say, standing up and stretching. "Time to return to work."

The gear room thrums with a tension that words can't capture, and we all lock into the task with a clarity that only experience brings. But the stakes aren't typical today—this mission carries weight beyond any assignment completed in the past.

Simon unfastens his Bergen with the calm precision of a man who's done this a thousand times in hostile terrain. Hands move without hesitation — vest unbuckled, mags checked and rechecked, every clip, knife, and tool scrutinised with the eye of someone who understands that one misplaced item might cost lives. It's muscle memory, with intent behind every movement.

The blade of the combat knife catches the light as Simon inspects the edge, which is razor-sharp and lethal, before replacing the knife into the sheath with a click that sounds final. Satisfied, he slings the Bergen over one shoulder and strides from the prep area, boots thudding against the concrete.

Simon pushes through the door to the control room. It's cramped, fluorescent-lit, and humming with muted tension. Dave's GSS team is clustered around a wall-mounted screen displaying the terrain overlay — transport routes, choke points, and red zones blinking in digital urgency.

Simon doesn't waste time. "Vehicle readiness?"

Dave nods. "Four ATVs prepped, thermal camo netting loaded in a box on the rear. The equipment will be on-site when you arrive."

Simon's eyes scan the screen, processing every detail. "Exfil routes?"

"Depends on the start point. Suppose you leave from the RV. The north ridge is compromised; a satellite picked up movement last cycle. You may need to reroute around the eastern ridge. Ten klicks extra, but no eyes on that trail in the previous 72."

Simon grunts approval. "Smart call."

A younger GSS operator says, "When you are nearing the exfil point, radio through, and I'll have the air transport en route to extract you."

"Make sure you do. We might be coming in hot," Simon replies.

The room stills for a second, the weight of the words settling in. Simon turns, the Bergen settling into a place like armour, and disappears through the door.

Derek's focus sharpens on the comms array. Brow furrowed in that no-bullshit, don't-talk to me, unless it's life-or-death expression he wears when in the zone. Movements are deliberate — no second-guessing. Every dial, every switch is touched with the precision of a surgeon, the calm intensity of a man who's lived and bled by signal strength.

"Encryption holding steady," Derek mutters, without looking up. "Signal clean. Satellite bounce is stable across all bands."

I move closer, watching as Derek fine-tunes the last frequency. The faint hum of power vibrating through the unit is subtle — but to Derek, it's a heartbeat.

"You hearing anything?" I ask.

"Interference out of the eastern ridge. Might be atmospherics. Or someone testing a jammer. Either way, I've patched a fallback route. If we lose contact, I'll bounce us through the Omani uplink," Derek replies.

"Thanks. I'm not dragging the team into the hornet's nest blind."

Across the room, Lucy's workspace is surgical. Interrogation tools, data packs, signal intercepts — all laid out with unflinching precision. Lucy's not just prepping gear but building a battlefield inside her mind.

Lucy lifts a handheld signal sweeper and thumbs the power button. "Battery full. Memory clean. Range tested. I've got spectrum analysis for every frequency they're likely to use."

"Redundancy?" I ask.

"Built-in," Lucy says, eyes not leaving the screen. "Triple-layer backups and rotating encryption keys. If Viktor so much as breathes on a comms line, I'll detect the message. If we land one breathing... I'll strip answers clean," Lucy mutters, a quiet promise wrapped in steel.

I give a single nod. I don't need to say anything. Years with Lucy speak louder than anything, I might add.

George is planted on the floor, cross-legged, with both sniper rifles stripped. Hands moving — methodical, precise. The barrel gleams under the dim light, a cold, silent promise.

George doesn't speak; he just works, as if the rifles are extensions of him. Scope alignment, windage, zeroing — all muscle memory. Picking up the scope, he peers through, turning the adjustment dial like tuning a piano before a symphony of violence.

"According to the weather satellite, the wind blows from the west," George says, not looking up. "I'll compensate. Elevation'll need fine-tuning once we're in position, but I've memorised the range cards."

"You always do," I reply. "Double-check the suppressors. If we need quiet, I want surgical."

George smirks. "When have I ever missed?"

"Don't start a list," I shoot back. George grunts in amusement before returning to the bolt assembly.

I sit in silence, laying my gear out in front of me. My rifle slides open, breechblock slick and polished. I chamber a round, check the action, then holster my sidearm. Explosives — clean, dry, and wired for immediate deployment. Each charge is pre-cut, each wire colour-coded, and fuse lengths checked twice over.

The gear room hums with unspoken tension — metal clinks, bag zips, and the occasional click of a mag locking home. The scent of oil, cold steel, and yesterday's cordite hangs in the air. The metal of my rifle is cool in my grip, steadying and anchoring me.

Simon walks in, tightening the webbing straps. "Final checks are done. Vehicles are fuelled and hot. Derek, are you keeping us on the grid?"

"Until the satellites fall," Derek replies, tapping the headset into place.

"Extraction routes uploaded. I also have heat maps showing recent movement. Appears they're shifting patrol patterns. Might be getting jumpy. The traitor here might have alerted someone that we are coming," says Lucy, packing the last data pack into her Bergen.

George finishes assembling the sniper rifle, the sound of the bolt locking home clean and crisp.

I rise to my feet, the weight of my gear settling across my shoulders like an old friend. I glance around at the team—everyone is dialled in, focused, ready.

"This is it," I say. "Once we move, stay sharp. Protect each other's backs. And if anything seems off... trust your instincts."

Everyone acknowledges. No bravado. No war cries—just calm, lethal readiness. Glory doesn't factor. The task comes first, last, and everything between—clean execution, clean exit.

"Alright, team. Let's go over last-minute intel," I say.

Simon leans over the open map, fingers moving over marked routes, aligning our transport plans with precision. Paths crisscross, marking our intended flight and ground routes across the Outback, every step locked in with Dave's team's input.

"Flight plan to Broome confirmed," Simon states, "once we arrive in Darwin, Australia, we will be taken to the insertion point five miles outside the target zone by helicopter. From LZ, it's a short hike to our FRV."

"Thanks," I reply.

The terrain is rugged and unforgiving, perfect for hiding a relic. Already shifting to what's next, Simon wastes no time coordinating with the pilots, confirming our flight plan and double-checking every piece of kit. Trust is absolute; Simon will ensure we're clear when the moment demands.

The last adjustments fall into place as Derek locks down the communications grid with multiple redundant channels, ensuring we stay connected even in the remote and challenging terrain of the Outback. Fingers fly over the keyboard, double-checking frequencies and encryption codes.

"Comms are up, secure channels are in place, and we'll receive continuous updates on any hostiles or potential dangers," Derek reports.

Standing in the control room, I'm reminded that the stakes are higher than ever, and the consequences of failure are unthinkable. Thoughts turn to Lucy as our eyes meet from across the room, walking toward me, face set with quiet resolve.

"Steve, we need to be prepared for anything. Viktor won't make this easy," Lucy says, resting a hand on my shoulder.

"Understood," I reply.

With a stern expression, Derek approaches. "Steve, after reviewing the intel, it's clear we're walking into a hornet's nest. Viktor's surveillance is extensive."

"Figured as much." My hand grips Derek's shoulder. "That's our edge. Adapt and overcome — our speciality."

Simon steps in, voice firm and clear. "Transport is ready. Departure in 30 minutes."

After one last check, weapons are checked one last time, and packs are in place. The team braces for what lies ahead. Each of us is lost in thoughts of what's at stake. Every step from here leads us deeper into the fire.

As the clock ticks down, I address the team one last time. "Remember why we're here. This mission is about more than stopping Viktor. It's about preventing a catastrophe and avenging Billy. Stay focused, trust each other, and we'll come through this. The flight to Darwin will be lengthy; take advantage of this time to relax."

Once aboard the aircraft, everyone fastens seat belts, taking their places for the journey ahead. Moments later, the engines roar to life. The next part of the mission is underway, the first leg of multiple stops until we reach Darwin, Australia.

The steady thrum fills the cabin, setting the rhythm for focused minds — minds fixed on the objective. Simon studies the flight plan, focusing on the tablet's screen. Derek tests communication frequencies, securing every encryption layer. Lucy analyses Viktor's latest intel. Ever the quiet presence, George runs a cloth over the sniper rifle.

The engines keep their steady beat as hours blur together. Discussions tighten around the crucial details — contingency plans, tactical manoeuvres, enemy intel — every word bringing us closer to the action waiting on the ground.

With Darwin on the horizon, I walk over to Simon, leaning in just enough to break his focus. "How are we set for transport when we hit Darwin?"

"All systems are go," Simon states, still focused on the task. "The helicopter will be waiting for our arrival. We have a five-mile exclusion zone surrounding the target, which means rapid deployment is critical upon touchdown."

"Fantastic," appreciating the thoroughness. "Derek, what's the latest on enemy communications?"

"Nothing of consequence," Derek says, glancing at the tablet connected to GSS. "Same old communication, but the area is locked down tight."

Lucy's eyes flick over the satellite feed, a silent dance of infrared overlays and thermal imaging scrolling across the screen. Figures shift like ghosts along the perimeter of the mining facility and beyond.

Glancing up from the screen at me, "I've been tracking Viktor's movements along with Dave's team for the last 24 hours. High-resolution satellite passes picked up multiple heat signatures—rotating patrols, elevated watchpoints, and canine units. From appearances, Viktor is doubling security across sites. That's the centre of gravity. Reinforced checkpoints, UAV sweeps every few hours, and no blind spots in their perimeter."

Lucy taps a corner of the screen—an infrared blur flares red, then fades.

"That's not a coincidence. The GSS traitor may have already tipped someone off. We're not just against Viktor's paranoia anymore—we're against a prepared enemy waiting for us to walk into the kill zone."

"Then we'll give them something to worry about," I say, the determination in my voice evident.

The moment we land in Darwin and the aircraft comes to a halt, we disembark. We exit the plane and leave behind the refreshing chill of the cabin, replaced by an oppressive heat that crashes over us.

The tarmac buzzes with urgency. Workers hustle, shifting crates, ammo cases, and specialised gear from the jet to the waiting helicopter. No wasted movement. Just that cold, focused efficiency you only witness in people who comprehend time's a luxury we don't have.

The helo isn't your standard bird—it's a goddamn predator in matte-black skin, a flying fortress dressed for war. Chin-mounted cannons, infrared deflectors, radar dampeners—the works. It's not here to transport. But here to deliver death.

The rotors spin up with a deep, rising thrum that cuts through the night, each revolution like a war drum beating out a countdown. Every pulse of air slaps me in the chest, reminding me—this isn't just another op. This is the kind of job that leaves scars… if you're lucky enough to come back with your skin still intact.

Simon slaps the side of the bird with a nod of approval. "They've brought out the evil toys. Someone upstairs wants this done clean."

"Or dirty," Lucy adds, climbing in ahead of me. "Depends which side you're on."

Derek angles toward the cockpit, hand adjusting gear, tone flat. "Comms frequency?"

The pilot's already strapping in; an older, grizzled man—one of those lifers with a stare like he's seen a thousand insertions and buried dozens of mates. His voice crackles through the internal comms.

"Channel seven. Encrypted. We'll go dark once we're inside five klicks of target airspace. Terrain masking all the way in."

Derek nods, already tweaking gear. "I'll keep us linked until the last possible second. After that… we're on our own."

I climb aboard last. The transition hits me the moment my boot hits the deck—one step from a world of structure and systems to the stripped-down, metallic brutality of war. No comforts here. Just harnesses, anchor points, and reinforced plating designed to keep us breathing for the first few seconds of chaos.

The aircrew work around us like ghosts, securing crates and locking down gear. One gives George a quick once-over before sliding fresh boxes of 5.56 and 7.62 rounds into the storage net.

George glances up. "If I need more than that, it's already too late."

The crew chief leans toward me, shouting over the whine of the turbines. "ETA to drop point—40 minutes. The weather's rough over the ridgeline. You want a clean LZ, better pray someone upstairs likes you."

I grunt. "Think he might not be taking calls tonight."

I drop into the jump seat, buckle in, and pull the maps from my Bergen, unfolding like the battlefield itself—lines, ridges, potential kill zones. The cabin light paints everything in a red glow. I trace the route with my finger, and terrain features come alive: elevation, visibility, and enemy patrol vectors.

The bird lifts off with a lurch that slams reality home. The city lights fall away beneath us, swallowed by black. The vibration runs through the deck, into my boots, up my spine. Everything we are, everything we've planned—compressed into the gear strapped to our chests, the steel in our eyes, and the ghosts we carry with us.

No one speaks now—not because we're afraid, but because we're ready. This isn't the calm before the shit storm—this is the storm.

"Gather around," I state, maintaining a steady yet tense tone. "We're venturing into uncharted territory, and readiness for any eventuality upon landing is paramount."

Lucy studies the fresh intel, eyes narrowed. "Dave's team confirms Viktor's reinforcing the mine compound. Appears like they're bringing in more firepower. But here's the twist—another team is closing in, camped a short distance from the relic's suspected coordinates," she says.

Wildlife and environmental hazards require attention. Vast and unyielding, the Outback conveys a menace without uttering a sound, hiding peril beneath the surface, poised for the unwary.

"Do you remember Steve's expression when that small snake appeared?" Lucy says over the intercom.

"Yeah, the numpty jumped so high, almost took me down, fucking wimp," Derek says, a laugh escaping.

"Don't worry, you green numpty, us donkey wallopers will keep you safe," comes the reply from Simon.

Rather than dignify a response, I extend my middle finger upwards in Simon's face.

"Our insertion point lies here, by the dry riverbed. It's the nearest location where we can approach undetected. Next, we head to the compound, where the ATVs are ready at the RV, arranged earlier through local channels. Routes are mapped out. Should a rapid exfil become necessary, options are lined up. The terrain will be an asset, but readiness to change course remains vital," says Simon, indicating a spot on the map.

"Appreciate that, Simon. Those will be useful, but for now, we're tabbing the first leg," I reply through the intercom. The helicopter hums with intensity as I outline our mission. "After securing the relic, focus on gathering intelligence about Viktor's operations and dismantling the cartel. Follow the plan, but be prepared for anything. The unexpected can always arise."

As we fly over the rugged landscape, Viktor occupies my thoughts. The man's ruthless, and we're about to penetrate occupied territory. By now, people might be well-acquainted with the land, giving them a tactical advantage.

The ground shifts from sparse scrub to raw wilderness, painted in the fading glow of sunset. The intensity within the team is almost tangible. Minds run through why we're here, each anchored by a personal reason that fuels the mission.

With a casual lean, Simon gazes through the small window before saying. "Once, I would have given anything to be part of missions like this. But now I'm immersed, each moment testing my resolve to stay alive, it's different. More real. More dangerous," says Simon, still looking at the ground below.

"Not the first challenge we've faced, mate, and won't be the last. If everyone sticks to their roles, we come out intact," I reply.

"I agree, do your job, and we're all back in one piece," George says, tapping the rifle's sights with a steady resolve.

"To me, this is more than a mission," Derek states, fingers tapping on the tablet. "Losing another man isn't on the cards. Billy's death cut deep, and repeating that would be a blow we don't need — unless, of course, the corpse is George."

"Fuck off, numpty; remember, I can slot a bullet in that space between your ears from half a mile away," retorts George, giving Derek the middle finger.

Lucy stares through the screen, not into it — hands still, breath shallow.

"Lucy, we've faced worse fires. We don't break now," I shout over the noise of the aircraft.

A flicker of intensity settles in Lucy's expression, somewhere between determination and worry. "No wild risks, Steve. You're needed for more important things — like moving house," Lucy says, a laugh under the surface.

"Got it, no reckless moves, and I'll be able to carry those boxes," I reply, the commitment in my voice matching Lucy's.

"We're braced for every turn. By the time Viktor catches on, it'll be far too late," Lucy declares, confidence a solid anchor.

The helicopter's interior lights cast a faint glow, illuminating the determination etched on every face.

Our path is defined: secure the relic, sabotage Viktor's plans, and honour Billy's legacy. Teamwork transcends function; we are a family united by loyalty and the unwavering pledge to bring each other home.

"We are approaching the target now," the pilot's voice crackles through the intercom, signalling our imminent entry into the hot zone.

The aircraft begins the descent, nose tilting as the rotors carve through the stillness like spinning blades of fate. Below us, the terrain stretches out — rugged and hostile, a broken expanse of rock, brush, and ancient earth scarred by time. It's the kind of place that doesn't welcome visitors, but swallows them.

The pilot's voice snaps n over the headset. "Dust landing, limiting visibility. Terrain's narrow but manageable. You've got 30 seconds, then we're gone."

"Copy," I reply, sensing the shift in the air pressure as we drop.

I glance at the team. Simon checks the harness one last time, "If this goes lateral, I vote we blame Derek."

Derek doesn't flinch. "I logged your death as 'accidental incompetence' 10 minutes ago."

Lucy smirks without humour, eyes locked forward. "Focus. Twenty seconds."

The chopper dips lower. Dust and gravel explode outward in a vortex, slamming against the hull, roaring like a beast trying to shake us loose. The ramp slams down, and the wind hits like a punch to the face — dry, sharp, laced with something ancient and feral.

That's the Outback. It doesn't care who you are or what you came for.

The bird touches down hard, a jolt snapping like a warning shot through the floor. Standing by the rear door, I signal the team with a clenched fist. No fast rope this time. Just run and vanish.

"Go, go!" the crew chief yells, voice almost lost in the thunder of rotors. "We've got 30 seconds on the ground. Make each count!"

Derek and George are, first off, running fast. Rifles raised, eyes slicing through the dark. Lucy follows, silent as a shadow. Simon is right behind, moving like he's already in the fight. I take up the rear, boots slamming into the dirt, the roar of the chopper swallowing everything.

The Outback embraces us without mercy — dust curling up, swallowing forms as the bird lifts away. The storm from the rotors rages for a moment, then dies as the aircraft vanishes, leaving nothing but silence and the echo of departure.

We don't speak. Don't need to. The rhythm takes over — silent, instinctive, burned into us through years of hard graft and harder battles. Formation clicks into place with the kind of precision no amount of training manuals can teach.

I take point, eyes locked on the terrain ahead, boots landing soft but sure, rifle raised and scanning. My senses are stretched thin, feeding on the tension that clings to the Outback like static before a storm.

Derek shadows me, close and quiet. I detect the faint adjustments on the comms rig and the almost silent press of fingers on toggles and switches. Derek's tuned into the frequencies; the atmosphere, the unspoken signals in the dirt and the wind — reading the land as much as the tech.

Lucy moves behind Derek, steps silent, surgical, alert even in the dark. The data rig is pressed tight to Lucy's side, every motion economical and lethal. She's watching everything — body language, shadows, the way the air shifts around us.

Simon follows Lucy, already tapping into terrain elevation data, marking visual checkpoints, and tracking our progress, eyes flicking between the GPS display and the ridgelines. Simon will find the way if a better route through this hellscape can be located.

George brings up the rear. Silent. Constant. Rifle moving in slow arcs, sweeping our six like a sentinel carved from stone. Anything tracking us makes a mistake. George will catch the movement before intent even forms.

The Outback stretches in every direction—barren, broken, and indifferent to our presence. It's not a place that welcomes people. The silence here isn't peaceful—but loaded. Even the wildlife sounds distant and cautious. As if it comprehends that we don't belong.

The shadows tighten around us, and the landscape is thick with twisted brush and jagged outcrops. The moon briefly breaks through, casting long, skeletal shadows across the scrub. Everything appears to want to reach out and grab us.

Branches claw at our gear, thorns bite into gloved hands, and the scent of earth and iron is heavy. It's slow going; stealth over speed. The dry leaves beneath our boots crackle, and every step might echo into something waiting out of view.

Ten minutes pass in silence—minutes that stretch as a wire pulled tight. I raise a hand. We halt, each dropping down, eyes scanning, ears tuned to the subtle shift of wind and undergrowth. I crouch, hand resting on the cool steel of my rifle, eyes sweeping the terrain.

The Outback breathes around us—alive, ancient, indifferent.

Derek whispers through the comms, just about audible. "Thermal's clean. Nothing on the ridge. Yet."

Lucy slides up beside me, "Air's too still. Animals are quiet?" she says.

"Like the land's holding a breath," I reply.

Simon angles toward the faint ridgeline ahead. "Something waiting in the night—and it's not guessing anymore," says Simon, pointing to the bush ahead.

After a few minutes, nothing warrants investigation, so we push forward, each step a calculated risk. Broken earth and patches of dense foliage stretch out before us. The moon emerges, throwing a silver wash over the landscape, shifting shadows, creating fleeting illusions that blur the line between solid ground and hidden traps.

A rustle, sharp and distinct in the night, disrupts the stillness. Then, a deep and guttural growl reverberates through the dark like a chilling warning. A hand signal brings the team to a halt. Muscles coil tight as our weapons hold steady, eyes fixed on every angle of the darkness, waiting for the slightest movement to betray a threat.

Sound drains from the air, stripping away the usual sounds and leaving a void on the edge of breaking. Instinct flares, sensing an unspoken danger woven into the night's fabric as shadows shift, warping the landscape in waves as the wind churns around us. Sweat collects on my brow as the team holds position, waiting for the signal to advance.

The moment hangs, drawn tight like a bowstring. A firm grip on the rifle heightened senses, searching for any trace of threat while seconds stretch, dragging in the silence. The growl remains elusive, leaving only the wind to carry faint whispers across the desert, empty but charged with hidden intent. With one quick hand motion from me, we press forward.

Ahead, the brush opens into a narrow clearing, and I motion for the team to halt, as I drop into a crouch, while everyone vanishes into the depths of the shadows. From my jacket, the Splashmap and compass come out as Lucy settles beside me, eyes on the perimeter, ready for whatever comes our way.

With a fingertip, I navigate the map, each contour guiding us toward the next objective. "We're here," I murmur.

Lucy's attention darts between the map and the rugged landscape beyond. "Agreed."

With everything stowed, we fall into a single line and push forward, our footsteps muted but firm. Trees thin, making way for more complex ground, rough rock replacing the forest floor. The shift underfoot signals that we're entering a different arena.

A steep drop unfurls before me, plunging into the valley. "Spread out," I whisper over comms, watching the team dissolve into the ridge's cover, each aligning to the ground facing different arcs of fire.

Through my night vision scope, the world bleeds green and black—harsh edges, warped shadows, any movement a potential threat. I scan the horizon, slow and methodical. The RV emerges in the distance, an unlit silhouette crouched against the skyline. Almost invisible in the blackness—except for a faint glint of metal where moonlight kisses the edge.

From my vantage point, the RV stands like a fortress—something dead and buried in the bush, dug in and daring anyone to come closer.

The compound sprawls in jagged pieces—an industrial carcass stripped bare by the wind and the years. A sharp and unforgiving structure dominates the centre, like a place no one enters without permission… or a death wish.

A couple of storage sheds litter the perimeter, scattered like spent brass. Shapes lean at odd angles, rusted and neglected, but not useless. They are perfect for concealment, ideal for an ambush.

The ground between us and the RV is bare, open ground with hardly any cover. Cross the space wrong, and you're announcing your death with every footstep. The kind of kill zone that doesn't forgive mistakes.

I keep scanning. Every contour, every shadow. Nothing moves. But that's what makes my spine tighten. It's too still. The kind of stillness that hums in your ears and wraps around your chest. Shadows cling to the edges of the compound, undisturbed, untouched. But I've seen silence like this before. It's not peace. It's patience — a loaded weapon with a finger on the trigger.

Derek shifts beside me, a whisper in the dirt. I don't need to check. Derek's eyes will be locked on the same thing. Lucy will already be running thermal sweeps. George will be checking the rooftops. Simon will be calculating every route in and every way out.

"All clear?" Lucy asks, voice just above a whisper.

"For now," I reply, lowering the scope. "But out here, this means nothing."

With a subtle hand motion, Derek eases into position, disappearing into the rock's dark contours. Years of practice have made our silent communication seamless.

A tap on my comms. "All callsigns, the compound's right ahead. George, hold a position on the ridge and provide overwatch. In case everything unravels, eliminate any opposition and control the scene. The rest of us will move in and lock down the RV. Over."

The radio comes alive with George's voice. "GD, copy, I've got coverage on most of the camp, but the structure in the middle is in my way. If you go behind, I won't be able to cover you."

"S3, Roger that." Adjustments to the plan take shape in my mind.

Holding a position on the ridge, George steadies the sniper rifle, zeroing in on the compound as the rest of the team pushes forward. The jagged path compels a silent approach, each action sharpened by silent understanding forged over countless missions. We vanish into the cover 100 metres from the core building, allowing us to track any signs of activity before moving.

"Derek, Simon — take the left flank and lock down the small structure. Lucy, stay in close. We're taking the primary target."

With a quick thumb signal, Derek and Simon vanish, melting into the night and blending with the shadows. Lucy and I angle right, moving toward the largest structure, knowing the rear falls out of George's sightline. Calculated risk — that's our currency here. Thick scrub slows each step, deliberate and steady, eyes sharp for any movement, crouching in the blackness.

Chapter Eleven — Tactical Disagreements

An expectant quiet fills the space, a charged pause before the storm. Viktor stands poised at the table's head, attention dissecting every subtle movement, every restrained gesture. The polished black surface reflects nothing but shadows, as if the light refuses to touch.

Blue light flickers from the tactical screens, cutting across Sergei and Natasha. They're focused; their attention split between the data and the unspoken weight pressing down on all of us.

Impatience ignites as Sergei taps several fingers on the table, a rare crack in his usual composure. Natasha stands motionless, gaze fixed on the scrolling numbers and maps, calculating and always a step ahead.

My reflection fades beneath me as the tension tightens around us — there is no time for lengthy speeches or elaborate plans. Sergei and Natasha are my chosen instruments. Both understand what lies ahead. The screens flicker with images: satellite feeds, convoy movements, target locations — all laid bare. And yet, the real battle hasn't even begun.

The buzz of the electronics hangs in the background, a faint hum beneath the sharp focus in the room. The aroma in the air reeks of stale coffee lingering from hours of work, a scent that blends with the cold sterility of the tech around us. None of that matters — only the mission.

First, I meet Sergei's gaze, then Natasha's. Silence hangs between us. The gravity of the situation already rests on their shoulders, visible in the strain of their expressions and the rigidity of their postures. They're poised, waiting for my command.

Pressure saturates the moment like a storm on the verge of breaking. Every decision moves us closer to our goal, and both sense the urgency.

"Everything required is laid out before you. The operation will be rapid and relentless. Steve's unit won't detect the danger or recognise their confinement," my voice slices through the stillness.

Sergei's lips curl into a faint smirk. He's already visualising the confrontation, already seeing the blood hit the dirt. Natasha remains calm and focused, acknowledging thoughts of logistics and calculations, refining chaos into exactness in her head.

The plan unfolds, and the pieces shift into place. Yet, beneath the surface, one truth stands out — the hunt is underway.

"The clock shifts against us." My tone remains steady, yet my words reverberate through the room. "This mission is paramount."

All eyes lock on me when I lift the projector remote and press the button.

The screen stutters, flickers, then settles — grainy and imperfect, like a memory forced into the light. On the screen — the relic — a weapon lost to time, veiled in dust, legend, and blood.

I take a breath, not because I need to, but because I want the silence to stretch, the weight of the task at hand to settle. Around the table, Natasha and Sergei sit frozen — killers and tacticians, both hardened, dangerous people who've burned empires for less.

Stepping forward, the projection casts a ghost light across my face. "This weapon is not just a relic of the past," I begin, voice harsh and commanding.

My eyes sweep across the room. Pausing on both Natasha and Sergei, I want the room to sense the years I've poured into this — every corpse, every bribe, every shattered lock and silenced voice that brought us here.

"Ten years. A decade of whispers, scraps of intel buried in dying regimes, half-erased files on obsolete drives. The kind of knowledge people kill to forget," I say, a grin forms on my face, slow and hard.

Another tap on the remote—schematics appear. Fragmented. Scorched. But unmistakable. "In our hands, this isn't history. It's leverage. It's deterrence. It's power," I say, pausing, letting the words hang like a noose.

"With this relic, we don't negotiate. We don't buy influence—we seize control. Governments collapse. Rivals vanish. And the world? I hold the image, distorted and dangerous. The world will witness a change as Viktor Readle reshapes order. I dictate the next chapter."

Sergei leans in, casting a shadow over the table. Narrow eyes reveal the task pressing down. Natasha remains still, focusing on analysing the implications and risks we face.

"The relic isn't some historical artefact," I continue, pacing in front of the screen. "This device belonged to a secret group of scientists during the war, a trial that may have shifted the entire conflict. The destructive potential is unmatched, even by today's standards."

Back at the head of the table, I let my words hang in the air before continuing. "This weapon restores balance, returning power to the rightful place. The one who wields the device commands the battlefield. Nations crumble, alliances fracture, and authority returns to the rightful owners—us. This relic embodies more than a simple trophy. Instead, stands as a pillar of dominance, embodying a form of control others cannot grasp."

Sergei lets out a grunt, shoulders tightening, fists pressing down on the table. "So that's why Steve's after the relic as well. GSS understands the implications."

"He's chasing shadows, trying to piece everything together. He's blind to the full scale. He's not ready for what's coming," comes my reply.

Natasha's voice cuts through the silence, sharp as a knife. "And if Steve's unit gets too close?"

"No chance." My expression remains cold and steadfast. "We lead, and that distance increases with every manoeuvre. Steve's team might push hard, yet they're chasing mirages. They arrive expecting control. Instead, impact meets them head-on—clean, silent, and done before resistance forms."

The atmosphere brims with tension as the stakes of our task become apparent. This isn't a fight; it's a shift in influence, and Steve's team stands as nothing but an obstacle to overcome.

My gaze shifts back to the radiant image on the display, the relic ingrained in my consciousness. The possibilities here are immense, connecting us to history while crafting our future. This isn't another operation—it's a turning point. Seize that weapon, and nations will quake at the sound of my name.

Silence wraps around the room. Sergei, Natasha, and the others comprehend the situation and the stakes—the intensity of what lies ahead. There is no room for failure, not when this relic holds such power.

"Prepare the teams," I command, my voice ice-cold. "This ends with us holding that weapon."

A brief pause crystallises the scale of what lies before us, with its significance settling into every fibre. This relic is more than just a tool; it forms the foundation of our dominance. Control over the underworld becomes ours.

Expansion begins. Resistance diminishes. Respect arises from force—earned through silence, not conversation. Fear garners respect faster than agreements. Any hand raised against Russia falls short of the mark.

This goes beyond strategy. Steve's torn through our ranks, wrecked our operations, and taken too much—people, resources, everything. He's made us appear weak, and I can't allow that. Not anymore. This relic isn't power—it's a shadow of retribution.

"The plan needs to be perfect. Petrov told us that the relic is hidden near Waterbank, in the Kimberley region. If the source holds, Steve's team operates from that sector. Assuming the locals have provided accurate information," I say, focus intensifying as I scrutinise the map on the screen, and every ridge and valley is memorised. "Locate the unit. Eliminate the command first. Sever the head — disorder devours everyone before help can react."

Sergei steps in, thick fingers stabbing at the southern edge of the tactical map, dragging along the contour, halting at a mark burned in with surgical certainty — the suspected location of Steve's hideout. Sergei's voice is almost a growl, carrying like a gunshot in the room.

"Here's where we start — the southern perimeter. We insert a recon unit. It's small and silent. If they're spotted, if a shadow twitches wrong, the operation fails," Sergei says.

"Once we have confirmation, we strike," Sergei continues, controlled but brutal. "No whispers, no finesse. A full-force assault. We roll in like thunder. Heavy ordnance, full-auto rifles, grenades, launchers — the works," pausing to meet my eyes, wanting blood. But more than that, Sergei intends to win.

"Two vehicles take point," Sergei says, tapping twice. "Mounted guns. Enough firepower to turn any RV into twisted scrap. We move at first light. Approach fast, loud — they won't detect us until they're choking on the dust."

With all eyes on the map, the weight of Sergei's intensity draws the room in like a noose tightening. Sergei's eyes are alive with a hunger for conflict. It's not recklessness. It's a certainty. And it's dangerous.

Natasha shifts beside me. Doesn't speak. But I sense the storm. Fury hidden beneath calm. Silence ensues. Disgust emanates. Crude tactics repel — Sergei's chaos insults precision.

Still, I say nothing. Instead, my eyes flick between the pair.

A flicker of satisfaction crosses my face, brief and sharp, which Sergei spots — and pushes forward.

"Once we breach, we split the assault." Sergei jabs again, carving paths into the map with a finger. "Team one drives straight in. Hammer to the front. Team two flanks left — cut any exit. Team three wraps the right and locks everything down. No retreat. No escape."

Sergei glances up, eyes locking with mine. Then Natasha's.

"Capture, if possible. We need whatever intel they're carrying. Any information might be the final thread that leads us to the heart of the relic's location." Sergei's gaze narrows. "Obstruct us, and everyone disappears. Erase the bodies. We clear the slate. No traces left. No one walks away.

"Our endgame? The relic is ours. Steve's unit? Nothing but dust. By the time they detect the first shot, we'll already be inside the wire — tight, fast, merciless," he concludes.

Natasha speaks, tone cool and sharp enough to draw blood. "How many bodies are you prepared to burn to achieve your goal? What happens if their satellite eyes pick up a convoy with mounted weapons tearing through the Outback? You want us on every agency's watchlist by midday?"

Sergei doesn't flinch. "I want results. Not another fucking digital ghost chase."

Natasha steps forward, challenging. "Brute force is a tactic that can counter. Intel and experience tell us that's how Steve's unit fights — overpower, outgun, survive. If we hit loud, we risk triggering a fallback plan."

"He's a soldier," Sergei snaps. "Not a prophet."

"And that's why you'll lose," Natasha fires back, eyes like daggers. "Steve doesn't need the whole picture — just enough to kill you in the middle of your plan."

The tension between Sergei and Natasha is steel and fire, raw and razor-edged.

Slapping my hand on the table. "Enough," I say, my voice harsh.

Stepping forward, my voice sharp, "Sergei's method comes with merit. It's decisive. Crushing. Loud enough to shake the bones of our enemies." I turn my gaze to Natasha. "And yours — elegant, surgical, quiet enough to leave no trace."

I gaze at both, then down at the map.

"This isn't about methods. It's about timing. Strategy. Psychological advantage. Steve's unit are many things — but most of all, they are people who react."

"OK," I remark, my voice steady but edged with danger. Sergei's eyes betray a flicker of understanding; he's on the right track. Instincts serve him well, yet I must push further. "What are the backup plans if this goes awry?" I ask.

Sergei doesn't miss a beat. Already prepared for the question. "Viktor, we'll have a rapid response team on standby, poised to move in an instant. If variables shift — resistance, evasion — this unit secures the flank and reconfigures. Flexibility ensures no route remains open for Steve's escape."

Finger-tracing along the map, Sergei marks a location. "Establish fallback position here. Strong defensive ground and a secure retreat route. This becomes the rally point for regrouping and a secondary strike if the primary offensive doesn't hold."

The location Sergei pinpoints stands out, and the options stack up as I assess. This approach hits hard, the kind of edge we're after. Sergei's thoughts are one step forward, anticipating moves before they surface.

With a steady gaze sweeping the room, Sergei says, "Speed is essential. Our strategy hinges on overpowering anyone in the area, not just Steve's team. We attack with precision and intensity, denying any opportunity to respond."

Arms crossed, Sergei moves back from the map, radiating an air of assurance. "That's my plan. Direct, aggressive, and with a high probability of success. Each second lost strengthens Steve's team, and any pause on our end shifts the advantage. Each minute squandered lets our enemies fortify their defences. A strike now is essential, executed with absolute conviction."

The weight of Sergei's words sinks in. They're bold and align with what the organisation needs to achieve. "Excellent. Confirm that your team is set. No errors, Sergei. This moment is critical, and losing isn't an option," I say.

"Understood, Viktor," comes the reply from Sergei.

My attention moves back to the map, thoughts racing toward execution. Efforts have converged to this point, and with Sergei's tactics established, the opportunity to take what belongs to us is at hand."

As Sergei takes a seat, the atmosphere crackles with tension. Natasha's expression shifts, revealing a blend of scepticism and respect. Standing with a commanding presence equal to Sergei's but charged with a different energy.

"Brute force attracts all the wrong kinds of attention," Natasha says, voice steady, almost clinical. "This isn't about force; it's about precision. We'll achieve far more with less risk if we stay discreet and leverage our tech advantage."

Natasha's fingers glide over a tablet computer, tapping a few keys, and the screen shifts, revealing a network of intersecting communication lines and marked infiltration routes. Studying the map with a keen eye, confidence radiating through every gesture.

"The strategy here is simple: breach their comms, plant false intel, and let Steve's team locate the relic for us. Then, we move in — small, elite units can create more chaos than a conventional assault. Without painting a target on our backs," says Natasha, hovering over the map.

Natasha steps closer to the screen, hands moving over the touchpad, highlighting entry points and vulnerable sections of their communication grid. Each tap marks another weakness, a chink we can exploit.

"Once we've breached their systems, we can access their communications. We intercept conversations and plant false intel; our units step through the breach by the time suspicion flickers," Natasha says as the map zooms in, centring on the possible location of Steve's RV.

Natasha's fingers trace the map, stopping at specific locations. "Position a team here to dismantle their comms hub. They'll lose connection with the outside, they'll be left blind and deaf. That buys our ground teams the freedom to slip in without triggering any alarms."

Looking at Sergei, Natasha's voice is as steady as a steel blade. "With their channels silent, our specialised units strike. Each unit is outfitted with advanced gear — heat sensors, night vision, and the latest covert tech. Ground scans reveal all positions. Movements align to rhythm — silent in approach, final in execution."

Natasha stands at the head of the table. A finger hovers over the digital map splayed across the table — compound details, heat signatures, patrol paths, all glowing in dull red against black. She's calm. Calculated. Lethal, without ever raising her voice.

"Our teams infiltrate through these approaches," Natasha says, tone sharp. Finger tracing the west flank before tapping the northern entry point, "Small units. Their orders are clear: neutralise any threats in silence. Both digital and physical."

Natasha glances up, straight at me. "Non-lethal force using cyber-attacks, where possible. Clean. Controlled. No bodies dumped in the sand for satellites to find. No mess. Minimal attention."

Sergei stands rigid beside me, arms folded, jaw locking. Friction pulses like a mine waiting for pressure.

"Non-lethal?" Sergei scoffs. "You think Steve's team will fucking go down with a syringe and a whisper?"

Natasha doesn't flinch. Instead turns to meet Sergei's glare without losing composure.

"They're professionals," Natasha replies. "That's why we don't fight on their terms."

I study Natasha. Every breath, every syllable is measured. She's thought this through and planned like a machine with blood running through its veins.

"Once inside," Natasha continues, tapping a cluster of icons near the command point, "our cyber unit locks the grid. No signals in. No signals out. The moment Steve realises something's wrong, it'll already be too late. Their comms? Dead. Backups? Jammed. Isolated. Trapped."

Natsha's eyes flick to me again—sharp, waiting for my reaction.

"Before realisation sets in, their fate already burns beneath the surface—quiet, merciless, ready to detonate," Natasha says, voice lowering, "We'll have the relic. We'll be gone. Leaving any interested parties choking on the dust."

I lean forward, letting my fingers tap once on the table's surface. "And if they adapt? If Steve's team punches through your digital walls and discovers the ambush?" I say.

Natasha's gaze doesn't waver. "Then we trigger contingency protocol. EMP burst, full blackout, drones on standby. I've accounted for every pivot. But we won't need to use it if we strike right the first time."

Sergei exhales through gritted teeth. "Mercy invites return fire. Leave their outpost smouldering and their names forgotten."

I turn to Sergei, letting my stare hold just long enough. "You want to fight a specialist fighting unit in open combat?" I murmur. "Be my guest. But expect a high body count."

Natasha edges back from the map. "Brute strength invites resistance. Precision dismantles faith. Erase the landscape piece by piece. Let absence spread while their boots sink deeper into false ground."

She's right. Not just the logic, not just in reason, but in precision. The brilliance lies in silence, not in warnings or fire, and controls the battlefield.

"Execute your plan, Natasha. No mistakes," I say, my words are final.

"Let's just hope fucking silence kills faster than bullets," says Sergei through gritted teeth.

I offer a thin, cold smile. "It does," I reply. "When only silence and consequence are left. Both approaches have their merits. Sergei, your plan is direct and overwhelming, but risks drawing too much attention. Natasha, your plan is precise and calculated but requires flawless execution," I say, after pausing for a few moments to consider both plans.

I glance between the pair — Sergei, rigid with leashed aggression; Natasha, poised and razor-sharp. The contrast is stark, but both are weapons in my arsenal.

"You work together," I say, my tone flat, final, with no room for debate. "Sergei, your unit creates the diversion. Loud, visible. You draw their attention. Natasha, your team infiltrates during the chaos. You exploit the blind spots, close their defences, and extract the artefact if it's in their hands."

I step back from the screen. The cold glow lights the map, the data feeds, and the outline of the possible unit we will take down from the inside. My gaze sweeps the room—each operative frozen in anticipation, no one daring to speak.

"The consequences of failure are not hypothetical," I say, voice dropping to ice. "This relic is not just a piece of history—it's leverage, legacy, control. Everything I have built converges here."

My gaze fixes on both. "Treating Steve's team like hired guns results in body bags—ours. Underestimating the unit is a mistake I cannot tolerate. They are all ghosts in tactical gear, killers. From what we understand, the team will fight and bleed to gain control of the relic."

Pausing to let the weight of my words settle like a noose tightening, "Strip fairness from the equation," I say, walking past the edge of the screen. "Hit the wall hard. Infect the heart. Let the collapse begin from within."

Sergei positions himself closer, "We move in fast, strike the target with overwhelming force, and secure what we need before anyone can react."

My attention falls on Natasha, who maintains a calm demeanour. "Sergei's right about moving fast, but kicking the door in might set off alarms we can't afford. A stealthy approach is essential to reduce visibility while increasing our effectiveness."

From my spot at the head of the room, I glance between Sergei and Natasha, reading their expressions. They're both sharp and capable—but different in their methods. That difference might break this mission or make the undertaking an unstoppable force.

Leaning toward the screen, I gesture to the satellite images flickering under the dim lights. "Mistakes are not an option. Sergei, your team delivers a brutal assault. Be the hammer, instigating chaos to divert their attention. Natasha," I redirect my attention, "you command the infiltration unit. Disable their defences and neutralise any threats."

"I can handle the diversion, but don't expect me to babysit a bunch of fucking tech geeks.," says Sergei, pissed off by the thought of babysitting a bunch of nerds.

Natasha's eyes flash with irritation, but she keeps the tone cold and controlled. "Your brute force is beneficial, Sergei, but you're swinging in the wind without intelligence."

As the argument threatens to escalate, I interject, "Collaboration is essential. This mission demands not just strength but also strategy. If we fail, we lose everything—the relic, our power, everything."

Silence hangs in the air as the impact of my words settles. Personal ties serve no function here. Obedience matters—nothing else. Each one exists to execute my orders without question.

Sergei grunts, teeth grind. One breath. "If failure lands at my feet, I erase the loose end myself."

Natasha's lips twist into a tight smile—more a show of teeth than an expression of amusement.

"Let's move forward," I say.

Strain bleeds from Sergei's throat before words surface—tight, brittle, lacking the bite required to justify the flare. One hand tightens near the edge, bone pushing through thick skin like it wants to speak first.

"They won't fall for this forever," Sergei growls. "When Steve's team strikes back—and they will—we must meet the assault with strength."

Sergei drips in the language of hammers—break bones, flood streets, erase names. Once effective. But the battlefield now demands silence and wires.

Natasha doesn't blink. Doesn't move. Eyes are fixed, calm, and lethal—like a scalpel poised above a beating heart.

"They're blind to our next step, Sergei," Natasha says, voice calm and unwavering. "Power thrives in the absence of anticipation. Clarity arrives too late—buried beneath precision and smoke." Natasha's words coil through the room like a slow-moving venom.

I let the tension breathe for a moment. Then I speak. My voice cuts through the air, sharp and absolute. "Every move counts."

Both freeze their eyes on me.

"Steve's unit isn't like the others we've erased," I continue, tone glacial. "They don't run when things get loud. Instead, close in, adapt and learn. Underestimate them, and we're not just exposed—we're dead."

Sergei straightens, jaw tight. Natasha's gaze narrows with thought rather than disagreement.

"Steve's team is relentless. Efficient. Intelligent. A force that doesn't make the same mistake twice. Every weakness we exploit will only work once," I say.

I let the silence expand around us, heavy with the weight of precision and consequence. My eyes move between the two. Natasha's posture is still collected. Calculating. Sergei's fists remain clenched, but he's listening now. That's enough.

"Adaptability is our weapon. Yours," I nod to Sergei, "is fire. Destruction. That's got a place."

Then I turn to Natasha. "And yours is silence. Smoke. The unknown. Also valuable."

I take a slow breath and step forward, the glow of the tactical displays painting blue shadows across faces. "Understand this — Steve's team is not playing a game. People like that... don't break easy. Just bury you."

Sergei's glare drops to the map, tracing paths and recalculating force deployment. Natasha glances away, scanning the digital feed for movement. The expression never changes — Natasha's already rewriting probabilities.

"Execute your parts, with no fuck ups. No glory. No deviation. And if either of you hesitates, even for a breath, you'll not face Steve — you'll face me," the tone in my voice leaving no room for an argument.

Sergei nods once. Stiff. Sharp. Then turns and exits, boots thudding like distant artillery fire.

Natasha lingers a moment, studying the screen again, then meets my gaze. "I'll handle the situation."

"Of course you will," I reply.

Natasha leaves the room without another word, the door closing behind her.

Silence folds back into the room, apart from the hum of servers. The faint flicker of satellite feeds. The map glows, and I'm alone with my thoughts — just me and the battlefield yet to unfold.

I lean in, hands on the table, eyes sweeping over terrain, markers, and possible movements. My mind begins cutting through the data, stripping everything to the bone.

Steve might already have the relic. Or he's still crawling through the Outback, blind, hunting ghosts. Either way, he will not be ready for what's coming.

Intelligence comes in fragments—fractured comms, broken transmissions. Whispers snatched from the wind. Nothing concrete. Nothing I can hold in my hand. But that's the game. The silence between the facts says more than the data itself.

Steve's team, every shred of intel we've pulled on the unit paints the same picture—ruthless precision, no margin for error. Every step is calculated three moves ahead. They don't chase shadows but wait for targets to enter their sights.

If a trap is waiting somewhere in the Outback, it's already set. Concealed. Primed. Waiting to spring the moment we falter.

If we're even a single breath ahead—that's the moment. The edge. The weakness. And I won't hesitate when I spot weakness. Instead, crush it under my boot.

Standing over the map table, the soft blue glow bathes my fingers as I trace the terrain—dunes, ridgelines, fault points. The relic's suspected location pulses in the dark, like a heartbeat beneath the surface, wrapped in steel and silence.

Natasha and Sergei move back into the room and stand beside me, eyes locked on the topography. But they don't speak, knowing better than to fill the air with words when I'm working. Sergei, impatient, leans in, breathing heavier and impatient.

"They'll dig in," Sergei mutters. "Fall back. Set up fields of fire."

"Wouldn't expect anything less," I reply, fingers tapping once on the southern trail node. "And wait for us to step into their trap."

Sergei grunts. "Don't wait. Cut air from their throats before lungs catch rhythm."

"No. We make GSS think they've won. We let the shit settle. Think they're close to securing the relic. Then we cut the ground out from underneath."

Natasha speaks up, voice like a scalpel slicing through the tension. "If we strike too soon, Steve adapts. However, if we draw everyone into a posture of control... they're committed. Anchor them."

"And anchored men can't run when the floor collapses," I reply.

My attention drifts back to the screen.

Every second must be accounted for. Every breach timed to the millisecond. If a single variable shifts out of alignment, Steve's team will exploit it like a blade to the throat. Steve's not just a tactician — but a predator. So am I.

Chapter Twelve — Operational Base

The approach is the silence that signals unrest—each step is calculated, deliberate, and charged with the weight of what's coming. The terrain stretches like a broken canvas of jagged rocks and scrub, offering little to hide behind.

Sharp bursts of motion mirror the breeze, every stride calculated and exact. The slightest shift in the bush stops us cold. The line between staying unseen and getting exposed tightens with every second.

I press the mic of the radio, "GD, status."

A calm whisper comes through the earpiece, "S3, still clear. No movement," comes the reply.

George's sniper scope sweeps the compound from high ground on the ridge, picking apart the shadows. Details aren't necessary. George's gut steered us right more than once. I move forward, sure he'll alert me if anything's amiss.

Silent figures spread out in formation, slipping through the terrain like ghosts. Derek's close breaths measured. Simon holds a position, eyes sweeping the rear. Lucy melds with the landscape, every movement calculated. Each comprehends the stakes—precision is survival, and one slip might light a fuse we won't outrun.

Shadows reveal the compound's outline, waiting in silence, prepared. The hush presses down, turning every motion into a tactical choice.

"Move," I direct, signalling the team to move forward. Heart pounding, the quiet hangs thick, as if hiding something just out of reach.

"Lucy, take the left. Simon, cover," I whisper into the radio.

Leaves rustle, and then they're gone, absorbed into the undergrowth with the ease of veterans.

Each step and motion is a refined calculation, smooth and practised from countless missions just like this. But the sense of something lurking and waiting gnaws at the back of my mind.

A brick structure stands in the distance, beige and unassuming, as if long forgotten. No movement means possible trouble, not safety. Something feels wrong beneath the surface.

"Hold," I whisper into the radio.

The team freezes. I take a second to listen—a faint sound, too steady to be nothing.

The radio crackles as George speaks, "All callsigns, I've got movement. Can't lock down where it's coming from, but it doesn't sit right."

"Might be a distraction," I murmur, scanning the predawn light.

Instinct sharpens, tension clawing up my spine. Or just empty air. Or the start of something lethal.

The beige structure rises ahead, a solid block of shadow that merges with the landscape, abandoned and fading into history. A lone wooden door breaks the wall's surface, paint chipped and worn, each crack a marker of long-forgotten use.

Lucy moves up, rifle angled, finger poised on the trigger. The other hand finds the door handle, and with a firm but quiet push, the wooden door swings open, the click just about audible in the stillness.

A hand signal sends Lucy ahead, and I slip in close behind. The air shifts around us—a stagnant draught, damp and stale, laced with dust that clings thick in the throat. The scent carries an ancient stillness, the kind only found in places left abandoned for years. The darkness presses close, absorbing movement and sound alike. The silence holds steady, waiting, braced, as though even the structure senses something imminent.

"Move," I whisper into the mic.

Lucy glides forward, rifle ready. Ahead, the corridor narrows to a tight passage, forcing constant awareness with no margin for error. This isn't terrain that forgives mistakes; every step demands precision, drawn with the knowledge of potential threats hidden beyond walls, floor, or the slightest crevice.

"Clear," I whisper into the radio, advancing deeper, the quiet amplifying the sounds within. The walls draw tighter, crowding in as we push through the space, subtle sounds sharpening against the encroaching dark. Lucy's steps sync with mine, precise yet charged, but the undercurrent of dread presses harder, a quiet force building in silence.

A faint ripple disturbs the black void ahead, a perceptible distortion brushing against the edge of visibility. The space stretches out, vacant and stark. Yet the stillness bites with unseen threats, as though something waits, poised and hidden just beyond the reach of vision. My grip on the rifle tightens, instincts sparking like a live wire.

This isn't just an empty passage. It's a confined hunting ground where shadows play their tricks, and the slightest lapse might mean our last step forward. The deeper we press, the more each corner and edge holds a whisper of threats unnoticed.

A quick hand signal at the intersection halts us in an instant. We are both pressing against the walls, weapons raised. I inch around the corner, pulse even, and glimpse the empty hallway stretching ahead. Each step forward leaves the passage behind undisturbed, yet an electric edge fills the air, like a trap set to spring the moment we cross an overlooked line.

The faint outline of a door at the end of the hall comes into view, hanging ajar and casting slivers of light across the floor. Lucy advances on my cue, every footstep crisp and controlled. Reaching the door, Lucy meets my gaze and pushes it open without a sound, disappearing into the room as I move in close behind.

A quick scan shows nothing obvious, but something is here — a wrongness that nags, buried beneath the silence. Even though the room appears empty, my training tells me not to trust appearances in a place like this. Whatever might be waiting in the shadows, it's near.

Moving outside, we assemble at the boundary, staying down and alert. The central building, a hulking silhouette against the sky. This is where the real challenge lies.

"GD, this is S3. Keep that rifle on the entrance," more for confirmation as I know he's already dialled in.. "Derek, are comms to GSS up?"

"All equipped, set, and primed," Derek replies, gear humming with readiness.

"Simon, Lucy, cover me. Breach on my go."

The team spreads out, every line of sight secured, every angle covered, shadows cloaking our movements. The doorway stands, almost as if daring us to make the first move. A quick hand signal calls Derek forward, crouching by the door, fingers on the lock. A loud click breaks the silence as the door swings open.

Stepping inside, the space holds a silent edge, shadows clinging like unseen predators, charged with hidden hostility. Corners are scanned with care, and each step is calculated. The team tracks without a word, weapons trained. Discipline is evident in every movement.

"Stay sharp," I repeat, as if the reminder isn't already burned into their bones.

The darkened edges hum with restrained danger, energy waiting beneath the surface, ready to explode. Steps land with intent, tension knotting tighter with every inch we close in as the air crackles; the promise of a volatile end lies ahead.

"Keep moving," I mutter, pushing forward. This RV remains locked down until we've swept every corner. Satisfied with the sweep, I turn to Derek. "Radio GD, tell him to move on our twenty," I say, voice steady.

Derek nods and relays the message. "GD, this is DR, on our location, over."

Moments later, George's acknowledgement crackles through our earpieces: "DR, Roger that, on my way." Navigating the descent, George's steps are placed with accuracy, tracing an unerring line.

Derek establishes comms to secure our communication channels with GSS. Simon shifts wide, eyes tracking angles. Lucy drops to a knee, rifle raised, posture tight. Threats don't get warnings.

"Derek, is the base communications set up?" I ask, my voice steady but urgent.

"Almost," comes the response, eyes fixed on the controls, hands working with practised ease.

Simon enters the small building to inspect the ATVs and equipment from Dave's contacts, ensuring every piece aligns for a swift departure. Lucy's hands move with accuracy, fine-tuning equipment, intensity carved in every action. My gaze sweeps the scene, confirming all elements fall into place, a cohesive display of preparation and expertise.

With the setup complete, the atmosphere shifts. Each of us moves with rehearsed efficiency, constructing our base camp. The kit is unpacked in sequence, and the command centre takes shape, a testament to meticulous planning.

Surveillance systems come together, gear goes live, and our perimeter locks into place. Despite the challenging environment, we remain focused on the task.

"Reminds me of our last trip to Australia," Simon says, breaking the silence with a small smile.

My eyes flick to Simon, memory slamming back. "Yeah, just like before," I reply, "even down to the heat and the fucking annoying insects."

"Remember Steve jumping when a snake slithered close by?" Simon chuckles, voice full of amusement.

"Funny, didn't catch you stepping up to handle the dam thing."

"Mad, not stupid, Steve," comes the instant response from Simon.

The team shares a moment of camaraderie, the bond forged in the fires of past missions evident in the easy banter. These shared experiences make us more than a team but a family in arms.

The memory snaps me back, and a smile breaks through. The team laughs, and our bond strengthens with each mission. Lucy remarks on how every challenge brings us closer together.

"Remember Ana's face as we got her on that plane?" Derek laughs. "She thought we tore through hell with nothing but grit."

A smirk edges onto George's face while scanning the horizon. "Took a bit to remind Ana—just doing the job, no superhero capes involved."

With the perimeter secured and gear in place, the next phase commences. We're not safe just because we're hidden. Not out here. The bush can turn on you in seconds—wildlife, weather, or Viktor's men crawling through the undergrowth with knives and malice. The ground needs sweeping. Every path. Every shadow.

I turn to the team, "We need eyes on the ground, scout the immediate vicinity, and identify potential threats."

Without saying anything, George walks over to join me. He understands why he's coming. Sniper discipline runs in his blood. George spots things before others. Threats. Movement. Anomalies.

His role isn't just overwatch now — it's surgical support. The rifle slung across one shoulder is a whisper away from judgment.

Simon joins me next. A rhythm to his presence, honed over years of driving through forests, deserts, and dead zones where maps mean nothing and instincts mean survival as a recce group commander. Simon doesn't track paths but creates them. He reads broken branches like headlines and spots boot imprints, whereas others only detect dirt.

We move out without making a sound, Simon and George following my lead as we slip into the forest, swallowed by thick foliage. Cover embraces us, shadows folding around our forms as if drawing us into the landscape. Silence hangs heavy, broken only by distant birdcalls and the faint rustle of unseen creatures shifting through the underbrush, hidden but always watching.

The forest vibrates with tension beneath the surface, an almost inaudible hum that sharpens every sound, an ever-present warning. Shadows press close against the trees, dark shapes melding into the bark, waiting to pounce at the smallest slip. The air sits thick and damp, weighted with the earthy tang of wet soil, grounding us in the reality that here, we are trespassers.

The route forward winds through scattered debris — twigs sharp as glass and dry leaves ready to snap underfoot, demanding exact placement with each stride. One misplaced footfall might shatter the silence, marking our presence in an instant.

Subtle shifts move across the underbrush, shadows merging with the trees. A dark rhythm that matches our pace. The track contracts, each movement honed, soundless, nerves wired to detect the slightest trace.

Before us, the landscape unfolds in muted layers. The thick canopy above blocks most of the early morning light, leaving the forest in a constant twilight. My attention is divided between the trail and the recce's formation, a well-oiled machine of coordinated and exact movements, ensuring no one drifts from the line.

Ten feet back, Simon trails with a precise rhythm, sightline cutting through the scrub, while George keeps our six clear, grounding our position with a steady readiness.

Our pace shifts, aligning with the contours around us, our movements sharp and concealed within the terrain. A river flows in a twisting line ahead, threading through the Outback. One quick gesture stops George and Simon, and I lower myself beside the stream. The crisp scent of freshwater cuts through the decay. My fingers trace along the mud, landing on a faint but undeniable footprint.

Simon drops next to me, studying the prints. "Human?" voice merging with the rustle of leaves. "Faint. Might be old, or they're trying to cover their tracks."

Shadows of movement remain in the terrain, fleeting yet definite. The water reflects a pale glow, the unbroken surface hiding truths too deep to surface.

"George, anything from your end?"

"Clear so far," George's tone carries the steady edge of control.

Simon shifts, tracking something across on the opposite bank, under the dense foliage. "We're being monitored."

"Remember, boys, this is the Australian Outback. That might be a predator with huge teeth and a bone-breaking bite, Aka Snappy, the crocodile. Recommend we put some distance between us and Snappy," George says over the radio, tone firm and measured.

I remain silent. The realisation hits, and I'm already pulling back. But something else, apart from Snappy, lies in wait. Every instinct screams that something's not right. But we don't have the option of turning back now. If Viktor's men are out here, they're waiting, biding their time.

The forest tightens its grip the further we push, and the air thickens, almost hostile. We spend an hour tracking the river's edge, scanning shadowed spaces, but no threat emerges.

Each stride takes me into a realm forsaken, an unsettling quiet apart from local insects, as if the earth itself had turned away. This silence eats away at me. A slow, grinding tension that promises something might lie in wait, ready to snap.

Beyond that, the land rises, a wooded ridge blocking any view of what might lie concealed. The spot contains all the hallmarks of a perfect ambush site — hidden and unpredictable — a place built for death.

So far, this mission unfolded as a constant test, where shadows and open ground play out like rolls of the dice. Each movement is a delicate balance on the line between life and oblivion.

"Check that elevation," I say, lips close to Simon's ear. "Focus beyond the ridge's edge — if something waits out of range, I need details."

With a raised thumb, Simon moves off, merging into the shadows without a sound. George and I stay put, slipping into the available cover, each of us angled to a different arc of fire. Our senses sharpened, and every creak of a branch or distant rustle becomes a potential threat. Time drags as the forest breathes around us, indifferent to our presence.

After 10 minutes, Simon reappears, crouching close to me and whispers, "Nothing evident past the ridge, more of the same terrain."

To my front, tangled cover sprawls across the ridge, clumps of green clawing at visibility. Open ground breaks the rhythm — nothing stands out. Then motion — quick, shallow — not wind. A presence lingers, staying just outside the kill zone.

Movement lingering on the edge of sight—a signal they're studying us as much as we're watching for movement. Possibilities line up in my mind. Whoever waits out in the Outback is working the long game, drawing us closer, pulling us into their control.

Grip firms on the rifle, posture taut. George reads the same signs I do. Both of us brace for that split-second shift from quiet to full-blown firefight. We're in enemy territory, their terrain, and every inch ahead might be wired with traps or hiding a gunman waiting for the right moment.

I signal George and Simon to advance again, each step calculated, the tension ratcheting higher with every metre we advance. The ridge looms closer, shadows dark and looming, like the threshold of something we're not meant to cross. But we don't stop. The mission comes first; we're prepared to break through if a storm in the shadows awaits us.

But nothing arrives, just dust and silence, where a presence once sat heavy, tracks swallowed by the land. I turn to George and Simon. "We should start heading back. For now, the area is clear."

Years of experience warn against retracing our steps—taking the same route twice invites trouble. A fresh direction is the only option, so we cut through untouched terrain.

Behind me, Simon and George remain alert, scanning the terrain and surrounding brush. The forest skews the acoustics, weaving together normalcy and danger, disguising threats within a natural rhythm.

After an hour's patrol, we're back near the RV. Stepping right in would be reckless. A swift motion of my arm, up and down, signals Simon and George to mirror the movement. We hold position, scanning and listening, combing the perimeter for anything out of place. The way forward appears open, yet something shifts beneath the surface—someone's making moves.

Turn and spot Simon crouched, eyes scanning the terrain. George takes point, moving into position ahead, rifle poised to cover us. The tension is suffocating, every second dragging as we wait. The landscape reveals no movement, no signs of life. But that's the problem. Derek and Lucy should've made contact by now. Their absence slices through the gut like shrapnel buried deep.

Twenty minutes pass with nothing breaking the stillness, tension clawing at my nerves until a flicker draws my attention— Lucy, moving near the camp. Just about visible between the trees, on the verge of giving the signal, when a voice cuts through the quiet from the undergrowth, 100 metres at my one o'clock.

"What's the Royal Green Jackets' motto?"

"Swift and bold," I reply.

A slight rustle, and Derek breaks from a concealed position, rifle locked in position, eyes hard and unblinking.

"I guessed you would choose this path. Anyone checking around would come through here. Sorry for the delay, but I needed to ensure nobody followed you. I've been watching the route. Spot anything?" Derek asks.

"Debrief in a few minutes," I reply.

Something is hidden beyond the trees, waiting in the shadows, whether it's Viktor's men or something else, I'm not sure.

The team assembles around the central point inside the RV, focused and ready for what's next. George faces the way we came, scanning the landscape for unwanted visitors.

The briefing kicks off. My words are precise and focused. "Dense terrain, thick with foliage everywhere. Plenty of cover out here for us and anything else moving. By the river, we picked up tracks a kilometre east. Footprints in the mud, so enemy movement in the area is possible."

"Shallow tracks indicate a light-footed group. Moved fast—recent enough for us to catch movement." George adds.

Clarity forms in my mind as the pieces lock in, revealing the emerging threats. "Stream. Your sector, mate. Anything that didn't sit right?"

Simon gets straight to the point. "Not much, Steve. That river's a strategic line—fast current, clear water, the banks usable. Either a lifeline or a threat."

"This location gives us a solid stance, though cracks remain, leaving parts open to probing eyes or a stray shot. The forest grants concealment, hiding us from view, but also conceals potential threats, while the river provides both a lifeline and a vulnerability. Better establish secure points around the perimeter," I say, switching to tactical thinking. "If they're patrolling, we can't risk being exposed."

"Supply drop included camera traps. Derek and I will take care of positioning the devices. We'll catch any activity," Simon adds, voice calm and confident.

"Hesitating isn't an option. This is about control, not just defence. The forest, the river, the ground we stand on—it's ours to secure, or theirs," I state, locking eyes with the team.

The discussion wraps up, and I glance around the team. Their faces are set with determination, their eyes reflecting the gravity of our mission. Moving with purpose, each person united in our commitment to the mission. The team scatters, everyone assuming their position with the precision of ingrained habits.

The air in the camp is still; the only sounds are the distant calls of local wildlife. A sudden intake of breath from Derek catches my attention. He's still, eyes locked on something near our equipment. My eyes follow Derek's and land on a coiled predator. Venomous and unblinking, body tense, eyes narrow, tracking us in the shadows, prepared to strike.

"Fuck, I hate snakes," slips out under my breath, nerves tightening. My adrenaline pumps hard as I motion for everyone to freeze. This team isn't backing down over something like this.

With a long stick, George advances, steady and deliberate. Movements carry a calm that's all-muscle memory, honed over years in the field. The snake, a spiral spring of potential danger, scales gleaming under the sparse light, ready to strike at the first provocation. The team, breaths held, waiting for any sign of a snap or lunge.

George inches closer, the stick extended. A gentle nudge, controlled but firm, and the snake reacts — a hiss, fierce and sudden, ripping through the quiet like a blade. The coils start to unwind, loosening as George maintains just enough distance, guiding the snake away from our setup, slithering across the ground, scales scraping against dry leaves and dirt. Without hesitation, George holds the position, manoeuvring the slithering bastard farther until the scaly fucker slips into the undergrowth, vanishing in the tangled shadows.

A shared release of breath signals the team's momentary relief, a tangible sign of the danger's dissipation. The air hums with leftover tension, an invisible reminder of the threat that almost slipped through.

"Reminds me of Malaysia," Lucy says, cutting through the quiet. "Ran into a king cobra once. Scared me half to death." A ripple of laughter follows, easing the edge of the moment.

The late afternoon sun bears down, turning the RV into a blistering oven. Heat saps focus and energy, but slowing down isn't an option. Gathering the team, setting the plan, and adapting fast is the key to making it through.

"Alright, we need to improvise," I say, scanning the camp's layout. Shadows are thin, scarce pockets of relief under the relentless sun. Heat bounces back from every wall, making the air dense and thick. Simon's our shot at a fix. "Simon, can you devise a way to protect our electrical gear from frying?"

Simon nods, already assessing the area with a seasoned eye. "No problem," his gaze sweeping over the limited resources — scraps, branches, leaves, anything that might hold moisture or create even the slightest shade.

Years in Iraq taught Simon well. Without missing a beat, he builds a cooling structure, stacking damp leaves on branches and locking everything down with stones. Skilled hands assemble a barrier, a defence against the sun's unrelenting heat.

"That should work," Simon says, stepping back and giving the setup a final glance. "Not a long-term fix, but will keep our gear from cooking for now."

The first problem is cleared. The heat is only the first hurdle. Derek and Lucy patrol the camp perimeter, tackling a hidden threat that's shadowed us from the start. The wildlife surrounding us isn't just a nuisance; it's lethal, and ignorance risks more than losing equipment.

"DR, LK — confirm sweep," I mutter into the radio, watching shadows shift near the treeline.

Canvas sealed, Bergens closed tight. One serpent slips through, and we're compromised before dawn.

"Traps are done," Derek mutters, weaving the vine into a tight snare.

Fingers move with precision, each snare positioned. With every knot precise, Derek places snares in the soft spots — simple setups designed for the job done. Barriers are assembled from sticks coated with raw onions, lime juice, and a stash of hot sauce from the rations.

The scent alone will be enough to deter most of the wildlife, as the slithering bastards don't have a liking for tobasco sauce. It's crude, but it's the kind of fieldcraft that works when options are limited.

Lucy moves beside one of the traps, giving the vine a sharp pull to test the tension, inspecting the knots for weakness. "This'll hold," she murmurs, half to herself. "Anything that tries to sneak through here will trip this before getting close."

We're as fortified as possible with the cooling rig set and the perimeter secured. The camp lies still, a façade of safety, but every shadow and rustle in the brush holds a silent warning.

The heat and wildlife are just part of the problem — this place isn't giving up secrets without a fight, and we're only scratching the surface. I signal the team, each of us braced for whatever's coming next.

"Fantastic work, folks," I say, gazing across the camp. "Out here, mistakes come with a cost. The heat bears down, the terrain fights us at every step, and unseen threats lurk in the undergrowth. Our past encounters here have taught us to stay alert for more than just the enemy. This camp's our base, and we're not releasing the area."

Simon's hand rest on my shoulder. "Camera traps aren't up yet. Derek and I will locate the devices before the light fucks off."

"Excellent plan. If it turns south, key the mic — and we'll come to you asap," replying to Simon.

Simon and Derek slip out of the RV like shadows, swallowed by the undergrowth. I track them for a few seconds before they disappear into the bush. Every movement is calculated. The kind of silence that takes years to perfect. The sort of silence that keeps you alive.

The Outback shifts around them. The air is thicker, dense, wet, and heavy, with damp soil and decay stench. The kind of scent that clings to your skin long after you've left it behind. Insects hum in the stillness, their drone mixing with distant bird calls and the occasional rustle of something moving out of view. This place doesn't sleep. It stays awake, waiting.

The river's faint rush carries on the wind, guiding them through the tangled foliage toward the target zone—the final trap, the pressure point.

Simon halts beneath a twisted tree, dropping his daypack to the dirt without making a sound before pulling out the camouflaged camera and uncoiling the wires.

"This'll do," Simon mutters.

Derek drops in beside him, crouching, laptop balanced on one forearm. "Angle's tight," Derek says, scanning the terrain. "Want the lens left or centre-weighted?"

Simon doesn't glance up. "Left. We've got coverage north. We need eyes on the approach from the creek bed."

With a nod, Derek is already adjusting the feed. "Done. Syncing now."

The camera clicks into place against the tree trunk, almost invisible beneath the layers of vines and creeping plants. Simon tightens the straps one last time, then adjusts the angle by two degrees.

Derek glances at the screen. "Feed's live. Grainy, but clean."

Simon drags a sleeve across his forehead, eyes locked on shifting foliage. "Forget clean lines. As long as it trips something before we do, it earns its place."

"Or catch them trying to outflank us," Derek adds.

"Either way," Simon says, "we spot them first. That's what matters. Out here, first sight is first blood."

The foliage sways with the wind. The air doesn't cool—it just shifts. Oppressive heat is replaced by something else. Anticipation.

Simon steps back, Derek beside him, both watching the screen now as the clearing comes into focus. Every angle is locked in. But we all understand the truth—cameras are only the first layer. The rest relies on instinct. Reaction. Timing.

Heading back to the RV, a sharp noise breaks through the rainforest—a dense rustling, something extensive and deliberate shifting through the undergrowth. Instinct takes over. Both Simon and Derek drop to the ground, weapons aimed, scanning the thick brush. The usual sounds die off, replaced by the steady crunch of something closing in.

Derek locks eyes with Simon and whispers, "You catch that?"

"Yeah, whatever stirred that dust possesses a threat—not natural, not random. Something massive shifted the surface with zero resistance. That path isn't carved by wind or wildlife," replies Simon.

The forest's bracing sounds blend into one, a silent meter ticking toward the unknown. As fast as it started, the rustling stops dead. Derek's rifle steadies, his finger a breath from the trigger, braced for the unseen to emerge.

"Changed my mind, it might be local wildlife," Simon murmurs.

Derek's attention sharpens on the treeline. "Whatever is coming this way, let's fuck off out of here."

Drawing away at a slow pace, Simon's focus hovers over the brush, a readiness built from the expectation of hidden threats embedded deep in the foliage. The quiet stretches undisturbed yet still present, with no easing up. Instinct warns us that silence, in these parts, is seldom what it appears to be.

To confirm the cameras are still operational, Derek and Simon stop halfway back to the RV and check the real-time visuals. "Systems checkout, all cameras streaming," Derek affirms, focusing on the display.

While Derek focuses on the monitor, Simon keeps an eye fixed on the dense tangle of bush. "Let's keep moving back to camp. Whatever's prowling out of view will reveal itself before we're caught off guard."

Nearing the RV, a voice calls out, the source concealed in the shadows. "What's Simon famous for?"

"Army chuck-in," replies Derek.

"Close enough," I mutter, stepping out from my concealed position in the thick vegetation.

With everyone back in the RV, we check the kit and prepare the RV for the night, with one person on a roaming sentry at all times.

Hours in, the makeshift cooler does the job, lowering the temperature around our gear. Derek and Lucy's traps catch dangerous wildlife, reducing the immediate threat in the RV. It's a smallish win, lifting spirits. Fresh meat adds to the boost.

The air cools as night drags its shadow across the Outback. The blistering heat that hammered us through the day starts to fade, replaced by a creeping cold that settles over everything like a second skin. The change is welcome. Just enough to remind the body that this land doesn't forgive hesitation.

The team sits around a shallow pit, dug earlier, masked with care. A small fire smoulders beneath a sheet of metal, hidden from above, controlled with absolute precision. No light escapes, only heat. Enough to warm our rations.

The crackle of the fire blends with the faint rustle of wind across dead brush. It's a fragile moment. Not rest—never that—but a lull. A breath taken between storms.

Simon handles the cooking like he's defusing a mine—careful, exact. Lucy scans the horizon, always watching. Derek is glued to his comms unit, fingers moving with the calm rhythm of someone who lives in signals and silence. George is out beyond the perimeter—posted with a rifle, a shadow among shadows. Watching. Waiting.

Predators stir as the night wakes in layers—distant calls, growls, wings slicing the air above unseen. The Outback changes after sunset. It becomes older, harsher, and alive with things that hunt and kill without hesitation.

"Impressive work today," I say, "We faced tougher challenges, but we adapted and got it done. That's our strength."

Worn faces reflect a hard day's effort, but pride lingers beneath. Stories circulate each testament to the risks we've tackled and the grit that kept us going.

"Tell us more about your snake encounter, Lucy," I say, after taking a long sip of coffee from my black mug.

Lucy relaxes for a moment, "Amazon, six years back. I walked straight into a den of vipers and thought, that's me a goner. A flash sliced through the gloom—too fast to register, too precise to dodge. Venom hit like a freight train."

Fingers skim over Lucy's side as if the scar of the memory still holds a sting. "Took out the snake with a blade, then all went dark. The rest of my team hauled me over the rough terrain. The unit held its breath, watching and waiting to find out if I would come through. I clung to survival, driven by nothing but raw determination, too stubborn to go down.

Derek sits still, gaze fixed on the fire, "Sahara for me. No water for three days. Sun scorching, sand everywhere. Lost half the team to an ambush, spent the nights crawling through the desert, dodging unseen eyes."

Simon jumps in, sounding more relaxed. "The Iraqi desert is not much better. Locals taught us survival tricks, such as soaking leaves and crafting makeshift coolers when the heat bore down like a hammer."

Stories like this are old ground for us—we all lived them. Yet Simon's tone, fading near the end, gives me the sense of something deeper he's choosing not to say.

The moment hangs for a moment, the past lingering between us. These aren't heroic tales. They're about scraping through the worst of what the world throws at you and still standing.

The fire's warmth spreads as the night wears on, the heat radiating through the metal, steadying us. The obstacles we've overcome have cemented our connection, forged through shared trials. For now, we settle into our routine and are ready for whatever comes our way.

"Rest up," I say. "Tomorrow's another day, and we'll need all our strength. But remember, we're doing this together."

The team disperses, and each member finds a spot to erect their bivvy bags to rest. The sounds of the Outback continue, a reminder of the constant vigilance required.

Pausing for a moment, the plan unfolds in my head, details of the next steps clicking into place. Out of the corner of my eye, I catch George springing up from his bivvy, swatting the right arm with the left.

"Fucking spiders," voice strained with pain.

The red beam of my flashlight cuts across the ground, protecting our night vision while keeping us concealed. The light exposes what I didn't want—dozens of venomous arachnids, slick bodies gleaming, swarming through the camp.

"Damn it, George," I say, ripping open the med kit and kneeling. The bite is already beginning to swell.

George clenches a fist, staying still as I work on the wound, cleaning and dressing the bite area. "Suffered worse," George mutters, but the expression on his face hints at the discomfort.

"Let's avoid making this routine," I mutter, tightening the wrap again. George's gaze remains steady despite the discomfort.

Field dressing secured, a quick pat on George's arm, and I settle back. "You're set," I say, aware the sting still lingers beneath a calm exterior.

"Better hope you don't grow extra legs," a raised voice comes from across the camp.

After inspecting his gear and reclining against a rucksack, a grin tugs at Simon's mouth. "You might be lucky, George, and develop some superpowers, mate. Spider-George."

"Or just start spinning webs," Derek doesn't miss a beat while giving George a sidelong glance, shaking out his sleeping bag. "Didn't expect you to lose your cool over a few insects, George."

George shoots back a glare, a flicker of humour breaking through the grimace. "Piss off, both of you. Let's find out who's laughing when one of those bastards sinks fangs into you."

With a smirk, Simon chuckles, tapping his boots to shake loose anything hiding. "Let the spiders make their move. They're the ones who'll be regretting coming too close."

Derek turns his Bergen upside down and taps the bottom. "Spiders taking you down? Not the enemy we prepped for, but perhaps we need to adjust the strategy."

"Keep pushing," George says, rubbing the bandaged arm. "Can't wait to find out how you arseholes deal with one of those things ends up in your kit."

The banter lightens the mood, easing the edge but not erasing it. Shadows press closer, a quiet presence that keeps vigil. The air holds its breath, broken only by the occasional shift of leaves or a distant call in the night.

The chatter dies, but Simon edges closer to Derek, a grin forming. "Spider-George. Sounds just right for George."

This is how we push through, pain and spiders be damned. The mission's hard enough without slipping. Take the hits, give some back, and stay sharp for whatever comes next.

The slightest movements ripple through the forest floor, branches creak, leaves whisper, and unseen things slide just beyond sight, challenging us with each sound. The land itself stands observing, reminding us that out here, who dominates here.

Hours crawl by as we take turns on stag, senses stretched thin under the weight of the Outback's midnight pulse. Sleep remains elusive, held at bay by the sounds that pierce the quiet.

Sitting down again, I survey the area, alert to movement. This place is unforgiving, but we've trained for worse. George's bite reminds us that this environment is as much an enemy as the one we're hunting. But we stick together, stay sharp, and keep each other safe. That's how we survive.

Chapter Thirteen — The Hunt Begins

First light crawls across the cracked horizon, a pale warning more than a welcome. The land shifts under its own silence, too still, too quiet. Shadows stretch long and low over scrub and stone, cast by nothing we can trust. This place doesn't wake—it stalks.

The breeze drags over the dust like breath through a clenched jaw. No movement beyond the sway of brittle brush. A single bird cries from somewhere out of reach, too far to trust, too close to ignore. The air remains cool, but the heat waits—coiled, certain. Every instinct screams the same thing: whatever comes next won't be gentle.

Soon, the sun will rise like a hammer, bringing the heat that makes people desperate. But right now, in this fleeting moment, we start to make a move before the world catches up.

I push out of the bivvy, joints tight, back raw from the ground. While packing my gear away, I scan the team. They're awake and alert, reading readiness in subtle movements. Sleep in this line of work is never real—it's just a shallow pause between one fight and the next.

Derek is hunched near the building, eyes narrowed, headset pressed tight as if he could force clarity out of static by sheer willpower. Fingers glide over the comms unit, tapping, breaking encryption codes and rebuilding them again. I saw him sifting through radio traffic through half-open eyes earlier, just before first light, hunting for whispers in the dark. Derek doesn't just monitor comms, he fights through signals.

Off to one side, Lucy is almost invisible beneath the mottled shadows cast by the twisted branches; sitting still, rifle cradled, eyes piercing through the morning light with an intensity that's become a signature. A silent guardian, watching for the smallest flicker of danger, every muscle coiled like a spring held at breaking point.

George is positioned by the RV's flank, sniper rifle angled down, gaze moving across the horizon, absorbing every line, every shifting shadow. Each sweep is methodical, mapping every detail into memory. If anything moves, George will spot the movement first.

I push myself upright, muscles aching as blood returns to limbs stiffened by stillness. I stretch — just enough to sharpen awareness, never enough to distract. My rifle rests undisturbed against my Bergen. Discipline is ingrained from years of repetition.

My hands move with instinct, checking gear and repacking the rest of my equipment, leaving nothing out of place. Habit is more than routine — it's survival. I lift my rifle, clear the chamber, inspect and polish the scope lens, and wipe the barrel — a ritual that keeps my mind razor-sharp, prepared for the chaos lurking beyond sight.

Walking around the RV, my gaze moves over the ground, noting each detail against my memory of last night. Checking clusters of dead leaves in the undergrowth, slight disturbances hint at something hidden beneath.

Around me, the morning light seeps over the horizon. The generator hums, Derek's keyboard's rhythmic clacking joining the morning ambience. From the Outback, the first notes of insect calls blend with distant birdsong.

Out of the corner of my eye, I spot Simon exit the building, and I give a quick drink gesture. Getting the message, strolling over to me with a smirk. "Patience, Steve. Unlike your lazy arse, I've already got breakfast and the brews on. Ten minutes, tops."

"Cheers, mate," I reply.

To the left, Derek still crouches over the keyboard, light spilling off the screen across a clenched jaw. Over Derek's shoulder, the satellite feed catches my attention — red markers dotting the map, possible vehicles or enemy patrols. From the look of things, he's cross-referencing intercepted messages, syncing each signal with the visual layout on screen.

"Viktor's men are concentrating here," Derek says, zooming the satellite feed in and pointing to a cluster of vehicles near a canyon. "They've set up something—might be a supply route or a staging ground. Whatever they're planning, they're moving fast."

"Tag the location. We'll move in before everything is locked down in the area," I reply, watching the screen as each point lights up, fixed on the layout.

Derek enters the coordinates, pinpointing the location. We've been tracking Viktor for days, and this is the nearest we've come.

"Alright," Derek signals, headset off, gesturing us in. The rest of the team surrounds the table, studying the maps, drone footage, and satellite imagery on the laptops.

"Viktor's positioned some people here," Derek says, finger tracing over the canyon on the map. "Intercepted chatter reports this morning, significant movement along this route." Tapping a narrow dirt trail winding through the scrubland. "Might be a supply line or staging area for something bigger."

George leans in, pointing to a location. "Spotted tracks here yesterday," circling another area with a marker. "Gear moved. Repeated trips. Staging something."

"They're funnelling everything through the canyon. Viktor's people might be guarding something vital or prepping for an ambush. That spot gives them the edge," I say, piecing together their strategy as the picture sharpens.

"We use the terrain to our advantage," Lucy states. "They've got the high ground, but moving along here." Lucy motions to the thick foliage, "Navigate their blind spots, position overwatch, and keep the advantage intact."

Derek opens the thermal scans on the laptop, pointing to a cluster of intense heat signatures. "Heaviest activity is right here. From the appearance, at least one of their camps is outside the primary base at the mining facility. Intercepted communications that trace back to this spot."

My gaze holds steady on the map, each possible scenario running through my mind, calculating outcomes and risks. Every route, point of entry and fallback position is laid out. "We move fast and quiet. Contact occurs when we decide. By that time, they're already bleeding," I say.

My gaze shifts to Lucy, who's studying the map with an intensity that's second nature to her. "Lucy, Derek," I say, pointing towards the perimeter. "You'll hold overwatch from here — electronic eyes on their movements. Relay anything unusual. If anything blinks, tell me."

Lucy acknowledges with a brief nod, her mind already charting the terrain, slotting herself into the field, and calculating lines of sight and obstacles as if she's already in position. Lucy doesn't just take in the landscape — she reads the landscape, predicting where shadows stretch and threats might lie hidden.

"Derek," I continue, "the comms are yours. Monitor every channel. I want enemy chatter the second things change pace. We need the intel fast for any twitch from their side, shift, or pause. Stay ahead."

Derek's hand goes to the radio gear, fingers running over the controls like a pianist prepping for a performance. Checking frequencies, making mental notes of possible interference, and gauging how much can be filtered without losing intel. With Derek on comms, we won't miss a heartbeat.

"Simon, George, you're with me on the ground," I say, tapping a route along the map, tracing a line that skirts the outer limits of their defences, avoiding the high-density areas where we would be easy targets. "We stick to this path. Our job is simple: gather what intel we need and bug out. If we're spotted, the objective dies before we cross the threshold."

Simon's eyes narrow, calculating the range and mapping each critical cover point; those split-second choices where a move or a hold might make all the difference. George studies the map with a sniper's precision, pinpointing ridges and knolls, marking every spot that offers a hidden vantage.

A scan of their faces shows a hardened stare from the team, commitment steady as always. They're with me, grasping the risks involved.

"Alright," I say, folding the map and tucking it back into my pack. "If they believe no one's near, that illusion stays intact."

We move out after breakfast. As my MTO in the army said, always eat when you have a chance. Next meal might be three firefights away." The team responds with curt nods.

Instead of the usual chuck-in, Simon sorted something better, getting rations delivered through Guardian Solutions' network on the ground. So, this morning's scran is a full English.

Once the meal is finished, and everything's packed, the weight of the day pack presses against my back, and every essential for the day is accounted for. Magazines snap into place. My combat vest is pulled tight, and the radio set. A tweak, rifle steady, and I'm ready to move out.

Simon and George kit up by my side. Simon studies the GPS, noting key positions, while George lifts the rifle and angles it across his front, ready for immediate use, movements stripped to function.

"Are we locked in on the comms?" I ask Derek, watching hands move over the controls.

"Clear and tight," comes the reply, not looking up from the screen.

A quick scan confirms everyone's ready. "Alright, let's move out."

We leave the RV in a single file. The vast Outback sprawls ahead of us, with the edge of the rainforest marking our path and the first waypoint. As we cross the near-barren Outback, light creeps over the horizon, casting long, warped shadows.

With GPS in hand, Simon tracks the coordinates Derek highlighted earlier. Every hundred metres or so, we halt, scanning the ground for any trace of movement."

A klick out, something catches my eye. Tyre tracks and a torn piece of fabric caught on a bush. Someone's been through here — perhaps Viktor's people or even someone else. That third party is still somewhere in the Outback, a factor we haven't accounted for.

"Simon, mark the coordinates," I whisper.

With the sun climbing, the early cool fades, and the bush thickens around us. Brittle leaves and twigs snap beneath our feet, amplifying every sound. Another 20 minutes through thick foliage, a discarded ration pack catches my eye, tossed on the deck, messy and exposed.

Down on one knee, Simon runs a hand over the ground. "Fresh tyre tracks leading that direction," analysing the tread. "Same pattern as before. And footprints alongside. Judging by the depth, I would say these tracks are hours old — no bounce-back yet."

Press the transmitter of the radio tighter. "DR, this is S3. Enemy signs confirmed. They're close."

Derek's voice crackles back. "S3, Roger that. Stay alert."

We didn't need to be told. Simon and George have eyes on the perimeter. Whoever or whatever passed through is either keeping an eye on us or has vanished.

The ground shifts as we move forward. The brush closes in, the sun beating down hard. We're almost at the location where Derek spotted a possible route or camp near the canyon. A faint movement catches at the boundary of my sight. I go prone, hand up for a stop. Following my lead, Simon and George shift their focus to the direction I'm pointing.

A blink, and the figure's just... gone. Only the emptiness remains. Light distortion, I don't think so. Every instinct tells me to stay alert as we press on.

As we edge nearer to the canyon, a backpack catches my eye, nestled against the roots of a tree, discarded and out of place to clean in the forest. If anything, my explosive and IED training taught me not to walk over and grab something without checking first for IEDs.

During the troubles in Northern Ireland, soldiers who snatched up an unattended mag often found the item rigged by the IRA, a lure that left too many paying the ultimate price.

After a few minutes, Simon checks the ground for any sign of an IED and decides the pack isn't wired. Instinct tightens every muscle, stretching toward the device, my focus sweeping for threats. Viktor's planning is too meticulous for anything accidental.

My gaze shifts to Simon. "Decoy?"

"Might be. But if this is deliberate, someone's playing games."

"Catch sight of anything or anyone, George?" I ask.

"Clear for now," comes the reply from George.

Proximity to the canyon flashes on the GPS. Tracks suggest presence—ours isn't the only journey cutting through this terrain. "Stay sharp. That next step might land us inside someone's crosshairs."

Weapons are drawn, eyes scanning the horizon. We push forward, no turning back now. Whatever's ahead—it's close.

*****

Back in the RV, Derek is hunched over his laptop and radio gear. Streams of encrypted signals and lines of code flash by, the result of hours spent scouring the communication networks for something — anything — that might give the team an edge.

Methodical strokes hit the keyboard, dissecting channels, honing in on anything that matters while filtering out the rest. Static fills the gaps, but focus holds. One overlooked blip and the electronic trail goes cold.

A faint blip appears on the feed, indistinct but unmistakable — a signal threading through the interference. Derek's back straightens, heart pacing faster as the dial twists, narrowing the frequency. The garbled voices sharpen, crackling through. Familiar code words emerge — Viktor's people. They're talking convoy, tactical units. The pieces lock together — they're in motion and within range.

With headphones tossed aside, Derek snatches the mic. "All callsigns, this is DR. I've got intel," each word charged with urgency.

Steve's voice, calm but sharp, crackles over the radio, "DR, what've we got? Over."

"S3, Viktor's people, unaware that we're listening, are discussing logistics — routes and RV points. They're prepping for something. Over."

Derek replays the transmission over the radio, looping back to the canyon reference, fingers moving over the keys to sharpen the audio. Derek's eyes cut over to Lucy, her face shadowed with intent. No words are needed; we understand what this means and where it leads.

"All callsigns, this is S3. They're on a tight schedule. We hit first," my words crackle over the airwaves, a clear command slicing through the interference.

Time pounds in Derek's head, the stakes sharpening by the second. The relic isn't something we can lose. Replays the essentials over again, focusing hard on the fragment—canyon, convoy, timing, locking in every detail.

Comms go dead without a hint of warning. Then, a new signal breaks through, dense with encryption, pulsing on the screen. A scowl darkens Derek's face as fingers move across the keyboard.

"Locked up tight," Derek says under a single breath, each tap chipping at the digital barricade.

Lucy moves, setting her laptop beside Derek's, programmes aligning in seconds. Fingers tapping in sync, Lucy brings her own skills to the task, cracking into the code with a confidence that speaks of years of experience, stripping back layers without missing a beat.

Minutes stretch long and dense. Lucy's focus narrows, eyes set on a stubborn code, but more challenging sequences have fallen in the past.

"Stay on it," Derek barks, voice flat and cold.

Code splits under pressure, keys clacking with purpose, minds locked on the objective. Each breach tightens the noose around whoever's hiding behind the feed.

The last barrier crumbles as the screen flickers, rearranges, and then drops into place. Derek leans back, lips tugging into a subtle smile.

"Got it," eyes gleaming with quiet triumph.

A breath slips from Lucy, and in an instant, relief morphs into fierce concentration. Routes, a hidden supply point, and the rendezvous location surface to define our next move.

"Right here," Derek murmurs, dissecting the intel. "Viktor's game plan, every move exposed," zeroing in on the strategy laid bare.

With a measured voice, Lucy points to the intel. "They've got supplies en route to a cache beyond the canyon, and something about a transfer... might be the relic." Lucy's gaze holds steady, eyes locking onto the crucial details.

Derek doesn't flinch, but the edge cuts deeper. "Clean work, Lucy. But it seems too clean. The pace smells wrong—like bait scattered across the wire. Wouldn't surprise me if they want us to chase."

*****

By the time Derek and Lucy secure their equipment and log the intercepted intel, I have already made the call. Instead of splitting up and pushing for the canyon, we will regroup at the RV. Moving with half the team into uncertain territory doesn't sit right with me unless the mission demands it.

The heat presses down on us as we emerge from the thick brush, sweat running down our backs, mixing with the dust and grit from the patrol. Each step through the Outback is a battle, the ground resisting at every turn. A scattering of trees offers a patchy shield, just enough to blur motion.

Hours in, and we've already been worn down by the brutal conditions. But deep down, I understand the most challenging part is yet to come.

Simon and George crouch down next to me at the edge of the forest, both silent. Their eyes scan the distance as we approach the RV.

With the standard challenge procedure preventing us from walking into a trap, Lucy is out of the way. We enter the RV, where Derek's hands dance over the keys as satellite feeds and drone footage flash in a dim glow.

Derek glances up as we enter but doesn't miss a beat, layering the latest intel onto the map. Lucy stands close by, studying the shifting images, piecing together every scrap of data.

"Got anything?" I ask, tossing my gear to the ground.

Glancing up, Derek replies, "It's processing. Almost finished. Dave's message says other groups are also looking for the relic."

"Any update on the GSS inside leak?"

Derek zeroes in on the screen, voice steady. "Still waiting on a solid ID. Dave's teams identified a few suspects, logging their movements as we speak."

Without a word, I step to the table in the centre of the room, where the detailed map is spread across the top. We started with fragmented intel—scraps that told us nothing definite. Now, everything aligns as Simon and George reinforce with their notes, mapping details, and GPS points.

Images load one by one on Derek's screen as a shift passes through us—a mutual recognition that we've been waiting for this. Viktor's men are almost within reach, plans aligning with each second that ticks past. The relic, our objective, lies in their path, and we're running out of time to stop Viktor.

"Gather in," I say.

The team closes in, shoulders tense, and everyone glances at the map's display. George locks onto the layout, absorbed in the details, as Lucy's sharp eyes move between the digital image and the map, calculating every pathway and approach angle.

"Let's start marking locations," I say, reaching for the small ball of cord we use to mark possible patrol routes. Outposts and enemy locations are identified by placing stones on the table one by one, each representing a vital part of the puzzle. "Patrols here," I tap the western side, "and another near the river."

George bends over the map, marking precise points where we've tracked movement and found traces of enemy gear. "Got fresh prints along this ridgeline," pressing a finger onto the spot.

"Might be their staging area, or perhaps they're keeping an eye on the route into the canyon."

Markers move under Lucy's hand, defining safe zones and pinpointing surveillance coverage. "A perimeter's coming together here. It appears they are trying to shield something important—might be the relic's location."

The intel falls into focus, exposing an organised perimeter encircling key locations with precision. A hand moves along the ridge on the map, marking the elevated ground under enemy control.

"This is where they've dug in," I say, tapping the high ground. "We adapt and take a route nobody will expect."

With careful strokes, Lucy marks the map, outlining potential routes. "Dense cover here gives us a chance. We move after dark, the best way to stay undetected."

Lucy's screen lights up with thermal images from satellite feeds, bright clusters marking the enemy camps. She centres on the hottest region, the concentration unmistakable.

"We're seeing increased movement in this sector," Lucy states, clear and composed. "The intercepted comms confirm—they're mobilising."

George scans the terrain, indicating critical locations. "Ambush from these positions. Stay concealed, remain close to monitor, and avoid overextending into hostile range."

Standing over the map, the weight of the mission sinks in. Every note and mark sharpens the focus on Viktor, leaving no room for missteps.

"This needs to be exact. One error and the advantage is gone. Analyse their setup—entry points, paths, next moves," I say, drilling the urgency into Derek. "Constant updates. We operate without blind spots."

Derek zeroes in on the laptop computer, and the equipment hums, "I'll lock down all signals. Noise won't go unnoticed. Reports will come in live."

"Setting an ambush might flush out what Viktor's people understand about the relic. Viktor's team might be sitting on intel we haven't seen." I glance around the room, catching a flicker of intensity in everyone's face, the silent agreement rippling through.

"This is our shot. The intel tells us that Viktor's convoy will be coming through here." My finger taps on a spot on the map just beyond the bend in the track, where the rainforest hugs tight on one side, and the terrain drops away on the other.

Planning the ambush in my head, I point to the map. "Take the left, George; Lucy, you've got the right flank," I say, my tone measured, my index finger marking each of their positions. "From here, you're set with a clear view of the road. George, aim for the front vehicle once we start. Lucy, lock down the rear. Anyone steps up, make sure they don't go far."

George locks the stock under his shoulder, breathes shallow, and focuses like a wire drawn tight across the kill zone. Lucy shifts stance, the scope turning in exact rhythm. Every shift is born from repetition, carved by combat.

The target's only part of the equation; they're already running the full op in their minds. These shots have to be perfect. A single second off, the entire play crumbles, leaving Viktor's men free to disappear.

"Derek, you're on comms with me in the centre," I instruct. "We hold the kill zone — keep updates sharp and immediate if anything changes."

Years of training have honed Derek into the kind of asset every team needs. Precision with intercepts gives us the edge, the only line between us and whatever move Viktor's crew might try.

"Simon, take the rear," I direct, highlighting the narrow route behind the ambush site. "Solid cover on both sides, funnelling anyone who tries flanking us. Make sure nobody escapes the scene."

Simon analyses the map, noting the way ahead. "I'll anchor at the rear, ensuring no threats slip through."

My army instructor always said, 'When making a plan, always give it a kiss' - Keep It Simple, Stupid. So our plan is just that—simple. Simplicity is what keeps us out of body bags. Viktor's crew is near, perhaps even carrying the relic; instinct flares, the kind built on hard-earned experience. Always something dangerous lying in wait, ready to surface at any moment.

One glance around confirms that everyone's dialled in. "This needs to be clean, contained, and fast. Expect at least three vehicles. We hit our marks, strip everyone for intel, and bug out before they realise what happened."

The focus shifts to the radio set-up. "No chatter unless it's critical. Signal if anything goes wrong."

No one speaks. They're running through the plan in their heads, visualising their movements, shots, and fallback positions. This isn't just another assignment. A single misstep here and Viktor's men fade into the shadows, robbing us of any edge we might gain.

"Everyone stays locked into their role. When we go in, it's with full force. Don't give anyone a second to think," I say, keeping my voice steady.

While the rest absorbs my briefing, I add, "This is the moment to hit Viktor hard. Any misstep, and we're exposed."

The team absorbs every word, "When we move, it's fast and precise. Until then, we focus on gathering every scrap of intel." The plan locks in after the final check—sequence set, roles firm, and everyone ready with exit paths and fallback moves if the worst happens. "We exploit any flaw we find and take them down before they catch wind of us. This is the shot we've been waiting for, perhaps the only one. Does anyone need clarification?"

"One thing. Viktor's no stranger to misdirection. What's to stop him from setting a trap with false intel?" George locks eyes with me, concern hitting the mark.

"Excellent point. I've cross-checked all the communications, but when Lucy and I worked on decrypting that message, I couldn't shake the sense that something might still slip through," Derek says, looking at George.

"Might be a diversion—deploying smaller units to mislead us, keep us circling while the relic is moved. Of course, that's if Viktor holds the device. We focus on reliable intel and stay on target," I reply, backing up Derek's analysis.

Mission prep wraps up. Focus sharpens, everyone is ready, instincts honed from countless operations. The plan's been refined to the last detail.

"At first light, we hit hard and clean. Until then, stay sharp— track every shadow, catch every flicker."

Lucy works on the sniper rifle, tweaking the setup with unhurried expertise. The sling is firm, the scope refined, and fingers glide through each setting. The rifle fits snug against the right shoulder, the barrel lined up with the fading light.

Lucy's gaze locks on the horizon, radiating a fierce, silent focus. Fingers stay close to the trigger, balanced on the edge of action, precision distilled to the purest form. Lucy is a force that can achieve the unthinkable.

Nearby, Derek sits cross-legged, locked into the hum of the comms unit. A crackle of static drifts as he fine-tunes each channel, engrossed in isolating clear signals amid the interference. His face hardens, eyes locked on the screen, tuned to the faint beats hiding in the static.

Nothing escapes attention as pieces come together, fragments others would miss. Locked into a zone, only Derek understands. More than our comms expert, he's our ear on the world. Filtering through a hundred different voices to find the one whisper that matters. Hand hovering over the mic, ready to catch any change or sign, we're not as alone as we think.

Simon stands near the portable stove, stirring the contents of a small pot. The mixture—beans, some processed meat, and something unrecognisable—bubbles and steams, releasing a faint aroma that's more industrial than appetising. But tonight, it's the fuel we need; consequences be damned. By dawn, we'll go dark.

Simon gives the food a final stir, nodding as if he's just concocted a gourmet dish, then glances at me with a half-smirk. Out here, with energy reserves stretched thin, it's fuel, pure and simple.

Next to Simon, George focuses on his sniper rifle, hands moving over the metal with a surgeon's precision. A bit of cloth glides along the barrel, each stroke deliberate, hands sliding over the components like craftsmen. Each component receives attention as George cleans, fits, and reassembles the rifle with perfect muscle memory.

The motion is seamless, the rifle settling into place, and the terrain beyond the ridge transforms into a hunting ground. That weapon isn't just a tool—it's a guarantee, and with George behind the weapon, our six is secure.

My kit is packed tight, checked and set for quick access. The rifle's barrel gleams under inspection, and every magazine is loaded, ready to speak when needed. This runs without a single hitch. Whether they've locked down the relic or left bait, I'm moving in with zero hesitation.

Flickering shadows stretch across our faces in the faint glow of the gas stove. Simon dishes the meal with a dry smile, muttering "Bon appétit" as we take our mess tins. The food isn't winning any awards, but the warmth does its part. We've all eaten worse, and tonight, this rough stew is a small comfort after hours of dirt, sweat, and tension.

With scran out of the way, Lucy heads out on stag first, vanishing into the night. In a few beats, she's invisible, leaving nothing but silence in her wake. Derek and George follow their steps as practised as ever. We've been on stag more nights than I would like to remember. Each of us carries out this familiar role with a silent focus.

Out here, with only the brush and stars for cover, every second is crucial. A single slip, a forgotten detail, and we're exposed, and this camp becomes a deathtrap. Stillness surrounds the camp, pressing into shoulders and clenching jaws. The silence bears weight, thick as packed earth beneath boot soles.

With the final stag, I settle into my bivvy, eyes fixed on the stars, the infinite sea above, visible only this far from civilisation. But the beauty's lost on me. Thoughts grind over tomorrow's plan, dissecting each part, probing for hidden weaknesses. Looking for an edge of something missing, a gap we haven't bridged. That third party's out in the wilderness, just beyond reach, waiting for us to expose a flaw, ready to pounce.

A brief and precise nudge from Derek rouses me for my stag before unfolding into his maggot, gear stowed with methodical ease. The icy air bites, sharpening my focus as I take in the darkness, tracking every shift, alert for anything out of place.

The trees sway, the wind whispers hints of something unsettled, insects hum in the dark, and the occasional bark echoes, a reminder of wild eyes out in the Outback.

The stillness around the camp follows every step like a shadow hinting at unseen threats. Crouched by a tree, my gaze fixes on the dim skyline, waiting for dawn's approach.

Chapter Fourteen — Ambush

The time, 03:45, glows cold and sharp on the watch face—time to kick things into motion. The team stirs at my signal; packs gathered, rifles prepped, Bergens locked tight against their shoulders, movements crisp and familiar in the dim light.

I take point, with the rest falling in behind me, with Derek behind me, ready to pass on any new intel that comes over the radio. Ten metres back from him is Lucy, concentrating on the right of the formation. Simon does the same on the left while George brings up the rear, covering our six.

A few minutes in, and the RV vanishes from view, swallowed by the barren stretch of Outback. Now, it's us and the vast, unforgiving wilderness, the landscape folding in tighter as we push further into the Outback.

The terrain dictates that our progress slows to a measured crawl, as one misstep could forfeit our advantage. The earth itself beneath threatens to expose us with a single sound, and I'm not taking that risk.

The sparse undergrowth offers no natural cover, just a false sense of security. The air is thick with the scent of eucalyptus and sweat, the intense heat clinging to my skin.

A gust stirs the leaves, too subtle to be ignored. The stillness is unnatural, as though the earth is on edge, sensing what's coming.

Moving ahead, the landscape gives nothing away—just sharp edges and shifting shadows. Something shifts deep inside me, a warning that we're being watched.

A wall of timber swallows the path, gnarled branches meshing into a solid screen, daring anyone to pass. The noise of the Outback fades as the forest awakens. Insects hum in the background, their annoying buzz a constant undercurrent as we push forward.

At the edge of the forest, I raise my right hand, the team halts, going to ground, and I scan the terrain. The stillness to my front is broken only by the faint breeze and the distant cry of a lone bird.

Entering the forest, the ground yields underfoot, firm dirt giving way to a damp, leaf-strewn trail that muffles our movement.

"Let's go," I whisper.

Above the canopy, what remains of the natural light is swallowed up, casting a muted glow across the path ahead. Shadows stretch long and dark, muting colours into shades of green and black, just enough to pick my way through.

The undergrowth thickens with every step. Roots and vines coil like traps underneath the surface, catching at boots and eager to trip up the unwary.

My movements stay slow and deliberate, each step a calculated effort to avoid an unsteady patch that could send me sprawling.

Behind me, a faint rustle marks the team's progress, George at the rear, quiet as a ghost trailing through the brush.

Every leaf responds as if part of a single pulse, the forest alive in its movements. Shadows expand and retreat between the trunks, moving like smoke. Overhead, branches sway, yet something about their movement goes beyond the wind, as though something unseen guides them.

Damp earth mixes with the sourness of decaying leaves. And beneath it all, a sharper scent cuts through, unfamiliar and out of place.

Moving deeper into the terrain, the GPS guides us toward the ambush zone, where the dirt track winds through a tight corridor — a natural kill box, whether for us or them.

After another 10 minutes, we're tucked into the rear of the ambush site, the trail just visible through the trees. I drop behind a dense bush, signalling the team to hold tight. Lucy melts into the shadows on my left, gaze locked on the treeline. Derek crouches nearby, hand firm on the rifle's pistol grip, breathing steady and controlled.

The forest's rhythm picks up around us. Insects buzz in an unbroken drone. Bird sounds far off. The layered sounds spark my instincts. My vision locks on the treeline, my finger on the trigger.

The forest snaps with a sudden, piercing noise—a sound that doesn't belong. Something shifts out there, just at the edge of my vision.

George's voice comes through the comms, "Movement right of me. Unknown."

"Roger that," I reply into the radio.

A sweep of the scene confirms that every position is locked tight with no enemy movement. This close to the ambush site, precision is key. One gesture from me fixes George and Lucy into position.

Anticipation of what's to come grips the terrain, an unspoken duel between forces waiting to strike. Whoever's out there understands the stakes, but so do we.

At the bend, George settles into position, rifle fixed on the path, scope sweeping the trees. Lucy anchors my right flank, her rifle primed and ready, aimed at the track in the direction we expect company to arrive.

Simon locks down the rear, positioning himself where he can spot any approach from behind, eyes sweeping for even the slightest movement. Derek's beside me, gripping the radio. One ear tuned in, blocking out chatter and, at the same time, listening for intel from Viktor's team.

The setup here is flawless. The thick brush conceals us, while the other side offers sparse cover. The bend compels any vehicle to reduce speed into our line of fire.

From our present location, Derek and I keep as close to the ground as possible, trying not to disturb the foliage in front of us, as we move the final 30 metres to our ambush positions.

Locate the perfect spot along the track that commands visibility in both directions, hidden behind solid cover that shields us from sight and potential incoming fire.

Once in position, I send a message over the radio, "All callsigns, this is S3, sitrep, over."

Within minutes, confirmation flows in from each location—everyone is in place.

"GD, in position."

"LK, covering track."

"ST, rear secure."

There is nothing to do now but wait. If the intel we gathered from Dave and the team at GSS and the satellite data is correct, just after first light, the convoy should roll along the track at the same time and route as the past three mornings, oblivious to the ambush lying in wait.

The first light of dawn slices through dense leaves, scattering fragments across the earth like broken glass. The rainforest takes on a sharp edge, and shadows cut across the trail.

My muscles are coiled tight as I focus on the target area in front of me, and my senses are sharp. To keep my brain active and me awake, I run through the ambush's setup.

On my left, George is stationed on a rock outcrop, sniper rifle zeroed in on the turn ahead. Lucy monitors from the far side, scope sweeping the length of her kill zone. Derek manages comms beside me, staying connected. Positioned at the back, Simon keeps a sharp eye on every angle, ready for the slightest hint of movement from behind.

Time drips by, the watch marking two slow hours. The forest stirs all around, yet the convoy is nowhere in sight. The birds overhead have started their morning calls, but their chirps and squawks appear distant and muffled.

Despite this, there's an eerie stillness to the world beyond that track. There is a sense that something is waiting to happen, but for now, we're left in the unknown, each second stretching into the next.

The urge to move gnaws at me, but I hold steady, two hours lying rigid in the dirt, muscles straining. Derek makes slight adjustments, fine-tuning the radio, waiting for any trace of Viktor's convoy.

Light edges in, shadows retreating, yet the target stays empty, untouched by movement. Thoughts churn — have they altered their route or caught wind of us? HQ's in the dark to avoid leaks. But the silence bites as if they're drawing this out on purpose, testing our patience.

My focus locks on the forest's edge, watching for even the slightest twitch, but it remains undisturbed, shrouded in silence.

Simon holds the rear. From here, his face is unreadable. But knowing the team well, I can guess where his mind is going. It happens to all of us when lying in an ambush.

In Simon's case, it will go back to those streets of Iraq, reliving that ambush. In this darkness, memories of earlier missions resurface in each of us, every detail precise and etched into memory.

A drink too many one night turned his tight grip on secrecy into a lapse, allowing fragments of truth to spill into the open.

In '03, he sat inside a Challenger 2 tank, the thick armour cocooning him during a vigil much like this one. The desert began to cook as the sun inched higher in the sky, heat pressing down like a slow hammer.

The troop was positioned along the edge of a dry wadi, waiting for an armoured convoy to come rolling down a stretch of highway. Concealed under camo nets, three tanks had their guns fixed on the bottleneck ahead, the only route the enemy could use.

As the convoy arrived, the sound hit like a thunderclap, echoing across the terrain. The ground vibrates beneath the sheer volume. The Challenger's 120mm gun came to life, sending the first round downrange. The impact shatters the lead vehicle into a ball of flame and flying metal.

The rest tried to scatter, but the desert offered no cover. Simon's words brought the moment to life — the surreal glow of his thermal sights, green-lit shapes shifting across the field, each a target. The team's rounds tore through the dawn light, his focus locked on each form as they took their shots.

Vehicles burned, and men leapt from them, screaming through the chaos. But once the dust settled, what lingered for Simon was the silence. A raw, unnatural quiet that followed, with shattered bodies scattered across the scene, louder than the gunfire.

Returning to the present, my ears strain for the sound of an engine, anything to break this unbearable waiting. Nothing stirs on the track; it's as silent as hours ago. Ambushes aren't like in the films — no thrill, just endless waiting.

Real-life ambushes get beneath your skin in a way nothing else does. You lie there for hours, sometimes days, with nothing but your thoughts running through the same procedures.

How many times have I checked my weapon, counted the rounds, and replayed the plan in my head? The process runs on repeat, with each move locked in and prepared for when things ignite.

That's the reality — nothing but waiting, body aching, muscles on fire, body stiff and burning, yet moving even a fraction isn't an option. Every rustle of the leaves, every gust of wind, makes you tense, ready.

The enemy never arrives on schedule. In real life, they don't show up within the hour like in the movies. The bastards force you to endure the wait, drenched by rain or baked under the sun, pushing patience to its limits.

Remember, once, spending days lying in the mud, cold biting through, every fibre urging movement, waiting under a wet tarp. The moment they stepped into the kill zone, chaos erupted — gunfire lighting up the kill zone and shouts tearing through the air. It's pure instinct, no thought, just action, over in minutes.

That's the reality. Hours of stillness, only for the quiet to shatter in an instant. Everything compresses into this heartbeat, the weight of the ground beneath, and the drill of preparation coursing through every nerve. Procedures hammer into place, the rhythm unbroken until the air splits and chaos detonates.

My fingers clamp down on the rifle, squeezing the stock hard enough that my knuckles burn with the pressure. Something I learned a long time ago is to focus your mind to prevent you from nodding off.

The mission and our way forward depend on this ambush. One chance to catch Viktor's convoy, stop whatever they're moving through this rainforest, and find vital intel.

The slightest movement behind me halts everything. Turning, I see Simon adjusting position. Apart from the subtle sound of a man fighting off stiffness, no sound echoes through the trees.

Light starts to creep across the terrain, cutting away at the concealment and making every movement a gamble. If nothing changes, I'll reassess the situation in another hour, maybe two.

As dawn's pale light creeps in, the terrain remains still, brushing against the unmarked path. My body's pressed low, every instinct telling me it's just a matter of time. The air is dense around me, filled with the sharp scent of damp earth and the hum of insects. Still, my hands rest on the cool metal of my rifle, fingers ready and alert.

Next to me, Derek studies the feed tucked underneath the foliage, eyes flickering between the screen and the terrain, waiting for any shift in the scene. Satellite visuals flash in succession, but nothing stirs.

Then it comes — a deep, rolling sound, distant but unmistakable, like thunder through the woods. The earth beneath me vibrates. Vehicles inbound.

"All callsigns, maintain eyes on target zone," I whisper into the radio.

From the ridge, George steadies the rifle's sights on the lead vehicle's driver, finger poised on the trigger for a single clean shot.

Lucy's rifle tracks the convoy's tail while Simon protects the rear from any flanking attempt. Every position holds firm, and the team is locked into formation.

A 4x4 lumbers into view, caked in layers of dirt and grime, dust thick across the windshield, cutting visibility to almost nothing. Moving down the track, ignorant of the threat waiting in the shadows.

I count the seconds as the following two vehicles file past: an open flatbed with armed men facing inwards on the back and another 4x4 close behind — the sound of engines grinding through the stillness. Right in the kill zone, the first truck slows to take the bend.

"Hold," I whisper into the radio. Every breath slows, bodies primed to strike. Engines echo through the terrain, the vehicles grinding forward, unaware of the storm about to hit.

"Now," I yell, my voice as hard as iron.

George's rifle cracks through the silence, sending a round slicing through the air, locked onto the target. The lead vehicle lurches forward, the front windshield exploding in a shower of glass as the driver slumps over the steering wheel, lifeless.

The car careens off the track, smashing into the underbrush. Lucy fires next, taking out the rear vehicle's tyres in a single precision burst. The flatbed is pinned down, with bullets flying from every direction.

The trigger breaks, recoil hammering into my shoulder as the rifle unleashes fury into the middle vehicle. Shots from Derek slam into the same target, punching holes through the metal and shredding any chance of order inside.

The battlefield erupts with the staccato of shots, drowning out all else as the ground absorbs the fallout. The roar of combat takes hold, the dry scent of gunpowder and kicked-up dirt thickening with each burst.

A sharp wave of rubber burning twists through the air, entwined with the unmistakable scent of fresh blood and gunpowder, making it impossible to ignore the carnage.

Men leap from the vehicles, stumbling into the open, some clutching their weapons, others caught in the daze of sudden violence, disoriented, scrambling for cover where there is none.

Their confusion works in our favour. There is no time to regroup or react as our rounds find their targets, dropping people at the point of impact. Screams from dying people deafening over the sound of gunfire, their bodies starting to build up on the dirt track, blood flowing like rivers before being sucked up by the dry ground.

One man breaks from the chaos, running for the protection of the woods, movements frantic, weapon ready—the break for freedom brief. The man falls hard, George's round stopping him short of the trees. Lucy keeps laying suppressive fire on the rear vehicle, picking off tangos with calculated precision.

The scene turns chaotic. Combat moves with brutal efficiency. Messy, as always. Gunfire rips through the air, bodies fall, heavy and lifeless. Cries break out, scattered and uneven, the unmistakable echoes of men trapped in a fight they didn't expect, drowning under the weight of the ambush.

Amid the turmoil, vulnerability sets us apart. An enemy soldier stumbles out of the flatbed, rifle loose in his grip, eyes unfocused, drifting somewhere beyond the present.

It's only just anchored to reality. There's a second where his vacant stare locks with mine, and its fragility threatens to crack. The battlefield doesn't care for the unready, and neither do I. George fires first, a single round taking the target down before I choose.

The fog of war settles thick, blurring the lines between instinct and decision. Combat isn't a perfect dance—it's a violent clash of will and survival, with every move dictated by split-second choices. You don't think. You act.

The final man drops, the shot to the chest halting him as he reaches into the wreckage to free another. His body collapses into the dirt, silencing the gunfire. At that moment, the forest reclaims the silence—leaves shivering, distant life humming on the edge of hearing.

On my feet now, I survey the devastation. The vehicles are torn apart, bearing the scars of the assault, metal frames riddled with bullets, bodies lie still in the dust. The aftermath. The point where we look back at what we've done and how we've survived.

"All callsigns, status," I say into the mic, my voice hoarse but steady.

"LK, clear," Lucy responds from the ridge.

"GD?"

"All good here," George says over the radio.

My focus shifts over the carnage, noting the impact and assembling the details. The convoy's neutralised. Objective achieved. But the quiet that follows — it's heavier. Surviving is one thing, but the images of what occurred will remain tucked away in the back of the mind, waiting for the right moment to resurface.

There is no time to dwell on what just went down. If these were Viktor's men, someone's already sent word, and reinforcements might be en route — time to search the bodies and bug out.

As I move toward the lead vehicle, black smoke lingers while the acrid scent of burnt fuel mixes with the metallic tang of blood. Dust swirls at my feet, kicked up by the ambush.

An eerie calm lingers, wrapping itself around the scorched earth, where violence erupted moments earlier. George is still perched on the ridge, rifle trained on the horizon, scanning for any sign of movement or help heading down the track. Lucy stays vigilant at the far end of the track, focusing on where the convoy came from. Intel isn't always bulletproof — another wave might still be coming.

A hand gesture brings Simon and Derek out from the cover of trees, their focus still razor-sharp. Tension hangs in the air after the fight. Your adrenaline simmers, waiting for another trigger. The ambush's far from over.

"Let's move," I say, still heading for the first vehicle, a 4x4 riddled with bullet holes, the windshield shattered from the fatal shot George put in the driver. The man's body is slumped over the steering wheel, lifeless, blood pooling across the dashboard, vivid against the cracked surface.

My hands rummage through the glove box, hoping to find something that explains who they are and why they're here. Something that reveals their identities and motives. Nothing. Just dust, maps stained with old coffee, and a pack of cigarettes.

Simon's already pulling the rear door open, dragging a bag out from behind the passenger seat.

"What's inside?" I ask.

"Convoy manifests," Simon mutters, thumbing through a stack of papers. "These might be for supply routes."

"Check for names," I say, moving toward the second vehicle — a flatbed. "Need to confirm if this is fucking Viktor's lot."

I step over a body sprawled on the ground. A young man in his 20s, rifle still in his grip, eyes wide with the shock of an end he didn't see coming. The reality hits for a fleeting second — he wasn't ready for this, not for the fury that tore through here. But war makes no allowances. I shove the thought aside.

Derek's on the back, lifting tarps off crates. "Just ammo and explosives," he shouts, pulling aside another cover. Hands freeze mid-motion, something unexpected catching his eye. "Got something here."

The edge in his voice catches my attention as Derek pulls a black leather case from the crate and slides the zipper open. Inside is a folder stamped with a mark I recognise — the Syndicate. Viktor's network. This is the confirmation we sought, yet there's another layer waiting to unfold.

"Appears to be orders," Derek says, flipping through the pages. "They're headed to a location further north. Might be where they're staging for the next move."

Flipping through the documents, patterns emerge. "The relic," I say, gripping the map with its bold markings. The lines converge on a remote target. This convoy isn't random. They're pulling everything together for a more significant move into the Outback.

The bodies tell a partial story, and Viktor's ambition extends beyond this scene. His men push north, chasing a prize for which he's willing to risk everything. The relic lies at the centre, and this convoy is a calculated piece in his design.

I call Derek over, "Take a look at your computer and see if this matches up with the places Dave and Dr Petrov indicated might be one of the possible locations of the relic."

From his Bergen, Derek retrieves the laptop, boots it up, and brings up a map marked with critical sites. After a quick comparison, he confirms, "That's one of them."

"Shit! Means Viktor is ahead of us."

"Maybe not. Sure, if that's the spot, they've got a head start, but who says they're searching in the right place?" Simon remarks.

"Good point, mate."

At the last vehicle, Simon searches the bodies for any ID, pulling a wallet from one jacket and flipping through it.

"Russian passport. Name matches one of Viktor's known associates."

The photo lands in my hand. A dead man's eyes meet mine, cold and unmoving, someone who won't be walking out of here.

The fog of war may still linger in the air, along with the chaos from the violence, but at least now, in the aftermath, there's clarity.

George is still monitoring the road ahead, scanning every detail. Lucy remains covering the opposite end, ready for any threats coming from the side. The situation's far from stable, but the intel gives us some of our needs.

"All callsigns, this is S3; wrap it up," I say over the radio, retreating from the vehicles. "Destroy what's irrelevant. Take the intel we need."

With me leading the team, we move out. The dance of combat is over, but the mission isn't. Time's against us, and Viktor's closing in on the relic. This convoy signals just the beginning; the real storm's yet to roll in.

The ambush site fades as we pass through the undergrowth and tangled foliage. Undetected like shadows. Leading the team, I focus on the ambient noise, analysing the environment, vigilant to the rhythm of the forest, and attentive to every change. The track fades behind, but the terrain presses in closer, its weight a constant reminder of its hold on those who tread it.

Simon moves behind me. Each step merges with the natural sway of the leaves, calculated enough to stay a whisper within the forest's song. Lucy and Derek follow, silent and precise, scanning the treeline, alert for anything that might intercept us. George keeps to the rear, covering our six.

The ground beneath shifts with each step, uneven ridges disrupting the rhythm of movement. Halts become instinctive as ears sharpen to catch the faint snap of a branch or a misplaced breath, sensing the possibility of something lurking nearby. Our senses are heightened to detect the subtle sound of disturbed foliage or the almost silent breath of something lying in wait.

The raising and lowering of my arm signals for the team to drop. Their bodies blend into the dense bush, vanishing into the undergrowth.

Twigs crackle beneath the weight, but silence soon takes over. The wind shifts, carrying a faint, acrid hint of smoke — a campfire, maybe, or the lingering trace of our earlier work.

Scenarios ripple through my thoughts — patrols returning to regroup or, worse, circling to cut us off further down the track. We are a unit, each attuned to the other's movements, a silent understanding binding us together.

The treeline shifts as Simon's subtle movement draws attention forward—his hand gestures to the thick cover ahead. The trees begin to thin, exposing glimpses of the terrain stretching beyond the forest.

The damp, tangled undergrowth gives way to dry, compacted soil as the Outback reveals itself again. Rugged ground stretches ahead, harsh and exposed.

A hand motion slows the team. Vulnerability rises as protection diminishes, with the open landscape offering no mercy. Treeline patrols could be within range, their position hidden by shadows, waiting for a clear line of sight.

Movement pauses again. Instinct warns—this is where mistakes turn mortal, where the open topography becomes a merciless foe.

Then movement emerges at the perimeter of the trees, four shapes skimming the edge of the dense undergrowth. They appear armed. Movements are deliberate, but too reckless for Viktor's supposed professionals. If they are who we suspect, their approach would reflect deliberate tactics. Or is this a new player stepping into the fray, unknown and unpredictable?

The terrain swallows the team, shadows merging with their forms until they vanish. A single sound or misplaced shift could bring those figures toward us in an instant. My line of sight finds Simon first, then shifts to Lucy, assurance exchanged in silence.

Concealed among the trees, we watch as the patrol halts, scanning the terrain ahead. My hand adjusts on the rifle, prepared to engage but hoping there's no need to use it. Giving ourselves away here could be a disaster. They're too close to the RV. Another step or two, and they might catch signs of our tracks or notice the camp.

The minutes crawl by before they pivot and dissolve into the vast, dark stretches of the outback. We wait, holding our position until I'm sure they've vanished from sight. George's signal from the rear confirms they're out of view. I move forward, motioning for the team to follow.

The RV's just up ahead, a couple of hundred metres out. A sharp gesture halts everyone. Instinct kicks in, and we break into our usual formation.

Simon takes the left, checking the far side of the RV. Lucy moves right, sniper instincts on high alert, while Derek and I hold the front. George remains in position, keeping watch on our back trail.

The team becomes part of the landscape, blending into its rhythm. Eyes scan the surroundings, ears tune to the faintest disruption that might betray our base location.

A few minutes later, Simon's voice comes through the radio. "No sign of movement."

"Same here," Lucy adds.

"Negative on contact," Derek confirms, tone sharp and unwavering against the backdrop of white noise.

"Let's move. George, Lucy, hold your positions until I signal clear." My words are firm, coming from my cover behind the enormous rock jutting from the ground.

Eyes sweep the area, paying particular attention to the two derelict structures. The compound appears just as lifeless as before, but I know better than to trust appearances. Not now, not after the ambush. There's a chance the RV has been infiltrated by someone we didn't account for.

"Eyes sharp," I murmur to Simon and Derek.

Simon acknowledges and heads to the RV on the right, rifle up. I move through the middle while Derek holds the left side.

The larger of the two abandoned buildings stands in the centre, paint flaking under the harsh sun. The RV has acted as our base, a momentary shield, but security is nothing more than a mirage out here.

Simon's fingers hover over the door latch, eyes meeting mine, waiting for the signal to proceed. A thumbs-up sends Simon forward, crashing through the doorway, barrel-sweeping the left corners. My rifle sights scanning the right as I move in behind, steps deliberate. Derek stations himself at the door, securing the exterior.

Inside, the air is stifling and stale. The odour of old sweat and dust hits me, but it's more familiar than unsettling. What a few hours can do to a place in the middle of nowhere is incredible.

The windows remain under Simon's surveillance while I clear the small table, pushing aside crates for a closer look. The corner yields no surprises, the trail staying cold.

"Clear," Simon shouts, eyes trained on the dark recesses while moving toward the rear.

After one last scan, I motion to Derek before we both check outside, then slip through the door.

We converge near the next building, Simon leading as I split my attention between it and the treeline where Lucy monitors the open ground, George remains steady as stone, both prepared to unleash precision fire.

The small, dilapidated structure sits ahead, its walls slouched and its roof on the verge of caving in. Far from ideal, though it serves well enough to conceal the ATVs. Moving toward the door, I signal Simon to cover the left as we approach the entrance. Derek remains in the rear, eyes on the perimeter.

The door hangs ajar away from the frame, just enough to expose a sliver of the room beyond. Positioned to the right of the doorway, back pressed to the wall, my hand pushes the door further open, slow and controlled. Eyes adjust to the dim interior, where light carves shadows along the floor. Dust particles swirl, and I watch and listen for any sound or movement.

Inside, dampness saturates the air, mingled with the earthy scent of decay. Simon moves along the left wall, while I take the right, rifle poised, avoiding the creak of weakened boards underfoot.

"Clear," I say, my voice sharper than I intended. Simon gives a short nod, and we move back toward the door.

Just the rest of the RV to check, including the rear of the building, which is hidden from the view of George and Lucy.

Shadows consume the rear of the edifice, cutting off the light as Simon edges toward the corner. I stay poised to intercept at the far end, behind the edge of the structure.

A moment of quiet focus envelops us before my voice pierces the comms, "Go."

Together, Simon and I leap around the back, hoping to find anyone lurking among the piles of scrap against the wall, along with old oil drums. But at the same time, trying not to shoot each other in any crossfire. This is where teamwork and those constant drills come into play. Both of us know our arcs of fire. The kind of precision that's kept us alive so far.

The team converges at the RV, heat radiating from the ground. Lucy holds steady in the shade, rifle fixed on the outer line. George scans the far edge, his scope tracing the horizon. My rifle locks into place as I exhale.

"All callsigns, this is S3. All clear, pull back now. Maintain eyes on the six," my words cut through static.

Chapter Fifteen — Recce of the Bunker

The RV is almost cleared when the midday sun slams down like a hammer, scorching through our fatigues. Packs drop with dull, exhausted thuds. We don't speak. We don't move more than we have to. Each of us scans the heat-shimmering horizon.

Everything fell into place in the ambush — measured, silent, and final. George and Lucy struck their targets, sniper fire tearing through the convoy before the enemy had time to register the attack. Vehicles stopped cold, bodies slumping over the moment it began.

But something's off. The objectives lined up, but the silence hums wrong — like we're chasing a setup, not a target. Something grinds beneath the surface — unseen, threading through the operation.

Viktor's crew hit the mark, but the setup ran too smooth. Patterns snapped into place like theatre — convoy must have been a front, disguised to hide something much bigger. Something more might be waiting, a layer beneath the surface we haven't yet uncovered.

"Alright," I say, cutting through the silence. "Let's debrief."

I spread the map across the table, the edges curling under the weight of too many red lines. Routes and ambush points are all marked in precise detail, and my mind runs over the possibilities.

Derek's focus stays on the map. "Their target's here," finger pressing into the marked area. "Abandoned bunkers, east of us. Intel indicates a lot of activity and resource gathering." The words come measured, but a subtle intensity underscores what's at stake.

Arms folded, Lucy comes over like a storm-gathering force. One glance cuts through the haze, grabbing everyone's full attention.

"From what we know, Viktor operates in layers. I'm with Steve, the convoy was a mere cover. Another agenda hides beneath — always does."

I stare at the map again, replaying the documents in my head that we pulled from those bodies — symbols, codes, messages buried in layers. The trail points straight to Viktor's people. Something's off. He's not the kind to leave a convoy exposed when we're this close. Not unless the convoy was part of a bigger plan.

"What's the purpose of coming through here? Why choose this route? Unless..." I stop speaking. The thought gnaws at me. "Something we're not seeing yet," I mutter to myself more than the team.

Derek's expression tightens, sharp and unwavering. "This is a trap," every word laced with the certainty of experience.

"Might be a diversion."

Even as I say the words, doubt creeps in. Viktor's too meticulous for something this obvious. Every action is deliberate. Something more might be going on here.

Simon's voice cuts through the silence. "So, what's the next move?"

"We split into two teams. Simon and George — head to the suspected camp. HQ's intel flags the location as a staging area. Find out what's happening and who's moving in and out," I say, surveying the group.

Turning to Derek and Lucy. "That leaves us three to check out the bunkers. From what we gathered, that's where they're looking for something, or perhaps preparing for something bigger." My finger presses into the circled location on the map. "If Viktor's team is moving, we need to move faster. The bunkers are our next step. If this connects to the relic, we extract the data and disappear. It's about getting inside, gathering proof, and pulling out clean."

Unseen dangers surround us, and every corner is a potential threat waiting to surface. Viktor's crew might be hidden, watching us. One wrong placement triggers steel, shrapnel, or worse — movement, pulling us straight into a kill box. Any sign things are going wrong, we're pulling out. Viktor plays a calculated game, and we're just the pawns until the entire layout's exposed. He's not worth the gamble.

"Need to act before we lose the trail," Derek remarks while adjusting the radio. "Something isn't right. It's too silent."

"Derek's right. The whole convoy setup stinks of a ploy. No backup, no distress flares — it's too precise, too polished, designed to pull us straight in. The intel checks out, and every piece of the plan is set, but certainty is a luxury. Viktor's always one step ahead; this might be another move in a playbook, " I reply.

After we break from the debrief, we each slide into our roles with the same efficiency we've built over years of working together. The RV is still and remains silent as we scatter across the compound.

Near the far end of the RV, Derek moves toward the storage shed. Inside the shed, every connection made locks our lifeline into place. Radios sit waiting in a line, silent but essential. Derek's fingers work fast, connecting each unit to the solar array and replacing drained power with life.

George is at the hidden stash, tallying our ammo. We went through a lot during the ambush. The metallic snap of rounds sliding into place echoes across the RV. Rifles undergo final checks, and hands operate with the precision of a sniper's detached calm, zeroing in on every detail without a word.

A burst of coded messages filter in as Lucy scans communication frequencies, jotting down key details and cross-checking against maps and logs, focus shifting between the incoming chatter and the documents laid out beside her. Connections form between locations, personnel, and a suspected third party moving within Viktor's reach.

Under Lucy's meticulous guidance, every scrap of information is dissected, reassembled, and layered into a roadmap, her fingers dancing over the keyboard, eyes fixed on the screen, hunting for any scrap of intel that might turn things our way.

With the maps still laid out, Simon is going over exit strategies. When the proverbial shit hits the fan, he's our ticket out, covering all the bases. Plotting the next phase and exfil, all routes and fallbacks are scrutinised. Tracking each line on the map with a fierce intensity dissects every detail. Accuracy is paramount.

I'm sitting on the step of the building, notebook in one hand, a Splashmap in the other, mind working through the subsequent moves. The camp and the bunkers are two critical objectives, and neither is guaranteed to hold what we're looking for.

Around me, the team moves like a machine forged in fire. The RV crouches like a coiled beast, concealed yet ready to strike without hesitation. Outside the perimeter, the forest waits, not in peace, but in that unnatural stillness before something breaks.

Above, the sky shifts—crimson bleeding into bruised violet, swallowed by the approaching dark. The staggered stag rotation begins, with George taking the first, melting into the shadows near the RV's flank. Rifle steady, body still, vision scanning like a predator on the edge of a kill zone.

The outer line comes into focus under that unflinching gaze. No gaps. No movement escapes attention. Nothing passes unseen. This is the edge—quiet speaks in riddles, and instincts write the rules. And George reads every line.

The stag passes from one set of trained eyes to another, George stepping down as Simon steps forward, the rhythm seamless and practised.

Inside my bivvy, time twists, minutes turning to hours. But soon enough, a rough boot against my bivvy wakes me, and Simon's voice cuts through my half-sleep. "You're on stag, you lazy bastard."

Rolling out of my maggot, the night air slices through the sharp and unforgiving landscape. The wind threads through the brush, carrying faint, distant sounds that drift like whispers—calls of unseen creatures hidden in the shadows. The night presses down, dense and unyielding, wrapping the camp in an unsettling stillness. The quiet holds weight tonight, unnatural, as though the land braces for something unseen.

The Outback stretches in oppressive calm. No rustling branches, no movement beyond the steady rhythm of insect chirps—an emptiness that hums with anticipation. The gut tightens, the instinct honed by years in the field, sparking with the subtle awareness that danger might linger just out of view. My fingers grip the rifle stock, sliding into place with the ease of muscle memory.

Boots press into the dry, cracked earth as I start a slow circuit around the perimeter. Rifle poised, eyes sharp, pausing every few paces, scanning the shadows for anything out of place. A faint rustle from the brush catches my ear—likely a wallaby or some nocturnal critter, but I stay motionless, letting my senses absorb the darkness.

The Outback plays dirty—warping shapes and sounds until nothing seems real. Shadows stretching out too long. The breeze whispers too sharp. Every noise fights for priority, demanding judgment. Friend or foe. Nature or threat. One wrong call and the land claims another.

In the quiet, memories creep in. Billy's face flashes before me, his grin lopsided, and his eyes squint from laughter, clutching a pint and sloshing beer down his front after one of his jokes. We took that trip to Spain in our 20s — a blur of resort bars, lousy decisions, and no plan other than chasing girls we never caught.

We didn't care. We were reckless and naive, with our lives stretched out like an open road. Billy developed a knack for grounding things, creating an illusion that nothing would go wrong.

Things shift over time. Edges become sharper, the laughter fades, and the weight of choices presses deeper with every passing day. The Outback doesn't forgive mistakes. Out here, hesitation kills. Out here, the ghosts walk closer than most would ever dare.

Billy's memory hangs heavy, not haunting — anchoring. That grin and careless words carved into who I've become. No one replaces that presence. No voice cuts the tension quite the same. No energy matches that reckless joy.

Wish for one more mission together, side by side, shoulder to shoulder, storming hell with pint-fuelled courage and foolish hearts. One last stupid joke, cutting through darkness like fire at the worst possible time.

Circling back toward the RV, I let my eyes drift over the bivvy bags scattered around the camp, each sheltering a teammate. We've been through too much together, so experience tells me nobody will be in a deep sleep. Not here. You rest, sure, but not real sleep.

Sleep always has an edge, that part of you that remains alert, ready to jolt awake at the slightest hint of danger. Hanging thin, more pretence than relief, a thin layer of hypervigilance. Instincts hum beneath the surface, bodies trained to spring from calm to chaos in the blink of an eye.

I settle back into position, rifle cradled in my lap, gaze drifting over the dark expanse beyond the perimeter. Out in the darkness, the enemy lies in wait. Their presence lingers, motionless, poised, and disciplined, mirroring our restraint on this side of the shadows. Every sound or movement may fracture the equilibrium. But out here, nothing else matters but survival, the mission, staying alive, and completing the mission.

The clock shows 02:30. Shift's done—it's Lucy's turn. I stand a few feet back, having learned my lesson about a dislike for abrupt wake-ups.

A careful tap on the bivvy and a quiet, "Lucy, you're on stag."

She's awake and alert in an instant. Within seconds, Lucy's up, weapon over the shoulder, sleep forgotten in one fluid motion.

Lucy moves with vigilance that wraps the RV like a second layer of protection; every movement is precise, and every glance is tuned to what might hide in the stillness. Survival demands that readiness never falters when apprehension fuels awareness.

My stag over, I slip inside the bivvy, and the memory of that first standoff with Lucy resurfaces. Started off as opponents on the Isle of Wight, doing a job for Mark. The ache from a bullet that sliced my arm serves as a reminder. But once Lucy switched sides, and patched me up, that's when it hit me—her loyalty stands as unwavering and solid as the shot that found the target.

Time slips away as I drift between wakefulness and dreams until a firm, sharp poke from a boot from Derek rouses me. "Time to move, fat boy."

Drag my sorry backside out of the bivvy. Take a moment to glance around. Lucy's already packing gear. Simon's over by the small burner, fixing up breakfast. A slight rustle comes from George's direction as he pushes himself up, brushing the remnants of rest from a weary face. To my right, sitting on the steps, is Derek. At first appearance, the night appears to have passed without any disturbance.

We're not the only ones rising from slumber. The Outback is also waking up—the distant calls of the local wildlife echo through the RV. Movement stirs in the underbrush, faint but deliberate, reminding us that unseen eyes track us.

Dawn stretches over the horizon, pulling shadows across the RV and the fractured remnants of nearby structures. The cold air lingers between the retreating night and the heat of the day yet to come.

We gather around Simon, each grabbing a steaming brew and a plate piled with his legendary army chuck-in. The aroma mingles with the rising steam of the coffee, warming my hands. Pushing back the chill as I turn toward the horizon, I take in the view with each bite.

"Quiet night," George mutters, still half-asleep but alert enough.

'Too quiet.' The words press against my thoughts, unvoiced.

That's the nature of this game. Silence is just a placeholder in this world, biding time until everything erupts into chaos.

With gear squared away and breakfast eaten, it's time to move. My day pack presses firm between my shoulders, weight balanced and ready, rifle resting steady in my grip. Lucy and Derek stand prepared, readiness written in the way both hold themselves.

The intel from the ambush and HQ points to two crucial locations. One is a suspected enemy encampment tucked away in a ravine deep in the bush, and the other is a half-buried bunker hidden in the forest.

Last night, after the ambush and the debrief, a decision crystallised. Two teams are needed for today's recon, and two viable targets have been identified. With that in mind, George and Simon are already heading toward the camp.

George's sniper prowess and Simon's recon expertise make both ideal for the long-range recce. Our next move depends on their ability to catch any crucial detail. Until then, we will remain in radio silence.

Lucy and Derek are with me; the bunker is our objective. Soon, information on whether Viktor's men are entrenched near the bunkers will reveal itself. The problem is getting in close without being seen.

Out here, the terrain is both a blessing and a curse, and that's why we are moving in daylight rather than using the protection of darkness. Should be enough cover to move undetected, but every step might betray us if we become sloppy.

"ST, this is DR, radio check, over."

A crackle comes through, followed by Simon's voice. "DR, this is ST. Loud and clear, over."

"ST, Roger that. Keep the airwaves clear unless you've got eyes on something," I speak into my radio, adjusting the earpiece. "Stick to the plan. Stay sharp, and hold off on combat unless unavoidable. S3, out."

A glance from Lucy, rifle poised, gaze tracing the edges of the treeline. Beneath her measured stillness lies power waiting to unleash when everything breaks loose. That's why she's by my side. Precision will be crucial if we encounter anything worth engaging. Viktor's men will not offer a second chance.

We slip into the underbrush, concealed from prying eyes. The brush is thick here, the red dirt packed and dry underneath our boots. The outback is waking up. Birds are screeching overhead, and there's a rustle of leaves as small animals and reptiles slither or crawl through the undergrowth. The problem is that every sound might mask something else, something human.

The path leads us toward the ridge that will, with any luck, lead us to the bunker complex.

I take a point. The rifle is tight in my hands, ready for action. Lucy keeps pace just behind me, Derek trailing at the rear. One ear is tuned to the comms, listening for updates from George and Simon, nearing their objective.

Shadows deepen as the forest canopy thickens, filtering scattered light just enough to guide us. Rocks thrust out of the soil like forgotten relics, encircled by dense patches of brush, forcing careful steps forward, drawing us deeper into uncharted ground.

My attention alternates between the tracks underfoot and the terrain ahead, scanning for signs of movement. Out here, threats take many forms—creatures lurking unseen, Viktor's men, or something more deadly.

The trail cuts into the dirt, angling off into the bush, fading as we press deeper into the undergrowth. A silent fist signal prompts Lucy and Derek to freeze. Dropping into cover, attention locks onto the disrupted trail. Deep imprints mark a hasty passage, accompanied by torn vegetation, suggesting something sizeable pushing through.

The brush ahead stirs, slow and deliberate, too controlled to ignore. Whatever is out there, movement grows closer, each pause between the sounds stretching, sharpening the silence around us. Training takes over, instinct syncing with the quiet urgency of potential contact.

The foliage splits, revealing hulking shapes. Muscle-bound wild boars carve into the ground with their tusks, gleaming in the dim light. Their movements are calculated and deliberate, the kind of confidence that comes from being one of the apex survivors out here. The ground beneath hooves, cutting out roots, oblivious to anything that doesn't threaten.

Lucy's gaze locks on me for a moment, a wordless exchange that says everything. These creatures are more than nuisances. They're unpredictable, aggressive when provoked, and lethal in groups. We've learned that lesson before, during the Outback hostage rescue—an encounter burned into memory.

The wind shifts in our favour, masking scent and sound but offering no guarantee. A single wrong move, a snapped branch, or an errant shift in position might cause the boars to charge. Their snouts twitch, searching, while their beady, dark eyes sweep for signs of movement. Fortunate for us, pigs root and snort, oblivious to our presence yet primed to react in an instant.

Time stretches, each second pressing down, before the boars fuck off at last, blending back into the dense undergrowth, the shadows swallowing them whole. Rising from the dirt, my movements stay cautious as we fall back into formation, each step measured, pushing forward into the unknown.

"Fucking close one," Derek mutters, grounding himself in the moment.

"For sure," I respond, a wave of relief hitting me, "but staying here isn't wise."

As we press on, the sun climbs higher, the heat pressing down with unrelenting force. The air is thick and saturated, and every breath drags through layers of exhaustion. Moisture gathers under my gear, pooling in places best left unmentioned and soaking through my clothes.

The brush closes in tighter with every metre, snagging and clawing, demanding more effort to push forward. The ground beneath cracks and crumbles, dry and unforgiving, another obstacle in a place where the land becomes the first adversary.

All around us, flies swarm in relentless waves, their annoying buzzing a constant assault. Wings brush against exposed skin — the sound drills into the head — a maddening, unrelenting noise that refuses to fade.

It's not just a fucking annoyance. It's a warning, a reminder of the Outback's rules: survival isn't guaranteed, and patience will be the first thing the Outback steals.

Branches block my way; I push them aside with one hand while the other grips the rifle. The heat presses harder, making each breath a struggle, like pulling air through a wet rag. This stretch of Outback offers no mercy. According to the map, the bunker sits ahead, buried deep in this terrain, hidden in a stretch of land that guards secrets.

An old line, a half-forgotten joke from an Australian postcard, resurfaces in my mind: "One Bridge, One Opera House, Eleven Billion Flies". The thought almost pulls a grin, but the buzzing around my head reminds me that humour won't outlast the heat, the insects, or the mission. Flies and this relentless heat are nothing compared to the enemy waiting ahead. The bunker isn't just a target. It's the operation's next step, and here nothing else matters.

After 10 minutes, we find a dirt track broad enough for a single vehicle. Dropping to one knee, I signal Lucy and Derek to mirror me, just in time to see an SUV rumble down the trail, the engine loud in the morning stillness.

Sitting in the back are four figures — three men and a woman, all dressed in thin black jackets with something written across the back. From our position, I can't make out the lettering. They're not Viktor's people, that much is clear — different attire than the ones we killed in the ambush.

The engine's growl diminishes, disappearing into the treeline ahead. I take out and study the Splashmap.

"According to the map, their route aligns with the direction of the bunker complex. So let's follow," I whisper.

Staying close to the treeline, slipping through the dense foliage, after about half an hour, the trail spills into an open space, revealing two parked Land Rovers near a basic camp setup.

Six individuals with weapons are moving around. Three are inspecting wooden crates piled up on one side. Two others head off into the undergrowth, rifles slung across their backs. That's when the writing on their jackets becomes visible: 'Broome Explorers'.

Lucy's already positioning herself, her sniper rifle trained on the clearing. Turning to Derek and Lucy, I point at the two men disappearing into the forest, "We need eyes on where those two are headed."

"Agreed, you and Derek go find out. I'll monitor the rest of the group," Lucy whispers.

"OK, radio us if you have any issues, then eliminate the threat, or vice versa, depending on the situation."

With that, Derek and I start to circle the camp, staying concealed and hidden from view, all the time with one watchful eye on the two figures who've wandered into the bush.

A few minutes later, a complex comes into view. Remaining unseen, Derek and I stay flat against the ground, buried in the thick brush.

To my front, concealed under a curtain of greenery, two small bunkers lie silent, their existence obscured by creeping roots and thick brush. Outlines blur amidst the chaos of the undergrowth, the dense vegetation revealing only a faint hint of their shapes.

Four men and a woman circle the entrance to the bunker, steps calculated, deliberate. As if handling a live mine. An unsettling calm seen only in professionals trained to kill without making noise.

A stocky figure emerges from the brush — green shorts and a sweat-darkened T-shirt — stopping short of the entrance before hacking at the vegetation with a machete. The machete swings in slow arcs through the thick foliage, its blade glinting in the sunlight. Each stroke lands hard, carving through overgrowth with the fluidity of someone born into violence, not taught.

After each cut, the door emerges from the tangled mass of vines, its edges and surface revealing inch by inch. The man pauses, sizing progress, then attacks the task with renewed determination, stripping away the layers of green that obscure the entrance. Two men try to yank the door open, but it doesn't move. It's not just built to block an entry but to repel anyone trying to enter.

A shift at the edge of my vision catches my attention. Another figure is at work, placing a tripod on the uneven ground and adjusting the legs to balance a camera aimed at the door.

The methodical adjustment of the lens carries an undercurrent of intent and actions layered with something deeper than any standard protocol. This isn't just an entry operation—it's calculated. Whatever's behind that door isn't just important—it's a message. This is about recording something pivotal, something that warrants documenting.

I lower my binoculars. This isn't a hit-and-run; their setup suggests layers of planning. Something nags—why document every angle? What's hidden away inside?

Beside me, Derek stays locked in, body relaxed but ready. "Thoughts?" he asks, voice cutting through the whisper of the forest around us.

"Broome Explorers, they're not just poking around—they're executing a strategy," I say under my breath, after analysing their actions.

To my right, a lone figure stands off from the rest. Just at the edge of their activity, a woman wearing a black jacket matching the ones from the vehicle. There is something about her that's different. She stands with her arms folded, her gaze sweeping the treeline, searching. A calculated patience, poised for something specific as if a spark might set things in motion any second.

Adjusting the lens of my binoculars brings the woman into focus, revealing an unreadable mask that betrays nothing, yet commands everything. The subtle gap between her and the others highlights dominance, an authority woven into every move.

Seconds drag under the oppressive heat. The man hacking at the vines commands my attention, a machete cutting through the green with relentless efficiency. Swipes reveal more of the door—a weathered steel slab, the surface scorched by years in the desert, guarding whatever secrets lie behind.

The woman, still standing off to one side, signals two men forward. Tools appear in their hands, and they head towards the door. These aren't amateurs; this kind of work comes as second nature. Each set on the door with intent, focus unbroken, working as though both comprehend what waits behind is worth the effort.

Even though the woman stands apart from the activity, her attention shifts between the bunker door and the surrounding treeline. Movements aren't random—she's waiting, not for the door, but for something or someone. The unease gnaws at me, a signal buried in my gut that I can't decode but can't ignore either. Something in stillness tells me the door is only part of the equation.

Whatever lurks in the shadows behind those crates promises chaos. My senses sharpen, and adrenaline coursing hot through my veins, the unseen threat prepares to tilt the scales.

To my right, the woman's fingers dance over the rough wooden edges, deliberate, unhurried, drawing invisible lines only understood by their maker. Each careful motion betrays purpose, exposing hidden layers beneath an innocent façade. This isn't curiosity. The methodical precision screams covert intent. We've stumbled into a silent storm.

"They're getting ready," Derek whispers.

Minutes stretch into irritation. The man gripping the crowbar snarls out a curse, stepping away. The crowbar drops and clangs against the door as the man leans back, face twisted in annoyance, swiping at the sweat running down his dirty face. A companion's knife scratches at the surface, but it's clear the steel won't yield to brute strength alone. Those secrets remain well hidden.

Derek signals me with a tap, eyes tracking the figures by the door. "They're not done yet. Heavier gear or extra hands might be inbound soon.

This isn't a bunch of rookies fumbling with a locked door. Movements line up too clean, timed and practised. This isn't guesswork. Someone behind this plays with precision, shaping chaos into something sharp. And then we have the woman in the black jacket, who remains on the sidelines, gaze shifting from the bunker door to the shadows in the forest, almost expectant.

My focus is not on the door; it's on the woman. Whatever she's withholding is something significant enough to disrupt everything. "They're not giving up," I whisper. "They're waiting."

"Waiting for what?" replies Derek.

"No clue," I admit, studying the perimeter again. "They didn't come all this way without a fallback plan. This may be a stall tactic. Perhaps the door's just smoke, maintaining attention while something more significant is in play."

We wait for another half hour, hoping for a breakthrough. When none comes, we pull back to meet up with Lucy.

Coming near Lucy's concealed location, a soft, quiet voice comes from the bushes, "Name my kids, or you are a dead man."

"Abbie, Bethanie and Hadley," I whisper.

Kneeling near me, Lucy's voice cuts through the stillness. "Anything stand out? Does the bunker give us a lead?"

"Yeah, found the underground shelter. They're working on the door, but no luck breaking in yet. Won't be long, though."

Slipping away through the half-light, shadows stretch across the terrain as the bunker fades behind us. Our footsteps fall in a controlled rhythm, Lucy close behind, rifle poised for action, while Derek holds the rear, radio in hand, scanning the frequencies.

A sudden crack, sharp and jarring, tears through the stillness, slicing the quiet like a blade. The sound ricochets off the trees, the echo expanding outward, rippling through the air.

Another follows, deliberate and calculated, layering over the first, the tempo shifting, the silence shattered. Every shot lands with purpose, a force that carries more than sound — a warning of what's coming.

We react, dropping to the ground in unison. Movements flow with precision, a testament to preparedness from countless drills. Bodies blend into the terrain. Adrenaline surges, sharpening awareness, turning shadows into looming threats.

The dim light of the Outback twists the edges of vision before gunfire tears through the stillness again, relentless and growing closer, hammering the fragile quiet into submission.

Behind, the sharp staccato intensifies, bursts echoing through the trees with increasing urgency. The source points to the bunker, the direction undeniable. The forest distorts the details, the natural density swallowing specifics, but the message is clear — something escalates.

Small arms crackle with frantic energy, punctuated by the heavier, deliberate thump of larger weapons. Each discharge pushes against the air, tearing apart the uneasy calm and replacing it with raw chaos.

The area quivers with the force of the unfolding fight, the serenity unravelling thread by thread. Whatever's sparking this conflict hasn't finished. It's moving and expanding. Something is unravelling, and it's about to find a way here.

"Sounds like automatic fire," says Derek.

The treeline surrounds us, obscuring the action. The noise carries, ricocheting off the tree trunks, filling the space between us with the chaotic rhythm of combat.

Balanced and poised, Lucy scans the scene. Decades of experience sit in every motion. The variables change, but the danger doesn't — one wrong step and the mess we've held at bay will rush in unchecked.

A rifle's bark echoes, the distance shrinking with every resounding crack. Shouts follow, muffled by distance, the words swallowed in the chaos. The ground vibrates under a deep explosion, the shockwave rattling through the air. Grenades or something heavier — this is not just a skirmish.

Soil grips beneath each step, the space shrinking as the clash advances, a tidal surge ready to engulf anything in its path.

"Broome Explorers... so who's on the other side of this battle?" with a hint of confusion in Lucy's expression, gesturing toward the commotion.

Derek leans in, "Viktor's people... might be the ones launching the attack?"

"No clear answer at the moment, but I think you're onto something," I say, keeping my tone measured.

Names and faces — they're irrelevant right now. What's critical is keeping a distance between us and them and not getting pulled into the firefight. The plan is clear — gather intel, not engage until we have to. But every instinct in my body is pulling me toward the sound.

Something is happening back in the woods, and my intelligent part understands we're not ready to take care of the situation. But the soldier in me wants to understand what's waiting around that half mile of dense undergrowth.

The bursts of fire taper off, leaving only stray echoes before everything falls still again.

I rise, signalling for Lucy and Derek to follow. "Let's go," I mutter. "The RV is our next move. This fight isn't ours. Yet."

Merging with the forest's shadows, the sounds of gunfire trail off. Tension rises, but we keep moving, knowing it's not far behind.

A firm grip lands on my shoulder, halting me just as the forest fades into the rough terrain of the outback. Lucy brings a finger to her lips, and without a second thought, we all drop to the ground, instincts snapping into gear.

Hidden in the dense undergrowth, every inch of my body is coiled, ready. The RV's just beyond the treeline, and something's coming.

Lucy's hand moves, a slight gesture, pointing to an advancing patrol. Four people moving along the rock outcrop about 500 metres away, closing in. Precision radiates in their approach, weapons positioned for immediate use, bodies tuned to the demands of their mission. They're not just here for a stroll; they're hunting someone. At a guess, us. This must be Viktor's people.

Derek catches my eye, and he's already tracking the patrol's approach. We've danced this line more times than I care to remember. Keeping this quiet is the priority. Concealment takes precedence. A measured advance closes the gap, their presence pressing against the edges of our position. A single misstep, and we're in their crosshairs.

A firefight risks exposing us to anyone nearby. The weapon fuses with my hand, unbreakable and exact, an unspoken promise of precision. They're near enough that sweat glistens on their brows, dirt clings to their boots, and fingers hover, poised on triggers.

The question gnaws, hovering — did they find us by luck or plan? With no alternatives left, Lucy's silenced 9mm sits ready. An instant of connection triggers motion, the decision solidifying under mounting pressure as we shift in perfect synchronisation.

The patrol closes in. Fifteen feet. Ten. Five.

"Now!" I shout.

Lucy moves first, a muted shot cutting through the air like a predator in the dark — quick and lethal. The impact leaves the man sprawled, limbs twisted, swallowed by the shadows.

Another round slices through the air, Lucy's mark precise, striking the next man before the others react. The bullet punches through the man's skull, and the torso goes slack, crumpling to the ground, emptied of purpose in a second.

Launching forward, the blade becomes an extension of my hand. The world fades, narrowing to the target in front of me. My knife sinks into the soft spot at the base of the person's neck, driving deep.

A brutal snap ends a life, a breath catches, terror locked in a final gaze, life already ripped away. The body is taking time to catch up. Their knees buckle, sending the corpse crashing to the ground, collapsing into a pile of raw muscle and sinew.

To my left, Derek is a blur. Movements are fluid, practised — one step, two, pushing the knife deep into the final man's chest. It's over in a heartbeat. The man's gasp is the only sound before life drains out, his body hitting the ground, sprawled beside the rest, still and silent.

The fight concludes, but the moment stretches, heavy with the confusion that comes after violence. The fog of war settles around us — not the literal kind, but the type that clouds your mind and dulls your senses.

After every battle, there's a fleeting moment when you question whether it's over or something is still lurking beyond sight. A controlled thud echoes inside, aligned with the rhythm of muscle and mind operating as one.

Everything returns to quiet except for the whisper of the wind through the trees and a lone bird singing in the distance. No sound betrays us, and the forest goes undisturbed by our actions.

Lucy stands, gaze sharp, scanning the surroundings, alert to any lingering threat, breathing steady, calm, and controlled. The chaos is sealed away, buried somewhere unreachable. Her focus is razor-sharp, as if untouched by what just unfolded. Blade wiped clean on the dead man's shirt. Derek rises, expression hard as stone. But that mask doesn't hide the truth. The unspoken truth lingers—we each bear the silent weight of the lives we've ended.

A sweep of the treeline reveals no movement, no threat—just an unnatural silence —the kind that presses in, begging to be trusted but never should be. Green hides the truth as much as covers. Nothing stirs, yet risk hangs sharp. Silence never clears the field. Complacency breeds body bags. Anticipate contact.

"All clear," Lucy announces, eyes darting across the perimeter, taking in every detail.

Beside me, Derek stands, blade wiped clean, a cold stare in place. "No other movement," he says.

"We need these hidden, and fast," I order, grabbing the nearest corpse by the ankles and hauling the corpse into the dense shadows, avoiding a scene any incoming patrol might find.

No room for sentiment or hesitation here—just the cold, methodical work of cleaning up. Their gear is stripped of identity, and no trace of allegiance is visible. Through collected intel, this is typical of Viktor's operatives: zero ties, blending into the shadows around us.

Derek and I drag the bodies into the undergrowth, leaving Lucy to conceal any traces of the fight that took place moments ago, each swipe of sand across the blood blending with the dust and dry leaves. The heat and the barren earth soak up the rest, leaving nothing behind but scorched ground.

Light cuts through the treetops, raw and unfiltered, exposing every inch of the aftermath with brutal clarity. No forgiveness lives here — only consequences. Another life erased, one more breath silenced in a war that never ends.

Stillness hangs heavy, denser than the shadows cast around the kill zone. Blood sealed in dust. Boots return to position. The threat is neutralised, but a deeper current builds. This isn't closure. This is the prologue.

Leading Lucy and Derek back toward the RV, the patrol is down, but the real threat sits on the edge of dawn. Whatever's coming, we're ready.

The heat bears down as we approach the RV. Time's running short, and answers are what we need — fast. Viktor's crew, the Explorers — something's brewing in the bunkers, and it's about to unravel.

Chapter Sixteen — Recce of the Camp

Both Simon and George leave the RV and step out into the outback's heat and silence, and vast, unforgiving ocean of red earth and jagged stone. Nothing moves. Nothing blinks. The RV is a ghost now, a memory swallowed whole by the shimmering horizon.

We're alone—just George and me and this brutal, sun-baked wasteland. I lead the way, boots crunching over fractured ground, every muscle coiled and ready. Behind me, George moves like a shadow, silent, watchful. My eyes stay fixed on the ridgeline ahead—dense scrub and spindly trees jutting up like sentinels. Somewhere beyond them lies the camp, and whatever secrets it's guarding.

A burst of static breaks the silence. Then Derek's voice, cool and clipped, cuts through with military precision. "ST, this is DR. Radio check. Over."

I press the transmitter. "DR, this is ST, loud and clear, over."

"ST, OK, over."

"S3, out." Steve's voice crackles over the radio. "Simon, maintain your position unless the situation shifts. Engage as a last resort. Stay grounded, sharp, and out of view. Out."

"S3, this is ST, will do. Out."

Pushing forward, every step stirs up dust, dry particles hanging in the air. The Outback stretches out vast and unforgiving, the kind of place that tests your nerves.

This should be routine, but something's brewing—a charge that hums beneath the surface, waiting to explode.

The ridge comes into view, jagged rocks tearing the skyline apart—a brutal barrier set to test every ounce of strength. I stare ahead, sensing the gravity tighten, aware that this obstacle demands focus.

George holds our six rifle-steady, shoulders balanced for an immediate response. Small movements telegraph lethal readiness — trained, precise, and lethal.

"Two klicks to the ridge," George calls out, gaze penetrating shadows, tracking unseen threats.

Ahead, the trail snakes toward shadowy relief, tempting yet dangerous. "Cover's close," I mutter, guiding us forward.

Safer ground awaits ahead, but shadows breed predators. Dark corners hide dangers sharper than blades, with patience as their weapon. Blind angles promise ambush.

Beneath my feet, dirt crumbles — deceitful and unstable. Shadows ripple, twisting into phantom threats that might mask enemies poised to strike. My heart pounds against my ribs, marking seconds toward confrontation. My pulse races, each beat signalling precious moments closer to compromise. Instinct screams caution. My body braces for the moment when concealment collapses.

Stopping in my tracks halfway to the ridge, a hand motion brings George to a standstill — the faint sound of rustling hits. Dropping to one knee, I scan the treeline.

Moving closer, "Spit it out," George murmurs, tone measured, eyes darting to the treeline.

"Something shifted by the rocks." The words drop firm as my arm angles toward the jagged edge of the ridge, tracking the shadow that lingers by the outcrop. My focus tightens.

George steadies the sniper rifle and surveys the terrain. "Might not be anything," though a measured breath tells a different story.

"Or more than we're ready for," I reply, lowering my voice.

The bushland retains a language, speaking of something hidden, watching, waiting. The pace eases as the terrain ahead becomes more challenging, thick with tangled brush and narrowing into a choke point. A natural kill zone, dense foliage, and steep ground funnel movement into a path no one would take without conviction.

I drop into a crouch, gesture for George to follow. The foliage provides cover close to the ridgeline, but it's a false sense of security. Misplace a step, and these stones beneath our feet will turn traitors and give away our location. I indicate the thicker cover nearby, off to one side, sparse but better than nothing.

"Slow," I whisper. "No noise."

George gives me a raised thumb. Every placement of a boot is deliberate. The breeze scatters through the brush, concealing some sounds and amplifying others, a constant reminder of how exposed we are.

A whisper of a sound from the ridge. I freeze mid-step. Kneeling, I scan through the jagged patches of shadow, searching for movement that might betray a presence. A brief wave prompts George to advance. Progress turns deliberate, pace adjusting to match the proximity of the ridgeline, its nearness a silent reminder of what might be waiting beyond.

A thick and unforgiving clump of bushes closes in around us. According to the map, the camp is beyond the ridgeline, hidden by the foliage and the jagged rise of the ridge.

As the sniper, George advances, scanning the terrain, searching for the perfect vantage point. No instructions are needed. He's done this so many times, it's instinct now.

With my eyes locked on the ground, I'm careful not to snap a twig or disturb the earth in any way that might give us away. The forest is alive, but not with the usual sounds of wildlife. My hand tightens around my rifle as we push through the final stretch of the bush.

"At our 12 o'clock," George whispers, pointing to a slight rise ahead, just about visible through the trees. "That ridge offers natural cover, a thick wall of leaves and branches that will conceal us while giving a broad view of the camp below."

I nod, and we move into position, crouching close to the ground as we make our way up the incline.

The ground is uneven, and loose dirt is shifting under my boots. The climb is slow, but we've got time. Viktor's men, or whoever is in the base, are unaware of our presence.

Reaching the ridgeline, George kneels to survey the terrain, ensuring he doesn't skyline himself. The area remains still, with no sign of movement or danger. A slow Bergen drop follows, hands moving to unfasten the observation gear without breaking the silence.

The tripod comes out of my Bergen, adjusted to the right height. The binoculars click into place, and the setup is complete. To my left, George secures the camouflage netting, breaking our outline against the topography.

The sniper rifle settles on the bipod, legs planted firmly in the dirt. George's alignment leaves no margin for error. The stance mirrors the calm readiness of someone who's done this countless times before.

Below, the camp reveals nothing obvious but the unnatural sway of leaves. I scan the camp below through my binoculars, sweeping for anomalies — a flicker in the foliage, a shadow slipping where none should be.

The sun beats down, relentless, sweat tracing the curve of my neck as the camp below moves like a well-oiled machine. Patrols move with intent, vehicles shift, and crates are hauled as though every second counts.

Subtle changes in their rhythm speak of a greater purpose, an unspoken urgency woven into their actions. This isn't routine — something significant brews beneath the surface.

Rows of trucks line the edge of the camp, their placement orderly and deliberate. Not an ideal place in my opinion, as some idiots like us could creep up, lob explosives in one of the trucks, and the lot goes up.

One vehicle stands apart. The movements around it are tighter and more calculated, the guards more alert. The activity around that vehicle pulses sharper, a signal clear as day — whatever lies inside carries weight beyond the standard haul.

George lies flat beside me, the scope tracking the guards circling the truck. Breath measured, the weapon becomes an extension of George, precision built into every motion.

"That truck's drawing too much attention," George's quiet voice breaks the air. "Guards are locked on like it's holding more than cargo."

I raise my binoculars and bring the truck into focus. The movements around the vehicle leave no question — whatever they're guarding, it's critical.

"Take a photo," I whisper. A couple of seconds later, the soft click of George's camera frames the activity below.

Dropping the binos, the camp stretches out in front of me. In my experience as a recce troop commander, and from what we have witnessed, their actions reveal deliberate intent, with every guard's motion calculated and each patrol's exact timing.

Notes are sprawled across the pad on the dirt beside me. Shift rotations are mapped, patrol routes dissected, and weak points marked. Every detail on the page feeds the picture forming in my mind.

Movement flickers near the ridge far beyond the camp, a shift at the edge of perception. The binoculars come up, focusing on the jagged line of rocks and scrub stretching across the horizon, half-hidden by the shimmering haze rising from the ground.

Stillness dominates, and the ridge offers nothing but rock and shadow — a barren stretch baked under the relentless sun.

But something shifted. The grip on the binoculars tightens as the search continues, sweeping every crevice and shadow, hunting for the faintest sign of life.

The terrain shows no figures, no tracks, only the unyielding landscape. The heat distorts the horizon and plays tricks on the mind. The Outback's illusory nature breeds doubt, but doubt in this place gets men killed.

The ridge's jagged lines make it an ideal route for unseen movement, the perfect cover to slip past unnoticed. The land here is both a shield and a weapon, concealing threats in plain sight. Instinct whispers to keep eyes on that ridge.

George lowers the camera, voice breaking the focus. "That truck holds more than they're letting on. It's not just cargo."

"I agree, mate. We'd better ensure we note any relevant details," I reply.

My attention shifts back to the camp. The guards don't just stand — they're positioned, stiff in posture, heads scanning like predators sensing a shift in the air. Their movements betray more than routine; they're braced for something. The notepad comes up, recording another layer of their behaviour, the patterns that don't match, and the calmness people want to project.

A man stands in the compound's centre, arms crossed, barking orders that move the others. Gear marks him as someone different from the rest.

"That's the guy in command," George mutters, scope locked on a figure at the heart of the camp.

The binoculars stay locked on as the man strides between the trucks, sharp gestures slicing through the air as commands fire off.

The way the man moves leaves no doubt—he's in charge. "Keep him marked," I say, the lenses dropping long enough to log the time. Identification comes later—back at the RV.

The faint click of the camera cuts through the ambient noise to my left, a sound as steady as the man giving orders. George anticipates the angles I miss, capturing layers of detail that'll matter when the dust clears.

A fresh plume rises as another truck grinds into the camp. Armed figures close in, their movements tight and fast, surrounding the vehicle as if it carries more than crates. Their urgency leaves little to question, though instinct forces the words out.

"Might be supplies," my voice just about audible.

George shifts before whispering, "Or it's bigger. Perhaps the relic?"

The dynamics shift. This truck doesn't seem routine, and whatever's inside changes the game. Another scan of the camp pulls focus to a weak point near the south fence—an opening they've left exposed. I nudge George, pointing at the breach. The note hits the page before the words land. No security is perfect; this one just cracked open a door.

The trucks keep shifting, gears grinding, equipment clattering, but the man in charge slips away, swallowed into the shadows. George takes one last shot, the lens pulling the final frame of the scene.

After hours of observation, documenting every detail—vehicle shots, the men, their weapons—patrol patterns are locked in my mind and recorded in the notepad. I've marked the weak spots in the camp and noted their security lapses.

"We're done here. It's time to move," I whisper, my hand firm on the binoculars. "We'll leave the rest for the next move," I say, turning my head towards George.

George begins packing away gear. The netting is folded and stowed in moments. We might be back, but the game will have changed when we are.

With a final sweep through the scope, George scans the camp below, checking for any shift that might hold us here. No changes, just men locked in their usual patterns. Routines bring comfort—and, with it, the risk of fucking up.

Notebook in hand, I scan the rough notes—vehicles, weapons, personnel—all the details laid out, a roadmap for what lies ahead.

Tucking the notepad back into my vest, I whisper to George, "Time to fuck off."

Crawling back from the op position to a point behind the ridgeline to avoid detection, haul Bergens onto our backs and set off back towards the RV.

George keeps pace 10 metres behind me. Years of training flow through the quiet rhythm of our progress. There are no unnecessary signals or wasted gestures, just the efficiency ingrained through repetition.

Halfway back to the RV, movement shifts ahead and shapes materialise through the trees—five figures, four men and a woman advancing on a direct course. Their presence isn't part of the equation, a variable that goes against the plan.

Our goal is clear: remain invisible, shadowed, untraceable. Any deviation risks turning this into a confrontation we can't afford. This encounter has already begun to edge toward dangerous ground, and the margin for staying undetected narrows with every step taken.

We melt into the undergrowth, blending with the available cover. As the patrol starts to close in, steps crunching over dry earth, their pace closes the gap too fast. The rifle's grip presses into my palm, steadying focus, movement in a body locked tight, muscles curled under the consequence of silence.

People make mistakes—hesitation, lousy timing, sloppy moves—and that's the thread we're relying on. Time slows, the absence of sound turning seconds into an eternity.

Boots scrape closer, their presence pressing against the space around us. Moments later, the patrol passes close enough to draw breath from the same suffocating heat. A snake slides past George's position, body rippling through the dust, but George holds, unshaken. Tension builds with every heartbeat, each second stretching longer than the last, straining like a wire pulled to the limit.

It must have been seconds, but it felt like minutes—maybe twenty, before the patrol moves past, drifting toward the shadows ahead. Relief flirts at the edges of thought, but it's short-lived as they stop, bodies pivoting in unison. Their steps reverse, aimed straight back to where we hold position—the chance to stay unseen vanishes, dissolved in the snap of their turn.

Instinct drives motion and leads the charge. The calm shatters, giving way to decisive action as I surge forward, closing the gap fast, blade flashing in a single arc. The man catches only a flicker of motion before steel slides into his throat, a practised thrust that cuts deep.

A choking sound slips past parted lips, hands scrambling to cover the wound, but it's done. Life spills through my grip as the body slumps, lifeless, hitting the ground with a dull thump.

The woman standing behind the man I've just dispatched moves one foot, sliding back, chest tightening. Lips part, not for a scream, for realisation. It's too late. That flicker of alarm never reaches her throat. My blade's already slicing through flesh, clean and specific.

George moves in. The blade cuts a direct path, slipping into the narrow opening between the ribs and puncturing the heart in a single, decisive motion. The victim releases a sharp gasp, body folding as life drains away. George steadies the descent, guiding the corpse to the ground.

The others open fire, ripping through the silence. The uncertainty vanishes. The fog of war is gone — chaos reigns now.

Actions unfold through muscle memory, movements precise and lethal. Rounds from my rifle split the air and sear into awareness. The rifle recoils, grip secure, barrel aligned.

Heat bites flesh as a round slices past my head. Wood from a tree explodes inches above my head, splinters sharp as knives showering down. Bark scatters, marking where death missed by moments.

My breath deepens, heart pounding against ribs, urgency guiding each movement — survival hinging on these instants. I twist, lunging hard at the attacker as more rounds hammer into the tree, the wood shuddering beneath the impact.

Enemy nerves fray, rifles jerk. Once soldiers, now scattered prey, cohesion ripped apart by fear as random fire punctures the surroundings; any discipline long gone.

George moves beside me, shadow-like, steady amid the carnage. Rifle poised, breath measured, one clean shot punctures the noise. The target jerks, skull snapping backwards, dead before impact with the ground. Precision dismantles resistance, discipline overpowering the unravelling threat.

Another freezes, fear-locking muscles, eyes open in paralysis. A heartbeat seals fate. The trigger squeezes, the rifle recoiling into my shoulder. The round strikes the centre mass, forcing breath from the lungs. Knees buckle; gravity claims another body.

Bodies lay in the foliage, nature uncaring. Calm asserts itself, and dominance is clear. Both George and I hold formation and structure intact in the face of collapse. Discipline brings victory; hesitation brings death. The forest reclaims the quiet, leaving their panic as nothing but an echo.

The noise stops, almost as if the world itself takes a breath. Heavy and oppressive silence presses in. The air is thick with the acrid stench of gunpowder, mingling with the sweat on my skin and the coppery scent of blood seeping into the earth. My breathing is shallow and measured, but my heart is hammering in my chest, the adrenaline still burning hot in my veins.

The fog of war lingers for a moment, that disorienting haze that blurs reality and instinct. But then, clarity sets in. I step forward, rifle raised, scanning for any sign of movement. Nothing. The bodies lie still, their blood pooling in the dirt.

The fight ends in our favour, but calm never follows clean. Thick and watchful shadows cling to the treeline. Something waits — not fear — something else. A weight behind the eyes. The sense of unfinished work is buried deep and rising.

We both scan the area, fingers resting near the triggers. Nothing moves. No sound beyond leaves brushing against bark. Smoke drifts close to the ground, curling around roots and boots. The quiet is earned but false. Peace never lasts out here.

George signals all clear. I nod, though doubt remains. This ground is held, not won. The next threat waits just beyond the silence, sharpening its edge.

"Better hide these bodies, mate, in case someone stumbles upon them," I say, heading to where they fell.

The first body is slumped forward, neck twisted, eyes open — glassy. Jaw slack, lips parted mid-scream. Blood leaking from a chest wound, dark and thick, soaking the uniform. One boot missing, leg bent the wrong way. Fingers still curl around an empty rifle.

I grab the collar and drag the corpse through the foliage. Branches tear at their face, peeling skin. Flies gather near the open throat. No warmth. Just the stink of blood and sweat. George pushes dead foliage apart, forming a shallow grave.

Another man lies sprawled, back arched, ribs shattered by impact. A red smear runs from ear to jaw. Pockets torn open, gear scattered. I pull the body closer, head lolling against my arm.

We press all into the ground, limbs folded, faces down. Rocks anchor the bodies. Branches pile high. The forest reclaims what the battle discarded.

With bodies concealed, we continue towards the RV, now a klick away. Buried in dense foliage, our focus sharpens on the RV's surroundings.

The RV appears empty, doors sealed tight. No movement disrupts the heavy darkness pressing in. The RV reveals nothing, like a mouth sealed over a secret. One misstep and the whole situation might escalate into a firefight.

A quiet shift from George, gaze fixed ahead, reading every detail in the terrain. No words are needed. This is familiar ground for us. Movement carves through the terrain, the brittle crunch beneath the fractured earth daring to give us away.

As we approach the RV, a voice cuts through the fading light. "What's the grenadier's motto?"

The trigger waits under my finger, the moment suspended. George speaks with a calm tone, cutting through the pressure. "Evil be to him who evil thinks."

After a pause, my hand tightens on the grip of my rifle.

"Admirable try, but not quite," Lucy replies, a laugh lacing behind the words. "The real motto is, 'If it doesn't move, clean it'."

"Fuck off, spook," comes the reply from George.

*****

Relief sparks and vanishes as we step into the RV. Lucy moves in behind Simon and George, crossing to the largest empty buildings, rifle secure across her back. Derek and I sit around the small table; Maps and gear are scattered across the table, illuminated by a faint red light. Fatigue fights for dominance, though concentration remains sharp and unwavering.

"Quick debrief before we settle in," I say, steadying my voice. "Derek, Lucy, and I followed a vehicle along a dirt path. Ended up taking us to some abandoned bunkers."

Simon cuts in, sharp. "Might be where the relic is."

"Correct," I say, maintaining my gaze on Simon. "A group gathered at the site. Some stayed with the two vehicles while the rest hacked at the vines covering a solid steel door. Three bunkers overall, but the primary target is the larger one. All wore black jackets with 'Broome Explorers' on the back. So not Viktor's people." I glance at Derek and Lucy. "Anything to add?"

Derek leans forward, "A woman stood off to one side. Late 50s. Didn't flinch. Supervised machetes like they meant nothing. Something about the woman's presence—quiet, calculated. Petrov came to mind. Maybe academic or more."

"That may mean Petrov isn't the only one digging into the relic. Tomorrow, we'll contact GSS and find out if they can uncover anything about our mysterious person," I reply.

"You kept an eye on the rest of the group. Anything unusual?" I ask, turning to Lucy.

"Nothing useful. Just leaning on their vehicles, drinking. Lazy bastards," replies Lucy.

"Final point for now. Engaged Viktor's patrol and eliminated several people. The bodies are stashed, but discovery and concealment are fragile, a secret the terrain won't hold for long. Simon, what did you find out at the camp?"

Simon's gaze moves across the team. "Cheers, Steve. Same situation on our end. Hostiles needed to be neutralised not far from here. The gunfire may have caught your attention. Bodies are stashed in the forest."

"Fuck me, the woods around here are starting to become a graveyard!" proclaims Derek, smirking to himself.

"As for the camp, it's larger than the intel suggested. Five trucks and a small army of a dozen men, strapped with enough firepower to hold their ground. One man appears to be calling all the moves. George captured a few shots."

Lucy reaches for the camera. "These go straight to GSS. Perhaps they'll be able to name the guy."

"Anything else?" Simon asks, looking over at George.

George leans closer. "One truck drew attention. The minute the vehicle pulled up, guards swarmed around the back. Whatever was loaded in the back, it's something they don't want to be compromised."

Time moves unchecked as the RV remains motionless. A deliberate stretch shakes off fatigue. "Today brought pieces, not the whole picture. Rest now. Tomorrow, we dig deeper." Words sink in. "I suggest we do the same as last night and set up a roaming patrol. I'll volunteer to take the last two-hour stag."

Chapter Seventeen — Natasha

The command centre's hum vibrates through the air. Voices murmur into headsets, punctuated by the staccato tap of fingers on keyboards.

Satellite images flicker on the screens surrounding Natasha, displaying overlapping grids of barren outback terrain, abandoned bunkers, and convoy routes. A faint hint of ozone wafts from the server racks as endless data streams are processed.

A map stretches across the table before me, marked with overlying red and blue lines — Steve's unit, the unidentified group, and ours. Three paths converge on a single target. A small circle inked near the bunkers draws her focus.

The artefact stays exposed for now; the retrieval depends on perfect calculation. Push ahead without thought, and concealment fractures; hesitate, and another will seize the opportunity.

I trace one line — a third-party movement charted from intercepted communications that don't belong to Steve's team, but their purpose is unmistakable. The data suggests the group may be mercenaries, private contractors, or professionals. Their presence complicates everything, as they might be potential allies or adversaries, adding another layer of uncertainty to our mission.

The chair creaks as childhood memories surface unbidden, piercing the meticulous analysis. Late nights in my father's study, the aroma of aged leather and bourbon. His steady voice explains the power of patience.

"The one who strikes first loses. Always make people think they've won." The words are etched into my mind.

The images of my parents' deaths follow, as vivid now as when I uncovered evidence in the MI6 archives. British agents. Assassins operating under the thin veneer of diplomacy.

No arrests. No justice. Just silence from the people sworn to uphold the law. The vow I made standing over their graves of who ordered the killings fuels everything. Viktor understands that drive and clarity of purpose.

The satellite feed sputters, snapping me into the now. A convoy advances near the bunker's boundary: four vehicles holding a tight pattern. That isn't Steve's team. They never opt for head-on tactics; From our intel on Steve, he always dissects the field first.

Proof came with the ambush—an attack launched against the decoy convoy sent to mislead and divert from the actual location. It was a costly manoeuvre, measured in lives, yet Viktor deemed it essential to secure the relic.

Viktor underestimated the unit once. No further missteps will be allowed. A faint grin suggests a measure of respect for the precision behind Steve's team and their recent manoeuvre.

Sergei enters the room, his frame casting a shadow over the table. Impatience is brimming just beneath the surface, but he doesn't interrupt. His approach—direct and forceful—stands in contrast to my calculated strategy.

"They're waiting for us to make a move," Sergei mutters.

"This delay speaks volumes," I interject, marking the convergence point. "Steve's team is predictable, but this isn't their game alone. The unseen players are manoeuvring for the position— every second lost edges us closer to a disadvantage."

"Paralysis by analysis," Sergei scoffs, but I focus on the data. Frustration is a distraction I can't afford.

Lines connect in my mind, each piece falling into place. The relic isn't just a prize—it's leverage—something far greater than Steve or this unknown group of people might comprehend. Viktor's vision takes shape, and mine edges closer to reality.

This artefact can redefine power structures, driving Viktor's obsession and the path we're forced to tread.

"Deploy the drones," I order, my tone slicing through the hum of equipment and the subdued chatter of the operations room. "Keep both groups under constant surveillance. When their next step begins, those details are ours to exploit before they even realise they've been exposed. No mistakes." My determination is absolute, echoing through the room and reinforcing the gravity of our mission.

The cyber unit springs into action. Fingers fly across keyboards, each keystroke translating into swift execution. Monitors light up with data streams as the systems come alive, feeding visuals from the drones launched outside and now streaking into position. Our meticulous planning is evident in every move, the technology meshing seamlessly with calculated human effort.

The atmosphere shifts the casual energy of moments before, replaced by laser focus. The hum of machinery intensifies, punctuated by clipped reports from the team. Contours of the land ripple through the monitor, their lines feeding into the algorithm. Each fluctuation sparks recalibration.

Movements are synchronised to track the slightest disruption. The operation breathes with methodical efficiency woven into the constant evolution of data. The target, oblivious to the encroaching force, faces a noose drawn tighter by the second as roles merge into an unbroken rhythm.

The air vibrates with purpose, and each individual in the room is attuned to the task. Voices hold back, reserved for commands.

Actions align, eliminating hesitation. The hunt unfolds, and I can sense movement in the charged silence—the game is ours to win, their downfall already taking shape in the glow of the monitors.

The tactical table glows under the map's faint backlight, the surface crowded with layers of shifting data. Red vectors sweep over the grid, outlining the movements of assets. Satellite feeds cycle through angles, stitching together a story from fragments of intercepted communications and thermal scans.

A pattern materialises, distant but deliberate, tracing a route that edges too close to the suspected site of the relic. They're careful, testing the ground like wolves circling prey. Patterns materialise — no mistakes in their timing, no deviation in their course. They are predictable in their precision. It's not recklessness. It's confidence.

A section of the landscape draws my attention — a bottleneck, perfect for an ambush. Small icons mark positions where their approach might falter. Possible counterpoints emerge in my mind. The terrain forces choices that rely on accuracy.

The third party adds complexity, their presence shrouded in ambiguity. Their movements appear random at first, but a closer examination suggests otherwise.

Decisions align, and one priority becomes clear — control the timeline — any delay, even seconds, tipping the balance.

Static hums faintly in the corner, a rhythmic pulse mirroring the quiet precision of the comms team. Screens shift with tracking data, and operators read signals like an unfolding script. Viktor's voice breaks through, steady and sharp, the cadence an anchor for the operation. The relentless demand for progress mirrors the control I wield.

Reflections surface in my mind, contrasting with the present. Childhood images intrude, fragmented and sharp: my father's deliberate pacing in the study, the crackle of old records spinning on the gramophone. The rhythm of my dad's voice carved clarity into my perspective, each syllable forging a sharper understanding. "Control the board. Let your opponents move first; you've already won by the time they realise their mistake."

Another fragment intrudes. Mother's whispered warnings, trust corrodes, comfort blinds. Their executioners remain unknown, but time will expose the truth: British hands, agents who justified their actions behind political lines. But the question remains, who ordered the killings and why? The system that took my parents away gave me my purpose. It isn't revenge — it's correction.

Returning to the map, possibilities cascade into view. A counterstrategy begins to form, connecting dots that are stretching too thin in Steve's formation. They'll cover the obvious routes but fail to predict the path we carve.

"Push more recon drones over that sector. I want feedback from our people on the ground," I say, pointing to the ridge that shelters the convoy. "Mark any heat signatures near these coordinates. I want a full readout of possible assets."

Movement around me signals action. The team executes commands with sharp efficiency, as Viktor demands. Analysis shifts from hypothetical to actionable. The relic rests within reach, a fragment of something much greater. Viktor grasps power, while I perceive leverage as a tool with potential that far exceeds mere control.

Adaptation defines Steve and his team's strength, shifting with precision. They'll adapt, pivot, outmanoeuvre. But the board's been set, and my pieces are moving first.

A final glance at the map confirms the next step. Control isn't just a strategy — it's the only option.

The table gleams under the harsh glow, its surface dissected by crisp shadows. Across the table, Sergei locks into place — spine rigid, chin lifted, a warning etched across every angle. The message doesn't need a voice. Challenge bleeds from posture alone, daring me to shift first.

Frustration carves into Sergei's tone, cutting through the charged atmosphere like a blade. "The convoy cost us. Steve's team dismantled everything, and now they're repositioning. Resources thrown away."

"Incorrect," I reply, my voice calm but deliberate. "The convoy served a purpose, a calculated diversion. Their attack confirms the decoy worked."

Sergei's hand slams onto the table, the sharp crack reverberating. "That's your idea of fucking strategy? Baiting Steve's team while we sit idle doing fuck all? We should be at the bunkers, securing the relic. Waiting is a luxury we don't have."

Sergei's impatience grates like sand in a wound, but losing composure now would give ground. "Charging in risks exposure," I say, pointing at the map. Predictability is their strength and their weakness.

Their obvious strategy captures their focus — straight lines, loud angles, and central fire. They spread wide across broken terrain, chasing phantoms. We slip past where floodlights fail, moving between their blind arcs, slashing through the gaps their plans overlook.

Viktor's chair shifts, leather creaking beneath controlled weight. Silence holds, pressing tension to the edge. Sergei turns toward Viktor, eyes searching for alignment.

"This approach drains resources and time," Sergei says. "A strike now secures the site before any regrouping begins."

The stillness fractures as Viktor's hand moves forward, calm yet commanding, "Natasha, highlight the weakness in Sergei's argument."

The opportunity is a blade, sharp but double-edged. "The flaw lies in visibility," I say, heading toward the screens. "Natural terrain wraps the bunkers in a chokehold, forcing any movement through the valley into plain view. A direct path becomes a trap."

I pause for the information to sink in. "Steve's unit isn't alone on the field. Our intel suggests a rival group is carving a steady path toward where the relic might be located, their movements too calculated to dismiss. Their approach signals intent, methodical, and unyielding. Meeting them head-on shifts the advantage to their favour — a risk I won't permit."

A sharp intake from Sergei disrupts the quiet, heavy with rebellion. The sound lingers, daring me to falter, but I press the momentum forward, refusing to yield to his disruption.

"Discipline aligns the strategy. Their focus on the convoy buys us an opening to slip through unseen, dodging Steve's team and the unmarked force."

Viktor's eyes narrow, scanning the table. "The convoy. Steve took the bait, then?"

"Correct, the diversion worked. Movement shifted away from the site. We slide in between beats, sharpen our edge against any pause, and transform hesitation into gain, " comes my response.

Sergei's voice cuts through, laced with a low snarl. "And if this third group moves faster? If they reach the target while the strategy stalls?"

My fingers hover over the map, tracing deliberate lines where paths converge around the relic. "Their approach shows calculation, not confidence. They're probing the terrain. That uncertainty is our opening," I say, precision in my voice.

The scrape of Viktor's chair echoes through the room as he rises, gaze shifting between us like a hawk searching for any weakness.

"Natasha's strategy stands. Sergei, direct that energy toward strengthening the advance team's readiness. Errors are unacceptable."

Each word lands with force, cementing authority in place, silencing dissent before it can take shape, and quelling resistance beneath a command that invites no defiance.

Shoulders tense as Viktor's words strike home. Sergei's jaw tightens and turns, boots scraping once before leaving the room in silence.

As the door slams shut, Viktor's stare lingers on me for a beat too long for comfort. "Do not fail, Natasha." The words land with the finality of a trigger pull.

I move over to the bank of computers and sit at one of the desks. The screens above me stretch along the walls, displaying lines of cascading code, satellite overlays, and comms data. The glow paints sharp angles across the faces of the people sitting nearby, their focus unbroken. A map of the region blinks to life on the centre console, a red marker pulsing over the area of Steve's location.

My fingers move over the keyboard at the central terminal, bringing up a secure channel. The implanted agent's feed flows into the system, streaming clipped blasts of intercepted chatter.

Guardian Security Solutions operates with blind confidence, oblivious to the steady siphon of intelligence from its core. The operative, planted deep within their ranks, dispatches transmissions in coded bursts, each piece aligning with Steve's team's calculated move west toward the encampment veiled by vast stretches of wilderness.

Viktor's shadow lingers at the edge, directives blunt, impatience cutting deeper than words. Detection remains out of reach — for now. Precision demands the perfect moment.

Sergei's disdain simmers beneath the surface, frustration with calculated pacing clear. Brute force grinds like a stone on glass, close to breaking the structure that remains intact.

But modern warfare thrives on nuance and deception, where precision and timing shape the outcome. Sergei's approach, locked in the days of raw aggression, fails to account for the intricacies of today's battlefield.

The art of strategy lies in mastering control and using hesitation as a scalpel, cutting through the enemy's resolve with calculated intent. Strength is nothing without the precision to exploit weakness.

A cursor hovers — still, waiting. One breath, one blink, and the strike begins — the command drops. Circuits obey. The infection moves like venom, weaving into their system, unseen until it's too late. The order is relayed. The team executes the next phase. The cyberattack begins with new intelligence from the informant in GSS, targeting Steve's communication.

Bandwidth collapses, folding inward. Static crawls through the seams. Words meant to guide now choke in digital fog. Commands fracture mid-transmission. Gaps widen. Confusion spreads, masked as delay.

Each signal hits a wall, rebounds, and splinters. Their rhythm stumbles. Precision breaks apart, piece by piece. No order lands in time.

Data floods my screen — chaos converted into patterns. I sift through the noise and pull truth from the fire. Every frame, another blade, each line drawn with intent to destroy.

Blank signals pulse across their networks. Words reduced to codes, devoid of thought. Their silence isn't peace, but fear masked in protocol, a language lacking conviction spoken behind mirrored glass.

But no system is flawless. Every machine dreams of control — until something more substantial takes the wheel. That control now shifts.

This isn't sabotage. This is architecture collapsing from within — my design, my hand. And their downfall begins not with gunfire but a whisper across the wire. The flaw lies in their assumption of invulnerability, a gap we will exploit.

The challenge comes from Derek's mastery over their network, sharp and seasoned in radio intelligence, which is a formidable obstacle. But his edge falters against the relentless barrage of our countermeasures. The field of radio warfare belongs to us.

Sergei's voice cuts across the room like a blade through the tense fabric, impatience demanding attention.

"They're moving, cut them off. Now," Sergei growls, advancing toward the console.

"Not yet. Disorientation clouds their movement. Let the disruption settle. Strategy dictates the field — we lead to where weakness lies." My reply is sharp and controlled.

Silence lingers, stretched thin by tension. Sergei steps back, a scowl marking the withdrawal. Brute force holds no sway in this phase. This requires precision.

A surge of activity floods the interface, their counterstrike unravelling in sharp bursts of intent. Each move is met with layered deception — ghost signals overlay their network, presenting false coordinates and splintered orders. Their systems falter, caught between truth and the chaos we orchestrate.

The time spent monitoring intel on Steve's movements and the info passed by the informant inside GSS is starting to pay off as the transmission cuts through fragments of dialogue and coordinates, piecing together a larger narrative. Steve commands with clarity, instructions carving a path through uncertainty, guiding the unit toward their intended position with methodical intent.

The encrypted line hums into life. Viktor's demand cuts through the silence. A response follows, calculated and exact, offering just enough information to placate while keeping the deeper layers concealed. No unnecessary details spill over—nothing that might shift attention from the surface.

Every step of the plan unfolds with ruthless efficiency. Actions are sequenced with perfect timing, each piece clicking into place. By the time Viktor and Sergei realise the magnitude of what's happening, their choices will have dwindled to nothing.

Satellite feeds illuminate the outback in fragmented light—bone-dry ridges, jagged gullies, and scorched silence. The terrain fractures into grids, and each section is monitored. A trail extends westward.

Steve's unit advances, their movements deliberate. Geometry unfolds, beautiful and lethal. Distance means nothing when the perimeter breathes with you.

Digital footprints mar the surface, faint but visible. Each one whispers of movement, enough to indicate position without revealing the truth. Decoys achieved their purpose. Attention is diverted, focus misled—just enough.

Sergei's earlier demands for a confrontation linger like static in an otherwise clear signal, a mindset forever chasing collision instead of orchestrating the trap.

For a moment, old memories surge back like a storm, tearing through the calm, unbidden and relentless. The scent of smoke clings to my skin as though seeping through walls, curling around me.

My father's desk—once the epitome of discipline—now lies in ruin, buried under papers and books tossed aside in chaos. Charred fragments speak in the language of ruin, their presence woven into the atmosphere. The room bears the imprint of destruction, as though the essence recoils from what transpired.

Men in dark suits stand motionless, their faces carved from stone. Their words carry no substance, just empty condolences that echo without definition. Eyes avoid mine, their practised detachment betraying their complicity.

Empty words spill from their mouths, void of conviction. "Tragic", "unfortunate" — those feeble attempts at sympathy fall into the silence between us, swallowed by the weight of their hollow meaning. Their words drip with rehearsed conviction, tailored to deflect suspicion. But the cracks show in fleeting glances, in the twitch of a hand, in the hesitation that betrays the polished act.

The space where presence once thrived now bears a hollow resonance, each surface betraying emptiness. Laughter, a melody that once bound the walls, dissipates into fragments too faint to hold. The air in the room holds an unnatural stillness, as though the absence itself shifts the balance, bending the space where my mother should stand.

Shadows stretch, shapes distorted as if the structure struggles to compensate for what it's lost. It's not just a voice that's vanished — her warmth, strength, and unwavering belief in the kindness that held us together. The void left behind grows like a storm, pulling everything into darkness.

For months, their promises lingered like smoke, fleeting and insubstantial. Grand gestures of justice made, only for the truth to be suppressed under a pile of bureaucratic tape.

The men in suits came and went, their words shifting from sorrow to deflection. Questions met with scripted answers. Buried facts encountered locked doors. I believed I wouldn't detect the cracks in their constructed façade.

At first, the flaws are almost imperceptible — whispers at the edge of my perception. One document erased without a trace. A schedule revised without warning. A chain of movements misaligned by hours. One detail misfires, and everything fractures.

Nothing breaks clean in this world unless someone forces the crack. The deceit built layer upon layer until the entire operation began to collapse.

The destruction of my family came by design, not chance. Every move followed a pattern built to lead us here. Their plan left no room for error and no space for choices beyond their design. We existed like pieces on a board, our lives a mere consequence of their calculated moves.

Clinging to the word 'justice', offering it like a bandage to a wound that runs too deep. A quick fix for the broken, a false promise that hides the truth. Justice isn't an answer—it's a distraction, a way for the weak to placate their guilt.

Retribution offers no comfort; it demands satisfaction, and—precise as a blade—it cuts through illusion to expose the hollowness beneath, each unearthed truth bearing the weight of the irreversible, revealing hidden scars until what remains is stark, unflinching proof of the cost exacted.

This isn't about fairness or balance. It's about righting the wrongs inflicted, about tearing apart the systems that allowed the men to act with impunity. Their operation destroyed my family. I will kill them.

I'm brought back to the moment as the map pulses with fresh data, highlighting a new intersection between Steve's route and an unfamiliar group that's remained in the shadows until now. A fresh element enters the equation—one I haven't accounted for.

Viktor's pressure to deliver results intensifies, Sergei's thirst for blood grows sharper, and my focus tightens on the one thing that matters: answers. My team stays unshaken, the strain of the mission unspoken, each member locked into the task with laser-sharp precision.

Orders pulse through the network, each one a blade drawn in silence. No flare, no chaos—just control. Signals shift, code rewrites routes, and every click feeds the storm building across Steve's comms. Rewriting the battlefield, moment by moment.

False intel floods their channels. Decoys drift across their screens—coordinates fracture. Targets blur. Delay creeps in, just enough to bend confidence into doubt. Communication falters. Movement stutters. Confusion grows where unity once held.

A strike team presses closer to the bunkers, concealed. Eyes fixed on the signal. Triggers ready. No movement until the net tightens.

Sergei growls behind the scenes—Viktor monitors from shadowed glass. Words fade. Decisions remain here. Pressure sharpens the edge. Control never leaves my hands.

Light from the monitor glances off the steel surface, cutting sharp angles that match the edges forged within. Viktor's machinations transform my hesitation into precision, shaping my resolve into a blade.

Commands pulse through the room, and the team is synchronised, waiting for the next signal. The atmosphere hums with focus, and screens flicker with the latest updates as directives cascade into motion. Each keystroke aligns with the plan, shaping the road ahead.

"Send the secondary unit to intercept now. Establish a perimeter around the bunkers and track all movement. Apply unrelenting pressure. Make sure Steve's team doesn't regain their footing. Strip advantage away, edge by edge. Let frustration tear at discipline. Force response through confined routes, where options fracture." My words cut through the operational chatter like a blade.

Commands ripple across the comms, tightening the latticework of control. Every directive strengthens the structure, a labyrinth where Steve's unit edges closer to their limits. Resilient, yes, but their determination only prolongs the inevitable.

The strategic landscape shifts under pressure, each movement narrowing toward the point of no return. Countermeasures only highlight the reach of control.

Pieces align with a precision unnoticed by those in motion, each step drawing the operation closer to finality. Control remains fixed, unyielding, and absolute.

Chapter Eighteen — Contact

The camp lies in shadow, cloaked in that dead hour before dawn when the world holds its breath. Cold gnaws at exposed skin, burrowing deep, a silent predator that doesn't let go. Every sound — or lack of it — feels loaded. The darkness isn't just empty; it's watching. Waiting. There's a weight in the air, not from the chill, but whatever's coming next.

Sixty minutes until the horizon bleeds gold. My watch ticks in my palm, the faint green glow of the dial slicing through the gloom. Around me, the team begins to stir — no words, just the muted shuffle of sleeping bags, the thud of boots meeting hard-packed dirt. Movements are slow and rehearsed. No one talks. We all know what today might bring.

Lucy moves first, stepping toward me. A tablet comes into view, its glow cutting through the dim light.

On a screen, the message reads: Viktor's informer identified. A person is being forced to send dummy information to a contact in Viktor's organisation, who is believed to be a woman named Natasha. I will keep you updated - Dave.

"Compliance will not be optional. Otherwise, they're headed behind GSS, one-way, ticket," I say.

"This isn't a game you play and walk away from. Screw up, pay the price," replies Lucy.

"If the informer is still alive when we return, I'll kill the arsehole myself. The bastard is as responsible for Billy's death as the one who pulled the trigger."

The faint aroma of cooking fills the air, drawing the others toward the makeshift kitchen where Simon is busy preparing scran.

Derek's face hardens as he sits down with the laptop. Fingers glide over keys before the screen cast a faint light upward. "A message from GSS states there is a 90 per cent chance the relic is at the bunkers we recce'd yesterday."

Silence follows as the information sinks in. The implication sharpens the edges of the morning. Lucy breaks the pause.

"Viktor's crew will show up at the bunkers, no question. So might Boome Explorers, too."

Plates scraped clean, boots kick out dirt, and the briefing begins. "The decision's clear — a full recon of the bunkers, enemy positions, entry and exit routes. Any weak points flagged. A fallback route to the RV is a priority if the relic's size forces relocation; Simon's ATV can handle the situation," I say, after sipping my coffee.

"They will be ready," replies Simon

This time, we secure the perimeter. Twice now, Viktor's dogs have sniffed too close. This area must remain secure when we return. The last thing we need is for some nosey bastard poking around and leaving us a gift of their own."

The camp defences take shape with systematic accuracy. Simon kneels by the building's entrance, securing a tripwire across the doorframe to the detonator of a small IED. Invisible in the half-light. Patting the device before moving on to the next step.

Shadows settle against my back as I dig a shallow hole at the entrance of the storage shed. A square bit of wood lies nearby, rough and bare for now, but ready for war.

Five-inch nails line up along the surface, each one spaced with care. The hammer rises and falls with measured strikes. A rhythm builds as I hammer each nail into the board. The underside transforms into a nest of teeth, each point waiting for pressure.

I remove ammo from my pouch, the brass casings catching a faint glimmer. I place small springs into position over the nails, coiled steel ready to compress. The percussion caps of the round nestle inside against the sharp end of the nail, the tension balanced on a razor's edge. The setup isn't complicated; it's efficient.

A second board rests beside me, its corners punctured by sturdy nails. These anchors guide placement, aligning with the construction below — the top layer hovers, poised to collapse under pressure, free to move to ensure maximum impact.

The assembly lowers into the ground, fitting like a key into a lock. I carefully place a thin layer of dirt and debris across the surface, masking the device's presence. The ground's texture blends seamlessly, deceptive in innocence. Nothing hints at the violence beneath.

Every element answers to a singular command — destruction. Pressure slams the upper board downward with no resistance. Nails drive into percussion caps, and brass shells ignite in an unforgiving and absolute vertical eruption. Contact means detonation.

The trap breathes violence. Nothing ornamental. No excess. Just steel, wood, powder, and the cold certainty of outcome. A lesson carved into the earth: misstep once and vanish in the fire. Efficiency becomes the executioner.

Moving back, I clear my exit path, the area stripped of any trace of presence. Twigs repositioned. Prints vanish under stones. Dirt settles without leaving an imprint. Nothing clings to the path. It's cleared and closed — ground seals over like flesh over a scar that never wanted to be unveiled.

The trap lies dormant, silent, yet alive with potential energy. Waiting without mercy, design flawless, purpose singular. A careless stride crosses the line. The trigger bites back without warning. The blast punches the lesson deep. The ground rewrites the boundary in shrapnel and silence.

Derek drops to one knee behind the RV, threading thin twine between anchor points — trees, rocks, broken roots. The lines stretch like veins just above the surface, each a silent tell-tale of infiltration.

Across the ground, twigs snap into place at pressure points, fragile enough to break under the softest step. The layout funnels movement, shaping choices without permission. Paths now don't belong to chance, but a perfect trap for those who trust silence.

Derek straightens, expression blank, posture tense. Trap set, ground ready. The ground now wears the trap like a memory — buried deep, never forgotten. No markers. No flair. Just pressure, primed to answer missteps. A thread. A foot. A consequence no medic can reverse.

Lucy crouches on one side of the RV, hands working fast, stretching vines across entry points — thin, silent, placed with care. Each one is pulled tight, tension balanced. A web of twigs ready to speak through the slightest touch.

Now, there is no safe route through for the uneducated. Every line forces contact. Movement means disturbance. One brush leaves a trail no eye trained in this craft would miss.

Twigs scatter across the floor, placed like bones in a ritual. Each one is aligned to snap clean and sharp under movement. One step, and the sound will cut through the RV like a shot being fired.

This system tracks movement signatures — heel pressure, gait variance, and timing. One rushed step signals adrenaline. One shuffle conveys a different story — hesitation, perhaps malice. The floor interprets what words cannot disguise.

Lucy shifts back. Eyes sweeping through angles like a laser guided through glass. Defences stretch across ground and canopy — not to strike but to capture, to warn. Surveillance lingers in stillness, cloaked by the illusion of emptiness.

Every crunch, drag, and shift will be logged. Misplace one step, and the entire perimeter activates — not loud but lethal in response.

Gravel compresses beneath George's boots, as stones are arranged with reason. Lines are drawn without ink. Intrusion rewrites into something structured, something deliberate. Lines cross at deliberate angles. The earth will whisper before steel speaks as natural debris becomes a signal.

Wind may hide breath, shadows may hide form, but the ground will not lie. George reads terrain like a map, then rewrites it for war. Each placement funnels intruders into a point of exposure near the entry points.

Veins of fractured stone carve the trail in patterns too deliberate to ignore. Each scatter conveys weight, speed, and timing. The route does not meander. But targets — alive, aware.

To a wandering eye, this is just earth — dry, broken, forgettable. But here, nothing is forgotten. Every footstep writes a name. Every scrape shouts a warning. The line between stealth and failure runs through this soil, waiting, watching, ready to speak.

Lucy's voice crackles over the comms, reporting that the tripwires threading along the other side of the camp are set. Markers will signal direction, complementing George's handiwork. Together, their defences turn the RV into a sentinel, alert to the slightest intrusion.

The RV's defences snap into place — laser grid taut, sound traps primed. The perimeter hardens, silent but ready. Bait wrapped in camouflage and consequence. Terrain woven with strategy. One step in, and it's game over.

Every crunch, every shift of weight, will betray the invader's intent. The defences are set, their silent warnings waiting to explode into action at the first sign of infiltration.

The rendezvous point becomes a monument to espionage, not just a camp but a fortress built from the ground up to defy anyone who might want to enter.

Each element of defence lies hidden in plain sight. Wires stretch invisible along entry points, triggering a symphony of destruction for the careless. Hand-dug pressure plates and improvised traps blend seamlessly into their surroundings.

Near the centre of the RV, our equipment is checked and rechecked. Magazines snap into place, blades slide into sheaths, their edges honed for the unspoken contingencies we all anticipate.

Daypacks bulge with essentials, water bottles, comms, and survival tools. Extra kit waits in a cache just beyond the perimeter, buried beneath a thin veil of disturbed earth on the outskirts of the camp.

George rises without a word, weapon slung tight across his back. Derek leans forward — zips closed, straps buckled, clasps snap shut like a sealed order. Lucy adjusts the earpiece with a flick, then locks into silence. No one speaks. Breathing syncs. Each inhale lands on a shared beat. No glances exchanged. Memory, not orders, sets the rhythm.

A Splashmap unfolds at my feet. My fingers trace the route, stopping at a point not far from the bunkers. "First objective is here," I say, pointing to the location marked in red. "About 500 metres from the target area. Once on location, we confirm their positions, routes, and numbers. No engagements unless necessary."

"Understood," George replies, tone clipped, ready for action.

"Normal formation on the way out," I add.

With everyone ready, I lead the team out of the RV. The Outback coils around us, wide and watching. Dry air carries a trace of iron — rain long gone — cut with the sting of eucalyptus hanging heavy between the trunks.

I take point, each step is measured, boots shifting dust over cracked red earth. Derek falls in behind, frame tight, breathing controlled, scanning for threats I might miss. Lucy watches the gaps between movement, eyes sharp, every muscle coiled beneath a calm exterior.

Simon drifts in behind Lucy, alert and tracking the high ground. George brings up the rear, eyes sweeping our six, the pressure of every footfall absorbed in silence.

A thin stream gurgles off to the right, the sound threading through the brush. Nature is breathing around us, masking movement, but only just.

A sound in the bush 100 metres away, close to a ridgeline, has me hitting the deck. My hand cuts the air, the signal sharp. Derek shifts closer. Lucy nods once. Simon and George adjust without a word. Bodies shift into concealment, the dense foliage swallowing figures.

Weapons press firm against frames, angles dividing the wilderness into interlocking fire zones ready to respond to the slightest provocation.

Branches shift above, scraping, brushing, and murmuring like breath through clenched teeth. Sound hovers — steady, unnatural, mimicking the stillness below. The ridge ahead offers two promises: shelter or contact. One angle conceals the advantage. Another holds death.

After a few minutes and no imminent threat, we move towards hidden cameras, placed days ago. They remain silent witnesses, their lenses fixed on the secrets that brought us here. Their recordings hold answers — answers we intend to extract.

Positioned close to the camera, ready to cover Derek, the trigger lingers beneath my fingertip. George moves to the high ground, eyes sweeping the ridge's crest. Lucy shifts left, her position commanding the stream's narrow curve, while Simon covers the way we came.

By the first camera, Derek crouches, hand reaching for the pack resting against a thigh, and retrieves a laptop. A square of camouflage netting mutes the faint glow of the screen. Fingers move across the keyboard, bringing the feeds to life. The first camera reveals the sunlight bouncing off the water's surface, the forest's reflection shifting with the current. Nothing stirs.

Derek scrubs the feedback of the second camera, frame by frame, then flicks two fingers — close, urgent, precise. Calling me over, "Five-man team. Armed. Pushing upstream," Derek whispers — just loud enough to carry only as far as needed.

"Timestamp. When did the patrol cross this point?" I whisper.

"Thirty minutes, give or take," Derek replies. "They're still in the area."

"Perfect," I mutter, a bitter edge creeping into my voice.

Remaining quiet, I navigate between cover, circling the team and moving with stealth through shadows to relay vital intel. Each footfall is adjusted to maintain balance without making a sound. The ground doesn't forgive clumsy — never has, never will.

Tension hangs in the silence, stretched taut between tree trunks and low underbrush. There are no echoes, no birds, just an oppressive stillness, thick like blood.

Bushes snag at my sleeves. Dust infiltrates every fold of my gear. Branches snap under no weight, only the pressure of the air. The earth registers every motion, and I ensure there is nothing for it to remember.

Light filters through the canopy in broken beams, gold slicing through bark and bone. Resin seeps from ancient wounds, its scent sharp enough to carve into my lungs.

My heartbeats align with my footfalls, the rhythm of war reverberating across the landscape. My muscles are disciplined; my joints are loose yet poised. The body instinctively knows what is necessary before the mind issues a command.

The silence is not comforting—it serves as a warning. I am attuned and prepared for whatever may come.

Moving off again, the Splashmap in my hand guides us along the edges of a dry creek bed snaking through the forest. The ground ahead narrows into a natural choke point, perfect for an ambush.

Fingers trace the route one last time before signals pass back down the line. The formation adjusts, spreading into a staggered arc. Each member slots into place, arcs of fire overlapping, areas of dead ground are covered, and every angle is accounted for.

Derek tracks behind me—close enough to cover, yet far enough to manoeuvre. Boots crush dry dirt. Pack shifts, the short antenna catching the light like a signal blade. Radio pulses faint through static—message thread alive, stitched into our movement. Left ear tuned to the op net, eyes locked on the scrub.

My left flank moves with determination—Lucy's silhouette aligned with the terrain. The undergrowth breaks under the scan, sliced into distinct zones. Movement meets the rifle before any thought catches up.

The muted glint of sunlight catches the telescopic scope for a fleeting second before Lucy adjusts. The treetops sway above, their rhythm steady and unthreatening.

Simon mirrors Lucy on the right, posture embodying readiness. Rifle sweeping the opposite flank, scanning for signs of intrusion— subtle disturbances in the natural order. Simon's stride matches Lucy's, deliberate and unhurried, steps a counterbalance to the tension that underpins the team's movements.

George holds the team's six, the anchor of the formation, covering the ground behind. Vigilance hangs heavy, the kind that ensures no corner of the terrain escapes scrutiny.

The trail curves ahead, ascending a gentle incline, the ridge's crest obscuring what lies beyond. Dark shadows cluster at the edge, reminding us how easy the Outback conceals secrets.

Kneeling below the ridge, I raise a clenched fist. Movement stops, and the team fades into the scrub. Rifles aligned, sectors claimed without a word.

Trees scatter across the open ground. Shadows stretch between trunks, each one a possible ambush. The landscape breathes uncertainty, every gap a question with no answer yet.

Moments later, the silence shatters — fur and power erupt from the shadows. A kangaroo spans the distance in three precise bursts of muscle. Dirt scatters beneath its feet, suspended in a haze, then sinks back down like a breath being released.

Derek props the laptop against a tree before removing it. Under the camouflage netting, its glow remains muted, and the faint hum is the only intrusion into the forest's natural orchestra.

The satellite image resolves into a valley below, where a dense bush interlocks like a fortress wall. In the centre of the picture, five figures materialise within the frame, their movement disciplined and deliberate.

Their movements align — measured and deliberate. Random turns angle toward the treeline. From the way they are moving, each figure spaced out, I would say they've done this before.

Derek shifts, the screen angling to catch the light just enough to sharpen the view. A hand glides across the image, tracing their course. "They're heading east. If their pace holds, a course correction would put us on a collision path," Derek whispers just loud enough for me to hear.

Signals ripple through the bush, silent commands passed through narrowed eyes and subtle shifts. The ridge ahead no longer stands as a barrier but becomes leverage. Height grants control. Lines converge. Arcs lock into place.

A cold readiness takes root. The formation reshapes in silence. Rifles cradle into shoulders, steel braced like a promise. Angles sharpen, interlocking like teeth. No dead ground remains. The terrain doesn't welcome; it disciplines.

Movement draws consequences. One false footfall turns stone into confession. Air presses down, thick with the kind of quiet that listens back.

My body drops low. Knees grind into dirt. Scope tracks the valley's curve. Shadows stretch long under the trees, but the details stay burned behind my mind — five armed men moving with intent. Their direction narrows options.

Caution. Pause. Time fractures across decision points. One wrong conclusion brings fire.

"Visual confirmed," Simon murmurs. "Two with AKs, one heavier. Might be a squad lead."

"Saw the same," Lucy adds. Their pattern's too clean. Not locals."

Derek's voice cuts low. "Interception route's shallow. We let them pass or set the net."

"No shots. Not yet," I say, the words sharp and final. "Let them pass. We track."

Trigger pressure eases but doesn't vanish. Sightline remains. One breath carries the fight forward or folds it inward. Distance holds, but not for long.

The intersection waits. Timing will demand blood or restraint. One misread shifts survival into loss. For now, the valley remains quiet. But not still. Never still.

After 20 minutes of watching and listening, we move off. Boots press into the dirt, trying to avoid loose rocks and branches, and any sound blends into the natural hum of the Outback.

The trail descends into a dry creek bed, the sandy bottom littered with animal tracks. Kangaroo prints crisscross in chaotic patterns, the occasional drag of a tail marking the ground. Lucy drops to one knee, studying the impressions. Simon shifts, rifle sweeping the contours of the surrounding brush.

The creek's edge rises, loose rocks shifting underfoot but holding firm. Heat intensifies. Sweat beads beneath layers of gear. Shadows shorten with the passing day, the forest breathing a slow, steady rhythm.

The Outback shifts under the wind, its movement subtle and almost scripted. We halt. Positions melt into terrain. Silence thickens, not from absence but from understanding. This place speaks in a code of pressure and stillness—those who are fluent move forward. The rest disappear.

"Simon," I murmur, nodding toward a stretch of disturbed brush. "What do you see?"

"Trail reads wrong," Simon replies, voice low. "From what I can tell, weight here. Pause there. Someone watched. Then backed out."

A trail marks the ground ahead. Broken branches lean at unnatural angles. Rocks lie scattered; not fallen, but placed. Too calculated. A message sent without words.

The forest hums with a threat not yet shown. Roots twist like veins through the earth, splitting the soil. Shadows gather at the base of trunks, pooling like dark water.

Overhead, the sky fractures through the canopy, shattered into shards. Silence cuts sharp, like a wire strung through leaves. No sound drifts without reason. Stillness crouches. Each breath of quiet drips with purpose. This ground does not warn. It waits.

A rustle of leaves draws attention to the left flank. Lucy shifts position, rifle angled toward the sound. The undergrowth sways as another kangaroo bursts into view, its movement abrupt and energetic. It bounds away into the thickets, leaving only a faint trail of bent grass. The team maintains focus, reading the moment as part of the larger symphony.

The forest whispers in the hum of insects and the creak of branches. The snap of a distant twig punctuates the stillness. The Outback doesn't offer reassurances. The quiet doesn't promise peace but demands vigilance. Hesitation costs lives; respect earns survival.

Hand signals ripple down the line — sharp, clipped, urgent. The path tightens. Trees press close, their bark almost brushing kit. Light cuts through uneven angles. Shadows drift like traps waiting to be sprung.

George maintains the rear, weapon sweeping in controlled arcs. Each shift covers angles left vulnerable as the team advances. Steps remain steady and deliberate, a metronome of focus anchoring the formation. Nothing moves in the distance except the sway of the canopy, patterns hypnotic but dangerous to follow.

The trail crests a slight rise, revealing a change in the terrain. The depression flattens into a clearing, the surface littered with fallen branches and scattered debris. I signal for a halt, prompting the team to fan out and secure the perimeter.

Lucy crouches near the clearing's edge, rifle steady as eyes trace the treeline. Simon moves toward the opposite side, taking a position that secures a clear line of sight. Derek lowers himself into the undergrowth. George holds a position at the rear.

The clearing speaks of past disruptions. A log lies, split near the centre. Jagged edges are worn but unnatural. Scattered leaves pile up on the deck, their arrangement disrupted by something recent. The forest here appears louder, the sounds of insects and birds amplifying as if filling the space left by human absence.

After confirming that the clearing is void of life, I signal the team to move back into the forest, forming a tight line as the clearing recedes into the distance.

The terrain shifts again, rising toward another ridge shrouded in thicker growth.

Sweat slips down my neck, caught beneath the collar. Focus holds firm. No glance wasted. That ridge line marks the next frame — could expose a route, or a threat.

The slope ahead tightens. Feet are placed with caution. Derek slips — stone shifts beneath tread. It's a short scrape, but loud in this silence. Lucy adjusts left, posture widening, sector stretched without command.

Simon blends into bark and leaf — silent, surgical. George anchors the rear, rifle slicing the path behind, eyes never still.

The ridge breaks without warning. There is no plateau — just a drop and a view. Trees roll across uneven, dense, and angled ground. The creek carves through, shining, then loses direction, becoming directionless.

Around the river, nothing stirs — yet the bush tightens like a breath held.

I am about to say, 'Derek, check where that five-man patrol is now', when movement stirs in the distance, a flock of birds erupts from the canopy, their flight sharp and erratic — signs of interference that demand answers.

Their flight carries faint hints of a presence and blurs the natural and deliberate lines. All ears strain for the faint crunch of movement. Eyes scan for the smallest shift in shadows. The ground becomes a map, every detail offering a clue to the unseen hand behind the disruption.

After a few minutes, I stand up and move down the slope toward the disturbance, with the rest falling behind me. Just as I reach the bottom, a crack from a rifle splits the air. Dirt kicks up inches from Derek's boots, followed by another sharp crack of incoming fire. The enemy patrol wasted no time revealing their intent.

Instinct strikes. I surge forward, rifle locked, arcs narrowing across exposed dirt. No hesitation. No pause. Flesh and steel merge. Every motion born from drills. Every breath edged with purpose. The rhythm finds me—cold, precise.

"Left, now!" my voice cuts through rising chaos.

Simon disappears into the brush. Lucy follows. George holds the ridge. A single crack from above—George speaks through his trigger. One person down.

Derek crashes behind jagged stone. Rifle set before dust settles. No words. Only motion. A shared glance locks the rhythm. His rifle mirrors mine—ready.

Rifle fire splits the canopy. Falling splinters rake my face as I drop behind timber, heartbeat spiking. Sweat creeps behind the eyes. Every sound matters. Every second shrinks.

"Three centre. Closing," Derek yells. Calm. Focused. No panic in the voice.

To my front, figures flicker through trees. Movements staggered. No discipline—only panic. I adjust. A burst from my rifle cuts through brush. One person falls. Another bolts.

"Simon—cut right!" A second later, Simon's rifle answers. Bark explodes.

"Lucy, cover rear!"

"On it!" Then, quieter—"Let's not let anyone else sneak up and introduce themselves."

The terrain ahead grows more difficult. Brush brushes against the equipment. Derek shifts left. Displaced rocks scatter the path. Broken branches litter the ground. The signs are too recent. A hasty trail shows itself.

Movement — someone breaks cover. My aim sharpens. I squeeze the trigger. The target collapses. A swift drop. No sound. No fight.

Lucy fires one round. No need for a follow-up. Precision triumphs over panic.

"Eyes left! Movement!" Simon yells, tone sharp, clipped. Always scanning.

I turn. Fire. The rifle recoils, and a shadow drops mid-step.

George's voice cuts in over the radio. "Topside clear. Four down. No runners. And no autographs."

Panic engulfs our attackers as they navigate the tangled brush. Footsteps pound the dirt. Their sense of direction blurs, and instinct abandons them.

"They're breaking," I mutter, already moving forward.

Arcs of fire overlap. Breath unifies. Movement flows like water. The field contracts.

"Push the line," I say — every step measured. Every shot is delivered with purpose.

Formation becomes more organised. Shots hit their targets. Territory is regained. The battle relies on instinct rather than conscious thought.

Lucy weaves between roots, her rifle slicing air. Her barrel halts, then fixes. The direction is chosen, and the target is waiting.

Simon swings left. Flank opens. Muzzle leads. Every step is a trap. The enemy just hasn't figured that out yet.

Derek secures himself behind the moss-covered bark. Barrel blocking the corridor of death, leaving no room for escape. No confirmation is necessary.

"Contact, north-east!" George yells from 100 metres away.

The crack of my rifle flies through the air. One person drops, silence filling the space where the man once stood.

Rounds scream past. Dirt erupts. Another person sprints through cover. George fires again—the woman is dead before the stride finishes.

"Flank right!" Lucy fires. Another body folds.

Derek moves up. Kneels. Three rounds. One chest caves. One target erased.

"Left side thinning," Simon calls, eyes tracking the gaps.

"Hold the line," my voice anchors the moment.

Near a tree, something flashes in my sight. I shoot. The target twirls and falls. Derek moves to the right with a single burst of fire.

George anchors high. "Crest clear. Still the fucking worst view I've ever had."

Then—steel glints. One person charges at me. Rifle slung. Knife drawn. His blade swings wide, and he stumbles. As he does, I pivot hard. The trigger squeezed—my round cracks bone. The body falls, hitting the deck—blood pools. Another life ends.

"Nice catch," Derek grunts, somewhere behind the cover.

"Stay focused!" I yell.

Another makes for the creek. The crosshairs from George's rifle sight find their target. A single round leaves the chamber. The man drops—a perfect shot from the team sniper.

"Two more!" Simon shouts, tone tighter now.

I hear the crack and thump from Simon's rifle as a life is ended. "Last one's pinned!" I yell back.

Lucy shifts her position and fires her shot, slicing through the air.

"Clear!" Simon calls.

Dust settles. Formation shattered. Will broken. Discipline outlasts fury. Every time.

George descends. Calm rests across his face, but the rifle never lowers.

Lucy wipes grit from a bleeding cheek. "Next time, maybe they'll bring biscuits."

Simon reloads. Brass clicks against stone. "Or bring something useful, like intel. Or a map."

Silence returns—not peace, just a pause. The Outback listens. The team moves.

The battlefield settles, the sharp edges of combat fading but not forgotten. The clash of gunfire and shouted orders hangs in the atmosphere, a grim reminder of how quick violence reshapes the moment.

Tension hums beneath the quiet, a current that refuses to dissipate. Weapons remain trained on possible angles of approach, arcs covered. The team holds steady, braced for a retaliation that might come.

Overhead, the canopy closes over blood and brass without a pause, no judgment, just bark and shadow reclaiming the ground. Trees don't mourn; the ground doesn't flinch. No trace lingers where the forest chooses to close in. Conflict ends. The terrain moves on without care.

This pause offers no comfort, only the demand to move forward. Victory here is a fragment of the larger mission, a brief interlude in the relentless drive toward the objective. The battlefield is silent, broken only by laboured breaths and the subtle rustle of shifting gear.

My orders cut through, sharp and direct, "We don't have time to stand around. Recce of the bunkers remains the objective. Search the bodies for any useful intel."

The team moves to check the bodies. Weapons and ammo pile beside the first corpse—standard-issue rifles, mismatched webbing, and a scattering of spent magazines. Derek kicks over bodies, checking pockets, but comes up empty. Simon rifles through packs, retrieving rations, a basic medical kit, and a half-empty water bottle.

Lucy crouches beside a corpse. Leather glints in the sunlight. Notebook—creased, stained, authentic. She flips through the pages: sketches, signals, grid markers. No fluff. Just intel. One outpost is positioned too close.

The body beneath Lucy shifts, a sudden groan pulling at a weapon lying on the floor within arm's reach. Without hesitation. Lucy's knife flashes, efficient and final, the blade drawing a crimson line across the man's throat. "He's dead now," says Lucy.

"Clean strike, Lucy. Let the wildlife sort the rest," I say. Blood pools near my boot. Flies arrive fast. "Anyone close will have caught the noise already. Stealth's off the table." My boot grinds a shell casing into the dirt beside the corpse.

Simon and Derek tend to the others, blade ensuring that no one else is doing an impression of a possum.

"Point well made, Steve." Simon's voice carries a grim satisfaction.

I open the notebook and flick through stained and torn pages. Names, symbols, and crude coordinates—every mark confirms the enemy's identity. Viktor sends amateurs. Sloppy kit, rushed drills, no plan. Just bodies pushed forward—meat tossed into gunfire.

Aligning the map with my own, I mark the outpost near our path on my map and slide the notebook into my pocket. From this point, the mission reshapes itself. This encounter changes things, and every decision must account for new variables.

Splitting the team opens the field. Control expands. Options multiply. Lucy, Derek, and I form one unit. Simon and George shadow right—50 metres, staggered advance. Two paths. One goal.

The gap between groups forms a blade—sharp, purposeful. One sweep triggers a flank—fire from two sides. Contact becomes lethal—every step is measured. Every angle is cleared.

Training guides the pace. Experience sharpens judgement. Arcs of fire remain clean. Each rifle covers a lane. Every movement reflects battles fought, survived, and learned.

The forest swallows light and sound, each step deeper, pulling us into something older than combat. A narrow path winds through trunks twisted by time, undergrowth thick and damp.

Branches fracture sunlight from above, scattering like evidence too perilous to leave intact. No ray of light lands unbroken, and no warmth penetrates. The air thickens in stillness. Territory speaks in silence—something stalks with patience honed to a point.

A sharp sound cuts through the Outback—quick, off-beat, wrong. The team halts. Rifles lift. Angles shift. Derek glides left. Lucy covers right. The path ahead sinks into shadow, with no line of sight, the only promise of concealment—and consequence.

No visual on Simon and George, just faint disruption—the crunch of weight over deadwood, the rustle of gear against branches. The parallel line holds. The forest closes around us. Branches twist inward. The ground narrows. No breeze. Just breath and heartbeat.

Unease knots in my spine. Stillness grips the canopy like a sniper waiting for a pulse. Calm doesn't settle, but crouches. Possible ambush hides between bark and shadow.

Mist drifts across the ground, not with sound but with something older than noise. Edges blur — shapes smear. Thought takes a back seat — instinct pulls ahead with teeth bared. Skin tightens. Something presses from above, from below, from everywhere at once. The terrain carries secrets. Roots lie. Ahead, something waits — and tracks.

Chapter Nineteen — Skirmish

The firefight fades into memory, a ghost of gunfire swallowed by the thick wall of bush. Silence creeps in fast—unnatural, sharp-edged. The trees tower around us, ancient and twisted, their bark peeling in brittle curls like old wounds. Each footfall on the leaf-strewn floor is too loud, too dangerous. The forest listens. And if it listens, it can betray.

A withered branch drags across my sleeve—dry, splintered fingers scraping skin. The air reeks of eucalyptus and dust, hot earth steeped in the Outback's unforgiving breath. Ahead, a thread-thin trail slices through the undergrowth, a narrow artery pulsing with risk. My hand drops to my weapon. This isn't over. Not by a long shot.

Derek's straps shift against the weight of gear, the sound brief but distinct in the quiet air—every footfall lands where intended.

The crunch of foliage signals Simon's position past Lucy, just beyond the shadow of towering trees. Movements cut through the terrain like a whisper, calculated and fluid, a skill born from countless hours navigating unforgiving environments without leaving a trace.

At the rear, George blends into the dimness, outlines that are just about distinguishable from the thick undergrowth. The rifle cuts deliberate arcs, slicing through the tangled brush with a precision that leaves no space for chance. Without a word, the intent is clear—order here is absolute, and disruption will end in blood.

A quiet breeze stirs in the treetops, masking the distant rustle of shifting grass. It's unnatural. It's too consistent, too rhythmic. Not the wind. I send a subtle hand gesture down the line. Behind me, the team tightens. Instincts honed by years of operating in hostile environments take over.

The forest appears to hold a single breath, an oppressive silence replacing the earlier hum of insects. However, the bend in the trail reveals nothing but an expanse of parched dirt.

Yet something is off. The terrain ahead bears faint scuff marks and irregular patterns pressed into the ground. Perhaps an IED or warning device of some kind.

Simon crouches beside me and points to a thin line that is just about visible and stretched taut across the trail. Primitive but effective. Following the cable, the tripwire enters a small cluster of dry brush.

"That needs disarming, but by doing so, we might alert anyone in the area to our presence," I say to Simon.

"Only if they come and check. According to the map and my planning, this track is one of our escape routes once we have the relic," comes the reply from Simon.

"OK, let's leave everything in place, but disconnect the business end."

"Excellent idea, as you're the lunatic that likes to play with this type of thing, Steve, off you pop."

I creep close to the ground, my belly pressing against the dirt, my breath slow. The hedge conceals what lies in waiting, nestled among roots, clay, and fractured stone. Wires protrude from the earth like veins beneath taut skin. A hum of tension resonates through each wire.

I reach the casing—rusted tin packed tight. Dirt clings to every seam. A pressure plate bulges beneath a film of grit, flanked by coiled wire and a crushed AA battery stripped clean. Classic field-built IED—quick to arm, cruel to disarm.

Sweat tracks my temple. I pinch the ignition lead and lift, slow and steady. My blade slips under the plate's corner. I hold my breath. One flick—wire severs. No click. No tremor. I'm still alive.

The second line crosses the cap fuse, buried deep in plastic wrap. A tripwire links a broken branch and a half-brick, weight sprung. I clamp it just past the tensioner. One snip. My pulse slows. There's no feedback. The device is cold.

Simon passes word back. Arcs lock across the sector. Eyes track the treeline. Fingers press triggers without pulling.

I start the crawl back. Then — movement across the track. A shadow splits from the scrub. Low, fast. My rifle lifts with me. Another threat comes hunting.

George, who's now moved up and is covering down the trail, rests the trigger beneath a finger as the scope aligns, framing the source of the disturbance.

"Spot anything?" I whisper.

"Thought I did," comes the reply from George.

The undergrowth brushes against me as I sink lower, scanning the terrain for any sign of movement. Satisfied with the silence, I signal for Derek to move up to my location by pointing and placing my hand on my head.

We have crossed tracks like this without being seen many times, so everyone understands the procedure. Derek moves first, taking giant leaps to minimise foot contact with the ground. He lands on one foot, twists around, and then takes another leap, and he's over. Once there, finds cover before signalling the all-clear.

With Derek in position, the treeline is scanned in both directions, ensuring the route remains clear. Using the same procedure, I cross, slipping into the undergrowth. A quick signal prompts the others to advance, one at a time.

Beyond the trail, the terrain shifts into chaos — uneven, littered with stones and gnarled roots that threaten to snap an ankle. Sparse patches of grass cling to existence between dense clusters of bush.

The bunkers' location is closer now, an unspoken presence drawing everyone forward. Our separation from the target remains calculated at 500 metres to minimise contact.

A flicker ahead halts progress. The shape cutting through the undergrowth is fleeting yet unmistakable. Instinct drops me to the deck, the team mirroring the action.

A ripple of faint shapes emerges from the bush. Their black uniforms fade into the terrain, stripped clean of markings, denying affiliation.

Their movement follows a rough formation, not chaotic but far from refined, betraying the cracks of inexperience. These aren't seasoned operators but contractors, likely brought in for their willingness to act without question, not their skill.

A figure steps forward, taller than the others, emerging from the group. Weathered lines mark a face shaped by years in hostile terrain, visible even through the thicket. The head turns in a slow arc, scanning for any sign of danger but failing to spot the figures hidden within arm's reach.

The ground shifts beneath deliberate steps, the sound breaking the stillness as the figure edges closer. Just five metres stretch between him and Lucy.

Lucy's form dissolves into the dense foliage, indistinguishable from the greenery. The crosshairs of my rifle rest on the man's chest, finger steady, waiting for the justification to pull the trigger.

A hand signal from Derek confirms no other contacts beyond the column. The message lands, quick and cold. Lucy turns to stone, shape moulding with the scrub, pulse buried beneath roots and dust.

Patrol drifts past, searchlight eyes blind to precision. The rifle slouches down one arm. The grip is slack, and the body is unwired. Eyes drift. Focus fades. Confidence spills across his spine like sweat — warm, useless. Arrogance drips from overconfidence, blind to how close death listens. The crunch of brittle leaves tears through the quiet, setting nerves alight with a promise of what might come.

Dust shifts as a boot stops a breath away from my outstretched hand, the movement abrupt yet unalarmed. An exhale escapes before a few muttered words drift toward another figure nearby. The cadence speaks of annoyance, the kind that follows minor inconveniences, not danger.

My breathing slows further, muscles coiled without a tremor, rifle held steady but ready to unleash hell if the wrong move happens. Another command, sharper this time, and the group begins to peel away, their presence dissolving back into the bush.

The lead figure pauses, head tilting toward the treeline. Fingers brush the weapon's strap slung across the body, a fleeting movement betraying unease. With a sharp turn back toward the group, boots crunch once more before vanishing into the thicket, leaving the air heavy with unspent adrenaline.

Stillness wraps around the bush like a damp cloth, stifling breath. Nothing stirs. Pressure builds. Simon taps twice—signal precise. George shifts three steps left, barrel steady. Lucy edges closer, expression unreadable, but the intensity behind her gaze leaves no doubt about the moment's gravity.

A steady gasp of air escapes my lungs in measured control as I slide out from cover. Derek gestures southward, hand cutting through the air, indicating a ridge offering concealment. The task remains critical—mapping potential exfiltration routes from the bunkers to the RV and ensuring a fallback plan leads to the pickup zone.

The dance with chaos continues, rhythm as relentless as the heat radiating through the ground. The viscous and alive forest wraps around us, shifting shadows under the muted light. Tracks cut a faded path through the earth, crisscrossing the route.

Simon marks the map beside me, strokes fast and direct. Every mark tightens the route—roads to the bunkers, lines back to the exfil. No wasted motion. Just structure, drawn clean through chaos.

Branches crack ahead—soft at first, then deliberate—the brush parts. Four figures emerge, half-swallowed by undergrowth. Not a patrol. They're too still. My gut knots before thought catches up.

Hand curls around the mic. "All callsigns, Tangos ahead. This reeks of an observation post." My whisper cuts through the net.

Lucy moves left, George drifts right. Their weapons are already up. There are no gaps, no questions. Their formation speaks a single truth—contact is expected, and will be managed.

Derek adjusts the radio dial, shifting the channel to connect with GSS. The static fades, replaced by a voice delivering intelligence drawn from intercepted communications.

Switching back, Derek speaks into the mic. "All callsigns, intel from GSS. They've picked up communication. Viktor got multiple teams operating in the region."

"S3, Roger, this confirms what we already suspected: the bunkers aren't their only concern," comes my reply.

Through my binoculars, I can see four figures locked in routine, confident but unaware. One sweeps the treeline with a thermal scope mounted tight on a tripod. Another checks a handset, head tilting to listen. No panic or chatter, just controlled movements.

The setup reeks of experience. Their posture, their gear—none of this feels improvised. Not militia. Not green. Each man pulled from the same doctrine we know too well.

A direct hit draws too much noise. Reinforcements might already be shifting on the perimeter, waiting for the bait to snap. But we need their intel.

The plan forms. Nothing fancy. No margin for error. "GD and LK," I whisper into the mic, "sniper positions — cover arcs. The rest follow my lead. Quiet and sharp."

"GD, Roger," comes George's reply.

Lucy also acknowledges, "LK, Roger, moving now."

George presses forward, navigating the uneven terrain, boots planting hard on the rocky incline. Lucy moves behind, vanishing into a dense thicket, their presence swallowed by the foliage.

Both take positions with clear views of the target, rifles locked and aligned. Hands move in silent coordination. Signals are exchanged without a sound as scopes track even the slightest movements in the distance. George's trigger finger hovers, the rifle steady, every muscle primed for when instant action becomes necessary.

Simon, Derek, and I shift forward, bodies low, breath anchored. Thorns tear at fabric, roots jut like bones through packed soil. The trees bunch tighter with every metre forward. Visibility narrows. Precision becomes survival. Every step risks exposure. Every step demands control.

The undergrowth thickens. Damp earth absorbs some sound, but twigs still threaten. One wrong footfall breaks everything. Movement slows. Muscles tighten. Discipline wins ground. The forest breathes above — broad branches stealing sky, shadowing intent with dense canopy.

Ahead, four men work, unaware. Focus fixed. One adjusts metal kit. A clink rings out. We freeze. Muscles locked. Lungs suspend. No alarm raised. Motion resumes. Target unaware. The net draws closer, silent, patient.

A brief scan of their equipment confirms their purpose. The radio rests near a log, the aerial pointed skyward. Pages fan across dirt, bunker maps inked with routes and notes. Their world is laid out in careless exposure. Every mark adds weight. Every line feeds our next move.

Derek flattens, motion fluid. A glance passes — no words. Just a purpose. A shared decision. Intelligence over casualties. The line is drawn. Execution must match intent.

Simon produces a compact boom mic recording device, preparing to capture audio from their transmissions. The signal feeds into our recorder. My pulse stays locked in rhythm. A twitch, a slip, and this whole quiet world burns.

The radio operator shifts closer to the radio, voice quiet but sharp, fragments of strategy spilling out in quick succession.

Another man moves to the imaging equipment, adjusting its position to align with the route leading to the bunker entrance. The precision in their actions suggests preparation, an unspoken readiness for contact — whether with us or someone else.

We stay motionless, holding back any trace of movement that might give us away for the next 20 minutes. Then it's time to leave and continue exploring the area.

The information we've gathered carries weight, and pushing further risks everything. Simon tucks the boom mic into a pouch. At the same time, Derek and I backtrack, inch by inch, until the distance between us and the OP grows again.

The withdrawal echoes the approach, silent, calculated, and fluid. Vegetation consumes both motion and sound, erasing any trace of our presence. Lucy steps back into formation with George, focused unbroken, scanning for signs of pursuit. The setup ahead remains undisturbed, and the operators are unaware that their position has been compromised.

We move away from the OP, heading back into the dense forest with George shifting to protect our six. We'd only moved about a hundred metres when George's foot lands on a dry branch, sending a sharp crack that breaks the stillness. The sound echoes through the trees, shattering the quiet like a gunshot—tension spikes in an instant. Everyone freezes mid-step.

A figure steps out from the undergrowth. Movements are deliberate and carry an edge of vigilance. The figure pauses, its gaze shifting across the terrain, tracking the source of the noise. George moves, shifting position and pulling his boot free to avoid detection.

The man's head turns, scanning the terrain, his gaze brushing too close to our cover. Layers of greenery distort shapes, and the interplay of light and dark hides the outline of crouched bodies.

The air grows tighter, pressing against the senses, as if the forest waits for another misstep to break the silence. A rifle rests across the man's right shoulder in a loose grip, the stance of someone more accustomed to calm than chaos.

The sharp press of a sole pins my hand to the ground, sending a searing shock through my body like an electric surge. The instinct to pull back fights against discipline, muscles rigid, jaw tightening to hold composure. The gaze above shifts, catching something unexpected, me.

Actions come without thought, a primal response honed by training. Momentum drives me upward, my frame exploding from the earth. An arm clamps around his neck, cutting off air. The man's eyes widen in shock, the initial resistance flailing but ineffective.

A guttural sound tears through the air, raw and unrestrained, breaking the quiet. The cry ricochets off the trees, carried deeper into the forest by the wind. The gravity of the moment tightens as the sound becomes a beacon, a signal destined to bring others closer.

The struggle erupts with ferocity, breath rasping as strength collides in close quarters. My hand moves fast, my knife meeting flesh with a wet, visceral sound. The form jerks, the fight evaporating in an instant before falling lifeless into the cover of tangled plants. A controlled breath steadies me, the adrenaline dulling the immediacy of the act.

Branches crackle in the distance, urgency rising with every second. Shapes emerge, fragmented by the dense foliage. Three figures charge through the trees, their approach marked by the chaotic energy of men caught off guard but ready to fight.

The forest becomes a battlefield, movements sharp and deliberate, each action driven by instinct. Lucy steps from the cover like a predator in their element. Her blade arcs clean, opening the throat of the nearest target. Crimson streaks cover the leaves, the contrast stark and violent. The rifle falls to the ground with a dull thud as the body crumples into the undergrowth.

Derek's rifle rises in a decisive arc, a trigger squeezed, a round puncturing the target's abdomen with lethal efficiency. The faint gasp is the only silent sound before the lifeless drops to the forest floor. Every motion speaks of discipline honed through countless moments like this.

Simon engages and launches at the third person—one hand clamps over the woman's mouth, smothering the instinctive shout. The blade follows, slipping between ribs with the precision of a surgeon. The woman convulses for a few seconds before Simon drags the lifeless body into the shadows.

The forest reclaims the silence, the echoes of the struggle fading as though the violence never happened. Everyone holds position; every sense sharpened, the moment stretching into a fog of uncertainty. The immediate threat lies neutralised, but the weight of the situation remains.

"Fuck, the observation post stays active, and the remaining man might already be reaching for the radio," I yell.

No time for finesse now. George and I break from the team, cutting a direct path through the undergrowth towards the OP.

Twigs snag gear, and the uneven terrain tries to slow progress, but the urgency overrides all else.

When we arrive, the operator is already hovering over the comms setup, intent carved into every motion, attention drawn to the equipment. The man's posture offers no awareness of anything beyond the immediate task, leaving his position vulnerable.

George shifts to the left, positioning himself to cover the makeshift entrance, rifle sweeping the immediate surroundings. My blade remains steady in my grip, the decision already made— this one stays alive, at least for now.

A quick hand signal from me sets the operation in motion as I bust through the OP. The man jerks upright, hand pausing inches above the radio handset. George bursts in.

The man stands and turns, trying to flee, movements jerky and desperate. A well-placed kick connects with the knee joint, folding the figure to the ground with a harsh impact. The weapon tumbles away, left abandoned and irrelevant.

My blade presses against the man's throat, the steel biting just enough to freeze any thought of resistance. Hands jerk upward, trembling, surrendering every ounce of control. Breath comes rapid and shallow, colliding with the static hum of the radio.

Words tumble out in a broken mix of curses, fragmented and empty. The tone betrays everything—a man already shattered, the will to fight eroding with every second.

George sweeps the OP. The small hide holds no surprises, just the equipment seen earlier. After checking the frequencies, used to communicate with whoever's on the other end, George's rifle slams into the comms setup, the butt slamming down hard on the handset. The crack of shattering plastic reverberates, the last vestige of their communication severed.

The collar pulls taut in my grip as I haul the body upright, the motion sharp and unforgiving. A weak shove pushes back, reflexive and futile. I push the blade's edge deeper into the throat, just enough to draw blood, which silences any further attempt at defiance.

Two black cable ties slide from my jacket pocket and loop around both wrists, pulled tight with a sharp snap. Next, the rough fabric of a hessian sack is pulled from the day pack and slipped over the man's head. Three more ties secure around the man's neck, cutting off any chance of escape. Muffled protests bubble through the sack, words breaking into unintelligible fragments of fear.

George shifts one boot behind the other — tight, exact, no wasted gesture. My hand clamps onto the captive's arm — flesh yields beneath my fingers. The captive jolts forward. Stumbles turn into compliance. Momentum teaches faster than threat.

The team waits in the designated fallback position, weapons ready. Their eyes — sharp and unyielding — snap to the prisoner as I shove him onto the ground.

"Got you a gift, Lucy," I say, a smirk tugging at the corner of my mouth. "He's in the mood for a chat."

Lucy moves closer, her posture calm but radiating a contained energy. Lowering herself to the prisoner's level, her voice cuts through the air with sharp, mocking precision.

"Relax, my friend," Lucy says, every syllable dripping with deliberate malice. "We're just getting to the fun part."

The captive stiffens, Lucy's tone cutting deeper than any blade. The woods remain silent, bearing witness as the man's will teeters on the edge. The human element, fragile and raw, hangs in the balance, a reminder that war isn't just fought with weapons but with the mind — and this one is already ours.

After an uneventful hour of trekking, the forest gives way to the dry expanse of the Outback, the brittle crunch of undergrowth underfoot. Aside from shallow breaths, the only sound is the local wildlife off in the distance. The RV lies ahead. We halt just short, not knowing if the location has been infiltrated.

"Stay here with this one, Simon," I say, pointing to the figure on the floor. "Strays an inch—lock the bastard down hard."

"Try anything, and I'll put a bullet in the side of that fucking head," says Simon, standing over the captive rifle, touching the man's forehead.

Once we are ready, the two groups peel off, moving with stealth through the terrain. George and Derek veer left, their boots leaving faint impressions in the dry soil. Lucy and I cut right, skirting the edge of a shallow ravine.

The camp is near, but the unnatural stillness pulls me up short. A single gesture halts Lucy mid-step. The sharp outline of a snapped twig embedded in a slight depression along the trail catches my eye. Nearby, branches bear faint scratches and bent leaves, subtle signs of recent movement.

The radio presses cold against my lips. "All callsigns, this is S3. We have movement. Approach with caution."

The advance resumes; moving in short bounds, Lucy covers as I move forward, rifle trained on the path ahead. Once I'm in position and covering, Lucy moves past me and takes up a kneeled firing position. Over to my left, George and Derek's figures flicker through the trees, mirroring our actions. This continues until we are inside the RV perimeter.

Out of nowhere, a rustle shifts to the right, and a faint breeze carries the sound of something retreating into the brush. Then, a burst of motion erupts from the shadows ahead.

A pack of wiry and feral dingoes burst from behind the largest building into the open, their movements erratic and frenzied. One is bolting straight toward Lucy and me, teeth bared in a snarl.

My weapon rises, the sights centring on the lead dingo. I take up the first pressure on the trigger. At the last moment, the animal veers off, vanishing into the forest beyond the camp.

The remaining buildings are cleared, and every corner and potential hiding spot is scrutinised. The RV sits abandoned, the emptiness an unsettling confirmation of the task ahead. Derek moves back toward Simon, the captive frozen under the steady presence of the weapon still trained on his head.

Simon delivers a precise kick to the man's side, causing the captive to flinch before being hauled up. With a forceful push, the prisoner staggers forward, steps unsteady and reluctant. Derek takes over, steering the reluctant figure.

Inside the doorway of the building housing the UTVs, the IED lies untouched. A simple wooden block wedges the mechanism, ensuring the top board can't be compressed. The work is quick but thorough. The tiniest oversight may kill the next person who enters, and complacency isn't an option.

The perimeter holds quiet. Cicadas fill the air with their steady buzz from deep in the brush. Lucy moves, rifle tracking every possible angle of approach from the surrounding trees. I kneel by the device, sliding the final component into the trigger, sensing the mechanism snap into readiness.

The IED sits snug between the building's structure and a hidden path leading into the camp. The device stays discreet but effective enough to maim or kill any intruder reckless enough to approach. One last check ensures it's secure before I signal the task is complete.

Simon and Derek emerge from the far side of the RV, firm grips steering the captive toward the central building. The prisoner's palms press flat against the rough brick surface, arms outstretched. Feet forced apart, planted two feet from the wall, causing an awkward stance that strains balance and endurance.

The sack covering the head absorbs the muffled grunts, though no authentic sound has escaped since the capture. Sweat spreads across the back of the shirt, dark lines revealing the toll of heat and nerves. Derek loops thick restraints around the wrists, securing them to a rusted hook embedded in the wall. Enough slack is left to keep both hands flat against the surface.

"It's a solid anchor. No way will that man be going anywhere," says Derek, ensuring the restraints will not slip before collecting everyone's radios.

The small devices are placed in a neat row on the folding table, their charge cables plugged into the solar-powered battery banks.

Since the team departed, the panels outside have been soaking up sunlight. Their efficiency is the only thing between us and a total comms blackout. Derek connects the last unit within seconds, ensuring every device gets charged.

George slides through the building doorway used to store equipment. Seconds pass. The sound of ammo tins being opened comes from inside before George steps back into view, a sack swinging from one hand.

Magazines tossed from George's sack hit the ground. Their edges glint like teeth in the dark. The magazines are distributed to the team. Each team member checks gear, loads pouches, and snaps ammunition into place. A few spare skids across the floor toward my boots.

A faint breeze shifts the dry air, carrying the faintest hint of dust and distant eucalyptus. Simon moves position again, pausing to glance toward the prisoner to ensure he hasn't moved. The man tied to the wall offers no movement apart from a head tilting an inch or two under the hessian sack, as if listening to the ambient sounds of the camp.

The tension in the man's stance mirrors that of the team. Everyone is aware this isn't over. Viktor's people are too well-organised to leave loose ends. A counterattack isn't a possibility; it's a probability.

Lucy positions herself by the radio set, face drawn with concentration. Bursts of encrypted chatter punctuate the static hum. GSS channels flicker with updates, though nothing substantial emerges.

The coming hours promise nothing but unrelenting focus, every moment brimming with the potential for a fight. The RV sits in a square formation of three buildings, enclosing a clearing at the centre. Traps laid earlier surround the approach, an advantage if we spot movement early. If not, the open ground might seal our fate, turning the space into a death trap.

Derek rechecks the restraints, ensuring no slack. Questions simmer beneath the surface — what this captive understands, how deep he's embedded in Viktor's network, and why he's here. The answers won't come easily, but the captive remains a potential asset if he still breathes.

For the next few hours, the team goes about admin tasks, and everyone keeps their voices to a minimum for two reasons. First, we can detect if anyone approaches via the defences already set out.

Second, to unsettle the captive, fracturing the sense of time and surroundings, every shift or attempt to move earns a forced return to the stress position, limbs shaking under the strain.

Not wanting him to die from exposure to the heat, I pick up a metal bucket and throw cold water over the man's body, a calculated reminder that survival is tied to cooperation. The interrogator waits, poised to extract answers when the moment is right.

Words fire off under the sack, scraped raw with panic. "Please — whatever you need. Just cut me loose."

Moving with inches of the man's ears, "Let's start simple. The name Billy — ring any bells? And what's your name?"

"Ivan. That's my name," the voice answers, sharp and direct. "Billy? Why, is Billy missing? Perhaps I can help track him down."

"One of you bastards killed Billy. So I might want to repay the gesture."

With that threat now deep in Ivan's mind, I throw another bucket of water over him and walk away to join the others standing on one side of the RV, drinking from water bottles.

When I arrive, Simon hands me a black mug of coffee, "Think our man is cooked and ready for a conversation with Lucy," I say.

"Think you're right. I'll set up inside," Lucy replies, pointing to the building in the centre of the RV where our prisoner is tied to the wall.

"While the rest of you are doing that, Derek and I will go and patrol around the base, in case some idiot thinks about creeping up on us," says Simon, putting a black mug back in his Bergen.

"Thanks, mate," comes my reply.

Once Simon and Derek are gone, Lucy moves off, heading to finish preparations for the interrogation. George and I coordinate the final steps to ensure Ivan is ready.

Inside, Lucy drags a table to the middle of the room and erects a makeshift chair on either side. Before removing all other distractions, Ivan may try to concentrate on avoiding answering questions. To complete the setup, Lucy places a strip of hessian over the window to limit the light coming in.

As I untie the captive from the wall, Lucy shouts, "Bring him in."

One arm locked in George's grip and the other clenched in mine, the body drags like dead weight. Boots scrape against the concrete. Breath rasps. Tremors run through muscles with every step deeper into the structure.

A chair waits across from Lucy — bare, unpadded, unforgiving. We force the man down. No resistance. No strength left. The sack comes off. Sweat clings to the skin. Eyes squint against the light.

Adjusting to the room, his gaze flickers across the unfamiliar setting before eyes land on the person sitting opposite. Lucy's smile appears before words can depart parched lips, and a water bottle and a chocolate bar slide across the table. But the hostage's hand stops mid-reach.

Fingers hover near the ration. Lucy delivers her opening words like a scalpel. "Eat. Drink. Stay breathing. Enemies waste time."

Silence cloaks the room, the thick, raw tension coating every surface like dust after a blast.

The tray is pushed back, hands firm, jaw locked. Words grind out, "No thanks."

Lucy's stare doesn't waver, nor does mine. The gesture speaks louder than any scream. Pride or fear — unclear. It doesn't matter. Message received.

Chocolate splits clean in Lucy's fingers. A bite follows, slow, certain — no effort to share again. Lucy's focus stays on the person sitting opposite, ensuring every movement is analysed. As the man's gaze falters downward, my hand grasps his hair, wrenching the head back with a sharp tug.

"Care to share information on Viktor's movements before things lean hard?" Lucy asks, voice smooth but sharp enough to cut the air.

Silence holds. One deliberate shake of the head cuts through — slow, methodical, carved from something harder than fear. Refusal hums in the air, daring someone to shatter it.

"Strange," I say, words flat as steel. "Outside, I couldn't stop you fucking talking."

My fist drives into Ivan's cheekbone, snapping the jaw to the left. Skin splits. Crimson blood sprays in a red arc across the table — bright, wet, real. Lip torn. Silence shattered. My message delivered.

Lucy, still playing the agreeable person, pretends to yell at me, "That's enough of that shit, Steve, don't fucking hit him again. He's our guest here. Take him out so we can discuss ethics."

Following Lucy's lead, "OK, grab the other arm, George, and let's take our friend for some fresh air," my tone sarcastic.

Back at the wall, arms are forced back as restraints bite into wrists. The coarse fabric of the hessian sack is yanked over Ivan's head, cutting off the surroundings.

A series of kicks sends him crumpling into the stress position, body shaking under the strain. In a quiet voice, I lean in, "That woman inside plays kind. I don't. Billy's blood tags your boots, and I don't forget names stitched in red."

As I walk away, George picks up the bucket and throws cold water over the man on the wall. "That's your alarm. Round two starts when you blink."

Thirty minutes pass before the captive is hauled back inside and pushed down hard into the chair across from Lucy.

"So, Ivan, I overheard you telling Steve your name earlier," Lucy asks, voice steady. "Ivan still fine? Or does a new name fit better?"

"Ivan is fine," comes the hesitant reply — a slight tremor to the voice.

"Excellent, Ivan. Where are you from? I'm from Reading."

A few seconds pass before Ivan speaks, "I'm from St Petersburg, Russia."

Lucy continues with the questions to build an understanding and persuade Ivan to trust her. "Do you have a family and children? I have three: Abbie, Bethanie, and Hadley."

"Yes, I have a wife and two daughters, Maria and Kira."

"I bet you would give anything to glance at their faces again. I can make this happen."

Ivan's voice breaks, words stumbling, "I can't... Viktor won't stop. My family—he'll kill us all if I talk." The fear seeps through every syllable, dragging words into fragmented pleas.

"Tell us what we want, or I'll kill the bastards myself," I yell, punching Ivan in the head again.

"If you can't act like a normal person, fuck off," Lucy yells at me. All of which is part of the plan.

"Let's try again. We have contacts in places that can make them vanish before Viktor senses the shift. All you have to do is provide us with the necessary information," Lucy continues.

George and Lucy lead Ivan outside, the sack already concealing his face. The wall waits as he is positioned with arms stretched and feet planted. Lucy steps back, walking with me out of range, while George stands guard, watching over the scene.

"Think Ivan will break and give up info or play martyr?" I say to Lucy.

"No question about it. Right now, he's running through every possible outcome, trying to decide which one might save him," Lucy says with a knowing look.

"Will leave the interrogation in your capable hands, Lucy."

A twang of the tell-tale snaps through the RV. Rifles rise out of instinct, bodies pivoting into firing positions as the team orients toward the noise. Silence stretches, shadows ripple through the bush, shifting beyond the treeline. Then the shape becomes clear — two figures moving in.

Seconds later, Simon and Derek step into the open, their silhouettes unmistakable. Weapons lower a fraction.

"Spot anything or anyone poking around that we need to deal with?" My question slices through the tension as Simon reaches the edge of the perimeter.

Simon's voice carries a trace of unease. "Nothing moving. Too clean for my liking. Derek intercepted some chatter — Viktor's crews splitting up into smaller teams. No sign of any patrols so far."

Derek's gaze cuts to the prisoner against the wall, restraints biting into the man's wrists, hanging from the hook embedded in the building.

The hessian sack covering Ivan's head rises with shallow breaths. "Did you find out anything useful from our friend, Steve?" says Derek, pointing at Ivan.

"Not yet. Lucy's close to getting what we need. Ivan hasn't given up much — just his name and mention of a family."

Emerging from the cover of a weathered structure, Lucy strides toward Ivan. Sharp clarity defines her movements. A glance passes between us, unspoken but absolute.

Lucy drops, knees bent in front of Ivan. One hand grips the rough edge of the hessian sack, fingers tightening around the frayed weave.

Ivan's body twitches — small and involuntary. A flinch born from fear, not pain. Control slips. Not lost yet, but close. Nerves betray the control he's fighting to maintain. The silence becomes a weapon; every breath dares to break.

Ivan's interrogation isn't just about information—it's about time. Viktor's patrols are moving, and the window to act is closing. Lucy leans closer to the prisoner, filling the small space with a weight that doesn't require words.

Ivan shifts against the wall, the restraints creaking under the pressure.

Lucy speaks, "Bring the arsehole back inside," tone firm, each word cutting through the air like a scalpel. Ivan's silence isn't built to prevail. The clock ticks, the team holds, and the storm Viktor's people edge nearer.

Across the table, Lucy's voice cuts clean. "Choose, Ivan. Saint Petersburg with your family—or a ditch in this desert?"

The air in the room thickens, silence pressing in from all sides. Lucy's palm strikes the table with force, the sound cutting through like a gunshot. Leaning forward, her face stops, shy of Ivan's sharp and unforgiving voice. "Answer the question! Do you want to walk out of here or die in this chair?"

Startled by Lucy's response, Ivan yells, "I want to live."

Lucy leans closer, pressing into Ivan's space. "Fine. Start talking, or that man behind you—who's itching for payback because you took out our friend—will end this right now."

The tremor in Ivan's voice betrays the desperation behind the question. "If I cooperate, do I walk away from this?"

Sitting down, Lucy responds, rifle laid across one knee, jaw tight enough to snap wire. She doesn't blink. Doesn't flinch. "I promised freedom. Promised safe ground. My word stands—no matter the fire we walk through."

Lucy waits a few seconds for the message to sink in before adding. "Ivan—where did the guards rotate last Tuesday?" A test. Answers are already on our table.

"Start with location. Where's Viktor anchored?" The drone feed pegged a rustbelt ruin. Metal shells, dust-blown. Dead mine, breathing purpose again.

After contemplating for a few seconds, Ivan replies, "The HQ is in an abandoned industrial site – it used to be a mine but has been shut for a long time. That's where Viktor runs things."

"See, it's not difficult. Comply, stay breathing. Start with the convoy route first, then the objective. Don't stall."

Ivan pauses for a few seconds. "Bait, not cargo. The route is designed to waste your time, mislead, and not deliver goods." Jaw clenched, Ivan adds, "The plan was simple: drive to a predetermined location, double back, and return to camp. Viktor's real push? Buried deeper. Radio transmission lies and false reports were planted to lure you in."

Derek whispers in my ear, "I thought the intel came too."

Whispering back, "I think you're right. Plus, this proves how ruthless Viktor is, if he sends people out knowing they will be killed."

Back at the table, Lucy leans forward, words razor-sharp. "Appreciate the answer. Let's step up the pressure. Does Viktor have any clue about the exact location of the relic? And just how many operatives have been scattered across Australia to locate the device?"

A pause stretches as Ivan considers the question, words slow to follow. "Before you arseholes extracted Petrov from Heinrichsberg, Petrov disclosed the potential location for the artefact to Viktor. As for numbers, about one hundred of us operate within Australia."

"Does Viktor have coordinates yet?" Lucy asks, lips tight. "If so, how fast before he goes for the relic?"

"I haven't a clue, but I'm guessing soon."

Lucy glances at me as if to ask me any more questions. I shake my head. Before turning back to Ivan, "Thanks for the answers. As I said, I will let you go; Simon, untie Ivan."

Simon moves towards Ivan and cuts the cable tie, which splits under pressure. The plastic gives way with a brittle snap.

The three of us step back, hands rising in unison. Silent and unmoving, our eyes locked, open palms facing the prisoner. No one speaks.

I monitor the room as Ivan rises like a corpse from the chair. Legs tremble, skin pulled tight over bone—face, blank but not calm—caught in that gap where thought fights muscle—perhaps asking himself the chance of walking out of here alive.

Glancing around the room at the team, everyone stands back, arms in the air, as Ivan's boot scrapes the concrete, moving toward the door.

Now, the door is within reach. Freedom waits beyond the frame, but the air is charged, warning of consequences that need no voice. Ivan turns back to check that we haven't moved. I raise my hands again, giving him hope.

Each of Ivan's steps punctuates the silence. No sound from leather or wood—something more profound. A weight clings to his frame: shame, fear, guilt—take your pick. The walk confesses what words won't.

Movement halts at the doorway, with one more step forward representing life. Pausing as if bracing for the blow, hoping it doesn't come.

Out of the corner of my eye, I spot George drawing a 9mm. An instant later, a sharp crack answers Ivan's unspoken question—one round tears through bone. Ivan's skull splits—blood fans across the doorway. The body drops hard—no twitch, no cry—just meat and blood on old timber.

Crimson spreads, soaking grain and dust—silence clings to the air, broken only when George's voice, flat, unflinching, says. "Lucy said you can leave. Not the rest of us."

Chapter Twenty — Sergei Jeopardises the Mission

Sergei breaks from the mine complex, vanishing into the wasteland beyond. The terrain ahead is merciless—raw, blistered earth that gives nothing back and buries mistakes without ceremony. No cover, no second chances. Just heat, dust, and the kind of silence that kills.

Two units sweep out behind me, disciplined, deliberate, every move choreographed to survive. But theory doesn't hold out here—this is a place where decisions bleed. The weight in my chest isn't my gear; it's command orders written in air-conditioned ignorance. Natasha's voice still echoes in my head—sharp, detached, oblivious to the grit grinding into my skin. She's not here. I am. And Sergei's already off-script.

The plan floats like paper in a storm, lacking grip and substance. Combat lives in blood, not ink. Observation breeds frustration. Restraint frays the edge of control, and I keep it wrapped tight.

A break slices through the terrain—bend ahead, hills crouched like beasts with bunkers buried in bone. Steel doors rest beneath dirt and shadow. A flicker along the treeline. The twitch of fabric. My hand tightens. That's not wind.

Movement spills from the brush. Sloppy, untrained. No cover. No angles. Legs are bent wrong. Weight shifts like a drunk in the dark. Desperation, not strategy. Informers warned of hunger, not skill. That truth gnaws at the edge of my control.

Patience fractures. My fist shoots up. The world snaps still. Boots freeze. Gravel silences. Fingers drift toward triggers. The wind stops mid-breath. Nature itself defers to the kill.

A burst splits the calm—flash, bark, scream. Muzzle flash lights up branches. Lead chews through bark. Rounds snap past. One body drops, twitching. No call, no mercy. This isn't theatre.

Return fire rips from the formation—disciplined, exact. Suppression pins target low. Branches shatter. Dirt lifts. Movement scatters.

No cover saves fools. Each step forward narrows the gap. My barrel swings with the rhythm of breath. Steel answers panic. This fight doesn't last long. Only the living count the seconds.

Natasha's directives fade into irrelevance, consumed by the urgent need for immediate engagement. Electronic warfare might fulfil a purpose, but only as a crutch for those reluctant to confront their enemy. Broome Explorers establish a loose perimeter around the bunkers, a barrier that begs to be dismantled.

The equation is simple: action removes uncertainty, while hesitation risks complications that Viktor will not permit. Decisiveness now prevents future chaos, cutting through potential threats before they gain ground.

The fist of my right hand snaps upward, freezing movement in an instant. Gravel falls silent beneath my boots, and the dense, ancient forest draws a sharp breath that holds.

Shadows ripple through the undergrowth, shifting with the faint breeze and twisting into shapes that trick the senses. The ground beneath appears alive, as though testing resolve, waiting for weakness to surface.

The group holds firm, tension rippling through bodies pressed into the earth. Straps creak under shifting weight, the sound cutting sharper than gunfire in the stillness. Every detail tightens around us—the dense, suffocating layers of trees and brush that trap sound and obscure sightlines. The forest becomes a labyrinth of possibilities, each with potential for catastrophe.

Barrels rise in unison, steel extensions of will, stocks firm against shoulders. Veins stretch against hands, gripping tight, the tension transferring to weapons that now carry intent. A single breath moves through the team, the rhythm syncing into focus.

The surroundings compress into a maze of indistinct forms, where lines blur between potential cover and concealed threats. Every step requires calculation, yet the silence reveals nothing, leaving only the sensation of something unseen lingering at the edges.

A flicker of movement draws my attention to the right. Pavel crouches, head tilting as though the ground itself is whispering secrets. Eyes narrow in concentration, dissecting faint outlines that ripple through the treeline.

A shift in posture reveals the silent calculus at play, thoughts sharpening into decisions. Glancing in my direction communicates commitment, a measured blend of readiness and restraint.

The forest presses harder, the silence oppressive, shadows deepening into a suffocating veil. Doubt does not enter the equation, but calculation sharpens every thought. The narrowing of focus brings clarity and tension, the weight of consequence perched on a knife's edge. Time slows, each second dragging as options narrow into the singular certainty of what must come next.

The decision is made without hesitation. Two fingers slice forward, the signal clear, passing through the group like a wave. Movements synchronise with the signal, bodies shifting into formation as the well-rehearsed mechanism of combat comes alive.

Years of trust weld the team into a single entity, each action flowing into the next. The forest, once chaotic, now bends to the discipline of the moment.

A crack breaks the calm, measured, not random. Brush shifts with intent. Not wind. Not an animal. Something waits. The path ahead bleeds tension. Dirt turns hostile. Shadows stretch long and sharp, wide enough to swallow a man whole.

"Hold."

My word grinds low. I raise a fist. The unit freezes mid-step. Barrels sweeping in slow arcs. Sights tracing treelines and hollows. Gravel forgets how to speak. Even the wind steps back.

My focus narrows to a point—readiness, wired into bone. Ahead, shadows refuse to sit still—every movement feels like a threat waiting to sharpen.

Triggers rest against fingers, breath timed with sights. Forest blurs into a canvas of threat. The calm doesn't last. Calm never lasts.

Another motion—too smooth, too placed. Shapes ripple behind the branches. Not nature. This breathes intent.

"Weapons up," I bark. "Eyes sharp."

The formation shifts. Pavel drifts left. Dmitry sweeps the rear. Each step rehearsed in sweat and broken ribs. Nothing here is by chance.

A figure drifts through the trees. Stance loose. Shoulders down. Not ready for what's about to occur. Not expecting a firefight. Perhaps a decoy. Or a mistake.

"There," I snap. "Flank. Push wide."

Grass splits under boots. Branches snap. The charge comes hard. Silent, precise. Fire answers fire. Flash and thunder crack through the trees. Lead hisses. Bark explodes. One scream rises, short and wet.

Return fire flails wide—panicked, undisciplined. No structure. No hope.

"Crush it!" my voice roars across the line. "No one walks out of here alive!"

The rhythm of the advance builds. Each step is driven by purpose. This forest no longer belongs to ghosts or shadows. Control is taken, not given. We've come to collect.

A flash of movement catches the edge of my vision—a figure dives behind rotted cover 100 metres out, dragging false confidence like a shield. Alone. Exposed. The forest holds no loyalty.

My fingers move—a subtle signal. Dmitry glides away, consumed by greenery. Silent, instant. Leaves separate around him like mist. A hunter steps into the labyrinth. The rhythm remains undisturbed.

Target shifts—missteps, incorrect tempo. Lacking awareness. A dead man in motion. Dmitry appears like a purposeful shadow, with a blade held low. Steel slips deep into the ribs—one gasp. No cry. Just the body, folding. Dmitry lowers the corpse without breath.

We press onward. The rhythm remains unchanged, the pulse steady. The forest closes in, and the path constricts. Danger lurks behind every tree, and we linger there too. The enemy observes us, just as we observe them. There's no advantage to be found—only instinct, only the determination to complete what we've begun.

Ahead, the trail diverges. I lift my hand. A hush descends. Boots are planted firmly. Weapons halt in mid-strike. My mind races, charting every potential outcome—flank, crossfire, collapse. Decisions weighed in blood—no opportunity for a second chance here.

The silent fractures—two shots, crisp and precise. Two targets collapse without ceremony. No alert. No time. Dust clouds swirl around the others, chaos seeking direction. Training forgotten.

A man lunges behind rusted equipment, screaming nonsense. It doesn't matter. My left flank opens fire. Precise. Calculated. Another drops, clutching a hole that wasn't there a second ago. Blood jets, then silence.

A runner breaks from the treeline—legs wild, feet dragging. A shot cracks through the air. One round ends the sprint. The body hits the earth. No glory. Just finality.

The remaining group assembles by the ribs of a dilapidated supply shed. The wood is splintered, and the walls have disappeared. Nothing remains to provide shelter, and options disappear. With each passing second, the gap narrows.

Boots grind against stone as I advance, rifle held tight. Steps measured. This is the only sound now. Fire boils behind my chest. This ends here. Resistance dies today.

Brush shifts. A head rises — wrong move. My finger squeezes the trigger. Three shots. All hit. No flinch. Just collapse.

The radio crackles to life, a cutting tone slicing through the static. "Sergei, this is Natasha. Status report."

My finger hovers over the radio's transmit button. The air still hums with the aftermath of gunfire, the acrid tang of spent rounds clinging to the breeze. The bunkers lie ahead, their secrets close. Natasha's transmission is a tether I resent, a reminder of orders I've already disobeyed.

A glance at my team confirms the operation's success. Only five of my men lay dead in the undergrowth. But at least some people from the Broome Explorers have been neutralised, their presence erased from the battlefield. The bunkers remain unscathed, their potential undiminished. My hand steadies on the transmitter, words delivered with the precision of a sniper's bullet, each syllable demanding focus.

"Area secure. Moving toward the objective."

I do not mention the ambush or acknowledge Natasha's strategy in my reply. The battle is mine to fight, and the decisions are mine to make.

Time is running short, and we still have much ground to cover, so after regrouping the men, we head back into the forest of the Outback.

A small stream carves through the dense brush, its banks bordered by thick vegetation, forming a natural trap. The men's movement slows as my silent hand signals shift the group into position, fanning out. The moment vibrates with the memory of earlier violence, an assumed warning stitched into every breath.

Shapes glide between the trunks, figures keeping down as their outlines melt into the forest's texture. Figures navigate with unhurried precision, spacing purposeful, suggesting an elite unit—might be Steve's group, by the precision of their pacing. Their progress is calculated, though our vantage point keeps us unnoticed.

The thought hits hard—ambush. It's not just a tactic; it's essential. The landscape unfolds like an open wound, pleading for violence. Natasha's self-control disintegrates into nothing. Screens cannot withstand this. Warnings belong behind desks, not here.

"Pavel, Dmitry—cut wide and wait for my mark," I growl.

Both nod once. No words needed. They move into position, low and sharp. Blades of grass bend to their rhythm, rifles drawn tight, eyes locked forward.

I draw the others in, crouched low, moving slow. Growth becomes denser around us, the forest enclosing us like a fist. Branches scrape against my coat. Old leaves crunch beneath my heel. There's no room for mistakes. Every sound counts.

Nature conceals better than any algorithm. Shadows extend outward. Wind obscures the sounds of breath. Every step is deliberate. A single misstep transforms shelter into graves. Accuracy maintains a steady rhythm.

Hand signals move along the line. One quick gesture resonates more than a shout. We approach quiet and unnoticed. The upper hand tilts in our favour, akin to a knife against the neck.

The patrol moves closer, oblivious and vulnerable. Their pace lacks urgency. They remain unaware of the hidden steel lurking in the trees, and for the moment, their false sense of security remains intact.

A figure shifts through the undergrowth, angling toward better cover, only to be pinned down by a sharp volley from the forward assault. The cover of a toppled tree becomes an unwilling sanctuary as the figure abandons the effort under the threat of precise fire.

A new sound splits the air, shouting, rough and frantic. Suppose this isn't Steve's team. Then it must be the Broome Explorers. Their presence complicates everything. An allegiance to GSS or a festering thirst for vengeance from the bunker skirmish drags them headlong into the escalating conflict.

A crackling volley erupts from an unexpected direction, carving through the undergrowth and splitting focus between the advancing line and those sweeping the flanks. My control starts to falter under the weight of this sudden offensive, scattering the momentum of the orchestrated attack.

To my right, one of my men goes down, the sharp crack of a rifle cutting through shouts of pain. The forest becomes a lethal chessboard, each piece moving to survive, kill, and gain ground. The attackers push forward with more aggression than the last bunch we encountered, using their numbers to close the gap between us.

The opposition's lines start to fracture under relentless pressure, gaps widening as coordinated precision dismantles their attempts to hold ground.

Then, several silhouettes break through the undergrowth ahead, fast and fluid, rifle firing in controlled bursts. The movement screams precision, the kind of aggression only Steve's team can deliver. Fuck, it appears we are fighting on two fronts and Steve and Broome Explorers have joined sides.

Moments later, a figure steadies behind a weathered boulder, calm and composed, sending rounds slicing through the chaos with the precision of a surgeon. Our intel was right, George's sniper hallmark is unmistakable, forcing my first group into retreat.

The forest, which once offered shelter and hiding, now ensnares us in a labyrinth of shifting shadows. Steve's team's strength becomes evident. Quick, decisive gestures resonate within the ranks, pushing the remnants of my group towards retreat. As we withdraw, the underbrush tightens around us. Each motion turns into a battle against an unforgiving terrain that seeks to overwhelm us.

As the retreat commences, movements are intentional, and discipline holds panic in check. Rounds pierce through the foliage, tearing leaves and fracturing branches, transforming the forest into a tempest of bark and metal. Controlled chaos prevails, with each crack and impact underscoring the stakes of failure. The advancing force remains relentless, fuelled by rage, their fire wild yet resolute.

A sudden explosion of fire erupts nearby, splinters cutting into my arm as I seek refuge. A sturdy tree trunk halts my fall, its bark digging into my back while I steady myself. The instinct to survive trumps the agony. Another loud crack reverberates overhead, causing debris to rain down, yet I stay grounded, planning my next action.

My formation stays solid, firmly positioned without any indication of progression. Their discipline adopts a defensive stance that changes only to attack when opportunities arise.

Controlled bursts cut through the disorder, compelling the Broome Explorers to make disjointed advances. Their untamed energy collides with the precision of Steve's trained strategy. The disparity in skill is clear, yet the Explorers' raw aggression pushes my unit further into the terrain.

Signals flow within my group, our hands moving like blades that slice through the fog of battle to maintain our connection. As one, we transform into more than just individuals — an indomitable force moulded by necessity and crafted in the heat of conflict.

Pavel moves to the right, manoeuvring through loose soil and thorny branches, a skill honed by experience and resilience. Meanwhile, gunfire echoes among the trees, with sharp cracks accompanying each step, as the enemy's shots remain erratic but constant.

A sudden motion slices through the thick underbrush. I raise my hand. Dmitry is the first to respond, turning as he fires twice in quick succession.

The shots vanish into the noise of combat, but the distant thud of a body collapsing confirms their mark. The line holds for a moment, but the fight's tempo shifts again, twisting like a predator circling prey.

The forest stretches deeper, with the undergrowth swallowing light and sound, offering concealment and peril in equal measure. The fight fragments, and the terrain becomes a foe, with every step a gamble against unseen risks. Thorny vines tangle and rip, while the relentless pursuit presses harder.

Steve's team doesn't falter. Their movements synchronise without effort, defensive positions shifting to counter every attempt at regrouping. The Broome Explorers advance, caught between their target and their desperation to overpower. Neither force bends.

My team splits further with every exchange, survival stripping away anything beyond the immediate.

The radio screams in my ear. It's Natasha. "Disengage, now!" Her voice is hard.

The retreat becomes clear. The only way ahead is survival. Our boots dig into the moist ground as shadows wrap around us, pulling us further into the forest.

Gunfire cracks through the canopy, chasing us like a relentless predator, closing the distance with every moment we falter.

The mission collapses in my mind, the ambush fails, and the fight unravels into survival. Every step forward burns with the cost of failure. Each move is an attempt to salvage something from the wreckage.

Regrouping turns into a heartbeat in my throat. There's no map, no orders — only the instinct's raw, brutal pull. The plan is shattered behind me, left forgotten amid the flames.

The forest becomes hostile. Roots twist like traps. Branches claw with intent. Movement slows and becomes deliberate. Each breath is measured, and each step is earned.

No time to think. Only action. Only survival. This battle has transformed — untamed now. Unscripted. Intimate. But it's not finished. Not while I still take a breath. Not while targets are still alive.

The hunt will continue. Steve's team and the Explorers will press on. Their precision and persistence cut through whatever remains of our defence.

*****

Radios hiss and spit inside the command post, the air thick with tension and heat. Natasha stands over the operations table, eyes locked on the chaos sprawled across the maps — patrol routes, fallback zones, contingency plans now fraying at the edges.

Tactical feeds flash in stuttering bursts — grainy visuals, broken signals — each fragment another nail in the coffin of Sergei's reckless move. Coordination's slipping fast, the elegant choreography of command collapsing under the weight of one man's ego.

Then his voice cuts through the static—ragged, staccato, tinged with panic. Sergei's losing it. The firefight's gone off the rails, and now Steve's team—reinforced by the Broome Explorers—are tearing through their lines like a blade through paper.

Natasha's hands remain still above the console. Making a wrong move now could jeopardise the entire operation, but delaying any further might pose an even greater risk.

The decision forms like ice-controlled chaos to buy time. I order radio frequency changes, a deliberate shift to ensure Derek, the communication expert on Steve's unit, can intercept the message.

Calm yet intentional, my voice cuts through the airwaves: "All teams, prepare for fallback. Reinforcements are sighted northwest of your position. Break contact and withdraw to secondary positions."

The transmission ends mid-thought, leaving just enough ambiguity to fracture their strategy. The objective is to disrupt their rhythm and force them to recalculate their moves. Any pause buys valuable time, shifting control of the battlefield.

The true challenge lies not in the enemy's advance but in Sergei's ability to follow orders that value precision over aggression. The disdain for subtlety is no secret. This retreat will push the limits of Sergei's self-control like no battlefield ever did before.

An aide arrives with new reports from the monitor banks. The aide remains silent; the papers speak for themselves—bodies in alleys, blood on walls. Sergei's people flee like rats.

The weight of the report presses into my palm. Twenty names. All loyal. All dead. The cost of pride—Sergei's pride—burns hotter than the flames rising on the screen.

No plan. No discipline. Just a muzzle flash in the dark and bones breaking without reason.

Heat rises behind my temples—slow, deliberate like fire creeping across dry wood. Orders shift. This ends now—no more names engraved into cold stone.

Viktor trusts me to maintain the balance. My task now is to cut the cancer before it spreads. Sergei made the first move; I'll make the last.

The opposition strengthens its hold, capitalising on the territory that Sergei neglected in his haste to act. This reckless initiative has become a double-edged sword, jeopardising the very foundation of the operation.

Commands pour out, branching through the ranks like arteries, feeding life into motion. The flanking squads pivot on a single signal, blocking vulnerable escape routes while Sergei's irritated tone snaps through the radio.

"Natasha, we hold! "The ground we give up becomes a route straight to our location!"

"Negative," I cut in, my tone firm. "The fight is lost. Break contact and withdraw back to the base perimeter."

The silence thickens as Sergei grapples with his internal struggle. Pride clashes with the reality of his mistake, a fissure in his façade growing with each passing moment he holds it in. The command centre radio blares, gunfire resounding over the line, a relentless rhythm of battle. Finally, a reluctant acknowledgement escapes him, his voice low and rough.

"Understood. Covering retreat and heading back."

Natasha monitors updated visuals showing units falling back and returning fire at calculated intervals. Sergei's irritation ripples through the airwaves, though control remains firm.

Sergei's tone hisses across the bandwidth. It's not chaos—at least, not yet. Brass rains down while dust rises. The assault halts mid-step, and those seconds elongate like silk just before a blade.

Reports from the perimeter indicate that the enemy's approach is becoming more deliberate and cautious. Steve's team is advancing closer, their coordination tightening as they sense the shift in momentum. The Broome Explorers fight with less precision but greater ferocity, their numbers filling gaps where training cannot.

Markers move—too quick, too near. Lines fade on the display. Signals gather like vultures over fresh prey. With one mistaken tap, the whole grid ignites. Opportunity entices, while catastrophe hides beneath every pulse of information.

Outside, Sergei sharpens his focus on the mine, driven by a reckless surge devoid of structure or signal discipline. Tension escalates as each recalibration tightens the line, straining it to the point of snapping. The relic must not succumb—not to chaos.

Plans break apart, reshape, and come together. Patterns form, fade, and rearrange. My hands move quicker than thought, building safeguards like solid barriers. Each layer represents a commitment—nothing reaches that artefact. Not as long as I am alive.

I remind myself that discipline is the foundation of combat, understanding when to attack and retreat. Sergei's reckless ambition has cost us more than just lives; it has given the enemy insight into our strategy, allowing them to encroach on our stronghold. However, the fight is not yet over. Thoughtful choices and strategic misdirection can rescue what hasty actions almost ruined.

Sergei moves ahead, his anger palpable in a glare that invites no discussion. A slight crackle signals confirmation, as the voice of the flanking unit relays the news of a successful extraction.

The mine provides no escape from the stifling air, with each breath filled with the dust of defeat and weariness. Sergei moves forward with determination, though the burden affects his stance.

Other men reflect Sergei's weariness, a procession from loss and survival. Sweat streaks through the grime on their faces, evidence of a retreat that seems more like a defeat.

The heavy clang of boots on steel flooring echoes through the base as men disperse without a word, leaving Sergei standing in the command room.

Monitors illuminate with maps, observing enemy movements and the few remaining members of Sergei's unit. Natasha's focus transitions from the flashing screens to Sergei's steadfast presence that commands the room.

Sergei remains silent, jaw tight, arms stiff. Pressure oozes through his skin like heat emanating from a buried wire. Once propelled by confidence, now immobilised — held captive by uncertainty. Anger lurks behind ribs, bitter and unproductive.

For several minutes, silence lingers between Natasha and Sergei, heavy with static and tension. Screens flicker, and the power hums. No one makes a move. I don't raise my voice. I don't need to.

"You ruined everything, Sergei," I say, contempt in my voice. "For what? Fame? Lives for your reputation?"

Sergei pivots, boots scraping against the concrete, breath tight with venom. "That ambush teetered on the brink of success — until those parasites stormed in. Sitting behind screens doesn't secure the ground. Blood does. Risk does. But that requires spine, not signals," Sergei replies.

"Better than drawing the enemy closer to our base and losing our people?" The steel in my tone halts any protest. "Inviting the enemy into striking range — genius? That choice relinquished hard-won positions. Precision holds greater importance than bravado. A retreat lures them out. That chaos drew us in.

Sergei plants both boots like anchors, chest forward, jaw locked. The air chokes with tension, but no reaction comes. No shift. No fear. Power hangs heavy, but still, Natasha stands untouched. That insults more than words.

"Your plans bleed theory, Natasha," spitting out the name like glass. Each syllable digs into Sergei's teeth. "Ink on a page solves nothing. Blood answers faster."

Rage pulses behind Sergei's eyes. "On the ground soaked with blood, strategy bends," he growls. "Maps don't scream when shrapnel flies. Plans don't crawl when lungs fill with dirt. Under fire, clean diagrams die fast."

Sergei's fist strikes the metal table, creating an echo that barks back like gunfire. "Combat doesn't wait for permission. Doesn't pause for approval. Movement wins. Hesitation kills. Act now or step aside."

"That stunt shattered the advantage we held. Now, Steve's unit breathes down our perimeter. No amount of deflection will shield this. Viktor will smash through excuses—and Viktor remembers failure," says Natasha, staring at Sergei.

Sharp lines define Sergei's face, embodying both conflict and determination. "Viktor evaluates the risks and makes the crucial move. This isn't just about survival—it's about triumph."

Fury boils within me, but I keep my voice level. "Discipline produces results—recklessness leads to failure, Sergei. Viktor gets that. This mission focuses on the relic, not personal grudges disguised as initiative. A sacrifice without a clear purpose is not a sacrifice; it's sabotage," I reply.

The clattering of boots on metal captures attention as Sergei strides toward the central console. A hand strikes the edge of the table, shaking the equipment with the impact.

"You think you're fucking better than me? Smarter? Think Viktor keeps you around because you're irreplaceable?" Each word strikes with purpose, cutting deeper than the words themselves, revealing layers of purpose crafted to unsettle and provoke.

Sergei's following words spill out like venom. "You're nothing, Natasha. Just another pawn in Viktor's game. Think you're fucking unique, but you're just here because Viktor owes your family."

"That's a fucking lie, Sergei, Viktor owes my family nothing," I reply, anger in my voice.

A pause lingers, the room constricting like a noose. "Your family is dead. Because I fucking killed both of your parents. On Viktor's orders."

The breath in my chest feels like a heavy stone, solid and unyielding. The tactical screens fade at the edges, and the room appears to shrink. Sergei steps back, observing and anticipating an explosion or outburst that never happens.

Control takes over, suppressing the fire clawing at the edges of my restraint, forged from willpower stronger than emotion. The words sting, but also lay bare vulnerabilities he doesn't realise he's exposed. Sergei and Viktor have played their hands, and now I understand where to strike.

My tone turns savage, calculated yet lethal. "Do you think that changes anything? This only confirms what we already understand. Power eclipses brotherhood. Trust is sacrificed for chaos. Loyalty dies beneath ego. What remains? Just wreckage and betrayal oozing through the dirt."

The grin flickers, exposing an almost imperceptible pause that disrupts Sergei's composure. The tension escalates, infused with a silent challenge as I approach the tactical displays, my attention steadfast. "Keep swinging at shadows, mistaking noise for dominance. That road ends in fire — alone, forgotten, erased. Power without control breeds collapse. Victory demands more than rage and impulse."

The tread of my boots reverberates, carving a trail through the heavy stillness as Sergei remains motionless, shackled by the gravity of this monumental fuckup.

Layers of tactics crystallise in my thoughts, threads of opportunity converging into a singular focus. Arrogance clouds vision, blinding him to fissures that threaten to shatter everything he's built. Every miscalculation contributes to a greater plan, honing the tools to dismantle Sergei's hold piece by piece.

But for now, the relic remains the priority. Adjustments to our plans are necessary, and Viktor's trust must not falter. Arrogance clouds Sergei's judgement, leaving vulnerabilities that nobody can yet understand.

The reckoning will be quick, designed to eliminate any uncertainty regarding the power of the misestimated force. When the blow strikes, its precision will penetrate deeper than any weapon, highlighting the grave error of underestimation.

*****

The air in Viktor's office hangs thick with silence, the kind that presses against your lungs and refuses to let go. A single bulb flickers above, casting jagged shadows across the cluttered desk — folders stacked like tombstones, each a testament to failure.

Satellite imagery, intercepted communications, and field reports all convey the same message: miscalculation, weakness, and sloppiness disguised as strategy.

I don't blink as the tablet in my hand glows cold and unforgiving. Line by line, it lays bare the truth — Sergei's reckless ambush, the firefight spiralling out of control, and Steve's team closing in fast, now reinforced by the Broome Explorers.

Every pixel on that screen represents a wound. Every failure poses a threat to everything we've built.

I shout, "Natasha, Sergei, get in here now." My voice resonates with anger. The door's metallic creak shatters the silence, accompanied by the sound of footsteps as they enter the room.

Sergei enters first, posture demanding attention, while Natasha trails behind, her gaze steady and focused, exuding unspoken authority.

Sergei's stride cuts through the stillness — shoulders locked, chin high, daring the room to flinch first. Opposite, Natasha remains poised. Spine straight. Composure sharpened into a threat in waiting.

I slam the tablet against the desk with a sharp crack. Both of their heads snap toward me. "Do either of you understand the magnitude of what you've done?"

My voice cuts through the tense atmosphere like a sharp blade, leaving no space for doubt or debate. "One ambush, one firefight, and now Steve's team gains control — tracking us, perhaps even closing in on the relic. The losses bleed deeper than personnel. The exposure threatens the entire mission."

A measured stride shifts Sergei closer, the jaw betraying restraint. "Timing dictated survival. Their line fractured — disjointed, exposed. That strike broke encirclement before it sealed. Delay would have guaranteed the relic entombed in steel," Sergei says, no repose in his expression.

"Vulnerable?" My word breaks the silence "That so-called fucking ambush fell apart the moment they drew you in. What appeared fractured — designed. That bait pulled aggression straight into a trap. Reckless execution handed over momentum. Now they dictate the tempo," I scream at Sergei.

Natasha makes a slight movement, maintaining her composure. Sergei's rash decisions jeopardised the mission. The adversary took advantage of the disorder. A more calculated strategy would have enabled us to track their actions and respond with accuracy.

"Wars turn on momentum," Sergei growls, voice laced with the weight of held-back fury. "Not on pause. Not on planning. On movement. Relentless. Unforgiving. One breath missed, one second wasted — those cracks open the door. Chaos waits, fangs bared. A moment lost would've bled us out. Vulnerable. Exposed. Dead before thought formed," Sergei responds.

"Advantage?" My fist slams onto the desk, rattling the piles of reports. "You don't understand the meaning of the word. Action without strategy is suicide. And yet here we are, burying men because of your inability, Sergei, to think past the next fucking bullet."

Sergei steps forward, fists clenched, voice snapping like a whip. "And Natasha's strategy — staring at monitors while blood spills outside? War isn't won through signals and silence. Delay gives the enemy ground. Hesitation kills faster than a bullet."

Natasha's voice remains steady, the calm counter to Sergei's storm. "That stunt didn't break the line — it relinquished positions. Maps burned. Men buried. Charging without intel exposed soft flanks like an open wound. That wasn't bravery, but failure masquerading as an uncontrolled force."

Natasha places a collection of images and intelligence reports on the table, their contents undeniable and laden with accusation. "Patterns revealed gaps. Movement shouted exposure. Patience would have torn that front apart, clean and surgical. Instead, impulse seized the initiative. Personnel absent. Advantage wasted. All exchanged for noise and ego."

A charged silence settles over the space, thick with unspoken challenges. Sergei fixes an unrelenting stare on Natasha, a wordless assault that dares her to falter.

My attention shifts between the two, decoding the clash of intent in the charged stillness. "Enough." My word detonates — sharp, final. Silence grips the room like a blade pressed to a throat. "This mission demands results, not pride, not posturing. The relic

365

determines everything. Ambition dragged this operation into chaos. Time lost. Men buried. Secrecy shattered. Aggression accomplished one thing — exposure."

I turn to Natasha, allowing a moment of hesitation before speaking. "And you. Your intelligence and surveillance should have detected Sergei's movements." My fury pours slow, controlled. "This fuckup carries more than one signature. Missteps are matched by absence. This is your failure, Natasha, as much as Sergei's."

Natasha and Sergei remain silent, their tension heavy as smoke. "Natasha will take the lead on all planning and execution moving forward. Sergei, you will follow her orders. This isn't a suggestion. It's an order," I say, leaving no room for comeback.

Resentment snakes across Sergei's jawline, a flicker of muscle betraying the turmoil churning beneath a brittle mask. Control slips, and the scent of fear leaks through any thought of defiance.

Natasha doesn't blink. A stillness that feels like the pause before a blade sinks deep. A flicker — almost imperceptible — a quiet triumph veiled behind calculation.

"Plans evolve. Natasha, merge data with Sergei's strengths. Moving forward, focus on coordination. A single mistake could jeopardise everything," I say, gesturing for them both to leave my office.

The door shuts behind them, leaving only the reports strewn across the desk and the pressure of my decisions. Sergei's hostility lingers like a toxin, contrasting with Natasha's steadfast resolve.

Their fragile dynamic teeters on the edge of disaster, a single misstep from unravelling everything. The relic is within reach, but the margin for error narrows with every moment the enemy gains ground.

Chapter Twenty-One — Uncovering Clues

Ammo's restocked, water sealed tight, and every piece of gear double-checked—we're ready, but the air says otherwise. Pages lie scattered across the table, corners stained and curling under the weight of half-drunk mugs and urgency.

Lucy and Derek scan intel reports with sniper precision—eyes narrowed, words clipped, fingers moving fast over lines of data that might hold the thread we need to pull.

Simon and George step in, boots heavy on the floor, the room shifting as we close ranks. We crowd the table, shadows from a narrow window slicing across maps, photos, and handwritten notes. No one speaks. They're waiting for what Nancy told me just after the skirmish with Viktor's people before we pulled back to the RV. I take a breath, because what she said changes everything.

"According to Nancy, who appears to be leading the Broome Explorers, the bunkers are empty," I say, cutting straight to the point. "No relic, no weapons. Just disused barracks and storage. Either we're too late, or we've been looking in the wrong place."

A slow breath escapes Lucy, gaze fixed on the charts. George shifts, arms braced, silent yet attentive.

I continue, "Viktor's people wouldn't be here without a reason. That means something is still worth finding, but it's not in the bunkers."

Derek leans in, "Did Nancy say anything about what they're after and why?"

"They're working for the Australian government. The relic is a piece of local history, something buried and forgotten. The Explorers aren't a combat unit. They're archaeologists. Word is widespread about Viktor's no-nonsense approach, which leaves no room for hesitation when eliminating threats," I reply, scanning the team.

"As we know, anyone who stands in Viktor's way doesn't walk away unscathed. So, to even the odds, they've turned to hired hands. Mercenaries — trained killers gambling on a payday that might cost more than they bargained for."

"Why not let another crew do the heavy lifting. We move when they falter," says Simon.

"Because Viktor's listening," I say. "Nancy and I agreed — no transmissions. If we start feeding intel over open radio channels, we risk giving Viktor an advantage."

This new intelligence shifts the dynamics, but the goal remains unchanged. Viktor's after the same target, and now we're aware we're not the only ones with eyes on the objective.

Derek angles the tablet toward the group. The map displayed is dense with layered data — satellite imagery, historical overlays, and markers highlighted in red.

"GSS and Petrov ran a second pass over the records, cross-referencing everything with newer intel. Three positions stand out, but this one — " fingertip taps the screen, pausing over a marked point near the northern edge of the region, " — matches classified World War Two documents detailing a secure installation. It's not just an equipment stash or barracks. Deep within the ground, something sleeps, forgotten and sealed away for a reason," Derek says, adding to the briefing.

Lucy traces a finger across the map, linking points. "Fits too well to be a coincidence. Whatever's buried, someone wanted it to stay that way."

The discussion shifts to logistics. Satellite and lidar imagery show anomalies — irregular formations that indicate artificial interference. "The location isn't far from the bunkers, about a kilometre, but distance means nothing in terrain like this." With a marker, I mark the area on the Splashmap.

"One thing, Steve, the RV's been left alone too many times in my book. To date, we have been lucky. Nobody came across the equipment. Suggest we move the ATVs and stores. Conceal the stuff in the woodland to the rear of the RV."

"Makes sense, Simon," I reply.

Once the briefing is finished and the gear is packed away, the ATVs roll away from the RV, their engines humming as they move towards a sunken patch 100 metres away in the rough terrain.

Once on location, the motors are cut, and the silence swallows the last echo. The ground dips just enough to break the outline of the vehicles, offering natural concealment.

The battery charging units settle against the base of a fallen tree, their bulk hidden underneath the rising undergrowth, leaving the half-concealed solar panels still able to absorb sunlight and charge our gear.

Simon hauls the camo net over the vehicles, securing the edges while Derek and George weave branches through the gaps, layering irregular patterns. The Outback doesn't ask questions— but blends in and lets things disappear.

The ground offers no second chances. Dry earth packs tightly beneath the boots, a surface that betrays every movement to the trained eye. The stash is hidden, but this isn't secure. A well-placed boot and a curious hand, and everything changes.

A stretch of narrow terrain near an access point draws my attention. Hard-packed dirt, with just enough clearance for an approach, makes the location perfect for a tripwire. The fishing line unspools from the pack, stretching taut from one side of the track to the other.

The trap merges with twisted roots and scattered debris, hiding every trace. A thread-thin glint betrays the device, hidden so well that only trained instincts will catch the deception before the trigger.

Across the path, an empty compo sausage tin, courtesy of Simon's breakfast, finds a new purpose. Wedged into the undergrowth, half-buried, waiting. A grenade slots inside the can, and the line attached to the grenade, the metal casing of the can holds the safety mechanism firm.

The pin remains intact for now, a safeguard until the site is ready to be abandoned. A single tug and the world erupts. Another zone calls for the same treatment, another layer of defence beneath the illusion of untouched ground.

Loose foliage scatters over the final device, the roots above masking its presence. Any shift in weight or pressure against the wire, and the silence will end in fire and shrapnel. No warnings or second chances.

The traps are prepared. If anyone finds where the equipment is hidden, they won't live to tell the story.

Positioning herself at the perimeter, Lucy settles into place, weapon held, gaze locked on the terrain ahead. George checks the net, ensuring no unnatural gaps in the camouflaged layer. The team doesn't speak. This is routine.

A final check reveals that everything is secure. The gear stays hidden beneath tangled roots and dry earth, shielded by layers of nature and violence.

A final check ensures that every trap is armed, and every angle is covered. A careful tug pulls the safety pin free. The grenade nestled deep inside the tin: no chances, no room for error, just cold precision in the setup.

Metal pins slide into my pocket. Each is a decision—retrieval if fortune allows and detonation if miscalculation intervenes. One fuck up, and the area erupts in a firestorm.

Ground disturbance tells a quiet story — intentional placement, lethal patience, and an IED set without mercy that an untrained will miss. Some stall — questioning light, angles, tricks of terrain. That pause writes a name on a slab before the shot even breaks.

With the site prepared, we move back towards the RV, rifles settling into positions, barrels angled to any potential threat. Everyone advances, boots pressing into the damp earth, senses stretched, nerves wound tight.

Back at the RV, Splashmaps are stored. Documents disappear into waterproof pouches, insulated from the elements. Nothing valuable will stay in the RV when we leave for the recce. The site will leave no trace, leverage, or advantage to the enemy.

Rifles rest against a makeshift bench, straps secured, bolts verified, and magazines in place. No weapon is left unattended. Each glance is followed by another, reflecting the team's persistent vigilance. Gear is meant to serve; failure arises from assumptions, not malfunctions.

A pack opens, sealing electronic devices inside insulated pouches. Signals are muted, and data is secured. Derek deftly manages comms, ensuring no transmissions, vulnerabilities, or loose ends to pursue.

George drifts along the perimeter, rifle-ready. Movements are slow, deliberate, designed to scan, not to be seen. The rhythm of security never wavers. Stillness does not exist here.

Half an hour later, Simon emerges from the building. "Scrans up," in a voice that can only be detected in the RV.

I move in beside Simon, assessing the placement with a glance. "Just what we need. My favourite army chuck-in."

"Thanks, Steve. Water for coffee is over in the pot." Simon points to a flask on the floor.

At that moment, the rest join us and grab a plate of scran and a brew. Metal scrapes on metal as mess tins fill with chuck-in, black plastic mugs are cradled, and the scent of compo rations clings to the air as the day's weight settles in.

A slow stretch, muscles unwinding as bodies adjust to the brief reprieve. Steam rises from the hot brews, the heat cutting through the cool bite of the Outback. Conversations drift from tactics to something else — something distant from the battlefield.

Lucy shifts against her Bergen. "What's everyone doing with their share of the dosh? I found a place near home on the Isle of Wight. My share of the money from the job, combined with Steve's, covers the cost." Lucy's voice carries something rare, something close to reality.

Derek leans back, fingers drumming on one knee. "Dumping mine into my bar on St Bethanie. It needs more than a fresh coat of paint."

Simon lifts a mug, steam curling past the rim. "A cruise. Long overdue. Wife's been dropping hints for years."

George exhales a short chuckle, shifting his grip on the mess tin. "Camper van. Ample enough for the dogs this time. No more kennels."

My boots grind against gravel as Lucy passes me a fresh brew. "Being a coward, whatever Lucy wants to do with the money," the words come without thought, a smirk twitching at the edge of my mouth before I turn toward the perimeter.

"The best way, Steve. Avoids arguments, and to be honest, who wouldn't be scared of Lucy," George says, laughing.

The laughter lingers for a few minutes, the moment extending just enough to remind everyone of something beyond the mission.

As the night draws in, we each rotate onto sentry, pacing the boundary of the RV, weapons cradled, eyes fixed on the horizon. The breeze changes direction, bringing with it something hidden that challenges instincts refined over the years. In the dim light, shadows contort and elongate across the uneven terrain.

I'm on stag again as the night drags on. I cup my hand over my wristwatch to protect the glow of the dial and check the time. It's 02:45. As I stare into the distance, the Outback breathes in slow, rhythmic pulses, the wind shifting between the trees, whispering across the dry earth. Brief bursts of insect calls rise and fall, then swallowed by the quiet, the land embracing the darkness with an unbroken calm.

Then, at 03:00, something changes.

A sharp and sudden shift in the air and a movement about 200 metres away make the hairs on my arm stand up. The rifle stiffens in my grip, rising and falling to match my controlled breaths.

As I gaze upon the open ground, the night encroaches, wrapping around me like a predator waiting for the perfect moment to strike.

I kneel in a firing position close to the corner of the rough concrete building, which digs into my shoulder. I peer through the night vision scope, cutting through the void with an eerie green glow.

Something moves.

The rifle steadies, its crosshairs sweeping the topography. There is no precise shape or definite target, just the mass of something unseen.

Then, the air shifts direction. Dry stalks rustle, trading secrets with the stillness. Every one of my muscles lock, waiting for the telltale sign—movement, sound, the flash of something unnatural against the organic sprawl of the land.

Nothing.

Barrel steady, the sightline holds firm. While the Outback glares back, vacant and mute, something lingers beneath the quiet—a presence, either gone or still waiting in the undergrowth.

The situation eases, but the terrain unknowns remain, refusing to reveal if something or someone is watching or if the mind is playing tricks.

I resume patrolling around the camp, breaking the silence with the faintest crunch of dirt under my feet. Each step sounds like an IED going off in my ears, as I try to stay silent and move with stealth. The report will wait for a shift change.

At 04:00, Simon emerges from the shadows. Rifle ready for action—a brief exchange—all facts, no speculation. "Something moved. No shape, no confirmation. Might be nothing," I report.

Simon nods, no assumptions. Boots pressing into the dry earth as he moves into position, gaze fixed on the Outback. The darkness remains still, offering no further intrusions before dawn.

Twenty-six minutes into Simon's stag, the first hint of light edges against the horizon, casting a faint glow over the camp. The wake-up is scheduled for 05:15; this comes with urgency in this field. With no time to shake off sleep and no room for slow reactions, every second demands focus.

Simon glances at his wristwatch. The dial reads 04:45. Enough time to prepare something hot before kicking their last arses out of bed. Nothing beats something warm down your throat.

Inside the building, the kettle rests on the gas stove, rattling slightly from the heat. Steam spirals from the spout, swirling in the dim light, blending the scent of burning fuel with the air. Another burner is tucked behind a pile of rubble for cover and holds a pan where compo sausages, bacon grill, and beans bubble to life.

George steps into view in the doorway, weapon slung and eyes scanning the perimeter. "Getting a brew on, donkey walloper," says George, holding a black mug.

"Anything for you, fatboy, and if you're lucky, I'll let you polish the mess tins."

"Fuck off, you streak of piss. Appreciate the brew, though. Need something strong before we move." George exhales, propping the rifle against the wall.

"Are the rest up?"

"Not yet, mate. You can go and kick everyone out of their pits if you like—right after I finish my tea," George replies, cradling the plastic mug like it's the last decent thing in the world.

"Cheers, that will save me a job."

Outside the building, stillness clings to the camp, the horizon stretching into the unknown, with nothing shifting beyond the perimeter but the Outback, which remains silent and indifferent. Nothing stirs except for the usual rustle of nature, waiting, watching, and holding its breath before a storm.

After putting down the empty mug, George stretches once before stepping into the open air. Mission clear—wake the team. Derek is the first person to be woken up, with a shove and the words,

"Hands off cocks, on with socks."

Derek scrambles from his maggot, one hand gripping a 9mm. Sleep fades fast, instincts kicking in before the head clears the sleeping bag.

One by one, everybody rises from their pits, the familiar creak of equipment breaking the morning air. Weapons are brought up, fingers sliding over triggers, and eyes narrow, scanning the surroundings for any hint of danger.

Everyone shifts. Their senses are alert, attuned to each crackle of the underbrush, every distant sound that may signal a threat.

Everyone moves towards the building at the centre of the RV, the walls offering a little comfort in the otherwise harsh landscape.

The promise of breakfast ahead is the only thing breaking focus, a small reward in the grim morning routine.

"Anyone spot anything unusual last night?" I say after eating a Compo sausage and a slice of bacon grill. "I thought I detected something moving a few hundred metres from the perimeter, but it turned out to be nothing."

"Nope, all quiet on my stag," comes a reply from Lucy. The rest shake their heads.

After finishing the meal, the remaining kit that isn't needed for the recce is concealed in the hide, hidden under layers of scrub and loose rock. The RV is stripped of all signs of life, ensuring nothing remains that could jeopardise it or our plans.

The RV is secured with reinforced entrances and monitored access points. The spring-loaded IED is placed near the entry of the building used for storing batteries and vehicles. If anyone forces their way inside, only a mess of bleeding flesh will remain for scavengers.

The sky clings to the final breath of night. The horizon is emblazoned in slate-grey strokes. The team moves out with unwavering determination. Shadows stretch across the Outback, twisting through dry underbrush and rugged rock formations.

Derek advances, weapon sweeping the terrain, eyes cutting through the landscape. One ear stays tuned to the radio, fingers flexing over the grip. Lucy trails close behind him, angles of fire adjusting with the terrain, scanning every blind spot.

Simon moves behind Lucy, GPS tracking the route against the land ahead. The bearing remains on course, each waypoint lining up. George covers the team's six rifle firm, focusing on the path and the unknown to the rear.

The Outback vibrates with hidden dangers, its silence weighing heavy like a restrained breath. The wind weaves among the trees, stirring dry leaves and displacing the dust that adheres to the parched ground. The patrol advances, steady and measured, disappearing into the morning haze.

The arid and unyielding ground shifts beneath our boots, cracking under the weight of the recce. An incline ahead offers a natural vantage point. Stopping short, we pause just before the ridge, ensuring we don't skyline ourselves.

I signal to Derek to move left, while Lucy and Simon head right. In the meantime, George stays put, rifle directed at the barren ground beyond the ridge.

I survey the landscape. Every angle is scrutinised through the scope. Other than the wind rustling dry leaves, there is no movement. The second sweep verifies the first — nothing. The terrain remains vacant and still, concealing countless secrets.

With the area cleared, we begin our descent down the other side. Loose rocks crumble underfoot, grinding together with each careful step downward. Boots press into the shifting dust as balance shifts in preparation for the next step.

Distant peaks come into focus with the first rays of morning light. Beneath layers of sand, a hidden structure lies in wait, shrouded in secrecy and overshadowed by forgotten conflict.

The valley unfolds before us, scarred and defiant. Rock and scrub cascade down the slope, carved deep by age and silence. Trees bend under weight, twisted forms engaged in a standoff with the wind. Something waits — not seen but felt.

Footing becomes unreliable. Each step over loose stones demands focus. Nothing shifts by chance. Rifles raised, shoulders braced, eyes scanning. Breath slows. The wind moves wrong — too cold, too fast. A message, carried from something waiting ahead.

Stone outcrops tear across the ridge, shapes sharp enough to cut. Nothing flows naturally. My fist rises, and all movement dies. I drop behind cover, pulse steady. My eyes sweep the skyline for any shape that doesn't belong.

The Splashmap unfolds across the gravel. My finger presses against the contoured lines.

"This sector needs clearing. No shadows left standing."

"Agreed," Lucy mutters, scanning the data on her screen. The display shifts, refining the location with a calculated tap.

"After yesterday's ambush, nothing gets overlooked. George, Derek — set overwatch while the rest push forward and search."

"Understood," George replies, turning left with Derek and hiding behind a rocky outcrop. Both rifles aim at possible threats, fingers hovering over cold triggers. The terrain narrows into a funnel, making any approaching danger visible.

Lucy moves with caution, while Simon follows her lead, both aware of subtle changes in the landscape; the sun-bleached rocks that emerge from the ground, their fractured edges shaped by constant heat. As the wind sweeps through, it stirs up loose grit, displacing dust over a surface that remains unchanged by time.

My first sweep reveals nothing but barren stone and twisted scrub. No footprints, discarded gear, or indications of recent movement.

On the second pass, something catches my eye — roots draped over rock looking unnatural, the soil beneath sagging.

My hands press into the stone, searching for weaknesses. Dust coats my fingers as they move through the cracks. Vines pull free under pressure, snapping back with resistance. Beneath the roots, a hardened ridge reveals itself — out of place and far too precise.

I look at Lucy, then at Simon. A single nod confirms it. This line wasn't formed by time; it was sculpted by tools. Here lies hidden intent.

"Someone wanted this unnoticed," I mutter, voice low, more to myself than the team.

A void yawns open as more debris clears. A metal door slouches in the frame, rust streaking the surface. The edges are too clean, and the cuts are deliberate.

Air slithers from the dark — a breath long held. Stale, dry, untouched. The silence grips tighter.

I crouch, eyes sweeping the ground. "No tracks. Not even a stray scuff."

Simon steps closer. "Whoever sealed this… didn't plan to come back."

I nod once. "Which means we need to move with caution."

Derek's voice crackles through the comms. "S3, this is DR, traffic on the track. Two vehicles, military profile. Moving slow, over."

"S3, Roger, keep everything under observation. We've found something and are going in, over."

"DR, understood, out."

Lucy moves closer, weapon steady, scrutinising the entryway with a slight adjustment. There is no evidence of new footprints, and the dust remains undisturbed.

A sharp snap breaks the glow stick, activating its dull orange light as Simon hurls it through the entrance. The vivid orange stands out against the surrounding darkness, creating a captivating contrast.

The orange glow dances over the jagged rocks, writhing before disappearing as darkness consumes the final remnants of light. Ahead, a steep ramp slopes down into the passageway.

Jagged edges absorb the scant light that penetrates this section of the complex, swallowing every fragment of illumination. Precision-made cuts define the tunnel, with steel girders secured in position and rust seeping into the cracked surfaces like exposed wounds.

Derek's voice crackles through the comms. "All callsigns, this is DR. Traffic is still moving, slow. One klick out. No deviation yet."

"S3, if movement shifts our way, push the message through. Keep updates constant. The second they advance, report. Out."

As we start our descent, I take the lead. Our rifles are primed in case we run into an unexpected visitor who might have discovered an alternate entry.

The tunnel curves, leading deeper. The walls press inward, the silence suffocating. Each step lands firm, boots brushing against the dust of a forgotten era.

Glow sticks pulsate with a sickly orange hue, their light casting shadows over the damp stone and corroded metal, while humidity clings to the skin, infused with the odour of decaying wood, rusted iron, and water trapped in hidden pockets.

Soft noises echo in the vast space, punctuated by purposeful footsteps crunching on the uneven debris scattered across the ground.

Wooden containers stretch along the walls, their edges dulled by dust. Decay gnaws through splintered planks and corroded hinges. Faint symbols cling to worn panels, military stencils just about visible beneath layers of grime and time's relentless hand.

Simon pushes the steel through the deformed slats, twisting until the lid breaks loose with a sharp crack. A heavy gust of air escapes, bringing with it the pungent stench of decaying rubber and stale mould.

A respirator droops in the corner, lenses fogged, and the rubber cracked where time's taken hold. Fine powder adheres to the brittle material, shifting as Simon's hand glides over the delicate form.

Wooden slats from another crate collapse under pressure, the top fracturing with a sharp snap before caving inwards. Spent casings tumble forward, their surfaces corroded by oxidation, ammunition long since ceased to serve any purpose. Military harnesses lie undisturbed beneath the rounds, their fabric stiffened by decades of exposure and decay.

Turning on her red torch, the light bounces off the fractured walls, illuminating rusted fixtures and neglected equipment. "This isn't just storage," Lucy mutters, "It's a secret locked away, waiting for the right moment to surface."

A metal desk stands near the far wall, covered in curled papers with edges that are browned and brittle. One paper sits apart, sealed in plastic, untouched by the damp.

As Lucy turns the pages, inked coordinates reveal themselves beneath a gloved finger. Intrigue grows when a symbol, resembling the one Petrov discovered, is seared into the weathered sheet.

A dull creak echoes through the cavern, distant and unnatural. Dust shifts from the ceiling, tiny particles catching the glow stick's eerie light.

Something moves just beyond sight, invisible yet unmistakable. The silence grows threatening, signalling imminent danger.

At that moment, the radio crackles again. George's voice cuts through. "S3 this is GD, DR spotted something through the rifle's scope. Appears to be another way in further down the valley."

"DR, this is TS. Any info on the two vehicles, over?"

"GD, yes, vehicles turned off the track close to where DR spotted the entrance."

"S3, Roger. out"

As we move off, a near-silent click echoes through the chamber, followed by a sharp crack that ricochets through the chamber, too precise to be accidental, placed with lethal intent.

Lucy halts mid-step, a boot hovering above an almost invisible strand stretched taut between corroded anchors.

One shift in pressure or one slight miscalculation could cause the entire structure to collapse in a wave of fire.

A millisecond becomes a lifetime.

My fist grips the fabric of Lucy's jacket. A sharp yank pulls her backwards, away from the tripwire, with a force born of instinct, muscles reacting before thought can catch up. The momentum carries us both into the cover of rough stone, boots scraping against the rock as we slam into the alcove's edge.

The wire tenses and then snaps.

A soft click reverberates against the walls, a murmur in the darkness that hints at death. The air constricts, clinging to the skin, a mute countdown that allows no space for contemplation. A flash materialises, a brief moment of illumination.

The explosion erupts, releasing a monster within the tunnel's depths. Pressure blasts outward, a ruthless force compressing the air and transforming the tunnel into a weapon. Flames rush forward, engulfing the ground in moments, incinerating fabric, tearing at exposed skin, and stifling every frantic breath for air.

The walls seem to scream, rock and metal splintering into lethal fragments. Energy surges through the passage, crashing against the unyielding rock and forcing the blast into a constricting funnel of devastation.

A raw force rebounds, cutting through space and turning the enclosed chamber into an armed pressure vessel.

A deafening rupture tears through the chamber, sending vibrations deep into bone, shredding stability, and twisting balance into chaos. A crushing force seizes the ribs, locking muscles and driving air from the lungs in a brutal vice.

Twisted fragments rip through the air, cutting fast and lethal, slicing clean through anything caught in the blast radius.

A dense cloud billows outward, mixing with pulverised rock and broken steel, turning the tunnel into a suffocating void.

The acrid bite of scorched metal coats the tongue—thick, sour, like rust ground into ash. Heat drills into my chest. Every breath scrapes raw down the throat, my lungs dragging smoke where air should live.

Stone shifts beneath my body, rough edges grinding against my skin. A vacuum robs the space of sound and breath. The world compresses. Smoke curls into every recess, heavy and choking. Light dies in the haze.

Glow sticks flicker, scattered like fading stars. Their weak glow disappears into the swirling fog, consumed by smoke dense enough to cloud the mind. Shadows extend in every direction—some genuine, some imagined.

A low groan rolls from above. Steel bends, a sickening grind of fatigue resonates. Dust falls like ash. Every breath tastes of failure waiting to collapse in.

"Status!" my voice breaks through the noise, sharper than intended.

A cough answers from behind. Then Simon's rasp, "Still breathing. Mostly."

George slides closer, face a smudge of grit. "Tunnel's unstable. We wait; we bury ourselves."

No argument there.

Hands grasp the weapon first—familiar weight, scratched but intact. Elbows scream as I rise, ribs protesting with every inch. The body obeys because failure leaves no alternative.

"Lucy?" I call, forcing the name through a throat full of dust.

A flash of movement—her silhouette cuts through the smoke. Rifle raised. Nods once.

We regroup without words. Just pressure. Just presence.

The blast wasn't random. That charge had a purpose. Direction.

"Trap," Simon mutters, low and cold.

"Yeah," I reply. "And we just stepped straight into it."

Stone shifts again. Another groan from above.

Upon hearing the explosion, George and Derek sprint in from their OP, weapons raised, expecting to find bodies rather than survivors. Fractured stone shifts as the cavernous walls strain under the force, with cracks splintering outward and debris tumbling in erratic bursts.

Their shouts tear through the chaos, cutting through the aftermath, searching for confirmation of life amidst the wreckage.

"Steve!"

"Lucy! Simon!"

Stillness clings to the space, the aftermath holding everything locked in the grip of deafening static. A scuff of rubber grinds against broken stone, movement stirring beyond the splintered wreckage. Shouts tear through the thick haze, edged with urgency, slicing through the stagnant air like a blade.

Dust clings to tattered gear, the air thick with the acrid tang of explosives. Figures emerge from the devastation, shoulders braced, boots dragging through debris. Blood streaks through grime, and shrapnel cuts trace thin red lines over exposed skin.

Lucy pushes forward first, hand gripping the wall for support. Simon follows, steps unsteady, muscles burning from the blast's concussive force.

George crouches by the wreckage, his eyes scanning the tunnel's depths for anything unusual. There could be another device waiting to go off.

Vivid contrast pierces the atmosphere at the tunnel's exit, creating a portal between ruin and the expansive land ahead. Heat emanates from broken walls, accompanied by fumes carrying the distinct scent of melted iron and charred synthetic materials.

The team staggers into the open, regrouping beneath the ridgeline's cover.

Gloved hands run over equipment, fingers pressing against injured ribs and shredded fabric. There are no fractures or deep wounds—only burns, cuts, and the weight of a battle that might have ended within that tomb.

Derek exhales hard, "I thought we would be dragging bodies out." The words carry no exaggeration, just the truth of what almost happened.

Simon flexes his hands, adjusting the grip on the rifle. "So did we just fuckup?" No space for anything except fact. Survival cut close this time.

George turns toward the ridgeline, listening past the wind shifting through the trees. "That trap wasn't forgotten. Someone wanted the device found." The meaning settles deep, heavy in the silence that follows.

"I'm guessing someone planted that explosion to serve a purpose beyond destruction. A clear statement — turn back or face something far worse. The relic wasn't just hidden, but protected. Whoever set the charge didn't want survivors," says Lucy, pointing to the pack on the ground.

"Nothing about this is a coincidence. A deliberate design ensures this site will stay hidden forever," I say, shaking dust free from my kit.

Cracked earth shifts beneath Derek's feet, the ground still echoing with remnants of violent disruption. "That tunnel never stood empty. The enemy never retreated. Never planned to. Remaining unseen in the black," Derek adds.

"Yep, this place is designed to keep the relic out of anyone's hands. Whoever set this trap made sure no witnesses would remain alive," I say, taking a slow drag of oxygen into my lungs that scours raw tissue, burning from the strain of the blast.

Grit grinds through my throat, coating the inside like ground glass, turning each swallow into a struggle.

The bunker isn't just forgotten history. It's still in play.

After taking another breath of fresh, clean air, I ask, "Did anyone grab any documents, maps, or photos?"

Lucy replies, pulling a pile of papers from inside her jacket, "I managed to snatch a handful."

Chapter Twenty-Two — Military Facility

Tension thrums through the RV like a live wire. We crowd the central room, each of us wound tight, senses honed, eyes locked on the Splashmap stretched across the table. The fabric is creased and stained, the scars of past ops etched into every fold.

Red-filtered torchlight slashes through the gloom, casting fractured shadows over the topography. Every contour line becomes a potential trap. Waypoints marked in ink scream danger. Each symbol is a warning: choke points, blind spots, sniper nests. No detail is decoration. This map doesn't show land — it charts survival.

No one wastes breath. Silence rules. This isn't the time for bravado — this is the razor's edge. One slip, one bad call, and everything collapses. No extraction. No second chance. Just a fortified facility buried beneath dirt and decades, and the quiet understanding that we either take it... or it takes us.

"Target location confirmed," Derek says, tapping a finger against the map. "Separate complex. Near the tunnel we just crawled out of. Tracked vehicle movement here — entry matches the intel. It's real. And it's waiting."

Simon shifts forward, fingers tracing the map's edges. "Viktor's people move fast. If they arrive first, we're looking at a siege, not a retrieval. What's the window before alarms start screaming?"

Lucy pushes a document toward the centre. "Not long. Radio intercepts show increased chatter. Viktor's people do not have exact coordinates yet, but they're narrowing the search."

"A lead buys time, but not a lot."

My words land hard, measured, pressing urgency into the space between breaths. Quiet lingers, calculations tightening behind locked expressions, minds dissecting the next move.

Ten minutes pass, each second sharpening the strategy, refining the sequence, and eliminating anything that risks failure. All variables are accounted for and locked, and contingencies are stripped down. The only move left is a clean strike to recover an artefact buried underneath decaying concrete within an abandoned bunker.

"OK, let's run through the plan. Objectives: secure the relic and transport it to the exfil site. Speed and silence take priority. Viktor's people want the device, and the Broome Explorers claim interest. Trust is a luxury we can't afford. If either side moves against us, we return fire without hesitation," I say after a few minutes.

Simon remarks, "But money speaks. If Viktor invests, that backing fades fast." Simon's words linger in the air, heavy and expectant, urging a response.

"I'll contact GSS for intel. Before stepping off, we'll determine if they're working on both sides," Lucy says, tapping her fingers on her gear.

The statement hangs like a loaded chamber. Information isn't an indulgence — it's the difference between walking out or bleeding dry.

"We move out two hours before first light. With any luck, the sky will stay black, with no moon to give us away. Keep the momentum high. Any delay might lead to exposure. If compromised, cut contact fast, shift position, and push toward the target, any questions?" I ask, looking around the room.

George's fingers drag across a bristled jawline, "I've one. Are we sure we have the correct location this time? So far, the green numpty taken us to an empty bunker and almost got some of us blown to fucking bits," asks George, trying hard not to laugh.

"Fuck off, George. Intel drops in real-time, and the next move rides on whatever flashes across the feed. Any sensible questions?" I pick up a rock from the table and launch it in George's direction.

Simon smirks, "Yeah, I agree, George, that green numpty damn near turned us into fireworks and riding the blast wave home."

"No guessing this time. Lucy cross-checks everything before we move." The weight of my statement settles, closing any debate.

I continue with the brief. "Conditions: the same as always—hot, dry, and unforgiving. Hydration stays a priority. Two litres minimum, extra reserves in the cache. Nobody runs out in this terrain.

"Resupply isn't an option. What's carried in must last for the entire operation. The topography remains the same. Broken stone crunches under boots, unstable footing threatening balance. And no place to hide if things get loud."

Simon shifts his gaze, examining the map's terrain. "Wildlife?"

Words reflect deeper concern than mere curiosity. The Outback is deadlier than any bullet. Silence wraps around the scene, as the answer remains starkly visible, unmistakable and resolute, etched into the moment like a knife slicing through skin.

"Snakes, scorpions, anything venomous enough to ruin the day. Anti-venom in all packs. If you are bitten, administer straight away. If this doesn't work, Derek calls for CASEVAC—no second chances. Surplus bodies aren't accepted, but poor decisions don't warrant a death sentence," I reply to Simon's question.

The unspoken rule remains unchallenged—those left behind won't be breathing. The mission dictates survival, but survival doesn't belong to the careless. Precision keeps bones from bleaching under an unrelenting sun.

"Let's move on to potential obstacles and threats. Wait beyond Viktor's mercenaries—terrain, dehydration, the slithering kind that strikes before detection. Venom doesn't care about tactics or firepower. One mistake means a one-way ticket home in a bag, and the consequences of failure are dire.

An old warning lingers in the air. 'Lives matter more than relics.' This isn't about glory. It's about getting in, getting out, and staying breathing. Any questions?" I ask.

With no takers, I move on. "Roles: command stays with me. Simon takes over if I drop. Sniper support—Lucy and George. Breach team—Simon, Derek, and me. If the relic isn't small enough to haul, transport falls to Simon."

"What about surveillance?" Lucy's words land, stripped of hesitation, slicing straight to the point.

"That's you and Derek. Any signal that stands out, any electronic interference, inform the rest of the team before it finds us." My words are a simple reminder that unseen threats might hit harder than bullets.

Simon nods toward the vehicles, netting stretched over their frames. "Are we leaving those stashed, Steve?"

"Yes, keep the ATVs out of view. We run on foot unless a clean pullout demands horsepower."

Derek speaks up, "The safety pins for the grenades in case you're otherwise engaged or blown to bloody bits?"

A hand taps against the left-top jacket pocket. "Right here."

"Cheers, mate."

"If no one's got anything else, let's continue." A slow scan confirms readiness—four sets of eyes locked on me, all shaking heads.

"OK, procedures."

A measured sweep lands on each face, cutting through any distraction before the briefing moves forward. The air is thick with focus, each of us preparing for what's ahead. This is the point where everything clicks into place.

"Preparation: consider this the final rundown." I pause, letting that sink in. "When we're done here, make sure your kit is in order. George will distribute the last of the ammo. Simon — run diagnostics on the ATVs. If the exfil turns hot, nothing stalls. Derek, Lucy — reconfirm comms integrity. No blackouts, no gaps. If something shifts, radio the info through."

"Not a problem," Derek says, more of a self-confirmation than for the team.

"Launch phase: once on site, close to the objective, George and Lucy will break off. The rest of us — Simon, Derek, and I — will move towards the entrance, keeping concealed. We stop short, find cover, and wait for the go-ahead. Nothing happens until everyone is in position."

"Infiltration: standard entry procedures. What's on the other side dictates our next move. If it's clear, we take up firing positions — inside and out. When we have secured the area, Derek will signal Lucy and George to join us. Fast, silent, controlled."

I glance around. Four steady figures, ready, peer back. The drill is second nature, but hammering it home leaves no gaps.

"What about the kit?" Lucy asks, arms folded, eyes on me.

"Excellent point. The artefact takes precedence, followed by our gear." There's no discussion — tiny changes in posture indicate comprehension, and the plan is secured. So, I continue, "Extraction Team Deployment. The relic stays front and centre. Secure the package, verify control, and clear out before the situation shifts."

"Any safeguard laced into that hardware?" Derek asks.

"Petrov trained us for this, so we can handle the device, Derek. If it's too heavy, we will implement plan B and collect the ATVs. Speed is everything."

Derek nods, already running through scenarios.

"Extraction: once we have the relic, we head straight to the LZ. Derek, you call in the exfil flight the second we move. When our boots hit the deck, the aircraft lifts. Darwin waits. The GSS jet will carry us home." My authority slices through the air like steel, pressing down with enough force to extinguish any objection before it begins.

"Handled. Standby goes live after this," Derek says, fingers working the tablet, input crisp, movements locked.

"Now—contingency plans." I let the weight of the words settle. "If we become separated, we regroup at the ATV hide. If we're ambushed en route, we stick to our SOP. We execute the plan, or we die trying.

"Communication protocols are simple: keep radio chatter minimal. Derek handles all third-party comms and relays intel as needed," I say, concluding the brief

With the briefing complete, everybody goes about their business. Dust hangs in the air, catching the glow of the dim red light from a tac-lamp clipped to a vest.

Metal clicks as magazines slide into rifles, locking into place. Silence dominates the RV, broken only by the measured sounds of preparation, each contributing to the tension and anticipation in the atmosphere.

Steel scrapes rock. My blade sharpens with each pass, edge honed to surgical intent. Not for show. But for a purpose. A tool that won't fail when the noise starts.

Webbing cinches tighter. Every strap is secured. Nothing dangles. Nothing is loose. Everything is loaded where muscle memory demands. Gear speaks one language—function or failure.

Ammunition counts are checked again. Every magazine is full and accounted for. Grenades positioned for instinctive reach, secondary weapons secured in holsters or slings—nothing extra, nothing unproven, nothing that doesn't serve a role. Precision defines the unit, honed by repetition and necessity.

Heat radiates from the concrete walls of the buildings, trapping the scent of oil, sweat, and the distant sting of rusting metal. Boots press into parched ground, adjusting for balance, nothing more.

Distant wildlife calls out, a steady pulse against the mission's urgency. Gloves flex over grips, knuckles tight but controlled. The gap between strategy and action lingers, a razor-thin pause before the first move detonates the silence.

An hour remains before darkness settles in the Outback, enough time to lock in the night routine. Lucy assigns rotations and breaks shifts, keeping the team fresh without gaps in overwatch.

First in, last out—that responsibility lands on me. The cycle moves clean, and each rotation is set as the team shares stag duty.

With my rifle in hand, I survey the camp as everyone else clambers into their bivvies, settling into whatever rest they can steal before the next phase of the operation.

I make my way to the far end of the RV, scanning the darkness. The Outback extends into nothingness, a vast void hiding unseen dangers.

As I patrol, my mind runs through the plan, dissecting every detail and contingency. The weight of responsibility is familiar but never gets lighter. All the lives in this unit are my responsibility. But risks sit on every shoulder, accepted without question, carried without complaint.

I shake the thoughts off. Doubt is a luxury I can't afford. I exhale, pushing aside the unease. The night is calm, and the land around us is lifeless, save for the occasional wind rustling through dry brush.

Time moves in increments, each minute ticking by and dragging silence along for the ride — the quiet that can either comfort or warn, depending on the person's mind.

Air flows through brittle grass, carrying the scent of earth. Insects pulse in the distance, a constant murmur beneath far-off insect chatter. The perimeter remains silent and untouched.

At 20:00, the shift changes. Lucy crouches by her Bergen. Gloved hands double-check the loadout. Gear is locked in tight, and every strap is secured. Precision never wavers, and instincts have been drilled past hesitation.

I step closer, my voice no more than a whisper. "Quiet night. No movement. All yours." I glance around, confirming the others aren't watching, before pulling Lucy into a brief hug. It's rare but necessary. "Be careful tomorrow, honey."

"You too," whispering into my ear, a firm hand pressing against my arm as the stag shifts from me to Lucy.

I watch for a while as a silhouette moves — weapon raised, tracing unseen threats before I retreat to my bivvy, which offers shelter but no rest, as my mind remains focused on the mission.

Stillness surrounds the Outback. The night remains undisturbed, except for the occasional rustle of small creatures navigating the undergrowth and the constant hum of insects. Everything outside the perimeter stays quiet, with no disruptions or misplaced sounds beyond what is expected. A sharp knock against my shoulder jolts me from half-sleep, instincts igniting as the clock strikes 03:00 and I'm on stag again.

Gear settled, Simon remains unmoving, fatigue scratching beneath the surface, buried under sheer control.

"Critters. Nothing worth a second glance," the words grind out, voice worn down by hours of stillness.

Stag over, Simon retreats into his bivvy. Material tugs into place, securing warmth and leaving nothing exposed.

I settle on a large rock, rifle across my lap, eyes adjusting to the pitch-black terrain. The Outback is still apart from the occasional rustle breaking the silence. The wind carrying the scent of dry earth and distant eucalyptus, masking any potential human presence.

As it always does on sentry, time drags every minute more than it should. The stars overhead remain unchanged, indifferent to the mission below. Once more, I cycle through my mental checklist, including routes, contingencies, and extraction points.

Glance down at Mickey. The time is 05:00. It's time to move. Pushing up from my position at the edge of the RV, I stretch out stiff muscles before making my way around the team. A steady push rouses each one in turn.

Within 10 minutes, bodies are upright, packs tightened, and magazines checked for a clean loadout. Weapons undergo final inspections, bolts are racked, and chambers are loaded, confirming everything is positioned.

With the team prepared and rifles ready, I lead us out of the RV, moving in standard formation. I am at point, with Derek behind, then Lucy, followed by Simon, and George securing our six. No words are spoken, just motion.

Tangled vines claw at webbing, snagging buckles and gear. Every step becomes a negotiation with terrain designed to resist. Thorns tear at sleeves. Precision isn't a luxury out here—it's the difference between a mission and a funeral.

The soil shifts underfoot, slick with rot. Dead leaves mask unstable ground. Insects hum above the silence, pulsing like a warning. One wrong move could echo through the bush like gunfire.

The air thickens. Heat crawls inside every layer. Sweat rolls down my back, stinging. Muscles grind beneath the weight of silence and expectation. This land wants to break us before contact even starts.

Boots navigate around roots twisted like traps. I survey each shadow and flicker in the underbrush. No path greets us. No indication provides safety—just this careful, measured progress through a forest that watches for errors.

I crouch by a tree and raise one hand to signal a stop, with my rifle braced against a raised knee. I take out the Splashmap, the fabric spreading across rough ground, creases settling into place.

I remove my torch from my jacket and direct a concealed red beam over the inked markings, illuminating the path still left to cover. Elevated lines trace the ridgeline, the terrain mirroring what's underfoot.

Our goal lies just a few kilometres ahead, but this is not our only hurdle. The wind brings shifting sounds that require silence before determining their source. The canopy absorbs noise, distorting our perception of distance; still, every misstep triggers a silent alarm within the underbrush.

My fingers tighten around the rifle grip as I listen to the Outback, trying to detect any movement out of the ordinary, something that shouldn't be present. Sometimes, patience outweighs action in moments like this.

After putting the map away, lines are redrawn, bearings set, and the team presses forward. Our training kicks in—bypassing obstacles, skirting ridgelines, and keeping out of line of sight. The enemy has no knowledge that we're coming. We remain like ghosts in the dark—unheard, unseen.

Sweat trickles down my back as we push forward. Every step brings us closer to the mission's most dangerous phase—getting inside without being seen.

As dawn approaches, the first light seeps over the horizon, painting the sky in hues of orange and violet. I pause amidst dense foliage interspersed with gnarled trees, raising a fist to signal everyone to stop. The team fans out, taking cover behind the vegetation.

From a vantage point, I raise my rifle scope, scanning ahead. The objective lies about 300 metres away. Jagged cliffs conceal the access point, while vegetation clings to the structure. Nature reclaims what once belonged to a hidden past. It's a remnant of secrecy, long abandoned by both nature and people but not forgotten.

I key my radio mic. "All callsigns, GD and LK, peel off. Radio through when you're in position. Over."

Static hums before George's voice cuts through. "GD, Roger, will do. Out."

George and Lucy disappear into the brush. Their footsteps gliding across uneven ground, bodies adapting to the landscape, disappearing into the folds of rock and foliage.

Their path follows the ridgeline above the entrance, with altitude providing a perfect vantage point—unbroken sightlines, a sniper's ideal perch. Phantoms against the terrain are invisible unless exposure serves a purpose.

Establishing an overwatch location demands diligence—no sudden shifts, no careless movements. The environment guides every action. George selects a shallow depression, masked by knotted vines and brittle grass, which offers enough concealment without disrupting a firing line. Body compressed, limbs drawn close, the outline blends into the uneven contours of the terrain, dissolving any recognisable shape.

Lucy works at layering a ghillie tarp over the hide. Broken branches, loose soil, and native plants weave into the fabric. Muted silhouettes dissolve into the earth's uneven surface, erasing any trace of presence from prying eyes.

George lies behind the rifle, bipod biting into packed earth, breath steady as fine adjustments, counter shift wind patterns. Lucy lies flat beside George. The scope sweeping across the ridgeline, plotting vectors, wind adjustments, and elevation for the inevitable shot.

Below the ridge, Simon, George, and I await confirmation that the snipers are in position to cover our approach to the complex. Minutes pass in tense silence before Lucy's voice crackles in my earpiece.

"S3, this is LK. All set. Over," tone calm and controlled.

I press the mic. "All callsigns, this is S3. We have a go. Out." My grip tightens around my rifle. The mission is in motion.

A final sweep secures the landscape, dividing the ground into sectors. Every segment interlocks with the next, angles considered, terrain examined in methodical strokes, removing gaps where a threat might remain hidden.

The area seems clear, so Simon, Derek, and I silently move forward, weaving through the dense undergrowth. The closer we approach the facility, the more signs of recent activity I notice.

Fresh footprints in the dirt, tyre tracks cutting through the dry earth, and discarded ration wrappers. Someone's beaten us here.

I crouch and scan the ground. The treads are deep, indicating heavy vehicles. The boot marks vary, suggesting this isn't just a patrol — it's a force. My gut tightens. It might be Viktor's people or other interested parties, such as Broome Explorers.

About to move when Derek raises a fist, then taps an earpiece, eyes latching onto something unseen. Fingers twist the radio dial, adjusting for clarity.

A beat passes before he says, "I've got an intercepted message. We've got movement inside. Viktor's mercs."

My crosshairs fix on the entrance, tracking silhouettes that shift near the threshold. Rifles hang ready, and patience is evident in their stance. Nothing about them suggests routine.

They appear to be scanning for something unseen—whether a scheduled shift, an unscheduled incursion, or something slipping through the cracks—perhaps us.

With measured breaths, every sense is attuned to the unfolding scene ahead. Guards outside suggest that more might be waiting inside, hidden yet close, ready to react as soon as something changes.

Breaking cover turns precision into chaos, removing any advantage. Turning to Simon and Derek, I whisper, "We need to move closer—without being seen."

We advance in staggered intervals. I sprint forward first while Simon and Derek remain anchored, ready to provide covering fire if necessary. Dense foliage governs my every move.

Twisted roots and tangled brush necessitate careful navigation. Each action is adjusted to blend into the environment, controlled and deliberate, avoiding unnecessary noise that might carry beyond the immediate area.

Finding cover, I dive down, forearms pressing into packed earth, ribcage tightening against the uneven ground, sights trained on the men in the doorway, breath steady, weapon firm.

Simon advances with controlled steps, halting just ahead, ready to cover Derek's approach as he leapfrogs past Simon and me.

With both of us concealed, Derek follows suit. Progress remains slow, dictated by the terrain, which enforces discipline and prevents unnecessary exposure.

At 50 metres, we lower into the undergrowth. Thorns scrape at fabric. Sweat runs down my spine. Every breath carries the scent of churned soil and anticipation.

I outline the quick strategy, "Simon and I will neutralise the guards on the left and right at the entrance without a sound. Knives only. Derek will remain behind to offer cover fire if needed."

"Any last requests?" Simon whispers, adjusting his grip.

"Yeah," I mutter, "don't fuck it up."

From the rear, Derek chimes in. "I'll write something poetic on your headstone. Might even spell your name right."

Simon grins without humour. "Make it dramatic. He died doing what he loved — ruining my cover."

Focus returns. The plan is sound. The snipers above will provide overwatch. I press the radio mic. "LK, this is S3, moving in close. Provide cover if needed, over."

"S3, this LK, roger that, out."

Simon braces, body still, the blade an extension of thought. Every breath is a countdown. Mine drags slow and deep, locking nerves into rhythm.

One glance. My finger flicks the signal. Go.

I take the left, Simon the right. Vines tug at ankles, roots threaten to betray us. The distance vanishes — ten metres, five.

We surge forward. Knives rise, shadows move. Targets stand unaware. For now. But not for long.

A moment later, a crushing force drives the body against the unyielding ground. Lungs compress inward, air stolen in one brutal instant. Silence swallows the struggle. My hand seals over the mouth—tight, final. In my other hand, the blade carves deep, slicing through the flesh of the throat with practised force. No hesitation or mercy. Only precision.

Beneath me, the body kicks once, then again. Nerves fire wild, mind not yet caught up with the death rushing in. Hot breath breaks through teeth, fractured and fast. I hold steady. A final twitch. Then stillness. A minute passes, silence claiming what remains, a pool of crimson spreading, swallowed by sunbaked dirt.

A slight shift in my position reveals Simon kneeling, dragging his knife across the man's jacket, stripping away the stain of violence in a single, practised gesture. Simon straightens, blade pristine, the dark smear on a sleeve the only remaining mark of the kill. Steel catching a faint glint before disappearing.

Simon and I kneel on either side of the entrance, rifles raised, scanning the immediate area. The air is thick with tension, and the scent of damp earth and oil lingers. Shadows stretch across the rock face, concealing unknown threats.

Derek advances on our position. Each second spent exposed is calculated against the surroundings. Simon and I hover with our fingers poised on the triggers, barrels tracing potential hostiles, mapping openings before anything can unfold.

Once the unit regroups, positions adjust, weapons align, and the operation shifts from movement to execution, preparing for the breach.

Last night's plan unfolds in sequence. Motions follow a blueprint perfected through years of rehearsals. Circumstances evolve, resistance adapts, but precision never wavers. Entry remains methodical—identify vulnerabilities, establish clear kill zones, and mitigate risks before escalation.

I take point, bursting through the door first, my weapon raised and sweeping right. Simon follows, pivoting left. Close behind, Derek moves in, rifle steady and covering the middle ground. The space is empty. A narrow passage leads deeper inside, with walls pressing in, forcing us into a tight column.

Reinforced barriers punctuate the length of the passage. A single threshold remains ajar, swallowing illumination beyond its threshold. The environment carries a metallic tang, mingled with the damp rot of neglected growth suffocating within enclosed confines.

A flick of my fingers cuts through the dimness, directing Simon, barrel aligned, seeking the smallest disruption in the silence. With a steady movement, I advance toward a weathered door, hinges fractured, buried beneath layers of hardened filth.

My barrel presses against the surface, forcing it aside while the hinges groan and stale air curls out from within. Porcelain lies shattered across the floor, a rust-choked drain, and walls smeared with grime — only a forsaken washroom left to decay.

Outside, Derek stays anchored, rifle sweeping the terrain, body rigid with purpose. Fingers brush the radio.

"LK, DR, on our twenty. Awaiting confirmation. Over." The message flows, quiet yet crisp, through the secure channel.

"LK, Roger. Moving now. Out," Lucy transmits.

Speed matters, but precision comes first. One step forward, the other holds — battle rhythm drilled too deep for mistakes.

George advances across 50 metres, pressing into depressions in the ground, vanishing between fractured stone and thick brush. Lucy advances, senses tuned for disturbance. Both fade into the dim haze, bodies aligning with fractured silhouettes of the terrain. Unshaken focus dictates every motion. Two figures thread a battlefield, unseen, untouched.

We regroup just inside the entrance — silent, tight, rifles raised. The air is heavy, not with heat, but with expectation. Sights sweep the corridor, slicing through dimness. Shadows shift under our gaze. Every corner is cleared, every silence interrogated. We move only with cover. Advancing without certainty could mean death.

The place hums with wrongness. Walls press in. Stillness clings like a second skin. Whatever waits beyond doesn't breathe, doesn't flinch. It's not flesh, not steel — but something older. Something that doesn't move because it doesn't need to. It watches. It measures. It waits.

Training whispers: push forward. Instinct screams: hold. The thing ahead knows patience better than we do. It feeds off stillness, draws strength from silence. And now we're inside its home.

Narrow passageways close in with an oppressive quiet, the air stagnant and thick with something more than neglect. Our movements remain measured, purpose slicing through the space between. Footfalls claim ground without pause, a declaration of intent. Those who stand in our way will face more than mere shadows.

In the distance, a low hum resonates through the air — the unmistakable beat of a generator. This sound is faint yet consistent, suggesting that power continues to flow somewhere in this forsaken area. Either someone has restored the old grid, or they've modified their supply.

The upcoming corridor is slim, flanked by concrete walls adorned with corroding pipes and entangled wiring. Faint emergency lights flicker, creating elongated, warped shadows that dance with each movement. The air is heavy, humid, metallic, and tinged with the aroma of decay and oil.

Moving in tight formation, we set off, keeping close to the walls, with me taking the right and Simon mirroring me on the left. Lucy advances in the middle, against the right wall. Derek and George bring up the rear, silent rifles at the ready.

Nothing is left to chance as the path unfolds ahead. Our momentum adapts to the terrain, fluid yet controlled, every shift maintaining complete awareness of our surroundings. The corridor demands discipline, as our senses absorb and assess the environment before we proceed through the narrowing passage.

Boots skim over the fractured ground, dodging unstable patches and navigating dry dust without disturbing the silence. Precision governs every step. Motion narrows to necessity, erasing excess, stripping movement down to pure efficiency, and cutting through the space ahead.

To our front, the tunnel comes to an end and opens up into a vast room, dark, cavernous, and the air colder than the tunnels. Towering stacks of rusted crates and battered supply boxes fill the space, their faded markings just about visible. Cyrillic letters, numbers, and military insignia.

A shape lingers in the dim haze ahead, merging with the darkness. Faint distortions ripple along the corridor's edge, unsettling in their stillness. The mind processes possibilities — failing light or something, patient enough to allow the silence to breathe.

A heartbeat stretches into seconds. Muscles tighten, lungs compress, nerves coil beneath the skin. Instinct replaces thought. Senses extend beyond sight. Something moves where emptiness should exist — the waiting game shifts. The hunt begins.

The atmosphere unravels, fraying like a stretched thread. A disturbance radiates, distorting the void where nothing ought to exist. Dark edges distort, expanding in response. Something unwelcome bends the space around it, altering what should remain unchanged.

The stench of damp concrete and rusted metal lingers, obscuring more subtle scents. Then, the presence reveals itself. Rats. A blur of fur moves fast, claws scraping at concrete, their bodies twisting in unpredictable bursts. One squeezes through a splintered crate, vanishing through a gap gnawed into the rotting wood. The rest funnel through the opening, disappearing in rapid succession.

Amid static decay, something deviates from the natural flow. This shift isn't just a flicker of dying light—it's intentional. The mind stops guessing, as instincts respond immediately. The time for patience vanishes.

In the foreground, a work trolley lies shattered and twisted, a victim in the blast zone. The metal is ripped back into jagged strips, and the frame is distorted by excessive weight, not built to bear a heavy load. One wheel is absent, leaving the axle exposed and ineffective.

The scent of old grease clings to the wreckage—stale, bitter, wrong. I kneel beside the scattered tools. Handles split, and steel rust bled. These aren't just abandoned—but dropped mid-use. Someone left in a hurry, and whatever forced that exit might still be close.

A screwdriver pierces the cracked floor, wedged with a force that speaks of desperation. I reach for the implement but stop short. The handle bears a faint smear—rust or something darker. A tarp shifts in the stillness, unmoved by the breeze. Nothing moves, but my instincts flare.

Machinery lies hidden under layers of dust—more than just decay, more than just the passage of time. A heaviness permeates the floor, dense in the air and bitter on the tongue. This... this serves as a warning.

Simon signals left—two fingers, deliberate. Another tunnel yawns ahead, narrow and sloping downward. The generator's thrum thickens, a faint pulse rising from the dark like a heartbeat under floorboards. My grip shifts on the rifle. Whatever is hiding beyond, we move in.

Ahead, the corridor opens into a chamber shrouded in silence. The air is dense and sharp. Faint, faded footprints extend into the distance. They are neither recent nor ancient. Wooden splinters scatter the ground, remnants of crates that have long been broken and left behind. Someone has been here.

The place reeks of a forgotten war — metal, sweat, and rot. Desks line the walls, their legs warped under decades of weight. Shelving units rise like tombstones, grey and silent, coated in dust and nothing else. From the look of things, a command centre once thrived here, but now it is just an empty shell.

A glass screen protrudes from a rusted console. Dials, covered in corrosion, encircle it, now rendered ineffective. Behind, a sign clings to the wall with curled edges, words just about legible. The letters depict control and procedure, but that intent vanished long ago.

Chairs lie broken, snapped where force met panic — paper curls beneath the grime. Symbols scratched in haste. This has been stripped, fast and recent. Someone hunted, found nothing, and left in a hurry.

Disturbed dust indicates recent movement. Opened crates with their lids thrown aside reveal rotting equipment and empty compartments. Someone's searched this place, ransacked it, and almost stripped it clean. Whoever came through didn't waste time.

I notice a faded schematic sprawling across a dust-covered desk, its corners crumbling from prolonged exposure. Key sections feature numbers and odd markings, meticulously arranged and hidden beneath layers of classified intent, revealing patterns locked in secrecy.

As I scan the room, I observe that the shelves stand bare, crates are cracked open, and every container that might have held a hint of an answer is now stripped. The relic waits somewhere, its resting place hidden beneath layers of deception and misdirection.

Ten minutes later, footsteps echo in the distance, approaching, coming our way. Straining to listen, I detect Russian voices filtering through one of the tunnels—clipped, professional, and unmistakable. It must be Viktor's people.

As far as we can tell, no other Russian faction monitors the relic. Movement becomes tense, and individuals blend into the landscape, weapons ready for action. Discarded desks, rusted machinery, and broken shelving now provide makeshift concealment.

Fingers tighten around triggers, and safety catches are off. Stillness grips the room. Breaths are shallow and controlled, waiting to take the first pressure on triggers. Faint murmurs drift through the underground expanse, shifting in tone with each passing second.

The rhythm shifts, tones become sharper, and the closeness intensifies from an invisible source in the dark. Irregular walls disrupt the sound, altering its range and trajectory. With every passing second, the space narrows between hunter and hunted.

Lines sharpen beneath a gloved grip on the map, revealing a concealed passage that aligns with the muffled disturbances up ahead. The route twists through the structure, forming a narrow artery that leads to the source of the faint echoes.

A secondary route cuts through reinforced barriers, an overlooked break in the structure. Wedged between crumbling supports, a hidden access point opens into the depths, steering movement along a path unseen from standard vantage points.

An opportunity to seize control before the first alarm rings. A sharp glance at Simon, then Derek. Hands shift as silent commands are exchanged. The unit slips into staggered positions, threads through uneven ground, and advances in calculated movements to encroach on Viktor's position unseen.

Chapter Twenty-Three — Confrontation

The underground air reeks of damp concrete and machinery long past its prime, tainted with rust, oil, and secrets. Overhead, flickering strip lights throw sterile shadows across a makeshift command centre—metal desks, tangled cables, and monitors just about holding a signal. Down here, the past clings to everything, thick and suffocating.

Natasha moves through the corridors like a scalpel—precise, cutting through dust and disuse with cold purpose, scanning every wall, every junction, hunting. The relic is in this decaying maze—a piece of history buried in lies, sealed off by time and fear. And now, it's almost within reach.

On the other hand my counterpart, Sergei, of course, has no patience for riddles. Instead, pushes for force—boots in the corridors, guns at the ready. His men are outside, poised to strike first and question nothing. He doesn't care what the relic is; he wants blood on the floor before Steve's team puts boots through the door.

Viktor's words will no doubt burrow into Sergei, forging reflex over rage, obedience over impulse. I see it take hold—useful, dangerous. I run this operation, for now, clock bleeding seconds. How long I keep command depends on what I uncover before time runs out today.

Sergei stands locked in place, fists drawn tight. Breath dragging slow through clenched teeth, a warning beneath obedience. For now, control bends, but never breaks. Not yet.

It's a pause enforced by order, not by choice. That kind of stillness is not sustainable. Rebellion coils beneath the surface, awaiting the next fracture.

Dust fills the air. Filters hang useless in rusted vents. Neglected consoles scatter the area, their surfaces tarnished by time. The odour of failing circuits clings to everything—weathered wires, burned tiles, and faded memories.

Lines collapse on the screen, and code fractures. Intelligence splits in two, once-clear signals now severed into chaos. Icons blink without rhythm, a machine spiralling toward a single, final command.

Heat signatures fade into apparitions on my screens. Silhouettes warp with chaos, wavering under static; forms refuse to settle. Every stutter, every glitch, knots my chest. I can read the noise like scripture.

Something hides inside this distortion—intent and disciplined— static spikes; the display tears. Shapes become phantoms, disjointed parts trapped mid-motion. Red arcs scythe the fog—alerts flare, then drown under corrupted surges. Each flicker forces recalibration; I wrestle to feed back into truth.

Seconds drag the picture nearer. Lines ripple like disturbed water; code bleeds through unseen channels. Heat traces sketch the void, painting a battle not yet visible, a geometry of intent drawn in temperatures and timing.

A single pulse crosses the grid. Shadows manifest where no one should be, gliding in measured steps. They track a route I didn't author, a choreography that anticipates cameras and cones of fire.

Other movements drift too smoothly, too perfectly. Not random. Not human. A deliberate vector threads the gaps, testing thresholds like a surgeon's probe, mapping our blind spots while pretending to be noise.

Then the room shivers—one stretch too far, one vicious flicker. No origin. No pattern. It refuses to resolve. My systems claw for meaning; I sharpen mine. The threat lives in negative space— clever, cold, and closing fast.

Sergei's men wait at the room's rear, fingers tense around the rifle's stock, worn to a shine from hours of preparedness.

However, bullets alone do not decide the battlefield. The human element of war combines muscle, mind, and nerves strung taut. The moment is fragile, poised on the edge of chaos.

Steve's team might already be inside these tunnels, hunting and searching as we are. 'If they are, I intend to be two steps ahead when we meet,' I think to myself.

A lone pulse flashes on my screen, breaking the grid's quiet. There are no scheduled patrols in that corridor. Yet the readout blinks — controlled and intentional. Someone is moving through the space.

A clear pattern is developing. Movements appear exact, execution is impeccable, and the unit functions with discipline sharpened by experience. It must be Steve's team moving through the facility, thinking they are advancing unnoticed.

However, precision by itself won't dictate the result. Adaptation is what distinguishes survival from failure — yes, skills are crucial. But instinct also plays a role, and my instinct is infallible.

I smile slowly as I refine the data. The pieces are falling into place. Let Steve advance. Every inch gained is another door closing, another corridor narrowing, another choice erased.

A shift in posture, tension radiating from the other side of the table from me. Sergei's fingers drum once before clenching.

"Enough patience, Natasha. This is not war; this is surrender." The words grind out, edged with contained aggression.

"We track their move, Sergei," comes my response. "They're navigating blind. We push too soon, and we lose that advantage. Precision wins, not brute force." My statement leaves no room for debate.

A muscle ticks along Sergei's jaw, frustration bleeding into action. He steps back, arms crossing over a broad chest, the restraint more telling than words.

"A trap fucking means nothing if they're the ones hunting!" Sergei's voice punching through the static, jagged, raw, meant to force action.

A voice cuts through the radio — Viktor's, laced with annoyance, "Enough. This is an operation, not a debate. Execute orders, contain the fight, and stop wasting resources. Fail again, and replacements will arrive faster than excuses."

Sergei exhales hard, shoulders rolling, tension shifting but not leaving. I glance at him. "We move when I say so." The words land flat, resentful, but final.

The strategy is paramount, but the fire still smoulders below. For Sergei, the confrontation is inevitable. The only uncertainty is when it will occur.

Looking up from one of the many screens, "Sergei, we have movement in one nearby tunnel. Go and investigate. No contact unless necessary, understand?" The tone in my voice is clear and sharp.

"Of course. No shots without your fucking say so," Sergei says, voice steady, though something unspoken lingers beneath the words. "Remember, Natasha's your command only gives structure — until terrain swallows comms, and the window closes. In that moment, your orders lose meaning and decision shifts from paper to trigger."

Stillness encircles the room like wire — delicate, pointed, on the verge of snapping. One twitch, and the entire illusion collapses. Hands linger near steel, breath syncs into a rhythm, yet purpose is submerged beneath control.

Boundaries offer relief to the weak, a reassurance shrouded in deception. Sergei feels no comfort; instead, the weight bears down, fracturing the structure of his raw determination. Here, obedience builds no cages — only extends the inevitable.

Six men crouch around the map, eyes locked, breathing held. Sergei's voice, short and direct, carves through the silence. No time for debate, no confusion. The plan burns into everyone's memory. One hand signal propels everyone forward, trailing behind Sergei as they are swallowed by the corridor's darkness.

*****

Steel presses against shoulders. Fingers hover over triggers. Steps fall soft, measured by discipline rather than fear. Each movement gains ground. Every breath matters. The enemy lurks — near, hidden, anticipated.

Orders flow through encrypted communications, directing Sergei's units deeper into the installation.

Fifteen minutes pass. Then a scrape — incorrect, harsh, dragged out. Concrete grinds under a weight. It's neither the wind nor decay. Machinery hums from deep within, as old bones resist death.

I raise a clenched fist, bringing the line to a halt. Boots shift. Knees bend. Stone creaks under the pressure. Fragments break apart, sliding into voids left by others. The air feels dense, pulled taut around bone.

Ahead, a doorway fades into shadow. Rust eats away at the frame, its edges jagged like torn flesh. Beyond is unknown territory — waiting, silent, and cruel. 'Perhaps this is where we will at last come face to face with Steve and his team.'

Then, without warning, something stirs beyond the door. Not noise — presence. Wrong weight. Wrong rhythm. Too patient. Too precise. An unseen breath held too long.

Weapons rise—sights align with angles. Backs pressed against the tunnel's stone wall. Muscles are tense. No voices break the wait. Only silence lingers, heavy with foreboding.

Next comes movement. Abrupt. Definite. No time for contemplation. None required. Action takes precedence—instinctive, immediate. Muscle overrides reasoning.

I'm about to launch a full-on assault when static crackles through the channel, irritation bleeding through the voice on the other end. Natasha's voice comes over the radio, "Sergei, what's your position?"

"Better find out what that fucking bitch wants," I mutter between clenched teeth. A quiet breath before pressing the mic of the radio. "Not the time, Natasha. One squeeze of my trigger ends this."

"Intel just came in. One of the surveillance teams picked up movement on a sensor, too close for comfort. The reading isn't a glitch. Something triggered the motion, something real. The location is near the central hub. A presence registered, and nothing should be moving out here. This isn't a random oddity," Natasha replies over the radio.

"Return now. No delays. Whatever tripped that signal isn't waiting around, and neither are we."

"Can't the people at your end handle the situation? We're fucking busy!" comes my reply.

"Pull back. Right now. The location is confirmed." The words cut through the channel, sharp, final.

My hands twitch, restraint grinding against instinct. A clear shot, an opening begging to be taken. A target waiting to be erased. Yet Viktor's law is absolute. Disobedience doesn't wound—but festers, and Viktor never allows the infection to spread. Punishment always follows.

Bodies drop hard, and many die on Viktor's orders, bodies discarded without hesitation. Each one is a decision made. And when it's made, Viktor or I execute the orders. Life is snuffed out, and each decision is etched in consequence.

I know control demands sacrifice; I'm just not happy about it. Rage coils through my body, denied release. "The fight isn't over — just buried for now, beneath concrete, waiting for the spark," I say to myself.

Strikes are not born from weakness but from careful calculation. Delay enhances precision. Pressure accumulates in silence, creating something colder than anger.

Moving back to the control centre, boots scrape through loose gravel, each step cutting through the air with purpose. Movements are deliberate, and breaths are shallow. The unit remains tethered to an unwanted command.

The directive is unequivocal and conclusive. It allows no room for dialogue. A decision is inscribed in ink and presented as an illusion. To rebel would incinerate too fiercely. Compliance advances, devoid of consent.

Resentment accompanies every move. Not overt. Not instant. But accumulating. No system survives long under forced control when it appears wrong to the men on the ground.

I can see the fractures emerging in my men, not in their minds but in their actions. A strike is nearing. It's not a question of if, but when.

*****

At the command centre, Sergei pushes against the vast metal door, its rusty hinges creaking. Inside, shadows extend in erratic shapes under the flickering emergency lights.

On one side of the room, Natasha lays an old, faded map across a dented table, the edges curling from moisture. Her gloved finger traces routes, highlighting potential choke points. The underground labyrinth presents opportunities for control—bottlenecks, blind corners, and terrain that dictates movement.

With anger pulsating through every fibre of his body from being compelled to disengage from the enemy, Sergei paces toward Natasha, boots striking the ground with deliberate force. Hands flex, tension bracing each step—violence calls for an outlet, something tangible to crush. And for now, this is reserved for Natasha.

"Explain this, Natasha. That target begged for a fucking bullet." Jaw clenches, teeth grind. Fury surges, caged yet shaking the bars. "You ordered us to back off. Why?" Sergei's angry voice rips through the air, louder than gunfire and sharper than broken glass.

"Steve's team, maybe? But that's uncertain. The data suggests a different conclusion. There are new patterns—strange, but predictable. Activity stirs at the far end of the complex. That grid came alive with something. That area is uncharted and unauthorised. A presence lacking identification," Natasha responds.

Another map unfurls, creased from use, edges worn from too much handling.

"Someone is moving, avoiding primary access points, suggesting a single objective. Their intent is unmistakable. This is no mistake; the calculations are refined, and the adjustments make themselves. Establish kill zones here and here," says Natasha, her fingers pressing firm against the surface, tapping on marked zones with force behind each placement. "Cut off their retreat, close the net. Then, once the trap is set, only one outcome remains. Steve and his team draw their last breaths."

Sergei studies the map, eyes moving over the selected points in agreement with Natasha. Orders crackle through the comms as teams mobilise to act. An urgent energy surrounds him, propelling an instinctive drive to move forward without hesitation.

"Steve's unit is either advancing blind or carrying inside knowledge. Neither secures control. Either way, they don't control their approach. Movement bends to our design. We dictate the ground. Steve moves where we want him to," says Natasha, finger tracing along the map, cutting through marked positions. A pause lets the words settle, sinking deep. "This ground belongs to us."

*****

Once ready, Sergei leads his men move out of the control centre again into the tunnel complex, braying for blood and revenge for having to fall back earlier.

The corridor tightens at each twist in the tunnels, forcing the unit to huddle closer, where precision turns into survival. Turns spiral like veins, each drawing men further into the unknown.

Fifteen minutes later, I identify an ideal spot for ambush, aiming to funnel Steve's team into a tight space. I set up a trap to prevent anyone from escaping once they step inside.

The location limits movement and narrows their choices. All that's left for my men is to wait for the trap to be triggered.

Back in the control room, Natasha leans over the monitors. Reflections twitch like ghosts. Movement flickers — patterns begin to emerge.

According to the infrared, shapes move, closing gaps and filtering through dead space. This can only be Steve's team moving in. 'Our strategy is unfolding as planned, but plans mean nothing if they escape and grab the relic,' Natasha thinks to herself.

The feed adjusts with a flick of a switch. A thermal cluster near an intersection—one of the choke points marked earlier—where Sergei's men wait in silence.

A sharp inhale steadies her balance. Move too fast, and Steve and the relic slip through our grasp. Push too slow, and control of the engagement weakens. Each second shifts the odds, turning strategy into instinct.

"Let Steve's team commit. Nobody breaks formation. No one moves until I say."

Her words cut through the static, sharp and final. The radio hisses, then falls silent. The order stands absolute.

*****

Sergei considers replying but decides not to. Because once things kick off, he will ignore any commands coming from Natasha. The ground dictates actions, not someone sitting in a control room.

In the ambush site silence envelops, pressing against the skin and wrapping around the body like a second layer. The air thickens, heavy, immobilising everything. Muscles tense and breath halts, anticipating the shift ahead, the tension evident in the stillness.

Stone drags against stone—dry, drawn out, wrong. Not wind. A presence shifts beyond sight. Pressure builds behind my eyes. That sound speaks of something close, something careless, or confident.

Lungs constrict. Breath struggles past clenched teeth. Stillness lingers like a noose. Each second elongates the pause until it creaks. A blink too long, and silence transforms into blood.

Once more, a noise. This one lingers. A wire stretched taut against skin. There's intention behind it—calculated, deliberate. Not a beast. Not arbitrary. A hand extends, concealed in shadow. An essence colours the darkness.

Edges fade. The air becomes denser. Every breath feels hard-won. Eyes survey, fixed ahead, perceiving nothing, yet understanding. The hidden lurks with patience, coiled behind concrete and darkness.

A hiss on the comms cuts through the tension. Position confirmed. Orders are clear. No chatter. Movement resumes. Steps grow more deliberate. The tunnel tightens. The world closes in. The kill zone lies in wait, unseen, eager to consume.

Metal rubs against sturdy fabric. Boots scrape through dust, fracturing ancient stone. Sounds die fast here, yet their significance resonates. A finger lingers close to the trigger. It's reflex, not contemplation. Instinct governs this realm.

Flickering lights illuminate the space above. A weak pulse flickers down the corridor. Shadows shift uneasy. Angles warp. Despite the obscurity, the mind conjures threats at every turn.

The blow hasn't landed yet. But it's inevitable. Everything in this place suggests that. And I'm prepared to confront it head-on.

The last steps lead into the kill zone, where hesitation is out of the question. Steve's team advances, controlled and unrelenting, locked into a course with no deviation. Only two results remain — clear exit or burial. Both are accepted, but one is preferred.

My breath halts, body tensing, instincts locking against the stillness. A pause lingers, stretched to the breaking point. My command cuts sharp.

"Now."

The word leaves my lips before the tunnel ruptures. Light burns through darkness, bullets ripping air apart.

Gunfire shreds the silence, the first rounds tearing through the confined space. Echoes of combat slam against concrete. Brass casings ricochet, bouncing off walls, dropping lifeless onto cold stone. The sounds of battle leave ghosts, reminders of each round fired, every decision made in a fraction of a second.

A single casing skitters across uneven ground, spinning erratically and refusing to settle. The rattle cuts through the chaos, distinct and isolated, the last trace of a shot fired. The final revolution slows, hesitating for a fraction too long before collapsing into silence.

Stillness clamps down, thick and suffocating, pressing into flesh and air alike. The battlefield inhales and holds a breath, waiting for the next eruption. It is a temporary pause, not peace — never peace.

Smoke bursts from shattered structures, rolling in dense, twisting columns that cling to the air. It swallows what remains of light and refracts in violent slashes of red and white. The next strike looms, unseen but inevitable.

Light erupts in jagged bursts as figures oscillate in and out of existence with each explosion. The kill zone tightens, forcing bodies closer, driving the fight into close quarters where hesitation dies first. Boots slam through debris, crushing everything beneath.

Rounds crack through the air, cutting off breath before sound can follow. One of my men takes the brunt of the fire, chest catching a full volley. Limbs give way, weight tilts back, and the body collides with the ground before the pain registers.

As soon as one falls, another steps in, rifle elevated. A squeeze, then a burst immediate. The battle requires one to be present, without grief, without hesitation.

The fallen do not matter. The living press forward, spent shells hitting the ground before bodies settle. Combat does not stall for the dead — but tightens its grip on those still breathing.

Shouts tangle with the roar of automatic fire. Dust plumes, masking movement, muting angles. Shadows stretch and collapse as bodies press forward, some fading, others fighting. The slow hesitate—hesitation kills. The survivors push, bullets carving the path.

A sharp burst from the front snaps one of my men's shoulders back, rifle swinging out of control in an upward arc. Blood stains the concrete before boots trample past. Another of my men slams into the wall, chest ripped open, momentum carrying lifeless weight into the cold steel.

The ambush fractures. Steve's team shifts with calculated speed, moving through chaos with trained precision. Controlled fire breaks through the assault, measured and disciplined, a force refusing collapse. The fight tilts, the movement slipping from the hands of those who began the fight.

I shift fast, angling toward cover, tracking the chaos all around. A rifle slams into the ground, metal clattering against stone. No hands reach for the weapon. The owner lies sprawled. Limbs twisted, another mistake bleeding dry into the dust.

Scarlet blood seeps into the earth beneath the fallen, familiar with death. The fight allows no room for the slow and shows no mercy for the careless.

Nothing waits, nothing halts. Only action matters. The moment to decide is already gone. Survival belongs to those who act.

Bodies are slumped where reflexes failed, where hesitation dragged moments into death. Shell casings scatter, weapons abandoned mid-reach, limbs twisted from miscalculation.

A formation once designed to crush now fights to remain intact. Pressure builds, yet control slips away from me like sand through fingers. The battlefield twists, reshaping itself in ways never anticipated. Precision fractures and cracks widen where strength should dominate. Lines that were once solid now bend under unexpected force.

Momentum dies where force should surge. Flow fractures, not loud, but deep, splintering from the centre like a spine giving out.

Strongholds crumble. Lines buckle. The middle folds first. Edges realise too late. Collapse spreads with speed.

What once held together, now fractures completely. Gaps emerge. Angles extend. No more choke points. No more dominance. Coverage becomes sparse. Steel encounters open terrain.

Those who aimed to trap are now left vulnerable. The situation reverses. There's no security and no escape. Every advance attracts fire, not territory. Under stress, precision diminishes.

The prey remains still. There's no scattering or panic. Their determination strengthens while ours starts to wane. The equilibrium alters. The hunters hesitate.

Each step back reaffirms the reality—this struggle goes awry. The advance stops, the backlash starts, and the price rises.

A signal rips through comms.

"Retreat."

Clear. Cold. Definitive. The order is followed. No pride. Just survival.

Boots move. Flames dim. Ground is conceded. Not forever—but for now. Breathing is the sole triumph.

*****

Stone fractures beneath Steve's boots. Each step drives dust into cracks that have remained undisturbed for decades. Movement slows—rifle up. The barrel sweeps left. Right. Vision narrows to the corridor ahead—black as oil, deeper than shadow. No end. No reflection. Just void.

Silence thickens—not absence—but presence. Every breath weighs more than the last. This passage doesn't lie dormant. Something waits—not a sound, not a flicker—yet the sense sharpens. A presence sits ahead, coiled in the dark.

A sharp metallic sound cuts through the air. Exact. No mistake, no hesitation. A resounding thud follows—heavy and near. My gaze shifts to the centre. A grenade moves forward, spins once, its casing glistening under fragmented light.

"Take cover!"

My voice slices the stillness. No thought—just reaction. Boots tear across stone. Steel hits walls. Movement hits maximum velocity in under a second. No hesitation. A drilled response. The explosion detonates with a deep impact.

A concussive wave collapses my chest. Pressure tears through my lungs. Sound fades. The world dissolves into ash and static. A curtain of smoke pours through the air, dense with powder and memory.

"Flashbang!"

Simon's voice pierces the comms—distorted and frantic. Another bang. Light warps. Shadows contort.

Vibration moves through the air. This isn't fear; it's a calculated placement, where every choice is made with precision.

"Eyes up!" Derek commands. His rifle steadies, eyes focused.

Someone's steering the chaos. A strategy leaks from every angle. This isn't just noise; it's design. Fire erupts once more—calculated, focused, and direct. It's not random or an act of desperation.

Each shot pushes us back, narrowing the angles. I'm breathing gravel. Dust burns in my throat. My sight fogs. Shapes flicker. Vision wavers. A steel frame anchors my spine. Glass crunches beneath my knees.

My rifle rises; the barrel sweeps across the area. A figure materialises, then vanishes in a flash. I pull the trigger. A bullet speeds toward its mark. No sound of impact. No scream. Just smoke. No confirmation of a kill.

"Contact front!" Derek shouts, voice locked. "Two, 12 o'clock." Two rounds follow, striking their target.

Simon calls next. "Both ends. Multiple shooters. This isn't an ambush. This is a cage."

The layout clicks. This isn't a kill box, but a prison.

"Lay down suppressive fire! Lock down the flank before it seals!" I yell.

Figures glide through the smoke like apparitions—Sergei's men. Formation precise. Movements brisk. Close-quarters strategies emanate from their postures: composed, skilled, deadly.

Simon fires. Two rounds, midline. One drops. The second falters. The third round finishes the job with no mercy. George and Lucy fan wide. Cross angles set.

Barrel flashes rip through the corridor. I surge forward, every breath synced to the forward push. Sparks burst from the wall. Steel screams as bullets dig in deep.

A figure emerges from the fog, moving closer. I aim. Squeeze the trigger. The body falls—a precise shot. Momentum drives my shot. Moving forward is essential for survival.

The formation falters. Sergei's strategy is starting to fall apart. Each moment of hesitation costs lives. Their lines weaken. Gazes shift. Hands hesitate. I see it too. That brief moment of uncertainty. Doubt.

"Left corridor—opening!" Derek yells.

A gap in the net. It might be a trap or a mistake. It's irrelevant. Action takes precedence over contemplation.

"Seize the breach! Derek—hurry!"

Derek charges forward without a moment's pause. His boots crash against the shattered stone. It's an open area—there's no protection. All at stake. Each moment spent exposed is a gamble with life and death.

Rounds cut through the air. Metal ignites with sparks. Stone fractures under pressure. Derek pushes ahead, charging through the chaos. Each step pierces the quiet. That's dedication. That's self-confidence.

An old service panel sits next to the access point. It is ancient technology; rusty and coated in grime. Derek crouches behind a steel plate, hands on the wires, tools ready, causing sparks to fly.

Fingers twist copper. Panels hum with energy. Circuits resist the flow. Smoke ascends. The acrid scent of burnt metal fills the lungs. This is our final gamble. The panel must respond, or we will fail here.

A breath follows. Then another. The panel trembles. A pulse ignites aged veins. Voltage courses through a lifeless system. Machinery awakens. Controls submit—structure bends.

Red lights break through the fog. The strobe flickers. Shadows contort. Their strategy falls apart. Blind spots disappear. We dominate the arrangement now. Their confinement breaks down.

George moves ahead. A figure stumbles forward—incorrect gear. Not our team's. One shot. The skull jerks to the side—no further motion. The man collapses, the body crashing to the ground before the mind registers it.

Another silhouette slices through the smoke, moving nearer. Lucy turns, raising her rifle. Simon outpaces her. Yet another life extinguished by accuracy.

"Advance," I command, my voice unwavering.

There's no hesitation. Each corner poses a question, and each wall conceals secrets. Every step counts.

Darkness deepens. Light recedes. Only our presence holds this corridor. Forward motion carves a path. We own every metre.

Rifles survey the kill zone. Eyes focused. Fingers poised on triggers. This isn't disorder; it's precision. Aggression is delivered with calculated force, violence honed to an edge.

A round slams against the wall near my skull. George responds with one shot. Another man drops. Simon watches from the edge. No motion escapes his lens.

A bulkhead looms ahead. Rusted. Open—just enough. This could be our salvation or a coffin.

Simon and Derek press in. Shoulders collide with the metal. Hinges scream. A wider gap opens. Just enough. We move in through the doorway, rifle first, movement second. Simon covers the left while I take the right. Every angle covered.

Once we are all through, the steel slams back. The world is split in half. The thud echoes—a statement—a seal.

A low hum resonates through the walls. Energy seeps into this tomb. Weapons are primed. Ammunition is tallied. Smoke lingers. Blood intensifies the atmosphere.

"Any injuries?" I say, my eyes scanning the team.

"I'm good," Lucy calls out.

"Flesh wound," says George, pressing a hand to his bicep.

"Excellent. No delay. We proceed now," I say, after confirming I haven't been hit. The world doesn't freeze. Control surges. Momentum favours the one who takes action first.

"I'm fine too. Thanks for asking," Simon adds.

"I'm sorry, you need a plaster, Simon?" I fire back without turning.

"Fuck off, numpty." A smirk buried in venom.

The team resets. The game's not over. The board just changed.

Rifles are reloaded, spare magazines are slapped into pouches, steel-on-steel, and final checks are complete. Pressure builds in the lungs, thickening the air like smoke before a storm breaks.

One chance. No repeat. No retake. Precision wins. Hesitation buries the brave. This moment is ours to claim or surrender. Nothing in between. Action dictates survival. Delay invites death.

Leaving the room, a corridor yawns ahead — narrow, wet with condensation, flanked by pipes coughing rust. Light flickers overhead, weak and twitching. Concrete walls press in, squeezing movement into a single thread. My boots lead the charge down the near-dark tunnel, rifle drawn.

Silence stalks behind. Each step from the others marks trust. No shuffling, no fidgeting. Discipline forged through years in places much worse than this. The point belongs to me — there's no better place to bleed than the front.

"Regrouping is inevitable," Simon's voice cuts through static, clipped and precise. "Minutes. If we're lucky."

Simon doesn't exaggerate A fresh wave approaches — trained, armed, committed. Our window shrinks with every footstep forward.

I glance at the map. My finger presses to the paper, scanning intersections. Choke points. Pressure valves. Options.

"We hold the junction. Anyone who gets close, we direct the fight. Force everybody into open ground."

Sound shatters the stillness. A mechanical groan, like ancient steel expelling its own spine. Pipes tremble. Dust falls from above. The tremor crawls beneath my boots, alive and hunting.

Steel shifts within the walls. A low grind builds — deep, guttural, unnatural. Something reconfigures out of sight. Machinery clutches breath. The enemy doesn't just fire bullets — they're rewiring the entire board.

Derek examines a nearby service panel. Wires hum with energy. Red lights flash in sequence.

"Control's compromised," he growls.

Doors bang shut further down the tunnel. One and then another. Noise reverberates like thunder against the concrete — Someone is managing the board's tilt beneath us. Paths disappear. Choices start to dwindle.

Lucy growls through gritted teeth, rifle tight. "We're getting boxed in. Driven into a trap."

Correct. This isn't just brute force. This is war through manipulation. The territory is being stolen an inch at a time.

"Think you may be right." My words land like stone. Calm. Controlled.

We move ahead. A bulkhead crashes shut behind us, sealing off our escape. In front, the corridor constricts once more, with the lights dimming further. This entire place seems to dance to Viktor's melody.

Angles vanish. Shadow swallows coverage. The rhythm of war is no longer ours. They're composing the next movement. Every note is wired to collapse.

Simon eyes the map. Fingers trace dead ends. One slow shake of the head.

"Someone is funnelling us. Nothing but dead ends ahead. If we stall, we're boxed, gunned, and buried."

Pressure mounts at the base of my skull. I sense the rhythm. We're on her stage now, moving to the wrong beat. That stops now.

Crack.

Gunfire rips out of the dark like a thrown chain. First burst hits pipework—sparks, shrapnel, ricochets. The second burst tags the wall inches from my head. Light vanishes behind barrel flashes. Shapes move fast and close. Disciplined.

One signal from my fingers—sharp, fast. George and Lucy peel off. Flank. Flank. Kill.

First shot hits flesh. Momentum breaks. Knees buckle. Face crashes to the ground. The next body dives behind a broken pallet—too slow. Lucy's second round finds the neck.

Spent casings clatter across concrete. The tempo shifts. Their fire drops. Gaps open. Opportunity breathes again.

The back wall is sealed off with a door. This could signify either hope or doom. There will be no more uncertainties.

"That override," I bark, pointing to the panel near the door. "Find it, Derek."

He moves, fingers flicking across the pad. Sparks fly. No response. Lights dead. Nothing gives.

"Give me a few minutes," he mutters.

"We don't have minutes," the words leave my mouth like snapped wire.

Derek slams a fist into the panel. "Locked out. Full system override. From our intel the person most likely to be controlling their cyber warfare has to be Natasha, Viktor's cyber expert, and he's got every circuit."

Red bloom flashes again. Another enemy pushes up. Simon's rifle erupts. The body drops hard, jerking as blood smears across the floor. One more gone. Too many remain.

"Push now," I shout. "Every second, Natasha pulls tighter. We either move or die here."

Boots thump forward. Shoulders drop. Rifles up. Hands firm. Training kicks in. Every motion flows from muscle memory.

I dash across the open area, the door looming ahead. Gunfire trails me like my own breath. Bullets pursue my every step. One round grazes my shoulder—sparks fly, pain ignites, but I dismiss it. The target takes precedence over the pain.

We stand at the door. Lucy slams a charge to the hinges. Wires twist. My hands cover her back. No voices. Just breathe and count down.

Three.

Two.

One.

The blast shatters steel. The door folds inward, choking on dust. Entry cleared.

The room cleared in a sweep. It is empty. The lights pulse red. A hum buzzes through the panels—another console intact. Power flows. Perhaps there's a way through.

"Derek, get to that system."

Derek runs over, slides in, plugs a device, and begins to override the system. Time drips away like blood. Every second without fire grants us a gift. Every second wasted invites death.

Behind us, metal rattles. Another bulkhead rising. Another wave is forming.

I give a single nod. "No more delays. When this opens, we charge through. No looking back."

Simon reloads. Lucy braces the door. George aligns his scope. Derek mutters numbers softly to himself.

The click of an unlocked door sounds louder than a gunshot— freedom beckons.

"Move!" I roar.

We charge through the breach, rifles blazing, shadows scattering. Nothing exists now but motion, fire, and survival.

*****

The room tightens in Natasha's command centre, and tension doesn't settle. The hum of circuits fills the void, a mechanical reminder that time keeps moving when nothing else does.

Data crawls across monitors, each detail a potential turning point, the difference between control and collapse. Screens throw sharp angles of light across surfaces, reflections twisting as the information updates.

Elbows press into the table. Tension braced in locked arms. Breath slips through clenched teeth, tight, controlled, laced with something raw.

Paths fold inward—cut, sealed, buried. The network tightens like a wire around the throat. Every signal is snared, and each route is traced back to silence. The trap awaits—flawless, patient, and inevitable.

Data flickers, revealing a fracture in the plan, while corridors open where they should be closing. Instead of collapsing, the map expands. Territory unfolds like an open wound, pushing the lines apart from the inside. Everything appears to be bleeding out, yet something moves unseen, rewriting the battle in real time.

Steve's unit should have crumbled, their movement crushed under precision strikes before a counteroffensive took shape.

Tactical lines were drawn, doors bolted, and pathways erased, ensuring no counter. Yet persistence carves into the structure. An imperfection lurks within the execution, a miscalculation breathing inside the design. The grip over this conflict remains, but fractures creep closer.

Plans fracture. Calculations skew. Steve's team refuses to break, slipping through cracks meant to close in. A slow burn presses deep, settling under the ribs like something foreign, something that shouldn't be. The weight spreads, coiling tight, refusing to ease. Pressure builds, pooling in the gut, sharpening into something precise.

"Your method fucking failed." The words land hard, not as an insult, but as a fact. "Brute force is predictable. Strategy wins wars." Natasha's fingers flick across the screen, shifting the map.

Sergei exhales hard, the sound sharp, controlled. "You waste time on strategy while Steve slips past your grasp."

A step drives forward, boots striking hard. The air between them is thick with something unspoken.

"Stacked parts mean nothing once fire hits the frame. Blueprints burn. Diagrams choke on dust. Plans lie — every damn one. Ground truth tears them open and reveals the rot beneath. The paper doesn't bleed. People do. Strategy ignites the moment I tear the board apart. You move. I erase."

Sergei doesn't shout, words emerge from deep within, with fury charging every syllable.

The map fractures. A corridor once marked dead now pulses green. Steve slices through the edge of prediction, carving a path into the unknown. A flaw? A miscalculation? Or something far worse?

My palm anchors the moment. Screens flutter with recalculations. Data breaks form. Routes falter. The rhythm slips. Every safeguard, once flawless, now questions itself. Steve rewrites the rules mid-play. Control slipping is one thing. Reclaiming is another.

A step lands with purpose, unshaken, unhurried. "Your choices, Natasha, just handed Steve's team vital ground," Sergei murmurs, an angry voice threading through the room like a slow blade drawn across a throat.

Natasha's lips pull into a smirk, slow and deliberate. "What will Viktor say about that?" The question hangs, waiting, taunting, daring a response.

Chapter Twenty-Four — Temporary Victory

The air stinks of gunpowder and blood — thick, metallic, clinging to the back of the throat. Emergency lights pulse like a dying heartbeat, throwing jagged shadows across the concrete as if the walls themselves are shifting. Silence stretches thin between breaths, broken only by the distant scrape of something moving just out of sight.

I lead the team deeper into the warren of passageways, pace steady, every step calculated. Rubble crunches beneath our boots, but we don't stop. Every corner could hold a muzzle flash. Every shadow could bite. Simon and George lock down the rear, rifles tight to their shoulders, eyes sweeping for movement. Lucy and Derek move centre, scanning for traps — laser lines, pressure plates, anything that might turn this corridor into a tomb.

Soon, we arrive at a reinforced and secure steel door. A quick sweep past the threshold confirms that the space beyond is clear — an abandoned operations room with intact terminals and secondary exits. Simon drags debris into place, reinforcing entry points by placing iron beams across doorways.

"Ammo count and injury check, everyone," I yell.

With that, the team remove magazines from pouches, reloading any depleted ones from the extra rounds carried in their mission packs.

George answers first, voice steady. "One hundred rounds for the sniper rifle. Four mags for the nine mil. Bleeding's done." A step forward, deliberate, weight shifting between feet, testing for weakness where none can exist.

A cut means nothing if the body still moves. The fight doesn't wait for pain to settle. An ignored wound is a wound that doesn't matter.

The rest of the team yells out ammo counts and injury status.

"Blood," says Derek. "Didn't spot the damage till now. Guess the rush kept everything else louder."

Static hums through Derek's earpiece, distorted voices breaking apart, fragments of intercepted transmissions slipping through the cracks. Enemy chatter shifts — orders, movement reports, something urgent; whatever they're planning.

"Grenades. Anyone holding?" Simon's voice pierces the silence, sharp and commanding.

"Five," says George, fingers tapping twice against the strap. "Never got to use the bloody things." A pause stretches enough to hint at amusement before a slow grin creeps in. "Plenty of targets ahead."

With the ammunition redistributed among the team and any new wounds dealt with, Lucy and I search the room for clues that will help pinpoint the exact location of what we came for. The documents collected earlier gave us an idea, but everything helps.

Maps unfurl over the dust-covered console, blueprints revealing hidden corridors and long-forgotten maintenance shafts. Lucy's gloved hand traces possible choke points on the map.

Derek deciphers intercepted radio chatter from Natasha's command centre. "Sergei's forces are regrouping, and it sounds like Natasha is assuming command. Hostiles consolidate, drawing lines in preparation for the next strike. An assault might be massing on the far side of that door, shifting into position," Derek says, still listening to the receiver.

The first shot will come soon — waiting for the advantage. We hit first. Make sure return fire doesn't come our way.

Simon takes up a position near the doorway, the barrel of his rifle staying locked, the stock firm, breath measured, waiting for the next threat to step into range. The trigger is a fraction away from the action. When the first contact lands in the crosshairs, the fight will begin again, when that time arrives.

George claims a vantage point, rifle settled. I prep additional charges on all exit points from the room, ready to blow if anyone comes knocking — an extra insurance policy against possible overwhelming numbers. The room is fortified, but containment is temporary. Time now directs the next move.

The plan begins to take shape in my mind — gaps, angles, and weaknesses waiting to be exploited. Sergei's reinforcements are the primary obstacle.

Cut the supply, sever the chain, and strip away options. Additional bodies mean a prolonged fight, one that might shift the odds. Silence the extra guns and break the ability to call for help. A wasted heartbeat invites the enemy to dictate the fight. Momentum stays with the one who refuses to stop.

One barricade, one blocked exit, and the fight becomes a containment kill. Open ground transforms into a choke point, with each step shrinking options, driving towards a predetermined outcome.

Sergei doesn't dictate how this ends. Cutting off the last exit forces action without thought and with no control. Pressure will build with every movement, pushing toward decisions that aren't Sergei's to make. Clinging to the illusion a second more — then ripping control from his grasp. Viktor's crew will stumble and be too slow to correct their course. A mistake measured in seconds. One breath too late.

Securing the relic matters more than the fight. Viktor's men push forward, steps tightening, distance shrinking. If Sergei's men dig in, extraction locks down. Dragging this out hands over the advantage. We must end this now before the ground beneath us belongs to the enemy.

With the target secured, one problem remains—staying mobile, keeping the ability to move before the walls close in. A dead-end means a death sentence. One chance exists to end this without getting buried.

With some plan sorted for the next move, I speak in a loud voice, just enough for everyone in the room but not anyone who may be on the other side of the door listening and ready to attack.

"We must depart from here and find Natasha's command centre before retrieving the relic."

Somewhere ahead, Sergei fortifies positions, closing gaps and forcing movement where advantage favours their position. Traps wait beyond sightlines, corridors narrowing into kill zones. A strategy unfolds, but the fight doesn't belong to Sergei alone. Step first, strike first, deny control.

Time shifts the balance, granting Sergei an advantage. Territory slips into his grasp inch by inch. Movement diminishes, paths collapse, and gaps that were once open have vanished.

Pressure surpasses control and acts quicker than sheer power, allowing no space for uncertainty. Take the initiative. Remove the issue. Leave no survivors, and seize control.

"To give us a better chance of getting out of here alive, Simon and George, I want you two to carry out a quick recce in that direction." I point to the door at the back of the room. "The rest of us will do the same, leaving through the other exit. We rendezvous at this location." I point to the map.

"What's the call if we spot or come under fire from tangos?" asks Simon.

"Send the message out first. If the line stays open, pass everything through. Engage only if you have no other option," I reply.

"Roger that."

"Last chance to speak. If not, we move." The order lands hard, leaving no space for hesitation.

George drops, one knee slamming into the concrete. The rifle is locked in tight, barrel fixed on the steel door. Breath held. Eyes calm. Kill-zone established without a word.

Lucy slides in beside George, steps silent, sight aligned, finger close but not committed. Control resides in the margin between now and never. The stare remains unwavering. The shot lingers, balanced on a knife-edge of tension.

Simon moves up to remove the blockade against the door. Fingers wrap around the cold steel beam. Muscles brace. Metal screams against metal, the sound tearing through silence—jagged, brutal, surgical.

The door gives one inch, then another. Hinges grind under strain. Every second stretches. My gut knots—not from fear, but certainty of whatever lies beyond the door.

The corridor remains devoid of life: no footsteps, no breath, just something unseen beneath the silence, waiting, watching.

Gaps like this don't happen by accident. Silence stretches too much, too open. Nothing blocking the path doesn't mean nothing is waiting beyond. Step forward without control, and the trap might snap shut.

The second exit gets the same treatment—checked, cleared, reinforced. There are no shortcuts or missed steps. Every door is either an entry or a trap.

Both teams step into the corridor, boots pressing against stone, the glow from flickering lights just about holding the dark at bay. The air hangs stale, heavy with something just beneath the surface—unspoken, unseen, waiting to be disturbed.

Concrete walls press in, the scent of rust and stagnant water thick enough to choke. Grates clatter under shifting weight, vibrations echoing ahead, swallowed by the dark. George moves first, rifle angled forward. Simon follows, barrel sweeping the tunnel, tracking movement before crap happens. A faint murmur filters through the ducts—a language neither speaks, but the tone is unmistakable. Russian. Orders. Commands. An operation in motion.

Shadows shift 200 metres away near an access corridor, bodies moving with purpose. Sergei's mercenaries are working fast, stacking crates, reinforcing barricades, weapons ready. It's a forward operating post in the making.

George raises a hand, fingers cutting through the dim glow. Simon drops, rifle lined up, breath measured, target locked. Eight figures advance, movements crisp, spacing precise. Rifles track unseen threats, barrels shifting in tandem. The air thickens, humming with the promise of violence held on a trigger's edge.

More might be tucked away, waiting behind cover, watching from angles unseen. Gaps exist in the view, pockets of space deep enough to hide more than just hesitation. The headcount won't matter when the first round fires.

Every number, every estimate, becomes irrelevant the moment bullets fly. Only those who strike without conviction dictate the fight. A stalled trigger kills faster than a loaded barrel. The weak hesitate, and the dead stay down. The final shot isn't about who fires first but who ensures the fight doesn't restart.

Near the supply crates, a shape lingers, body tensed, radio clenched in a firm grip. Lips part, shaping words without sound. No broadcast reaches the ear, only the promise of what follows. Signals don't linger unanswered. The intent is evident. They are requesting assistance or verifying preparedness.

Simon presses against the wall, breathing deep, eyes scanning the gap. Movement beyond the fence flickers—soft shadows framed by halogen light. The price of a single wrong move hangs heavy in the air.

George crouches forward, marking the terrain—crates, mud trails, broken ground. Every object appears as either a threat or cover. The fence line is stacked with loaded and empty steel boxes. All are dangerous.

"Two guards, west side," Simon murmurs. "Loop resets every 10 seconds."

"Four firing points, overlapping," George adds. "No clear lane. Yet."

Tactical patterns form in Simon's mind—defensive arcs, blind spots, and weaknesses ready to be exploited. Precision dictates survival. One mistake and this corridor becomes a killing field.

"S3, this is ST. Forward OP confirmed. Two hostiles are entrenched. Defences remain strong. No casual placement—this is deliberate. Over."

Static crackles, tension hanging in the air. Words descend like lead through the comms. The post isn't scouting—it's waiting.

"S3, Roger that, what's your twenty?"

Simon scans the passage. A faded mark stains the wall. E4 stands stark against filth and rust. Streaks of time strip the edges, but the code remains readable. Numbers scrawled across a torn map match the symbols on the concrete. Not random. A marker left behind, leading somewhere unseen.

"S3, we're positioned near a junction labelled E4," Simon's voice stays level. "Marking aligns with our 20. Confirming position, over."

"TS, closing in on a parallel track—near your corridor. Left approach coming in fast. Distraction required. Out."

Simon and George launch a controlled diversionary attack—fast, violent, and disorienting. Sharp, precise, relentless gunfire ripples through the silence. A deafening crack rolls through the air as spent casings scatter across rough ground, bouncing off rock and dust.

Burnt propellant lingers, sharp and raw, seeping into fabric, clinging to skin, embedding deep like an old wound. The air carries thick with the aftermath of gunfire, each breath pulling in the remnants of spent casings and scorched residue.

As we get close to the junction, a wall of return gunfire erupts to our right—sudden and punishing; the air fractures. Pressure crushes the chest, demanding motion with no time to think, only to act. Flashes tear through the dark. Each burst is a strobe of violence.

Every round carves the terrain. Earth splits, and concrete cracks. Movement becomes survival, not strategy. We push forward, teeth clenched, boots digging for traction across uneven ground.

The cover disintegrates under the second wave. Splinters fly. Metal shrieks. No mercy in that rhythm. Each shot tracks with precision; zero drift, zero waste.

Simon yells over the fire, "Flank left, push the breach!"

Lucy shifts beside me, eyes hard, rifle up. George breaks right, dragging suppression with him. The kill zone reshapes. We don't control the field yet, but the moment cracks. One weakness. That's all I need.

Simon pivots, locking the rifle into the right shoulder, breathing steady. The trigger squeeze remains deliberate, seamless, and uninterrupted. Brass spins from the ejection port, a rhythmic offering to unfolding battle. The barrel shifts, the sight picture clears, and another tango drops—then another.

George reinforces fire with an unrelenting hammer, striking the enemy's anvil. The push intensifies, forcing movement and corralling the disoriented opposition toward their demise.

Confusion spreads like an infection, hesitation growing in the absence of direction.

A head appears above the protection of the crates. George squeezes the trigger, and a single round carves a path through flesh, puncturing the man's windpipe with surgical precision. Crimson mist erupts, suspended midair before splattering across cold steel. The lifeless form crumples, limbs twitching as nerves misfire in the final seconds of existence.

A second man stares, eyes locked on the convulsing corpse, breath ragged, grip faltering. The ground shifts, rules break, and nothing follows logic anymore. Battle rewrites itself in real-time, shredding order and leaving behind a storm without direction.

The crack of splitting bone drowns out instinct before the mind registers the damage, the force snapping through muscle and driving the body back. A muffled burst pierces through flesh, ripping control away in an instant. The spine crunches against an unyielding crate, the collision absorbing what remains of resistance; the dull sound is swallowed by the silence that settles where life once stood.

A brutal burst tears through the barrier, sending jagged shards hurtling through the air. Bullets carve through like fangs, sinking into prey and devouring everything in their path. Debris scatters, dust thickening in the air as the structure buckles under the relentless impact, remnants spreading across the concrete.

No shield remains, leaving only exposure and the promise of something final—a killing ground waiting to be claimed.

A sharp command shatters the moment, desperation bleeding through the shouted orders. Sergei's men flinch, confusion splintering discipline. Rounds carve through the dust-choked corridor, a relentless cascade of controlled aggression. The air thickens with cordite and blood—the language of war, spoken in bursts of lead.

Muzzle flashes strobe through the murk, painting the walls with flickering ghosts of violence. Simon and George unleash a measured onslaught, each shot a ruthless demand for dominance. The enemy hesitates, momentum shifting, balance teetering on a knife's edge. Every movement pushes the battle toward.

A suppressed crack punctuates the chaos. One of Sergei's men stiffens, shoulders snapping back, knees buckling as the fight drains from rigid limbs. Blood spatters across the wall, soaking into the dust before a lifeless form slumps against jagged concrete.

Another combatant falters, rifle slipping from fingers that now disobey. The weapon clatters, echoing through the corridor, swallowed by the roar of combat. George steadies, breath controlled, gaze locked — another clean execution.

Four figures press forward, rifles swinging in frantic arcs, barrels chasing ghosts. Boots scrape across the debris, the desperation piercing the noise. Doubt lingers in the pause between orders, in the glances that measure the distance to cover.

The fight mutates with every passing breath, stripping away predictability. Hesitation invites a swift end, reaction carving the only path forward.

Firepower alone won't settle this — the one controlling momentum will. Whoever forces the next move determines who claims victory and who meets the ground.

A metallic snap cuts through the tunnel's din to the front as George lobs a grenade into Sergei's men. Steel scrapes against rock, bouncing twice before settling in the dust. The grenade lies motionless, a silent promise of destruction. The battlefield pauses for a heartbeat, then the world tears apart.

The team dives for protective cover as the detonation rips through the corridor, swallowing the darkness in a blinding eruption. A wave of heat and fragments slams outward, shockwaves rebounding off the walls, punching through anything caught in the blast radius. The barricade disintegrates, jagged shards slicing through the air, metal splinters seeking flesh.

Smoke churns, thick and choking, warping the battleground. Sound distorts, movement fractures. Boots scrape against steel, hurried steps fading into the haze. Sergei's men scatter, instinct for flight overriding tactics. Chaos reigns now — command lost to confusion, discipline collapsing under the weight of raw survival.

A second explosion shatters what remains of the OP. Rifles of those still alive rise in panicked response, barrels sweeping through the fog. Rifle fire rips through the air, rounds hammering into concrete, spraying dust, carving through emptiness.

Muzzle flashes stutter in erratic bursts, desperation choking precision. Control slips from hands, territory shrinking with every missed shot. This ground belongs to us now.

Rounds from the team snap through the air, weaving between barricades and cutting off options. Our advance presses on, a methodical force encroaching from all directions. Territory succumbs to pressure, leaving no room for retreat.

Five metres away, an arch, the frame ruptured, edges curled inward as though clawed apart. Oxidation spreads like an infection, with flaking remnants crumbling. Beyond the opening, blackness stretches deep, an open maw, hungry for movement, silent, watchful, concealing whatever lingers within.

Filth scabs across corroded walls, spreading rot where metal once held firm. Stale air lingers, thick with the stench of decay. The walls press closer, the corridor narrowing into a choke point where movement slows, and survival hinges on precision. Nowhere to dodge, nowhere to run. A hunter's dream, a soldier's nightmare — an inevitable kill zone for Viktor's men to enter.

Gunfire rips from my right, a relentless barrage anchoring the kill zone. Simon and George hold the line, controlling the battlefield with methodical precision. Trapped between overlapping fields of fire, Sergei's men fight like cornered animals, clawing at ghosts, grasping at a victory already lost.

A figure bursts through the smoke. Fast. Direct. A rifle swings out of control. Too close. No time to fire. My blade clears the sheath. Instinct leads. Muscle follows. The blade finds the gap beneath the man's ribs, sinking deep into muscle and lung. A sharp twist severs the last thread of resistance before silence takes hold.

A crack splits the silence, finality written in lead. The weapon remains still, unwavering. Crimson streaks creep across the fractured stone, leaking from bodies twisted at angles nature never intended. Crimson fingers trace jagged cracks, filling voids between shattered fragments. The scene is frozen, yet the blood moves, marking the ground with the last proof of life.

Derek lifts the rifle—no pause, no adjustment—just pure reflex. The shot cracks out, a single breath wrapped in violence, slicing through the chaos.

Flesh tears, bone snaps. The round drills through meat, carving a path no surgeon may follow. Red blood sprays out. Crates catch the fallout, and wood drinks deep. Splinters glisten under the blood. Grain darkens, soaking in the stain like confession inked in silence—one less threat.

A rifle slips from rigid fingers, crashing onto the stone, yet the body doesn't touch the ground by itself. Another shot pierces the silence, the bullet striking its target with surgical precision.

Another target jerks, head snapping back before the spine surrenders, collapsing inward. Scarlet mists the air, settling over debris and dust. One by one, resistance crumbles.

A figure hangs in the open too long—one shot fixes the error. The round hits hard, centre mass through the skull. The body folds into the rubble, thought never catching up to the consequence, one less threat.

The team moves forward. Tight. Focused. Barricades shred under the team's relentless fire, no place left to hide. Sergei's defence collapses, not in chaos, but due to overwhelming pressure.

"Left side clear," George shouts, voice cuts through solid and cold.

A doorway looms ahead, half-gutted, teeth of rusted steel and shattered wood biting inward. The frame absorbs bullets, each one carving into the past.

A body lurches forward. The impact of a single bullet folds the torso backwards. Arms flail, grip slipping. Another failed piece of meat is added to the threshold.

Another staggers left, clutching a torn limb. Flesh torn, bone visible. Eyes filled with agony and loss. The purpose bleeds out faster than the body can compensate — another step. Then collapse.

Smoke rolls close to the ground, thick and heavy. Vision narrows. Sound sharpens. The fog of war doesn't confuse — it refines. Every second now lives on the edge of a trigger pull.

"On your right," Simon yells.

I pivot — rifle up. Breath held. A shot punches through the flesh and bone of a man about to fire. The weapon clatters free. Another body falls. No scream. Just a body hitting the ground.

Lucy moves up. Firing a clean shot, drills through the woman's skull. The twitch is a reflex, nothing more. The body seizes. Then nothing. No name. Just another finished moment.

We pass through the carnage without pause — no room for mourning. The dead chose a side. So did we.

I exhale. Focus resets. Thought returns — but only for a breath. Strategy forms in motion.

"Push through," I scream.

Derek clears the right, George sweeps the rear, Simon shifts left, and Lucy oversees the high ground.

Battles don't have favourites. Precision beats passion. Sentiment weakens steel. I carry no hatred — just responsibility. The outcome matters. The rest dissolves in smoke.

Scattered spent brass covers the ground. The language of battle is expressed through casings and injuries. Each sound acts as a punctuation mark in a fiery sentence.

Those who wait, die. Those who doubt, vanish. The line between breath and burial lies in instinct and execution. The battlefield doesn't care either way.

I do what I must. Nothing more. Nothing less.

With no more fire from Sergei's men and not wanting to be hit by a stray bullet, I radio George, "GD, stand down. We are moving in, over."

"GD, Roger, we are coming up to join you," comes the transmission from George.

When I reach the once forward OP, crates lie shattered, splinters jutting upwards like jagged teeth. The remnants are now a death trap. Beyond the wreckage, bodies twist at angles nature never intended — spines warped, arms flung open, mouths locked mid-scream. Blood thickens in the cracks, turning dust into a paste, a battlefield stamped with finality.

Crimson blood streaks blemished, fractured stone, a liquid path marking failed escape. A man crawls forward, each inch stolen from death itself. Torn flesh drags over jagged ground, nerves firing on impulse, refusing surrender.

Air rattles through crushed ribs, ruined muscle shudders, and a body functions on instinct alone. Nerves misfire, and legs are lifeless. They stretch out behind. Movement slows, but survival urges forward, even as life spills away. Each pull through the wreckage is slower than the last, as fingers scrape through dirt and grit, desperate for traction.

Boot leather scrapes across shattered stone, skimming past spent casings and splintered wood. Legs refuse to answer the command to rise, dead weight dragging beneath ruined fabric.

Blood spreads through the torn weave of fatigues, soaking into the dirt, marking territory that will never be reclaimed. An arm stretches forward, fingers clawing toward the threshold, reaching for salvation that doesn't exist. Survival remains a lie — one that instinct still believes.

A mercy round. A cleaner end than the alternative. Some might flinch. Others may hesitate. Neither changes the truth of what is about to happen. Lucky for me, my PTSD grants me a lack of empathy. A single round ends the struggle, piercing through bone and plunging what remains into silence — no last words. No regrets. It's just a problem removed.

Nothing lingers. The last flicker of resistance burns out. One moment drawn tight, the next surrendering to stillness. Not justice. Not cruelty. Just another step forward. Blood cools, drying in thin streaks over torn fabric. The world doesn't wait, doesn't mourn. The only kindness war allows is the quickness of an end.

We move through the wreckage — weapons raised, instincts sharpened. Spent casings crunch beneath every step. Smoke coils low across the floor, seeping into every fracture, thick enough to breathe — no movement, no sound — just the aftermath stitched into stone.

Bodies litter the ground — some folded in clean collapse, others twisted mid-motion, frozen before impact finished the job. Nothing is assumed. Each form gets checked. One twitch, one gasp, and it's over — protocol over pity. Survival refuses sentiment.

"Clear left," George mutters, rifle tracking low.

"Two down, far side," Lucy responds.

No emotion. Just the facts. Always the facts.

Simon signals a sharp turn. Angles adjust, lines converge, and fire arcs narrow without uttering a single word. The terrain of death reconfigures solely through muscle memory.

"Strip the gear," I order, sharp and controlled. "Take what keeps us alive."

Derek moves in fast, dropping beside a corpse. Fingers work fast, pulling a loaded mag from webbing. No hesitations. No pauses. Tools, not trophies. Each item becomes a step closer to the next breath.

Beneath us, blood spreads like oil. The dead clutch their weapons with frozen defiance — grip locked around steel, as if still fighting. Pride doesn't survive bullets.

Combat vests strain against rigid frames. Pockets bulge with unused rounds. Grenades stay cold, pins still in place. Everything was ready — nothing got the chance.

Steel lies where it fell. Safety switches remain off. Gauze unused. Tourniquets are still folded — no time for treatment. The wounds outran the response. That's how fast this game shifts.

Shells scatter across fractured stone. Magazines untouched. Rifles half-loaded. The hands that once aimed now rest open, fingers limp, purpose gone.

No resistance meets us now. Ammo swaps hands. Knives slide from sheaths. Equipment lifted and reassigned. Survival demands no ceremony.

Rations get passed along — vacuum-sealed, stripped from cooling corpses. Fuel for the living. Calories for muscles are still needed. Nothing wasted. Nothing revered. Death feeds purpose.

No breath left for names. Just gear, weapons, and the will to press forward. What mattered minutes ago lies quiet and silent beneath the stench of burnt cordite.

No emotions involved; just calculations. Unnecessary burdens are abandoned. Anything deemed unhelpful is thrown away. This is the rule in such environments.

Viktor trained soldiers, who now fuel the fight against him. Explosives are repurposed, magazines are reassigned, and steel is turned back on its sender.

Every second counts. War moves in fractions—an inch, a trigger pull, a decision made under fire. That's the currency we trade in now.

Victory values neither rank nor bravery, only swift action and fierce determination. The one who seizes the next moment claims the territory. Nothing else determines the outcome.

Casings grind underfoot. Steel splits bone. Limbs twisted in ways no body should bend. The ground drinks deep blood, filling every crack, every fault line.

George kneels beside a body. Gloves peel back webbing. Pockets open to yield mags, wires, a worn knife blade, chipped but still sharp.

Knuckles scrape across concrete. Lucy finds a sidearm—chamber still loaded. That weapon switches hands. Now it fights for us.

Rigour claims muscle, not metal. The cold doesn't stop the gear. Rounds stay ready. Steel outlives flesh. The fight continues, just with new hands.

Our boots advance, leaving death in our wake. The divide between the fallen and the next victim blurs with each step. There is only one path left: forward.

Paper clings to damp skin, ink spreading in broken lines yet refusing to vanish. Coordinates, transit schedules, coded instructions—the last remnants of a dying mission traced by a grip that failed before the job finished.

The dead do not speak, but secrets remain trapped in their grasp, worth more than the life they surrendered. Information lingers, buried beneath ruined flesh and smouldering ruin, waiting for someone ruthless enough to extract the info.

Numbers press through the red, refusing to fade. Names buried under layers of war reveal something more remarkable than supplies, something more dangerous than bullets. Not all weapons are fired from a barrel. Some are written in ink. Some are spoken in hushed meetings before the first shot is fired.

Twisted wreckage sprawls across the ground, the remains of men and metal indistinguishable in the debris. Something foreign glints under torn webbing among the ruins — pale, rigid, untouched by fire.

A keycard, discoloured and cracked but unbroken. Lucy rips the badge free, plastic scraping, ridges sharp against damp flesh. More than an entry pass. A gatekeeper. An unspoken invitation to whatever lies locked behind reinforced doors.

A sliver of plastic but far from disposable. Not just an entry pass, not just clearance — this unlocks more than doors. Secrets, blueprints, something worth more than the bodies scattered across this floor. Whatever's locked behind reinforced steel didn't stay hidden by accident.

Men don't kill for a keycard unless the prize behind the door outweighs the corpses left in the wake. Reinforced doors don't protect scraps or supplies, but barricade power — something that should have stayed buried, something worth more than the blood spilt.

Static crackles through my earpiece, an electric whisper cutting through the thick air. Derek's voice snaps in, sharp and controlled.

"I've intercepted their comms. Russian voices burst through, orders exchanged. Coordinates relayed. A response team is inbound. Expect contact." The words tighten the space between breaths, the clock already bleeding seconds.

Burning boxes spit fire into the darkness, casting jagged shapes across shattered concrete and twisted steel. The air vibrates with distant movement, and the battle shifts unseen beyond the wreckage. Muscles ache from the weight of the fight, but the mind remains clear, locked on the next engagement. This isn't the end. This is the moment before another storm.

A slow exhale steadies my grip. "A battle won, not the war." My words land hard, cutting through the lingering adrenaline — more for myself than for the others. "Weapons remain raised. This isn't over."

The team stays sharp. Fingers rest on triggers. The battlefield doesn't reward hesitation.

The air stirs through the exposed passage, dragging the acrid stench of spent cartridges through the throat like dry fire. Victory fades when left unguarded, slipping through grasped hands as quick as a pulled trigger. Lungs empty, limbs still, silence stretching where chaos once reigned. Nothing ends until the body stops trying to rise.

Derek's fingers strike the keyboard, slicing through security layers built to keep the past locked away. Code snarls, resisting the breach, walls of encryption slamming down, tightening like a noose. Strings of numbers flicker, symbols scramble — then the screen stutters. A fracture forms.

A vault, a second entrance, an entry point concealed beneath years of classified operations, a buried tunnel stretching through forgotten history — patterns align, revealing an unseen corridor threading through old battlegrounds. Every step pushes the mission deeper into a place never meant to be found.

Lucy's fingertips glide over brittle parchment she's found, a breath of movement sending invisible fractures through the frail material. Stains creep along the edges, soaking deep, the colour long set into fibres worn thin by time. Shredded remnants curl away, flaking from the surface like bark stripped from a dying tree.

Never designed to last, yet standing defiant, held together by something more profound than structure. Cracks splinter across the surface, jagged reminders of the battles once endured. Weakness creeps through every fracture, but purpose locks the foundation in place, refusing to fall.

Symbols twist where moisture carved through paper, the sharp edges of intent dulled by time. Fragments scatter, ink stretched thin, lines drifting into chaos but never erased. Stains stretch deep, bleeding through layers, each marking a fight between decay and preservation. Buried words hold, clinging to existence, waiting to be uncovered.

Light catches on the surface, shifting the contrast and forcing shapes from the wreckage of what once held order. Meaning rises from underneath destruction, letters aligning in a sequence never to be seen again.

Script etched in fading ink clings to the remains of war, a final testament to those struck from history. Fractures crawl along the edges, whispering of battles fought in shadows. Every letter holds the weight of purpose, challenging anyone bold enough to pull truth from the ruins.

The battlefield isn't pretty. Grit has embedded itself into fractured stone along the sides of the tunnel, swallowing meaning beneath the weight of the lost.

Scattered wreckage conceals more than memories, waiting for hands ruthless enough to claim what remains. Some serve as graves, while others hold something far worse.

Scorched fabric clings to the dirt, smothering what waits beneath. A single step chooses who walks away and who never moves again.

To deny Sergei's men freedom of movement, I erect several IEDS along the corridor. Wires stretch tight beneath crumbling debris, hidden threads of destruction primed for the first misstep.

Charges conceal themselves in thresholds and under chassis, buried where no one thinks to check — an invitation written in silence, ready to respond with fire.

Nothing goes to waste. Straps ripped from fallen gear secure detonators, explosives stripped from abandoned stockpiles repurposed for a new target. A twisted frame slumps over shattered concrete, lifeless but not forgotten.

Strangers mistake the quiet for an invitation, creeping forward with misplaced confidence. The promise of still ground tempts the untrained, pulling them into a grave too slow to recognise. The ground does not forget; it only waits.

Silence clings to the wreckage, a false lull stretched thin over the battlefield. Movement disrupts the illusion, boots grinding through dust already claimed. Somewhere in the complex, Viktor's forces advance, oblivious to the trap beneath their feet, the ground set to turn.

The ground does not negotiate, but takes what battle demands, swallowing the fallen without question. Lines drawn today will mean nothing tomorrow except for the bodies left behind. The only certainty here is that not all will walk away.

A voice cuts through the radio, quick, measured. Simon's words hit fast, stripped of hesitation. "Hostiles incoming. Rapid approach."

Beyond the barricade, movement thickens. Shapes push forward. The last body hasn't stiffened. Yet another wave closes in, weapons raised, decisions already made. Carrion birds don't hesitate. Neither do men with orders to kill.

Heat radiates from the shattered concrete, the scent of burnt powder and charred steel curling into the air. George adjusts, rifle firm, crosshairs floating over a heartbeat that doesn't realise their time is measured. One pull. One kill.

Angles shift. Escape routes vanish. Across the gap, figures move in a calculated dance—regrouping, adjusting, reading. Patterns emerge in the chaos, the shape of the next push taking form. Whoever delays writes their ending. The losing side does not make the last decision in combat.

"Move. Now."

My command lands with weight, slicing through the air, leaving no room for hesitation—a single order, absolute. The vault remains the only objective. Viktor's men cannot claim what waits inside.

My grip tightens around the rifle's stock. A fight awaits beyond this threshold, not as a possibility but as an inevitability.

Muscles settle into purpose. Boots grind over grit, shifting into practised formation, weapons aligned with the unknown ahead. The silence before impact never lingers, a fleeting breath before metal and intent carve into resistance. Reinforced steel does not conceal treasure, but it conceals something buried by time and blood. Some vaults store artefacts. This one locks away power.

Chapter Twenty-Five — Digital Battlefield

Gunfire tears down the corridor—short, violent bursts carving the air into chaos. One of Sergei's men breaks cover, rifle up, ready to fire. I don't hesitate—one shot. Centre mass. He folds before the barrel smoke clears—sharp, clean, done.

A body jerks backwards, dragged by the fist clenched in his collar. Another shot cracks. Skull, not chest. Messy. Final. The weight slumps, breath rattling once before silence seals it. Blood seeps out in slow waves, thick and dark, pooling through fractured concrete like the floor's trying to drink it.

Rounds slam into the barricade ahead—wood, steel, whatever holds shape under fire. Crates splinter. Screams twist through the smoke. Limbs flicker in and out of view, flailing, ducking, caught in the storm. It's not a firefight now. It's a slaughter line. And we're walking straight through it.

Flashes of impact slash across the ruins, momentary bursts revealing the destruction in fragments. Broken ground shifts under relentless fire. The battlefield is alive in shifting tides. The scene twists in violent unpredictability, momentum shifting with each shot fired.

Bursts of gunfire tear through the wreckage, exposing shattered barricades and figures frozen mid-motion. The dark swallows people just as fast, erasing everything in an instant. The battlefield shifts, unpredictable, the next moment unwritten. Viktor's fighters edge backwards, slipping from one defensive point to the next, keeping their lines intact, retreating but not collapsing.

Rifle fire answers every shadow. The team opens up, a wall of force sweeping the ground clean. Rounds cut through soft targets before positions can form—no time for thought. Movement dies under weight and the velocity of fire.

The first line breaks. Limbs buckle. Nothing but silence follows, broken only by the last few rounds clearing what remains.

I push forward, my heart hammering against my ribs. No emotion—just focus. Eyes scan for the next threat, not the last mistake. Brass bounces underfoot, rolling through red-soaked stone.

Another wave of rifle fire slams our line. The team lay down another barrage of fire slamming through open ground, shredding the staggered formation before an escape can take shape.

The few that move now drop mid-step, cut down before momentum becomes an escape. One by one, the fight bleeds out. No mercy. Precision over noise.

Yet again, the ground holds bodies in pieces. Unreadable. Twisted. Blood seeps into old fractures, finding depth where nothing human should settle. The stench in the air turns thick.

Burnt powder clings to the air, cut by the raw scent of open wounds. Bodies lie tangled across the shattered ground, frozen mid-motion, where force abandoned hope. Spent casings rest against exposed flesh, their heat fading faster than the lives ended.

Boots grind against lifeless forms, pushing past the wreckage left behind. Nothing moves except those still clinging to life. The dead hold no threat. Only those with breath remain unfinished business.

A single round carves through the exposed ground, tearing through anything caught in its path. Simon fires once— unwavering, deliberate. The round buries deep, cutting movement short. Limbs convulse, forced back by the sheer force of impact.

Our route cuts through bodies torn apart, some reduced to silence, others thrashing in futile resistance. Survivors pull themselves forward, reaching for cover or a last desperate shot, pain drowned beneath sheer will.

Silence claims those who stop moving, their presence nothing more than discarded wreckage on a battlefield that doesn't wait. The battle drives forward, a force without patience, dragging what remains into the next kill zone.

Loose fragments shift beneath a measured, deliberate stride. Progress unfolds with a sharp efficiency, with nothing left to chance. Speed matters, but discipline matters more — one misstep invites trouble that doesn't allow corrections. I scan the shifting lines to my front in a calculated motion, breaking apart only to reform elsewhere.

At last, the firing thins as the enemy withdraws beyond range, leaving the area littered with bodies and weapons scattered across the dust-coated concrete.

Routes close and reopen, forming lanes that guide rather than scatter. The exit isn't a scramble — it's controlled. Someone orchestrates the retreat, adjusting the pieces and preparing for whatever comes next.

"Let's fuck off out of here," I yell, turning and indicating down the passageway behind me.

"Right with you," comes Lucy's reply as we sprint away from the latest firefight.

After 100 metres and several turns, I raise my hand, and everyone goes to the ground. Barrels track entry points and overlapping arcs of fire, ensuring no space remains unchecked. Footsteps adjust, a constant calculation, positioning dictated by experience.

The kill zone is controlled. Nothing enters without consequence. A silent agreement pulses through the team — everything outside this perimeter is a target until proven otherwise.

I examine a paper map that splits along fractured seams, a relic of the past. Routes intersect at deliberate angles, funnelling movement into spaces that trap rather than guide. Walls close in, narrowing, shifting passageways into a controlled funnel. The air grows thin, choices wither, and hesitation seals the outcome. No turns, no backtracking — only a singular path ahead, one step away from a final reckoning.

Routes slice across the map like fresh wounds, expertly crafted to mislead the trusting. Openings widen to entice, then funnel movement to narrow passages without an exit. A sniper could be lurking, scope focused, breath controlled, finger poised on the trigger.

On the wall to my left are the words F7. A fingertip drags across the blueprint, tracing walls and junctions, counting every turn. The vault should be within striking distance, assuming the access card's data holds.

However, we need a secure room not too far from the objective, to prepare and gather information on Natasha and Sergei's movements before recovering the relic.

I keep movement tight as I slip through cover to reach each team member. Execution demands clarity. Anything overlooked becomes an advantage for the enemy. Nothing progresses until the pieces are set, locked in place with no weak links.

A single mistake means the last thing I detect might be the crack of a round meant just for me. The next decision falls to whoever's left standing. Whoever makes the call won't matter where I'm going.

When ready, I lead off, stepping forward with each footfall measured and deliberate. The tunnel stretches ahead in silence, minutes pass, the air thick with the scent of damp concrete and old circuitry.

A shape emerges from the grey. A doorway. Fortified. Steel hardened against anything less than full commitment. Bolts recessed. No latch. Just defiance welded into the frame. R5 — marked bold, high, unforgiving.

My hand rests against the frame — pulse steady, mind focused — but something stirs beneath the surface. This door doesn't block access, and it doesn't open to options; rather, it eliminates them. Steel forged for finality, not passage. Whatever awaits beyond carries mass, the kind that shifts air and alters outcomes. My gut senses pressure long before contact.

I make a swift gesture with my left hand that sends the unit forward. Boots surge ahead, rifles locked in, as bodies slice through the gap without pause.

The doorway collapses behind us as space shifts. Movement is controlled. Each step is measured with intent. The right falls under my scope, barrel locked on. Simon flanks left, sweeping the blind corner, while George holds the centre, cutting off any frontal attack.

Lungs seize, breath trapped tight, refusing release. A step grates over the silence, raw against the absence of sound. The stillness isn't empty — it waits, listening, calculating. The slightest misstep isn't forgiven. Here, hesitation and death are the same thing.

One reckless idiot, one desperate move, and the whole operation spirals. A hidden gun, a last-minute charge — anything turns lethal in a fight like this.

Silence tricks the untrained, a false comfort waiting to be broken. A breath starts but never completes. Movement follows calculation — nothing steps forward unverified, and no weapon lowers until the next space confirms itself empty.

Hesitation isn't a weakness here. It lingers long enough to prove fatal. When the trigger is pulled, the decision lasts less than a heartbeat — bodies will fall, deprived of choice.

Barrels sweep the dark, tracing every fracture in the stone. Crates lie overturned, shadows thick between broken supports. Each corner is sliced apart — no noise, no movement, just waiting.

Boots grind through dust. Every sense pushes forward. Emptiness never equals safety. Silence often masks the worst.

Dust clings to undisturbed surfaces, untouched by the battle that might have never arrived. The vacuum of inaction presses against the walls, stretching the seconds before reality asserts itself.

Cabinets lean, twisted by time and force. Doors hang loose, hinges groaning under dead weight. Shelves sit bare, cleared fast or left in panic. Nothing accidental. Everything about this place speaks of purpose repurposed.

Prints in the console run fresh across the dust. Footprints are recent. Someone's worked here. Someone still might. Rusted dials sit motionless, stripped of signal, but the silence hides a potential advantage.

I tap Derek's shoulder. "Run comms from here. Push updates to Dave. Fast and quiet."

"On it," Derek says, placing the laptop on a dented metal table. Wires loop from the ports like exposed nerves, and fingers tap commands into the keyboard. A length of insulated cord snakes from the console, leading toward something unseen. If this links to an external antenna, the right frequency turns the room into an open broadcast.

Derek strikes keys in a rapid sequence, threading through encrypted layers like second nature. "Simon, grab that lead," he says, urgency spilling into motion.

Sparks dance from a cracked panel, circuits resisting their final override, the last step before completion.

Simon gives a pull on the cable that strains under the pull, knots slipping as tension shifts. Metal grinds against concrete, a drawn-out scrape that bites through the silence. Derek stands, unreadable, the moment stretching as reality cements itself, unavoidable and fixed.

The line snaps taut, stretched to the limit but missing the mark. Simon flexes, frustration bleeding through. "Bollocks. This bastard's too short."

Without saying a word, Derek jerks the table with the laptop into place, wires dragging along the grated steel. A sound cuts through the space, an interruption and a caution. His fingers strike the keyboard with urgency, eliminating the unnecessary, slicing through resistance like a knife through skin.

A concluding command secures control, compelling the system to comply or fail. "Sorted," Derek mutters, voice stripped of anything but certainty.

A sweep of the space exposes something crude yet deliberate — a rusted lever anchored into corroded steel. A contact breaker, thick with neglect and caked in dust, refuses to budge. George's hands clamp around the worn grip, and with one hard pull, the switch slams downward.

A mechanical groan rumbles through the silence. Old radio equipment rattles and sputters before a sharp whine splits the air, dragging something dead back to the surface.

Derek hunches over the laptop, keystrokes rapid and precise — each input a weapon slicing through layers of encrypted defences. Streams of information ripple and bend, flickering between corruption and control, a battlefield of shifting code.

Barriers constrict, reinforced with countermeasures, yet breaches unravel protections in real time, scripts locking into combat, a war fought in milliseconds.

Firewalls tighten, resisting the surge, but fractures spread like veins through glass. The system fights back, desperate to hold. The intrusion spreads, worming past protection and digging into the framework.

Encrypted walls fracture, sequences collapsing in succession. A controlled failure, systematic and precise. Weak points widen under the strain, peeling back layers designed to withstand any attack. The network haemorrhages security, defences giving way before containment becomes an option.

Streams of corrupted intel scatter into the void, unclaimed fragments waiting for whoever dares to seize control. Viktor's firewall remnants flicker, struggling against collapse, but the foundation crumbles, leaving nothing but an exposed network gasping for stability.

Static crackles through the comms. "I've got movement, faint," says George, positioned near the door and adjusting the grip on the rifle.

"Roger that, keep us updated," I say into the mic.

Simon adjusts, pressing deeper into cover, rifle aimed at the corridor's entrance. The sound of boots closes in, each step compressing the space between uncertainty and engagement.

George angles forward, the weapon locked into place. The corridor ahead is stretched thin between an empty passage and an ambush waiting to spring.

Death stands ready just beyond the door, arranged with precision, primed for anyone reckless enough to be the first to enter. Simon takes his stance, rifle steady, silently affirming that this frontline is under our control.

Static crackles split apart as Derek locks onto hostile chatter, stripping away the noise to expose the threat. Lucy hunts through the surveillance grid, mapping changes in patterns and marking the moment a presence shifts from passive to lethal.

"How far do you think those footsteps are, and how many tangos?" I ask Simon.

"I would say several hundred metres away. As for numbers, hard to tell as sound echoes in here."

Pressure rises—not from loss but from what lies beneath the surface. This fight shifts. Something personal weaves through the smoke—and is pulling hard.

Mission parameters faded the moment blood hit steel. This isn't about extraction or leverage. Something else rides this line—something with weight behind it. I understand the shape of calculated revenge.

I've worn that face—calculated, cold, built for purpose. The same stare lingers in the dark, reflected back with precision. No broadcast. No warning. Just a silent message—this ends with one of us.

Cyber walls realign in a single stroke, sealing vulnerabilities before scanners register the abnormality. Subroutines shift, diverting automated sweeps to dead zones, leaving critical areas unguarded.

Unseen lines weave through security gaps, slipping past unmanned barriers and locking essential entry points before countermeasures react. Systems lag, struggling to track the silent advance carving through critical junctions before resistance can be deployed.

Derek exhales, reading the counterplay. A decoy attack initiates, redirecting Natasha's focus. A false breach alarm at a secondary server mimics a real-time intrusion. The firewall pivots, isolating a non-existent threat.

Fragmented structures collapse inward, debris marking the route of a silent breach. Encryption layers falter as a concealed sequence threads through unguarded access points, slipping past broken security barriers. The surrounding fight rages, keeping focus elsewhere while intrusion deepens without resistance.

A secure data cache surfaces—encrypted, buried beneath layers of defence, but exposed for the first time. Derek breaks through the cypher and extracts fragmented files. Lucy scans the information on her tablet, piecing together coordinates, mission directives, and financial trails. It's a transaction, not an artefact.

Natasha's system retaliates. A counter-hack launches, with backdoor scripts attempting to brute-force their way into Derek's terminal. This offensive manoeuvre is designed to plant a trace and disrupt the framework. Firewall responses surge, and intrusion logs flood with false positives.

Derek floods Natasha's system with packet data, and intrusion logs overwhelm monitors. It's an orchestrated digital barrage. Derek pries through gaps, lifting deployment routes and extraction markers the instant Natasha's securities hesitate. Another weakness cracks open, exposing layers buried beneath encrypted shields.

Layers of reinforced security peel apart, crumbling in increments, every split widening as defences struggle to hold. Firewalls collapse in intermittent bursts, causing complete sections to shut down before the system can react. The breach cuts through unprotected code, disconnecting control with pinpoint accuracy.

After 20 minutes, Derek spots something: a hidden server cloaked under a labyrinth of dead pathways, a restricted vault of info untouched and unseen. Barriers collapse, cascading in a rapid breakdown as Derek dismantles layer after layer.

Encrypted walls rupture, sending corrupted signals surging through weakened infrastructure. Protective barriers split apart, collapsing in succession, with no failsafe engaging. Each breach widens the exposure, blind spots flaring, while critical systems flicker in and out of function, haemorrhaging control with no recovery in sight.

Processing thresholds shatter, and raw surges burn through relay points. System integrity fractures, and command chains shorten as safeguards dissolve. Permissions dissolve into hostile hands, rewriting root controls and purging balance in a cascade of destruction that no firewall restrains.

Natasha retaliates, launching countermeasures designed to sever the intrusion, but it is too late. Derek's fingers move with surgical precision, locking the stolen files into secured storage on the laptop before the system seals the breach.

Heat rises from the laptop's vents, carrying the remains of strained hardware pushed past safe limits. Light flickers across corroded panels, shadows stretching and retracting over metal, scarred from time and neglect.

Distorted fragments shift over jagged edges, stretching and twisting with each flicker of light. Once solid, now shattered, the remnants cling to an erased past, leaving nothing but splintered echoes of what once stood unbroken.

Lines of code spill down the screen, an unbroken stream of commands tunnelling deeper into Viktor's network.

The ground trembles. Outside the door, the sound of approaching boots gets louder. It's a countdown, not a waiting game.

Derek's fingers continue to strike the keyboard in controlled bursts. A decryption sequence unravels, exposing layers of encrypted communication logs. A priority message surfaces, and red flags are embedded in the metadata.

The monitor flickers, streams of intel tightening into focus. A pattern emerges, one that leaves no doubt. Viktor's men are inside the lower tunnels — this is ground chosen, not stumbled upon. The relic isn't unguarded. Presence lingers beyond sight, silent movements setting the stage.

A burst of sharp and immediate static cuts through the comms. Lucy presses a finger against the earpiece, isolating the transmission and focusing on Derek's screen. Data floods in, unravelling each fragment as a piece of something larger, something calculated.

An opening materialises, fleeting and volatile, straddling the line between opportunity and disaster. Data offers an edge, but only if wielded fast enough to shape the conflict.

Deliberate action carves through hesitation, reducing options until the outcome is forced. The cyber battle starts to dissolve, replaced by the silence of those who never witnessed the shift.

Deep inside Viktor's facility, a separate war rages. Natasha's gaze sweeps across the command centre, rows of security feeds distorting as Derek's intrusion spreads. A slight inhale, a slow exhale — calm under pressure. 'One move at a time,' Natasha thinks to herself.

Warning lights pulse through the system, slicing through obstructions with relentless precision. One layer collapses, then another, connections severing mid-transfer. Conflict thrives in the unseen, in the cyber battlefield of raw calculation, where the slow become ghosts before recognition sets in.

Firewalls reconfigure in real time, locking down vulnerabilities and sealing exposed pathways before a trace remains. Derek's digital presence dissolves, stripped from infrastructure with surgical precision. Detection scrambles to adapt, but the breach erases itself faster than pursuit can catch up.

The counter-sequence fires, purging stolen files and injecting decoys in their place. A digital sweep wipes files and plants decoys, but the timing fails. Empty signals rush to cover gaps already carved open. The real data is gone, lifted clean without a trace.

Code bleeds across the grid — structure intact, soul gone. A shell left behind, dressed in function, stripped of meaning. Nothing remains but silence. Derek stares at the screen, jaw clenched. Victory shouldn't be this hollow.

A move like that isn't just tactical — it's personal.

Natasha builds the next step. Keystrokes tap out a message, every line deliberate. Not noise — signal. Not threat — invitation. Precision disguises intention, but something inside me judges the shape of the move.

Fragments drift into Viktor's grid — disguised as error, shaped by intent. Too clean to be random. Too quiet to be innocent. Derek has built digital traps like this before.

An intercepted signal means nothing if the sender anticipates intrusion. A subtle yet intentional gap exists within the encryption. Encrypted bursts slip through airwaves, weaving into the right networks.

Invisible strands tighten, reinforcing control at every junction. Silent connections coil through hidden paths, securing choke points before an escape forms. The snare holds steady, woven deep beneath the surface, pulling tighter with every second wasted.

Lines shift with absolute precision, code slotting into place without delay. Each step measured, each turn preordained, a silent choreography unfolding in perfect sync. Commands drop, unspoken yet obeyed, the unseen hand directing from beyond sight, moving the whole without resistance.

"R1... Sergei, status update now. No response indicates you're compromised if the tunnels are lost. No loose ends."

"Trap... lock the access point. Cut the maintenance route before escape becomes an option. No one slips through. Break their momentum, force hesitation, and make the corridor a kill box."

"At the... orders locked. No deviation. Reinforcements are closing in — no wasted shots. Keep the net open. Allow Steve's team to wade in deeper. Let assumptions settle. Slam all exits shut.

"Door... seal the vault. The second the door buckles, unleash fire from both flanks. No mercy, nothing left standing.

"Relic... location secured. Move now. Retrieve the package before sector four is compromised. If necessary, abandon the personnel. The priority remains unchanged."

Static clings to the screen, and data streams twist into a tangled mess. Lucy's trained instincts cut through the clutter, hunting for order buried in chaos after years of counterterrorism, chasing whispers in dark corners, and tracking voices that never wished to be found.

Lucy's edge sharpens, breaking apart layers designed to deceive. Algorithms scramble, trapped in a defensive weave. Patterns shift, aligning in several messages that defy coincidence. A message punches through the noise, raw, unfiltered. "Relic at R1. Trap at the door." Not just a location. Not just a warning. A signal—but for whom?

Lucy's fingers dig into the table, skin pressing white against the surface. A breath drags deep, held for a moment before words cut through the silence. Precise, controlled—each one chosen with purpose.

"I think Natasha isn't alerting Sergei. The message is for us."

A brief hesitation hangs in the air, uncertainty twisting into calculation. Why? The enemy commander shouldn't be feeding intelligence to the opposition.

A single thought scratches at the edge of focus. "What's the play here?" I say to Derek and Lucy, eyes still locked on the darkened screen. "This can't be random."

"Doubt anything is left to chance," Lucy says, eyes fixed on the information. "Took effort to layer those messages, not something pieced together in haste. Either she's covering tracks or setting something in motion."

"We have a problem," announces Derek, as a flash streaks across the screen.

The data stream is interrupted and fragmented by unauthorised trace breaches. Natasha's system is counterattacking, attempting to locate our position.

Numbers surge on the interface, pulsing like a code-red alert. Endpoints scramble, closing in, but firewalls shift, dissolving before containment locks in place. A keystroke lands, clean and deliberate, sending disruption rippling outward, etching a new route through hostile ground, unseen but irreversible.

Every movement carves a signature—no gesture forgotten, no misstep ignored. Time thins. Natasha tightens the net, systems locking down with surgical precision.

Derek strikes the keypad. Sequence lands clean. The door yields. A rogue pulse detonates inside the grid. Firewalls collapse. Logs burst. Commands scatter. Amid the storm, we vanish—ghosts drawn from a failing system.

Static screams. The feed dies. One second stolen from disaster. Our location is scrubbed before coordinates lock onto our twenty. Interference smears the last frame—blurred, broken, gone.

A final pulse flickers, then fades. Circuits fall silent. Power drains. The line dies, clean. No trail. No past. Just silence.

The screen dims, signals go silent, and the network flatlines. There's no pulse, no trace—only silence in place of the presence that once thrived.

Machinery from the room hums. The severed link creates a stillness entwined with unease, an absence too deliberate to overlook.

Corrupt fragments weave through the wreckage, whispers of interference embedded in code. Natasha's footprint lingers, threads of compromised script spreading like fractures in glass, remains of an unseen battle refusing to vanish.

Derek exhales, slow and controlled. Fingertips press into a tense temple. Pressure builds behind locked muscles, the echoes of encrypted exchange still scratching beneath the skin.

War unfolds in the space between perception. Combat fought without steel or fire. No trigger pulled, yet Viktor's infrastructure buckles under precise dismantling. Connections sever, foundations weaken, and the remnants of any operation slip into a void.

"Natasha must have accounted for this. Not an oversight, but an invitation. A door left open on purpose." Derek's voice lands sharp with no hesitation, no second-guessing. Just fact.

The words coil in my chest. "We're not breaking through. We aren't forcing our way in. We're following a path she designed."

Lucy shifts, focus narrowing on the decrypted fragments: numbers, symbols, scattered lines of intercepted messages. The pieces don't form a complete picture, but the outline is waiting to be understood.

A question hangs in my mind about the encoded message. "Why would Natasha want to warn us?"

The implications twist deep, cutting through the already tangled battlefield. Information is currency, but not when it's given. Nothing in this fight happens without a reason.

Lucy stands rigid, arms folded. Voice flat. "Natasha wants the relic moving—just enough to stir the field. Guessing she wants Viktor to stay blind." The logic tracks, but the motive scratches deeper. Too neat. Too clean.

The room stays silent, tension stretching between unspoken thoughts. Natasha isn't protecting Viktor. She's manipulating the field, moving unseen pieces into place. The battle isn't just about the relic. It's about control.

Our path ahead fractures into three choices: follow the lead, gamble on the unknown, or dismantle everything in a single strike. Each option spirals toward the same conclusion. The fight never stops. The board shifts, but the pieces remain in motion, the stakes climbing with each decision.

Chapter Twenty-Six — Securing the Relic

We pull back fast, slipping into a secured fallback point beyond the corridor where Derek clashed with Natasha. One wrong signal, and silence shatters into a firefight. Data shields buy seconds— never safety. A trace lock activates. Something's coming.

A single bulb flickers overhead, throwing harsh shadows across the concrete. The air stinks of machine oil and old sweat. A battered table anchors the space, its surface buried beneath maps, schematics, and decrypted messages, bearing the scars of countless briefings.

Linked routes snake across worn paper, red circles marking trouble spots. Every scrap of intelligence paints a target—one step wrong, and the whole plan burns.

My fingers glide across the blueprint, identifying pressure points and chokeholds. The relic lies buried deep, protected. Layers of steel and purpose stand between us and it. Nearby, the command centre awaits. One nerve hub. Cut that, and Viktor bleeds.

A torn surveillance photo sits on the desk, revealing a corridor. Natasha's decrypted message underscores a potential trap at the entrance to R1, where intel indicates the relic is being kept. A single mistake at the threshold might trigger devastation. Disarming any device falls to me. One misstep and the sound of an explosion is sure to bring Viktor's people sprinting in our direction.

"Steve, this might change everything." Derek lays a faded blueprint across the table, a blade pressing against a forgotten exit. "Might be another way out. Might shave minutes off extraction, keep us from dragging the fucking thing through a kill zone."

"Might work. This passage winds through an abandoned service tunnel," my voice firm, calculating. "Enough space for movement, but expect collapses or worse. If this route goes hot, options shrink fast."

While the rest prepare for the following engagement and study the information, I develop a plan. The next part of the operation needs to be divided into three phases, each a calculated assault.

First, the recovery of the relic. Second, the control room must be closed down to deny communications and disrupt any coordinated counterstrike. Third, journey with the relic to the exfil point. Any deviation will demand immediate adaptation.

With everyone standing around the table, again checking out documents, one ear listening for movement outside the room, I lay out the plan's first stage: retrieval of the relic.

"Derek, refresh us on what we learned from you hacking into Viktor's network before I start." My words land with the weight of an order, not a request.

"Ten people inside the command centre. Viktor's office sits next door. Radio logs feed straight to the monitors, backed up on the server. Everything is recorded. Sergei's taken a force-out, sweeping the mining facility perimeter," Derek replies.

"Anything else, mate?" I ask.

Derek doesn't hesitate. The answer is primed, prior to my question even landing. "Found something that matters—Russian frequency. Lucy ran the translation. Viktor just confirmed possession of the relic. Plans are already in motion—destination, Russia. Timeline? Days, not weeks. If we don't move now, we lose the advantage and the relic," Derek says, scanning the data.

A slow, controlled breath pushes through clenched teeth. "Now Natasha's message lines up," Simon mutters.

Stillness grips the space thick and unbroken—no need for debate. Every person in the room reaches the same conclusion without a word exchanged.

"R1 holds the relic. Intercepted chatter confirms Viktor wants the relic gone. No doubt expects trouble; the entrance won't be clean. Wires, plates, or a dead man's switch. One wrong step, and the only thing leaving is shrapnel," I say as a hand drags along the diagram, marking key positions.

"One misplaced foot, and the walls might explode inward. Intel suggests Viktor engineers build for destruction, not alarms. The kill zone will not announce itself, and it will not negotiate. Threads of death wait, stretched across unseen lines, tuned for the slightest imbalance. Any device isn't just about blocking a route. It's about making sure no one walks out.

Any IEDs require certainty. If Natasha's intel is accurate, the verification task falls to me. Any trap lying ahead will be neutralised before anyone moves.

One mistake might turn the entire place into an inferno. Explosives sit primed, waiting for a command — mine or someone else's. Control remains locked where it belongs, with me. Nothing ignites unless I give the order."

"No argument from me, Steve. If you explode, I'll let Simon pick up the body parts, as he has had practice with that," says George with a stupid grin.

Ignoring George, I continue. "After I've cleared any IED, a controlled breach remains the only option. I will lead the entry and cover the right. Simon follows, sweeping left. George takes the middle. Derek clears the dead ground behind the door. Lucy holds the corridor, eyes on enemy movement. Entry rules are simple — don't die stupid."

George's voice slices through the stillness. "Take it anyone who stands beyond that entryway won't be walking afterwards."

No concern, no hesitation — just a stark reality. This isn't a negotiation. Their only escape is in a body bag.

"Correct. Once inside and the room is clear, Derek and I will check and disarm if necessary," I reply.

I throw a worn pack on the table. The dull thud is followed by the sharp clink of metal on metal. A disarming kit unfolds, tools arranged — cutters for wires, probes for hidden triggers, clamps to hold steady what shouldn't shift.

I continue with the briefing, "A weapon like this doesn't travel easily. Simon will have the final say on transport. If two people can carry the device, the extraction runs clean. It's a smooth lift, a direct route to the exfil. Anything bigger changes the equation."

"Roger that," Simon replies.

"A larger payload requires a shift in strategy. Wheels mean mobility, but add risk. Pushing the relic out the door turns the operation into a race against the clock — visibility spikes. Viktor's men will close in fast," I add.

"What about grabbing the vehicles before we grab the relic?" asks Simon.

"Smart call, mate," I reply. "If the package's smaller than expected, transport stays buried. ATVs don't roll until I say so. Nothing moves without reason or risk detection unless the mission requires it."

Air rasps through Derek's clenched teeth, sharp like a hiss through wire mesh. Laughter rides beneath — rough, jagged, ready to cut. "Simon, you lazy bastard," he mutters, shaking his head. "Trying to dodge another trek, aren't you? Next thing, you'll ask for an air-conditioned exfil and a protein shake."

Simon chuckles. "Just thinking ahead. I'd rather not hump a relic the size of a coffin across two klicks of sunbaked misery."

"Then pray it's small," I say, scanning the ridgeline. "Otherwise, you're the mule. We'll strap it to your back, paint a target on your arse, and call you bait."

Derek snorts. "Again? That's three ops in a row. We should get you a loyalty card."

"Fuck off, you green numpty," Simon responds.

"Moving on. If we can haul the thing out of here, we may need to rig something together from webbing, straps, or whatever we can find in the room. Any questions so far?"

"Nope, all sounds like standard stuff, "replies Lucy.

Boots scrape against concrete, shifting in the silence. "If the relic's retrieval is clear, we push forward onto phase two. Target—command centre. No alarms, no survivors," my words measured, cutting through the dim light.

A slow glance sweeps the team, waiting for suggestions. With the team offering only approving nods and no comments, I proceed.

"Communications, surveillance, tracking—everything runs through that room. And leaving anything operational or alive isn't a fucking option.

"A weapon of this calibre never moves unnoticed. If extraction includes the relic, nothing outranks the device's security. A dead drop gets prepped, out of view, out of reach. Once locked down, the focus shifts to the control centre."

A finger drags across the map, tracing the route. "What if securing isn't a choice. What happens if the whole task goes loud mid-move? What then? Contingency needs to be in play before we step out," Simon asks, voice firm.

"Then we adapt," I say, my words cutting through the stillness. "If this becomes fucked up, the relic moves with us—better in our hands than back with Viktor. Leaving the device behind means handing Viktor a loaded weapon.

"Relics don't sit on shelves in Viktor's world. Every piece will be wired to detonate, repurposed into something lethal. Viktor operates on momentum, not delay. The second it lands in his grip, hesitation dies each minute after, an unknown city shifts closer to erasure. Containment evolves into the impossible. Prevention ends. Reaction is all that remains.

Entry mirrors the first phase, with one change. This time, Lucy enters the command room, shifting from overwatch to direct assault. The corridor stays a kill zone, but the fight goes indoors."

George with arms crossed. "What's the contingency if the room's door is closed and reinforced? We can't risk getting bottlenecked before we enter."

My gaze moves to the explosives bag, the unspoken answer already at hand. "A timed breach paves the way. If those doors believe they're standing firm, they shan't be for long. A directed blast will transform any obstacles into rubble.

The second boots cross the threshold, the team splits—Simon, George, and I handle the bodies, quick and efficient. Lucy and Derek will dismantle Viktor's infrastructure, one keystroke at a time. Two sides collapse in tandem, leaving nothing remaining."

A chair drags across the concrete. "If failsafe measures are implemented, stalling is not an option," Derek says, examining the diagram. "Nothing stops a total shutdown. One stroke, and the data vanishes."

"Viktor's people believe they're invulnerable. That's their flaw. Before an alarm sounds, we're already inside. Their complacency dulls any edge—sitting behind reinforced doors, convinced no one can breach their perimeter. This belief makes them slow. When reality catches up, the fight will be over, and none of them will have time to bring their weapons into play. So, we move quicker than any response, clear the control room, and leave nothing but an empty shell," I reply.

"Roger that," replies Derek.

Continuing, "Intel holds power. Any intelligence left intact comes with us: hard drives, mission files—anything carrying Viktor's operations. Extract or destroy, no in-between. If the network falls, so does Viktor's reach beyond this compound.

"Every monitor, console, and relays are to be reduced to scrap. Ensure all monitors are shattered and circuits are burned. Remember, this isn't just a space—it's the mind behind Viktor's operation."

Viktor commands through authority, not chaos. Take that away, and his forces don't fight—they scatter. Coordination unravels, orders fall silent, and discipline fractures. A contract pays for skill, not allegiance. With no control, hired guns dissolve into individual threats; twitching, second-guessing, and reacting. The machine stalls, with no unit cohesion, just scattered fighters choosing to continue fighting or flee. Others act first, turning weapons toward the closest threat.

Disorder moves faster than strategy, and command dissolves in seconds. Trained soldiers become isolated bodies, hunting dangers they can't define. Instinct pulls them in different directions—some fire without thinking, some freeze, waiting for guidance that never comes, and some will choose to run.

Simon exhales, glancing at the team. "And if reinforcements roll in before we complete the job?"

"We stand our ground. We keep every inch we take; nothing stays breathing except us. The next fight can wait—we finish this first. Final call for questions on phase two. If something needs clarifying, speak now. Otherwise, phase three begins—exfil and extraction," I say, taking a firm grip around the rifle, heat from the barrel bleeding into my palm.

With nothing coming back from the team, I continue, and the last phase locks in. "The relic leaves Viktor's compound with us, one way or another. The first option runs clean. If the relic can be moved by hand, we advance on foot. A direct route to the LZ minimises risk—no unnecessary exposure. The package stays close, weapons up, heads on a swivel."

A knuckle raps on the edge of the map. "No cover at the LZ means an easy kill box. If hostiles dig in before we arrive, we step into a one-sided massacre. We walk straight into a bullet storm with no fallback," Simon mutters.

"Then we reroute. The secondary exfil sits here," I say, a finger pressing against a stretch of terrain marked for an emergency location identified by Simon back at GSS.

"A larger relic shifts the plan. ATVs become the only option. They stay hidden until confirmed necessary. If the relic is too heavy for transport on foot, we split up. George, Simon, and I recover the ATVs. Derek and Lucy hold a concealed position, securing the relic."

The schematic transforms beneath Lucy's steady hand. "If the hide is burned, we're stranded. There is a reasonable chance that Viktor's people may not wander, but patrol under Natasha or Sergei's control. If they stumble across our gear, those ATVs might not be where we expect them to be. They'll be stripped, disabled, or worse, wired for our arrival."

"Then the plan adjusts, no vehicles. No delays. We move on foot. Find solid ground. Extract clean, or not at all," I say.

George grips the back of a broken chair, fingers bracing against splintered wood, tension carved into knuckles; ready to ask the unspoken question that lingers, weighted, demanding an answer.

Silence presses close, prepared for the inevitable—spoken or not, the truth already exists. "If this gets fucked up, how much time before we move on?"

The query pauses, awaiting the verdict. No one breathes. No one speaks, anticipating a number that might determine one of the team's fates.

The words land hard. "No one remains left behind. Derek keeps comms live. Radio contact stays constant. The final push ends with the relic secured on the transport. The ride to the LZ determines whether this mission is a success, or another black file buried in intelligence archives," I reply.

With the briefing over, everyone checks their gear, ready for the next phase of the operation. A cocking handle slams forward, chambering a round. Metal snaps into place, breaking the silence like a gunshot.

Magazines stack in rows, fingers checking loads by touch alone. Straps pull tight, securing gear that won't stay clean for long. Once these sights adjust again, the fight won't be a battle anymore. A conclusion, not a skirmish. The weight of decisions already made will dictate who walks away.

Air thins, stretched taut between people locked in silent preparation. Hand strip and load mags, chamber rounds, and confirm safeties are off. Malfunctions cost seconds. Seconds cost lives. Equipment doesn't exist for convenience—it exists to function. Unchecked failure turns operators into bodies.

A firm grip tightens around George's rifle, the layout memorised in silence. "If this kicks off sooner than planned, what's our play?" asks George, the question slicing through the room, demanding an answer that prevents the operation from devolving into a hunt.

I glance across the table. "Same as always. Adapt. Hit harder. Move faster."

The words land flat, but the meaning lingers. A single mistake reshapes the battlefield in ways no plan can predict.

A fresh mag locks into Lucy's webbing, fingers brushing the worn surface. "Viktor still breathing when this ends, or are we finishing this?"

A question like that doesn't hang in the air for long. Decisions form in real time, stripped of doubt. This isn't a debate—it's survival.

A lull stretches between my breaths. "No prisoners." The weight of the statement presses into the room.

"Once we breach, radio contact stays clean. If the network drops, the fallback protocol kicks in," Derek says, adjusting his radio.

A curt nod moves through the room like a silent prayer no one will say aloud. No need to mention the obvious—some of us might not walk back out. The silence isn't empty. It's loaded, cocked, and counting.

"When we pull this off, first beers are on me," Simon mutters, trying to sound casual, like we're debating pub choices and not our mortality.

A flicker of amusement flits across his face, then vanishes. No one diverges from the task. Eyes remain forward. Focus remains locked. Victory is assumed. Cost remains unknown.

"Worth the fight if that tight arse is buying the drinks," George yells from the far side, checking his rifle with all the grace of a pub bouncer on his sixth pint.

Derek snorts. "Make mine a double if I lose a limb."

"Only if it's your mouth," I say. "Otherwise, you're crawling back and paying your own bloody tab."

Final checks move like clockwork. Magazines lock with finality. Safeties snap off like breaking bones. Knives vanish into sheaths. One glance, a single unshaken stare, and everything is understood. The line between life and death sits razor-thin, but no one plans on falling.

Silence presses against the skin, thick as concrete dust, heavier than body armour. One look passes between us. No blink, no flinch. The kind of stare that carries weight in funerals. The line we walk isn't just thin — it's fraying.

I lift my fist — signal cast. George drops to a crouch, eyes scanning, finger resting on the trigger like a promise. Motionless, yet barely held in place. A loaded spring with teeth.

Simon takes his place, spine straight, eyes forward, looking like a man who's seen too many exits close behind him. I mirror the stance, back against cold stone, grip tightening on the handle. Each second drips with pressure.

I count the breath, time the beat, and nod once.

The entryway breaks open with a hollow groan, revealing a vacuum. Static hums from wiring, fractured light casting unpredictable distortions across a barren floor. Wires drone like a throat trying to scream — light fractures. Shadows slither across scorched concrete like predators searching for skin.

No resistance, no presence, just a space that shouldn't be. Just absence — too quiet, too clean. The kill zone isn't empty. It's waiting, watching and preparing to decide who walks out.

"Either we ghosted through unnoticed, or they're watching the door." The statement lands flat, a dead weight in the air, reality pressing in.

A flick of fingers sends the team forward. No words. just movement. Bodies blend with shadow, rifles raised, edges sharpened by purpose. Each step placed with care. Ground ahead holds no welcome — only the promise of resistance.

The passage narrows. Formation compresses. One breath shared across five souls. I move right, boots rolling over dust, weight low, head on a swivel. Lucy ghosts behind, her rhythm locked with mine. Simon edges left, eyes forward, one finger resting above the trigger.

Derek slips between, gear silent, face set. George covers the rear, weapon tracking each corner like death riding on his shoulder.

Above, a soft vibration whispers through the vents – unnatural. Controlled. A presence masked in steel. Doors line both sides, sealed, numbered, unreadable. Each one hides something we're not meant to see.

My grip tightens. Pressure flows through my palm into the stock. Weapon ready. Targets unknown. Something might be lurking ahead.

Ten interrupted minutes pass before the door to R1 stands ahead of us at the end of the corridor. A dense steel reinforced with external locking bolts. The relic is now within reach beyond that barrier. The device everyone is here for. Weapons rise, sights trained, fingers resting near triggers. A single movement dictates survival.

The final check of the route to the door belongs to me. With the team covering, I move the last 30 metres. A greater distance would have been preferred in case of an explosion, but this is a luxury we don't have in the confines of the corridor.

Moving step by step, I clear the route in case a second IED extends from wall to wall, leaving no gap to bypass on the way to R1.

To my front, a disregarded plank stretches across the deck. Experience tells me this isn't random. Getting close, I take a prone position and inch forward the remaining couple of feet. A metal sliver catches my eye between the wood and the floor.

Beneath, a pressure-sensitive device mechanism, rigged to a dead man's switch due to its placement. Nothing about this setup is accidental. A misplaced wire, a half-buried plate – all too easy to spot. The real danger lurks underneath, set for those who believe they understand the game. A step too confident, a breath too relaxed, and the area ceases to exist.

One footstep in the wrong place detonates the charge. A close-quarters blast funnels straight back, turning the corridor into a kill zone. One misstep turns the team into scattered remains.

Derek's fingers tighten around the mic, the grip firm. "Any way through?" The words fall with authority, carrying the weight of someone who's witnessed too many barriers collapse, detonations transforming obstacles into open ground.

George shifts behind me, a sniper's patience honed over years of unseen war. A near-silent shift recalibrates the focus, the scope locking in without hesitation. The words break through like a round chambering — final, absolute, preparing for what follows.

"Contingency. Where do we regroup if this turns south?" asks George, words pressing into the moment, unspoken realities hanging between breaths. "Need an exit plan that doesn't lead to body bags. Well, for us lot. Don't careless about your ugly arse."

A necessary question, even when we all have an idea of the answer. I let a calculated pause stretch the moment, keeping control.

"Go back 10 metres. If this blows, only one of us goes with it." My voice is clinical, stripped of emotion. Facts, nothing more.

Lucy doesn't move. "Negative. If you're staying, so are we." Her voice didn't waver, just like her stance. Discussion won't change anything.

I inhale. The thick, metallic scent of disturbed earth and old explosives fills my lungs. The crude device beneath me is simple — coiled wires, a pressure plate primed to snap shut at the slightest excess force. The IED doesn't have redundancy, no second chances. My fingers tingle, the fine tremor of adrenaline a ghost beneath my skin.

My knife edge finds purchase, slipping between the IED and the wood. Steel shudders against the mechanism, a whisper of movement in my grip. Pressure stabilises the blade; control is absolute. A shift no wider than a breath, a lift finer than a pulse—the faintest rotation, the subtlest lift.

Oxygen remains trapped in the team's waiting lungs, with discipline overruling instinct. Every muscle is wired, and every thought is focused on the following action. Everything hangs in the balance on the razor-thin line between preparation and ignition.

One slip, one miscalculation, and my teammates are scraping pieces of me off the dirt.

Another fraction of movement. Another risk taken. Another silent battle between control and disaster.

The final adjustment locks the blade under the plate. The slow, deliberate lift disengages the connection, freezing the trigger's mechanism. The charge remains live, the explosives still deadly, but the pathway is severed for now.

Air escapes from my lungs in a controlled, measured, and steady release—knots of tension coil beneath my skin, muscles tight from holding position too long. Not a twitch breaks the stillness, discipline anchoring every muscle. The strain simmers beneath the surface, buried deep, contained.

A whisper of air leaves George's tightened lips, precision wrapped in restraint. A clipped and firm voice shatters the void. "Clear?"

I stare at the device for a beat more, making sure. "Clear."

Lucy shifts beside me. "You OK?"

I flex my fingers, rolling my shoulders back. "Still here."

Now, onto the door, a critical point in locating the relic. If Natasha's intel is correct, there is another improvised explosive device (IED) lying in wait just by the entrance.

Its design is created to catch anyone off guard and inflict substantial losses, sending team members home in body bags if we do not approach this situation with the utmost caution.

I make a slow, deliberate shift forward, scanning the corridor's surface for signs of irregularities. Any patterns that betray secrets, and fractures in the dust settle around imperfections, exposing the attempt to conceal. A solitary mistake could transform steel and concrete into an unmarked grave.

The entrance to R1 stands ahead, the doorframe thick with more than reinforced plating. Distance holds, instincts warning before logic catches up — Natasha's decoded message running through my mind. Layers stack one over the other, sealing something unseen within.

Search begins top to bottom, each half-metre divided, scanned, cleared. Fingers trace edges while eyes map patterns. Movement slow, steady — learned from scars, not textbooks. Every centimetre speaks a language. I listen.

Near the base, something disrupts the rhythm. Not a shadow. Not a flaw. A line, slender and taut, rests across the threshold. One mistake triggers a funeral.

Tripwire runs low, tension buried in silence. Seam cradles the line like a blade tucked beneath the skin. The cable holds more than steel; it holds intent.

Beyond the wire, danger compounds. Residue clings to metal — putty forced into cracks, masked by dirt and paint. No wires are exposed. No lights blink, just waiting to answer a mistake.

Explosives pack the frame. Not refined — just cruel. Fragments ready to rip, overpressure aimed to crush. The structure won't hold. Nothing here is built to wound. Purpose points to one outcome — no survivors, only names carved into stone.

My blade touches the wire. Pressure builds between steel and death. No sound, but a pulse hums through the edge — steady, alive. This isn't a guess. This wire sings with charge. One slip ends the mission in scattered bone and flame.

Fingers pinch the trip-line's anchor — thread-thin, glass-coated. Tension wraps around the frame, hidden beneath rust and grease. Sweat beads under my collar, each drop a weight. I angle the blade beneath the wire's core, not cutting but separating.

I insert a bypass loop — copper filament wrapped in resin, tuned to catch the live current. The hum shifts pitch. Contact holds. Energy reroutes. My thumb adjusts the line tension, applying feather-light pressure to stabilise the circuit.

A flick of my wrist sends a ceramic blade through the neutral point. Clean break. The snap comes soft — like a sigh. Circuit dies. No flash. No heat. Just silence where there should have been thunder.

Wires come next. Nestled in a hollow groove behind the frame, three twisted cores feed into a shaped charge — C4 laced with ball bearings. Crude, fast, and lethal, I slice the lead contacts, severing ignition from the payload before peeling the det cord from the block, one spiral at a time.

The charge rests inert now, dead weight without a voice. But death lingers close. This room wants blood. It just hasn't chosen who yet.

The trap is defused, but the battle hasn't ended. Natasha's intel places Viktor's men inside. The relic sits within reach, yet the entry reeks of something else. Whoever waits beyond the door dictates the next move.

A block of PE4 comes free from my jacket — cut and shaped, meant for moments like this. Wires thread into the enemy charge, not to defuse but to hijack. Control shifts. One signal. One press. Now, the device answers to us.

I move back as much as I can and check that the team is away from the blast. It should blow inwards, but it's best to be sure. After one final glance at the team, I ignite the short 10cm safety fuse, which gives me 10 seconds to move away from the blast area before the detonation collapses the door inward.

A sharp explosion tears through the corridor. Steel door folds inward, walls buckle, and debris surges ahead in a violent wave. Smoke rolls over the threshold, thick and choked with residue.

The haze consumes the breach. Movement vanishes into shifting grey. Light fractures through the smoke, casting broken shadows that ripple across half-seen forms beyond the entry.

Fragments of steel clatter against the floor, ringing before the silence returns. The air swells with the sharp tang of burnt explosives, wrapping the space in heat and warning.

The blast grants temporary control—an opening, nothing more. That kind of noise travels fast, punching through rock and echoing down every corridor.

If Viktor's men sit within earshot, they'll be coming now. Boots will hammer the floor, rifles up, eyes hunting through dust. Not to defend—just to kill before the dust clears.

Not waiting for the debris to settle, I push through, rifle raised, sweeping the area to my front. Every inch is covered. The air pulses with tension, the stench of explosives clinging tight.

Simon sweeps left, fluid and precise. George covers the right, steps sharp and decisive. Derek moves behind the door, covering blind spots—nothing is missed.

This isn't chaos. This is orchestration. Every move is built on experience and combat. My heart doesn't race, it drives. Focus sharp. Eyes cold. Purpose clear. No one walks out without going through us first.

Lucy enters next, rifle aimed at the corridor, leaving no room for error. Gaps are sealed, and areas are secured. Our warning is clear: step through and you drop where you stand.

Two figures take cover at the room's far end, the barricade absorbing the brunt of our incoming fire, weapons poised, tension locked in their stances. A standoff lingers between the lines, waiting for the signal to shift stillness into a storm of lead.

With AK-47s in hand, their grips trembling, they move with a palpable uncertainty. A brief pause exposes their intentions, showing either a lack of training or preparedness. A moment's doubt leads to grave consequences.

Sprinting forward and to one side, I fire two fatal shots that snap through the air, their muzzle flashes illuminating the near darkness. The bodies in front of me drop, their motion ceasing before understanding registers.

The relic commands the centre of the room, cables sprawled from the base like severed arteries. Blood spilled for this. Lives traded. The bodies stiffening near the barricade don't matter. This object changes everything.

Clearing the rest of the room becomes urgent. Simon moves first, sweeping the left flank, weapon tight. George clears right, checking dead ground beyond the overturned desks. The team moves, every person knowing their role, steps dictated by training honed through years of operations. Silence holds more weight than gunfire—no resistance remains, no more threats lurking in the shadows.

A glance with Derek exchanges intent. The device stands dormant, but nothing about this is safe. Viktor wouldn't leave this unprotected.

Delays, remote detonation, or automated triggers—each a calculated possibility. Assumptions lead to failure, and failure ends in bodies. A fresh scan tracks no visible tripwires, no immediate tampering. Meaningless. A well-set trap doesn't advertise its presence. The absence of a trigger only confirms one exists.

A step forward commits to the next phase. My hands track across the relic's metal shell, mapping the surface in silent coordination. Pressure sensors, tampered panels, anything out of place or appears wrong. A heartbeat passes, then another. The casing holds steady. The threat isn't external. But waits inside.

I dropped to one knee on the floor, the tool kit unlatched, and instruments ready for immediate use. "Give me a target area, Derek, to work on," I say, my voice clipped, direct. Our actions dictate whether this ends clean or in one massive explosion.

"You start on that side and I'll take this end," replies Derek.

One careful tilt shifts the panel, exposing the mechanism beneath. The failsafe reveals itself—a timed detonation, buried deep within the structure. A defined radius locks the charge in place.

Touch the device, move it beyond its threshold, and the consequence ignites without mercy. A network of destruction, set to devour the evidence. Wires thread through critical points, primed to ensure nothing survives.

One flick, and history rewrites itself in fire and ruin. Viktor's grip extends past the living—he destroys what he can't hold.

"Countdown activated. Five-digit code required. One opportunity to override."

Each word underscores the stakes, a breath held between function and destruction. No shortcuts are available. One misplaced digit spells the end.

Derek closes the distance, laptop balanced on one forearm, connection primed. "Pre-coded or randomised?" Derek asks. Hands hover over the interface, waiting for confirmation before engagement.

"From the appearance of the device, I would say pre-coded," I reply.

Viktor's arrogance relies on complexity, not unpredictability. With a measured shift, I expose the primary access panel. A countdown lingers, dormant yet present, a silent reminder that failure doesn't wait. The numbers remain inert—for now.

Derek's cables lock into place. The software syncs with the relic's aged circuits, bypassing the layers designed to ensure destruction. Keystrokes track across the laptop, peeling away redundancy and isolating ignition protocols. Each input thread between security barriers unravels Viktor's safeguard line by line.

As the final connection is severed, a breath hangs still. The display dims, and the countdown disappears. A thick, unmoving silence settles in. For the first time in decades, the relic stands without purpose.

George shifts his balance, rifle angled toward the entry point, listening, head tilted. "Viktor doesn't sit idle. What's the extraction time?" he asks. Nothing in his tone suggests doubt, only urgency wrapped in precision.

"As soon as we get the device secured for transportation," I reply.

Simon steps closer, assessing the weight and structure. "Can be carried. But this will slow us down."

I secure the panel, ensuring the device stays inert. "Your call, Simon. alternative?"

A plan already exists. "We grab the ATVs, load the vehicles and drive to the LZ, " replies Simon.

"That's the transport sorted. Moving the relic? That's the problem," my words sharp, as I scan the space for an answer. We need to find a solution, resolve the issue and execute. We don't have time to linger, waiting for second chances.

Resources spread across the room—steel sections, webbing, discarded fragments of a once-active operation. Each component is repurposed and shaped. A transportation rig materialises from the remnants and is reinforced to withstand movement. The relic's existing frame holds, keeping the mission intact without slowing extraction.

The relic leaves the ground as if it understands the cost. Not light. Not willing. Metal groans under strain, as if it remembers what came before and dreads what comes next.

Moving away from the room, I take point, rifle up, eyes locked down the corridor. Simon shadows the opposite flank—no words—just rhythm, breath, steel. Lucy covers the rear, her silence anchoring the team. Every step forward pulls a little harder.

So far, our luck holds, with the facility offering no resistance. Viktor's people will, without doubt, be regrouping elsewhere, preparing for a confrontation yet to come.

Two hundred metres from the command centre, I stop signalling for everyone to do the same—no need for reassessment or maps. The layout exists within our minds, memorised from countless briefings.

To my right, an open door reveals a concealed room that offers temporary concealment. Simon and I cover each end of the corridor, while the rest push the relic inside before closing the door.

A calculated pause holds the moment. The next choice defines the battle. The fight moves forward, dictated by purpose, controlled by experience.

Chapter Twenty-Seven — Assault on the Command Centre

Darkness closes in, thick as sludge. The compound breathes around us — vents wheeze, unseen machinery grinds behind steel. Viktor's control centre sits a hundred metres out. Between us and that door, kill zones and blind corners built to bleed intruders dry.

The air tastes of rust and damp, a rot that clings to the back of my throat. Circuits burn somewhere close. Condensation slicks the walls, dripping like a leaky clock counting us down. Each step forward cuts deeper into whatever trap waits ahead. This place doesn't feel abandoned. It feels hungry.

Boots ghost over concrete, a whisper of contact, each step deliberate. The surface beneath shifts in places — crumbling edges conceal fractures in the gloom. Rubber soles press into grit, weight shifting to mute the impact. Breath thins between movements, measured with precision, a calculation in silence.

A presence lingers past sight, watching. The unseen narrows in, patient, waiting for the misstep that never comes.

Ahead, a ray of light shines through an open door on one side of the corridor, something we need to deal with if we don't want the alarm to be raised, before the team is ready to launch the assault on the command centre.

Blurred shapes drift beyond the threshold, faint distortions in the fractured glow leaking through the opening. Shadows stretch around shifting forms, the hard edges of shoulders, the sharp cut of weapons at their sides. Voices rise and fall, muffled yet distinct, threading through the silence.

A clenched fist signals a complete stop. Everyone behind me fades into shadows, their bodies moulding into the surface, vanishing from view.

Breaths are rationed, and movement is stalled. Time stretches, pressing in from all fronts, silent but deafening. Nothing ahead hints at certainty—just risks, a threshold leading deeper into uncertainty.

Rifles settle, slicing through the murk, each locking onto a separate avenue of approach. Shoulders brace, nerves honed to a razor's edge. Triggers rest beneath calloused fingers, measured and unyielding.

A shift inside the scope will trigger a shot without hesitation—barrels lined with unwavering precision. One misstep into the open turns a heartbeat into a last breath.

Hands tighten, bracing against the inflexible steel. Rough stone presses into spines, breathing slows, calculated and managed. A presence past the veil of darkness—unseen yet impossible to dismiss.

Firing arcs mesh into a seamless kill box, leaving no blind spots unguarded. The grid holds firm, and a steady rifle claims each sector. Frames stand rigid, the surface betraying nothing of the unknown beyond.

Air sinks into still lungs, shallow to maintain the silence. Carrying more than dust, expectation lingers, as thick as oil. Weapons stay anchored, their weight evenly spread, guarding all areas. The moment elongates, drawing the team into a tighter readiness. One shift, one flick of a hand, and the mission propels forward.

With the rest remaining in the shadows, I move forward. Pressure flows through my boots, stillness assessed with intention. Concrete breathes under careful steps, vibration dulled to nothing. The closer to the frame, the higher the risk. The door is a funnel, a kill zone for anyone careless enough to enter or cross blind.

A direct glance through the opening invites death. I drop to one knee beside the frame, spine low, head angled beneath the line of fire. No part of me offers a clean shot. This isn't cover — it's survival.

Flickering light spills from within. A pulse, not a rhythm. Weak, uncertain. Stuttering, as if something is about to fail. The smell hits next — burned wiring, hot metal, stale copper. The scent clings to every breath.

A shape moves — too smooth, too slowly, with the wrong stride. There's no structure. It doesn't belong to a patrol. Shadows stretch behind it, yet none reveal a threat. The silence surrounding it tightens. It is not empty. It is not peaceful. Something waits. Watching.

My lungs seize. A single disruptive sound fractures the tranquillity. The odds change with each passing second. There's no room for error. A small movement of fabric. A breath that exceeds the previous one. That's all it requires.

The corridor remains shrouded in neglect, as no visible scans monitor its length or contours. The surveillance systems are limited in their scope, with their focus constrained to specific, anticipated angles, overlooking the subtleties and nuances of the surrounding environment. This predictability creates a false sense of security, highlighting a significant gap in the observation protocols.

My grip tightens around the trigger. Muscles steady. Calculations shift. Angles converge. Windless, measured space. Each breath adds weight. Each second brings new choices into play.

Sweat trails between my shoulder blades. The air thickens with unwashed bodies, scorched plastic, and chemical waste. A bulb flickers above cracked concrete, casting fractured shapes across the walls. Dark lines split through the stone, deep gouges filled with shadow.

Light scatters unevenly. Rebar protrudes from shattered cement, rust entwining every exposed edge. Pools of light stretch and collapse, sculpting the room into fragmented shards.

Beyond the doorway, heat thickens in the air. Drinks, decay, mould, and sweat mingle, the odour of lives spent in shadows. A fragrance that fosters misguided confidence. Complacency.

Figures slump in the dark. Shadows cover most, but not enough. One woman sinks into torn foam, her jeans stained. A bottle rests on her leg. Liquid rocks gently inside, unaware of what watches.

Two men lean near a scarred worktop. One swigs from a bottle, the other draws patterns in filth with a fingertip. Cups and cans litter the surface. A kettle groans on the side, a red glow alive beneath it. Steam winds upward — thin, slow, unnoticed.

Lack of structure. Absence of coordination. Merely negligence added to habit. A single bottle clinks on the counter. A narrative drifts in the air. Joyful laughter follows. There is no interruption. No reconfiguration. No trigger hand held close to a grip.

The scrape of a chair cuts across the room, jarring and sharp. One foot drags and then stills. More laughter follows. No awareness of the opening, just a metre beyond reach.

Spines droop, limbs lean against wood and stone. No readiness, no sharpness. Fingers wander over bottles. Rifles lean against the wall, supported without consideration. Oil stains tarnish the steel, subtle hints of attention. Yet no hands are near the triggers.

Words tumble from mouths. Slow. Relaxed. Blunt edges dragging across time. Stone absorbs the noise, swallowing everything before it can escape. The walls here trap sound. And therefore death.

My rifle remains steady. The target is locked in place. My breath is tight, leaving no room for error. It's either a silent kill or a bloodbath — nothing in between.

The doorframe supports my weight, with my team standing right behind me — quiet, unmoving, precise. Each of us is like a blade, focused on one thought, ready for one strike.

There are no glances behind, no nervous twitches. Nobody is shifting to check blind angles. Every warning missed, every sense dulled by the monotony of repetition.

One final scan confirms it; however, there is no alert, no defence, and the weapons are too far away. The distance is too great, and time is too short. These lives must be erased — clean, fast, and quiet. Any noise draws others from the depths of this structure, and any shout delays the breach of the command centre.

Moving back to the team, movement and breath controlled, every step calculated to avoid unnecessary noise. A glance at each — trained eyes meeting mine in a quiet understanding. No requirement for drawn-out explanations. Nothing spoken above a whisper.

Murmurs carry less risk than the sound of four sets of boots against cracked concrete. So, information is clear and precise, and nothing should be left to interpretation. I make my way around the team, explaining the plan to each person.

The plan is for Lucy and me to move forward and eliminate the targets with silenced 9mms. Lucy's target is a woman sitting on the sofa. I will dispatch the other two. The mission continues without a pause, the second the bodies hit the ground.

"If you're ready, Lucy, let's deal with the situation before the people inside come out and we are discovered," I say, standing up. Lucy's grip tightens around the 9mm and joins me heading to the kill zone, keeping close to the wall. No other words needed. Everyone understands their role.

Derek's posture is rigid, balance steady, control total. A silent figure within the dark, rifle drawn, tension humming just beneath the surface. Shadows stretch ahead, shifting, uncertain. Grip firm, stock pressed into a shoulder. A barrier holding steady, separating control from the void beyond. Muscles tighten, senses razor-sharp, time compressed into single beats.

Simon takes a controlled step, shoulders squared, body wired, narrowing the gap between the team and me. A calculated stride closes the distance, movement crisp and purpose absolute. One sign, one command, and the entry point ceases to exist.

George remains a ghost at the rear, presence more sensed than seen. A phantom in the dim light, hands tight around the weapon, awaiting the call to strike.

Thirty seconds later, Lucy and I take our positions against the wall close to the door. We can't risk one of us crossing the open gap, so Lucy tucks in by my side to the left of the door. The faint conversation continues inside.

I tap on Lucy's thigh, and everything shifts. Limbs tighten, vision narrows. The doorframe dissolves as both of us surge through, weapons raised. Suppressors choke each shot to a muffled hiss, but the impact screams through the room.

A shift on the torn sofa, a head lifting just enough to register movement. A whisper of compressed air splits the stillness, Lucy's round punching through flesh and bone.

The skull caves, tissue shredding, the back of the head vanishing in an instant. A red mist bursts outward, droplets suspended for a fraction of a second before settling on the faded upholstery. Limbs slacken, the frame collapsing inward, sinking into the stained cushions. The silence swallows the moment, undisturbed by the absence of breath.

A limp grip releases the bottle, a muted splash soaking into distressed fabric. The body folding into itself, crumpling without fight. A final gasp shudders out, chest sagging into the wreckage. Blood spreads, dark and thick, flowing into fractured concrete. The last tremor fades, leaving nothing but stillness, a shell crumpled in the ruin of what once stood.

Two men hunch over a table, for an instant too long. The first shot punches into the closest skull, bone fracturing beneath the round's force. A forced exhale struggles free, caught between dying and collapsing lungs. The man pitches forward, momentum ending in an abrupt collision—forehead splitting against unyielding wood. A hollow thud echoes, final and absolute.

Fingers release. The bottle twists mid-air, liquid sloshing before crashing to the ground, shattering on impact, foam bleeding from the jagged glass that remains.

The other man jerks, instincts flaring, a sharp convulsion gripping the frame, muscles tensing. Arms twitch, mouth cracks open, nerves misfiring; an empty gesture from a form already beyond repair. A second shot strikes true—centre of the throat—shutting down everything in an instant. Reflex kicks in as hands clutch at the wound.

A strangled rasp breaks free, a drowning gurgle swallowed in blood. Knees weaken. A slow collapse follows, hand dragging across the counter as balance vanishes. A body in freefall, dead before striking the floor. The thud of impact settles into the floorboards, final and absolute.

With any luck, nobody will have detected the sound of bodies hitting the deck. For now, the room remains still, where life existed seconds ago—a clean execution, leaving nothing behind but cooling corpses and empty bottles.

Bodies lie broken, sprawled across concrete like waste swept to the edges. Blood seeps into fractures, darkening stone with a silence louder than gunfire. No twitch, no sound—only stillness earned in violence.

Reflection has no place here. No value in names. The dead don't slow the living. This corridor records nothing. The world beyond won't notice a thing erased from it.

The team moves forward, focused and composed. Each step is purposeful. There are no questions, no doubt — only a relentless pursuit of a fixed goal. Walls close in, corners become narrower, and escape routes vanish. The command centre awaits just around the corner — a singular junction where everything either concludes or starts anew.

Footsteps shift as one, deliberate, fluid. Rifles carve through the space, tracking every angle, barrels unwavering. Index fingers rest against triggers, the first pressure held.

Corners split the area into kill zones, vacant places pretending to be safe routes. An open doorway, an unsealed vent, a flash of movement in the periphery — danger lurks in the quiet. A single wrong assumption can turn a path into a grave.

The corridor stretches onward, each shadow a potential foe, each door a possible death trap with no margin for error. The world outside fades; nothing exists past the next few minutes. The enemy is unaware of what closes in.

I stop short of a door 20 metres to my front, light from the command centre breaking through into the passageway. A signal from me and everyone goes to ground, diving behind, crates that line the walls.

From my position behind a broken box, I listen for movement in the passage. The only sound beyond the target area is in the distance. Footsteps that do not appear in a hurry.

After a final glance at the surroundings, I whisper into the radio, "OK, folks, we have a go, out." No need for a response, everyone knows their roles.

Keeping as quiet as possible, I move into my breach position to the right of the door. Derek moves in, standing by my side, followed by Lucy. After checking that no nosey bastard is looking toward the door, Lucy moves to the other side.

Any sudden movement here risks drawing unwanted attention. A casual glimpse from inside the control room. A calm breath, a steady step. Simon and George stroll towards their start positions, appearing relaxed. Their movements mimic a patrol, merging with the monotony of the facility.

A final glance at the team confirms readiness as a silent acknowledgement passes through the unit, bodies set, fingers braced around triggers. This is calculated destruction, a mission designed to prevent recovery.

Grenades are primed on a two-second fuse. Detonation will be instant. The first movement will shatter the quiet, leaving only the certainty of what follows — violence; rapid, absolute.

I give the signal, and Simon throws the first grenade through the doorway, bouncing once off the cold concrete floor before landing in the heart of the room. A small block of C4, on a short fuse, leaves my hand, arcing through the air, spinning and coming to a rest with a dull thud; sufficient to cause damage but not destroy the control room.

Time drags, thick and unnatural, stretching silence until it becomes a noose. Every breath weighs more than the last. Stillness creeps like fog before a storm, pressing in from all sides, waiting to crack under the pressure.

Lungs tighten. Pressure builds — something unseen coils in the air, ripe with threat. My chest heaves against the invisible grip. The moment teeters on the edge — one breath away from eruption. Every sense leans forward, bracing.

Then the blast. Violence erupts without mercy, splitting the corridor with raw force. The explosion punches through steel, ripping silence to shreds. Shockwaves slam outward, swallowing space in a brutal roar.

Walls convulse. Debris flies in all directions—metal, dust, fire. Fragments spin like shrapnel caught in a wind tunnel, smashing against anything solid. Chaos crashes through the corridor, tearing calm apart, leaving nothing untouched. The quiet is gone, replaced by destruction, screaming in every corner.

Shockwaves hammer through the structure, forcing metal to scream as it bends and buckles under the force. A split-second delay, then the fireball surges, swallowing the room, devouring oxygen, rolling out in a burst of shattered debris. A foul haze grips the body, with the unmistakable reek of scorched bodies and smouldering insulation.

Shrapnel from another grenade bursts in a lethal swarm, jagged fragments slicing through flesh, fabric, and failing equipment. Screams mix with the hiss of ruptured lines, a chorus of chaos from those caught in the kill zone. People crumple mid-motion, torn apart.

Smoke floods the space, dense and choking, curling through wrecked consoles and exposed wiring. The sharp bite of burning cabling clings to every surface, the scent of charred plastic mingling with something darker. Monitors flicker, desperate signals blinking from ruined control panels.

Sparks jump from shredded cables, circuits gasping as the system stutters, flickers, and dies. Screens hang in shattered silence, earlier pulsing with commands but now frozen in digital rigour mortis. Once a nerve centre of power, the command hub smoulders beneath collapsing steel and the acrid stench of defeat.

A signal flashes from a raised fist, and we breach. Boots slam over the threshold, the impact reverberating through metal and concrete. Weapons snap into position, muzzles tracking movement before thought registers.

Shadows shift, bodies flow through the smoke-choked entrance like phantoms. Dust swirls in the air, stirred by the assault's momentum. Wreckage sprawls ahead, and the control room is suspended in a twisted moment between order and destruction. Thick particulate clouds cling to the devastation, curling through shattered glass and deformed iron.

A figure stumbles from behind a damaged console, boots dragging through debris — glass, casing, cables. One hand grips the neck, breath is uneven. The air stings like acid, dense with chemical fumes. An arm rises, fingers outstretched, reaching into the chaos.

No direction, only instinct struggling for stability. Metal, paper, timber — none offer support. Twitches ripple through tensed limbs. Nerves spark without guidance. Legs quake, the body wavers, as the barrier between movement and collapse crumbles. One final breath tightens the frame, and then silence envelops it.

Fumes twist into my sinuses, dry and bitter, coating the throat with engine grease and scorched plastic. Muscles tighten. My jaw clenches. Reflex pulls back from the stench, but the focus stays locked.

My rifle snaps level, stock tight against my shoulder. One breath, then three rounds spit from the barrel, clean and flat, punching through flesh and bone. The centre mass erupts, the figure jolting back into a shattered console, glass shattering beneath.

Blood splatters the fractured screen, running slow across its lifeless glow. Fingers claw at the air, desperate for a last command. Eyes dull fast, panic fading behind a mask of finality. Another problem erased.

Movement ripples to my left — enemy frantic, hands scrambling for a dropped rifle. Too slow. Lucy pivots, firing a disciplined burst into ribs, bullets chewing through vital organs. The target folds, crumpling onto the blood-slicked floor.

A third figure lunges, desperation fuelling motion. I exhale, finger tight on the trigger — one bullet slices through the neck, severing intent from muscle. Momentum carries the body backwards, ribs cracking brutally against splintered metal. No scream follows, just the sound of another body hitting the deck.

The corpse lies across shattered glass, flesh tearing against embedded fragments. Muscles twitch, surrendering to stillness. Blood spreads, saturating circuits beneath, silencing the hum of machinery forever.

I glance to my left to see Simon sweeping left, rifle steady, barrel tracking across fractured consoles. Air pulses with heat, shimmering, distorting outlines in waves.

Above, the weakened girders let out creaking sounds, a haunting reminder of their precarious state as flames savage and consume the once-sturdy structure. Sparks tumble down from the flames, dancing in the air, threatening to ignite anything in their path and adding to the chaos of the scene.

George angles right, sight fixed, senses razor-edged. Shadows flicker uncertainly behind a barricade of debris. George fires without hesitation, rounds slicing through darkness, tearing muscle.

A silhouette tumbles backwards, its body appearing lifeless as it collides with the jagged and twisted metal surrounding it. The clash resonates through the air, a grim reminder of the violent forces that led to this haunting moment.

Derek steps into the gloom, rifle raised, every muscle tight. Shadows stretch long across broken walls, hiding secrets behind jagged edges. His gaze slices through the dark, hunting movement, reading silence like a map etched in fear and violence.

A flicker — small, but enough. Behind the wrecked furniture, something shifts. Not fast. Not bold. Just enough to betray the fear. It moves like prey that knows the end has arrived, yet stays rooted, caught in the final moments of choice.

Derek exhales one breath, one squeeze. The trigger breaks the silence, but the shot whispers rather than screams. It is suppressed, clean, and reluctant, like even the bullet mourns what follows.

The figure crumples. Darkness swallows the motion — no cry, no final protest — just a hollow stillness draped over memory. The space, once alive, now bears the quiet aftermath of someone who will not return.

Lucy moves ahead, carving a path through thick smoke, weapon glinting like a promise of death. Each footfall silent, focused; ghosts of fog curl around her frame, a lethal shadow drifting toward violence. I watch, muscles taut, rifle raised.

She halts, shoulders squared, eyes tracking unseen threats lurking in the dark. Her finger caresses the trigger guard, poised to unleash chaos.

"Movement left!" she shouts, voice tight. My pulse quickens, anticipation twisting like a blade inside my chest.

In the depths of the night, shadows dance eerily around, illuminated only by the occasional gleam of metal that catches the faint light. Lucy grips her weapon tight, as she takes aim, she squeezes the trigger, and the muzzle flashes, casting a momentary glow on a world steeped in darkness.

The deafening sound pierces the stillness, and bullets fly with precision, tearing through the flesh of the figures lurking in the shadows. The air is filled with a cacophony of pained screams, each cry a haunting reminder of the violence unfolding. Yet, just as quick as they erupt, the screams fade.

A chemical haze suffocates, sharp and unpleasant. Fumes burn the lungs, violently intermingling with the cordite that hangs thick in the still air. Sparks leap from a ruptured console, wires snapping, spitting embers.

Amidst the chaos, I take a moment to listen to my surroundings, listening for the sound of running feet in the corridor. I can't detect any footsteps rushing to reinforce. Viktor's men start to falter visibly — panic eroding discipline, fear destroying courage.

A technician cautiously steps out from cover, hands raised in an attempt to plead for mercy.

One swift round from my rifle silences the plea, piercing the skull with brutal precision. Gravity claims the corpse. No hesitation. Another obstacle is eliminated without thought as the mission moves forward without pause.

Feet scramble across slick tiles, figures desperate for elusive safety. Chaos breaks their ranks, bullets flying without purpose, ricocheting wildly off machinery, screens shattering into fragments. Magazines empty without purpose, panic dominating over precision.

My rifles bark again, rounds slicing deliberately, clinically. Bullets rupture flesh, bones fracturing grotesquely, bodies collapsing amid strangled cries.

With adrenaline surging through his veins, a fighter charges forward, weapon lifted high and ready for action. Instinct taking over, Derek responds without a second thought, firing three precise shots that tear through flesh with a sickening sound. The impact causes the body to stiffen, limbs convulsing out of control as if caught in a final dance of desperation, before it collapses into the debris, a stark reminder of the chaos that engulfed the battlefield.

At the back of the room, half behind a damaged console, a woman hesitates, indecision stealing precious seconds. Lucy doesn't and fires, a single bullet breaking bone in the woman's shoulder, spinning the body into a chaotic dance before hitting the floor.

George finishes off a man sprinting towards the exit, desperate to escape. With a steady hand, George squeezes the trigger, and the bullet sails through the air, hitting the back of the man's head with a sickening thud. The impact forces the man to stagger forward a few feet, legs giving way beneath, collapsing, lifeless, to the cold, hard ground. The scene's chaos echoes with hurried footsteps, now replaced with the heavy sound of finality.

Yet another enemy emerges from the wreckage. My rifle pivots, bursts hammering home mid-stride. Flesh splits, corpse collapsing back onto ruined equipment.

Casings are strewn over steel, their echoes drowned out by the rifle fire. Heat radiates from the warped metal, blending the bitter chemical residue with the acrid smoke. Breathing grows harder as the atmosphere becomes suffocating. Spiralling smoke trails cling to the devastation.

I scan the wreckage, confirming silence. Bodies sprawl frozen, triggers still gripped. Blood seeps across circuits, drowning without a sound in crimson pools. Consoles flicker before screens fail, and darkness claims Viktor's command post.

The empire Viktor tried to construct here in the Australian Outback crumbles in minutes, leaving behind only dead circuits and silence. Over the sound of dying electronics, a crack of gunfire shatters the moment. Short bursts slam into metal, sending sparks across the debris.

Rounds tear into an overturned desk, the impact jarring through the solid frame. Another burst follows, ricocheting off steel, too close for comfort. A separate room, tucked just beyond the central control room, holds the source.

Muzzle flashes flicker from the back of a tall cabinet, an entrenched shooter pinning movement. The angle is tight, and the cover is adequate. The bastard picked his ground well. The firefight resumes, a lethal dance dictated by angles and split-second reactions. A quick shift brings a new line of sight. Legs stretch beneath the cupboard, a brief glimpse before vanishing behind the reinforced frame.

A skilled sniper shot from George hammers into exposed ankles, bone splintering under impact. The scream cuts through the chaos, sharp and raw. As I move, I signal for George and Simon to follow me.

Fragments grind underfoot. Simon advances on my left, George on my right, weapons tracking the jagged terrain ahead. The wreckage stirs, tension thick, breath measured, trigger half-pressed. The injured man writhes on the ground, hands clawing for a firearm. Without flinching, I rest the barrel of my rifle on the man's forehead. A single round ends the struggle.

Lucy pauses near a shattered console, fingers pressing into a gap in the fractured casing. A slip of paper, edges charred, wedged between exposed circuits—maps, schematics, something worth hiding. The faded ink bleeds through damp fibres, numbers scrawled coded markings.

A sharp call brings Derek to Lucy's twenty, gaze locking onto the find. The pages shift, calculations lining the margins, coordinates buried in the mess. No hesitation. The stack vanishes into a secure pocket, sealed away.

Simon clears left, rifle steady, eyes locked. George mirrors the motion, covering high. Every step cuts deeper into the wreckage. Silence holds for one breath too long. Movement flashes at the entrance. Two targets—fast, aggressive, committed. Weapons lift. Triggers snap. The first burst shreds steel, throwing splinters into the air. The second passes wide. I hit the floor.

The team dives for cover. No command needed—just instinct. Simon and George fire in unison, shots drilling into flesh with surgical precision. Chests rupture, crimson splattering the walls. Staggering figures collapse mid-stride, legs tangling as lifeless forms crash through the opening, dead momentum dragging them into the kill zone.

The doorway clogs with remains, torsos draped over one another, weapons still clutched in useless grips. The moment ends before it starts, the fight erased with a single exchange.

A stillness settles, fractured by the crunch of breaking glass, as Derek drives a rifle butt through the last standing monitor, the screen collapsing inward with a hiss of failing circuits. Sparks snap, the command centre slipping deeper into darkness.

"Anyone spot Viktor, Natasha, or Sergei? Dead or alive?" My words cut across the silence, a demand rather than a question. Responses bark back, sharp and final.

"Negative. Not here!" yells Derek.

"Nope, no sight of the wanker!" shouts Simon from the other room.

"The fucking idiot has to be somewhere; keep checking. Might be in a concealed room hiding behind anything!" I shout.

The team continues to search for intel and hidden entrances. Weapons angle through the haze, scanning for distortions, the slightest sign of a waiting ambush. Desks lay overturned, filing cabinets gutted, drawers forced open in a rush. Gaps between doors and walls hide uncertainty. Hesitation invites a bullet from the dark.

As I lift my head, something stirs at the doorway. A ripple, subtle yet deliberate, disrupts the threshold. Silhouettes shatter the shadows, shifting through the murk, their forms defined by the doorframe. Viktor steps forward, fluid and unhurried, flanked by guards standing like statues hewn from war.

Then, in an instant, gunfire rips through the air, with muzzle flashes illuminating the shattered remains of the command centre. Viktor's men lift their weapons, their instincts sharp, but their reactions are too sluggish.

A burst of return fire from the team shreds through muscle, pushing bodies into jagged convulsions. The impact snaps torsos back, bones yielding under the force.

Crimson mist hangs in the air. Limbs give way as momentum forces the lifeless figures downwards, resulting in a pooling red blood that spreads beneath the contorted remnants.

Viktor lunged towards the passageway, heart racing as he sprints towards the passageway ahead. Every stride and step thundering against the floor, each echoing through the narrow tunnel.

Even with potential dangers hiding in the shadows, Viktor prioritises speed over caution, motivated by an urgent need to reach a safe destination as fast as possible.

"Lucy! George! On me!"

My voice slices through choking dust, sharp with urgency. Boots pound the concrete in a tight cadence, echoes booming. Every turn of the corridor tightens, space shrinking, guiding us forward into Viktor's labyrinthine trap.

The walls squeeze inward, narrowing options to single paths — no choice but to advance. Each corridor angles sharply, channelling movement toward a fatal outcome. The layout is precise, designed for one brutal purpose: to end pursuits like ours.

Ahead, Viktor slips ghost-like between shadows, swallowed by barriers built for concealment. Sounds splinter, ricocheting unpredictably, masking the actual location. My grip tightens on the rifle, heart pounding — every second counts.

"Watch corners, stay sharp," I command, voice low.

Each twist draws us deeper into suffocating uncertainty. Emergency lights cast harsh, flickering silhouettes across walls — each shadow hiding lethal intent. The distant crackle of gunfire fades into oppressive silence, replaced by rhythmic thuds of adrenaline-charged pulses in my temples.

A single door stands slightly open at the corridor's end, darkness spilling from inside. The space beyond beckons — a lethal invitation. I gesture forward, weapon raised, finger ready. One breath steadies nerves. Whatever waits within, we'll meet head-on.

The abandoned guard room looms ahead, door open. The stench of sweat, gunpowder, and old leather hangs in the stagnant air. A presence waits beyond the threshold, the past colliding with the present in an inevitable moment.

With George covering outside, Lucy and I head indoors. If Viktor inhales within these walls, the pursuit concludes here. Then, from the shadows at the rear of the room, a slow clap breaks the silence — deliberate, mocking, with measured intervals between each strike of skin against skin.

The sound slithers through the space, settling heavy like smoke from a dying fire. Viktor hovers near a rusted desk, shoulders relaxed and posture loose, an old predator toying with prey.

"Still one step behind, Steve," Viktor's words roll out, laced with something more profound than mockery. "Just like Oranjestad, when you killed my relative. Just like Billy, when life was ripped from his body." A smirk flickers across Viktor's lips, amusement masking a sharpened edge.

I take a slow, measured breath that pushes through my clenched teeth. My muscles tense, generating a conflict between control and instinct. Billy's name slices through the air, jagged and unforgiving. It tears through old wounds with surgical precision, stitched together by time, exposing raw nerves beneath.

A stillness grips the space, heavy and unbroken. Edges sharpen where sound ought to exist, yet nothing rises to fill the void. The past lingers beyond reach, a graveyard of choices left to rot, their remnants seeping through cracks too deep to mend.

Nothing reaches forward from the earth. Nothing distracts my attention from what lies ahead, cutting through the static, clarifying the contours of the mission, sharp as a knife. The only thing that matters is standing in front of me.

Outside the room, movement disrupts the gloom. A figure inches forward, unaware of eyes locked on him. The dull gleam of a pistol reflects the dying light, raised just enough to confirm intent. Breath hangs, suspended, waiting for impact.

From the shadows, George rises—silent, deliberate, rifle already aligned, breath already stilled. No hesitation. One round cracks the tension, slicing through the air like a scalpel. The shot hits clean, crushing windpipe and spine in the same blink.

No scream arrives, just a wet gurgle swallowed by blood. The figure folds in on himself, knees buckling first, weapon slipping from a limp grip. The body hits hard. Twitches. Then nothing.

George lowers the rifle without a word. Just another mark on the tally. Another threat erased before it could stain the room with death. The silence that follows is earned, but temporary. Something always comes next.

Back in the room, a breath lingers in the space between, neither moving, neither backing down. Viktor stands unmoved, shoulders loose, weight balanced, the smirk never wavering—a head tilt, a wrist flick, inviting, taunting, waiting for the strike.

"Same mistakes, same moves. Drop the weapons and the team. Just you. Just me. No excuses, no running. The way it should've been from the beginning." Viktor's words carve through, soaked in certainty. Arms spread, palms open.

A clean shot or a slow bleed — makes no difference to me. The only outcome for Viktor is death. The name Viktor Readle will never shape another war, never push another piece across the board. Billy's grave stays cold, but the man responsible will rot before the sun rises.

"Come on then, you fat bastard," I say through gritted teeth.

Viktor strikes first. A fist snaps towards my throat, not quick enough. I shift my weight, the blow glancing off my shoulder and instead of crushing my windpipe. He's exposed — my turn.

My fist slams into Viktor's ribs — deep, sharp, direct. The impact forces a stagger, breath caught mid-motion. Balance shifts, but my resolve locks in. I sense it in Viktor's movements, strength holding, but the edge is weakening. Not enough to drop him — yet.

Another strike lands at the same point and depth. It tests both muscle and will — flesh yields. The rhythm falters. Momentum shatters. This transcends mere power; it's pressure exerted until something crumples.

Viktor counters with precision and control, avoiding wild swings. A knee strikes upwards, targeting my centre mass. I pivot his kick, missing by a narrow margin. An elbow follows in a broad arc, quick and controlled, mere inches from making contact.

I feint — baiting him. A fraction of a second is all I need — Viktor bites.

A shift forward, where the trap tightens. My right hand cuts through, Viktor's temple absorbing the entire force as my fist slams into the side of his head. The impact rattles through him, body lurching, crashing into an overturned chair. Wood shatters, splinters scattering along the floor. Pressure never eases, the next blow already in motion.

Viktor lurches towards me, sheer strength propelling every inch of movement. A strike slices through the air, knuckles slamming into my cheekbone, sending a shockwave through muscle and sinew. Bright bursts flash in my periphery, my vision blurring at the edges.

Viktor grabs my jacket, yanking me towards him. The desk bites into my ribs. He's going for control. That's not happening.

My elbow slams into his side, a direct hit, deep and unforgiving. A sharp exhale rattles from Viktor's throat, grip failing as the body buckles for a fraction of a second. My right fist follows through, cracking against the jaw, bone shifting under the force. The head whips to one side, blood spraying across the table in broken arcs.

My boot catches on debris, causing a momentary imbalance. Viktor surges, seizing the opening.

Hands clamp around my windpipe. Crushing down. Cutting air. Vision tunnels.

Adrenaline swells within me as muscle memory kicks in.

A violent shift in weight, a knee slamming up into Viktor's bollocks. The hold breaks. I twist, reversing the grip.

Now I'm in control.

My knuckles drive into Viktor's face, a solid break shuddering through bone. Cartilage crumples, an intense crunch slicing through the chaos. Nose? Cheek? Makes no difference. A red spray streaks across the desk, dripping in thick, uneven trails.

A change at the edge of the fight—Lucy. A measured step forward, drawing Viktor's attention, a deliberate move. Testing response, trying to force an opening.

A quick pivot answers, the movement crisp and calculated, forcing Viktor's focus off balance for a fraction too long—half a second too long.

I strike. The side of my hand slams into Viktor's throat, crushing cartilage in an instant. A sharp gasp sputters out, breath stolen before a sound escapes. Viktor staggers, knees buckling, hands clawing at the ruined windpipe, body jerking in a desperate struggle for air.

My chest heaves. The air burns on the way in. Sweat drips into my eyes—blood trails from torn knuckles. Muscles burn, every fibre locked tight. One misstep away from the wrong end of the fight. The edge holds, not by luck, but by calculation and force. Close doesn't count. Only survival does.

Viktor's body jerks against the floor, limbs spasming. Blood spreads beneath, thick and dark. Breath rasps from a throat too damaged to speak. But the eyes still burn—rage, pride, failure, all trapped in silence. Lucy seizes the moment and binds his wrists and ankles, the plastic biting into raw skin.

Soft murmurs echo from the corridor, quiet but filled with urgency. The moment hangs heavy, loaded with unexpressed tension. Then a silhouette moves across the doorway.

Natasha steps inside, shoulders squared. Both hands raised, a 9mm dangling loose from an index finger, grip balanced between surrender and purpose.

George enters behind, rifle barrel fixed on Natasha's centre mass. A shift in my focus drags attention away from the heap on the floor, limbs twisted at unnatural angles, breath shallow, almost absent.

"Appears you caught a fucking live one, George?" I say.

George gestures toward Natasha with his rifle, saying, "Natasha sent us that message because Viktor's fate is already sealed. She's got a score to settle and won't let anyone else interfere."

Before I can ask any questions, Natasha stands still with her hands resting at her sides, breathing steady and controlled, each inhale deliberate and calm. She fixes her gaze on Viktor, drawing a sense of intensity from the moment.

Beneath her composed exterior, something enigmatic simmers, hinting at unspoken thoughts or hidden emotions poised to surface at any moment, creating an intense friction in the air.

Natasha's voice cuts through the stillness, sharp and unyielding. "You always thought no one would find out. You and Sergei murdered my parents. And now you're plotting to have me killed." Each word lands with weight, something jagged.

Viktor doesn't flinch. Doesn't bother with lies. His voice scrapes out—dry, worn, the edge of a man who's bled too much into lost ideals. "Yes. I ordered it. Both of your parents betrayed the cause." He pauses, eyes narrowing, lips curling with contempt. "Russia comes first. Always. They were weak. Sentimental. Dead weight dragging us into compromise." Viktor's glare cuts through the air like a bayonet. "I don't mourn traitors. I erase them."

Natasha takes another step, jaw clenched, muscles wound tight with rage held just below the skin. Her eyes burn—not with shock, but hatred, long-forged and sharpened.

"I trusted you. Like a damn fool. But the truth's out now."

Without forgiveness or redemption, Natasha's world narrows to one final act. A silent guilty verdict forms behind her eyes, carved in betrayal and blood. She doesn't blink. Doesn't flinch. The pistol rises fast, hand unshaking.

The shot cracks like a personal exorcism. A round slams into Viktor's skull, bursting through flesh and bone. The head snaps back.

Viktor's body gives up from his seated slump on the floor, as if his spine remembers the treachery. He buckles—slow, broken— and tips onto his side, dead weight thudding against the concrete. Blood crawls from the wound, spreading in thin rivulets—silent, steady, final.

She doesn't look away. Doesn't regret. Not for a second.

Natasha drops the 9mm. Steel kisses concrete — one brittle crack, then a skittering clatter that ricochets off bare walls. Vibration ticks up through my boots; oil and old cordite breathe into the air. Fingers unclench. The final act is sealed in the space between breaths, jagged at the edges, voice stripped bare.

"Viktor took everything from me," Natasha says, a breath slipping between clenched teeth, measured, restrained. "Killing him isn't justice. It's balance." The words drop, with weight behind each syllable. "Now, the score is even."

Natasha steps closer, gaze never wavering from Viktor's lifeless form sprawled across the ground. A slow shift in posture, just about perceptible, years of buried fury settling into the silence. A flicker of movement — a glance at the ruined face, then back again. Something stirs, but nothing is released.

"So what are we going to do with Natasha?" asks Lucy, taking away the pistol.

"Let her walk," the words cut through the space, controlled and "So what are we going to do with Natasha?" asks Lucy, taking away the pistol.

"Let her walk," the words cut through the space, controlled and keep it that way. Two rifles are locked, one breath away from turning your escape into a body drop."

With that, Natasha turns without saying a word and leaves.

"You gone fucking soft, Steve, she deserved to be put down," says George, confused.

"Not weakness, nor madness. Strategy. If that group resurfaces or the Russians start knocking, information becomes currency. The right whisper in the wrong ears, and Viktor's killer will be their next target. Let's move and grab the others."

Chapter Twenty-Eight — Tactical Withdrawal

Dust still hangs thick in the air as I push through the wreckage with Lucy and George. The stench hits first—burned circuitry, gunpowder, blood. Shards of glass crunch underfoot. Bodies lie where they dropped—abrupt endings written in red.

Through the haze, shadows shift. Two shapes move at the rear, weapons raised. Simon. Derek. Picking through shattered comms gear, eyes sharp for anything that might still bite. No words—just the quiet language of survivors.

The gunfire's stopped, but peace is a lie. This mission won't be over until we're back on British soil, if we make it that far.

I take a moment to glance around the team. Everyone's face is streaked with dirt and sweat; their uniforms torn, yet alive. Each step carries the burden of combat, exhaustion, tightening muscles, and relief buried under readiness.

Lucy drops the heavy barrel first, her breath steady and controlled, each movement precise and deliberate. The air around them still pulses with the residual energy from their earlier confrontation, the heat clinging to the devastation surrounding them like a dense fog.

Amid this chaos, Derek grimaces as he scrapes the dried blood from his arm; the wound, while still bleeding, shows signs of slowing, a reminder of the fierce struggle they have just endured.

George stands resolutely by the entrance, monitoring the silent void stretching beyond the doorway. His eyes scan the area with a mix of determination and wariness.

Meanwhile, Simon stands nearby, tapping the magazine against his palm in a rapid and methodical manner. His gaze flits around the room, taking in every detail before locking onto mine, an unspoken communication passing between us.

"Find anything useful?" I yell.

"Nothing new, just whatever Lucy tucked away," Simon replies.

Sharp glances slice through smoke-filled silence, the team speaking without words. Viktor's ambition lies crushed beneath smouldering wreckage, twisted bodies frozen in the stark clarity of defeat. Smoke curls thick, each breath scraping raw through lungs filled with battle residue.

Sweat stings across fresh cuts, adrenaline pulsing beneath skin. My grip tightens on the rifle, heart hammering against the silence. This victory leaves scars, etched deep and unyielding. The team remains firm, ready for whatever follows. Survival is about execution — precision carved in violence.

After 20 minutes of scouring for anything useful, "OK folks, let's fuck off and grab the relic and move our sorry arses to the exfil point!" I shout across the room.

With the team moving in closer, I confirm, more to myself than to the team, "If any of Viktor's people are hiding in the bay where we stashed the relic, we will execute a standard breaching entry procedure."

Boots move forward, with barrels scanning the surroundings for any signs of hidden threats. Nothing stirs.

When we reach the stash, we approach with caution, stopping and listening for any sound that might give away an enemy hidden from view, ready to pounce.

The area remains quiet and void of life for now. But a few minutes is all we need. Inside the room, the relic remains in position, its edges sharp in the dim glow of the cargo bay. No stray boot prints disturb the dust, and no shifting shadows hint at an unseen threat.

Spend a few minutes checking that the device hasn't been tampered with. Once I'm clear that no IED was rigged to the device while we were dealing with the command centre, "OK, let's haul this out of here," I say.

The team moves in unison — angles covered, eyes tracking every shadow, tension increasing with each step. Only the scrape of boots on grit and the soft hum of breath held too long fill the air.

The atmosphere thickens. Oil coats the throat and clings to the skin. Rust mingles with damp stone. Every surface oozes age. This passage is not welcome — it's a trap.

Concrete narrows the route. The walls press in tight. Sound vanishes the instant it forms, leaving a silence that breathes like a predator poised for movement.

Wheels of the relic's makeshift carriage grind over broken slabs. Steel against stone screeches, an uncomfortable echo. Vibrations creep through the floor and up the spine.

The tunnel communicates in broken warnings. Although I sense danger ahead, we have no time to stop until we reach the exit.

I raise my left arm. A single motion halts the unit, locking bodies in place. The tunnel's edge marks the threshold between concealment and exposure. Outside the facility, there is nothing but raw landscape.

Somewhere in the Outback, Sergei moves as though the land responds to him — unhurried, intentional, exposed yet pristine. No shelter. No fear. The terrain stretches across the Outback, yet that assurance conveys more than mere arrogance.

The silence is misleading. Stillness isn't tranquillity — it's a lure. I've walked that same route before, so I'm aware of what lies in the emptiness.

We cannot confirm whether one of Viktor's operatives slipped a message through, and Sergei has covered all the exits, waiting for us to expose ourselves.

At the doorway, my breath steadies, rifle gripped firmly. Shadows ripple beyond the trees, wind masking potential threats. However, my instinct says otherwise.

"Something feels wrong," I mutter, jaw tightening.

George peers out, eyes narrowed, scanning for trouble. Silence drapes thick, like the calm before an ambush. The lack of sound twists deep in my gut.

George nods once, voice hushed, "Too quiet. Ready when you are."

I glance at Lucy. She steadies the rifle, sights aligned, covering our move.

"Go. We've got your back," Lucy whispers, finger poised on the trigger.

"Simon — move now!" I bark, launching forward into open ground, zigzagging as I run. Adrenaline surges, boots pounding the earth, muscles tight. Every metre exposes multiple risk. The treeline looms, offering either shelter or death.

Heart slamming against ribs, the cover draws near. No gunfire splits the silence, yet danger pulses through the emptiness. Diving forward, I crash against dirt, roll beneath thick vegetation, and crawl into concealment. Simon mirrors my motion.

My rifle snaps up, scanning every shadow and angle for ambush. Finger tightens around the trigger, and my muscles taut, ready for instant response. Seconds pass, each stretched, the silence remaining unbroken.

"Hold position," I whisper to Simon. "Watch your arc."

Scanning the perimeter once more, I grip the mic, static hissing before clarity returns. "All callsigns, Area clear — advance to the treeline," I say, voice low and controlled.

"LK, Roger that, moving now," comes the reply from Lucy through the radio.

Moments later, the rest of the team advances, pushing the relic into the shadows of a thick treeline. A natural concealment, wrapped in jagged rock and dense foliage, blocks sightlines from every angle.

George braces against rough stone, rifle steady, eyes fixed through the rifle scope.

"Sector secure," he murmurs, calm masking tension beneath.

Lucy sinks beside the relic, weapon tracking every flicker of movement.

Once in cover, Derek inputs coordinates, transmitting our position through encrypted channels and confirming the location of exfil. "GSS locked," he whispers. "Extraction inbound. Standby."

I check again — no enemy movement is visible. My chest tightens. "Simon, on me," I say, breaking cover, boots pounding dirt.

My heart hammers, and adrenaline surges as my eyes scan the area. Every step feels like crossing a wire rigged to explode.

We hit the ground hard beside Lucy, dust rising around our knees. Our ears search for threats hidden behind deceptive calm.

Satisfied, my eyes lock on the team. "Right, stick to the plan," I instruct. "Derek, Lucy, secure this location and guard the relic. Simon, George, with me to retrieve ATVs from the hide."

"Understood. We'll hold firm," Lucy replies.

"Maintain radio contact at all times," I add, voice firm. "Call any issues through; the others will come to your aid if possible. OK, if you two are ready, let's move out," I say, getting up and leaving.

We melt into shadows, mission locked, survival hanging by a lone thread. The forest waits silently, threatening in its calm, concealing unknown dangers ahead.

A dry wind sweeps across the plains as we depart, dragging grit against my exposed skin like sandpaper. Each gust appears like a forewarning.

The Outback stretches before us, intensive and relentless — dust, stone, scrub, and nothing more. The intense heat distorts the horizon, conjuring shapes from the ground and warping distance into deception.

The land scrutinises, silent and unmoved. No birds. No insects. Just us — shadows navigating through the void, rifles at the ready, eyes locked in focus.

Boots crunch on gravel. The sound fades beneath the oppressive din of insects. Each step forward marks the passage of time, like rounds waiting in a magazine.

The terrain folds around us, dips and ridges forming natural kill zones, each a potential ambush site. Shadows creep over the landscape, stretching with the lowering sun and staining the sand with burnt orange and black streaks.

To my front, a dry creek bed carves a scar through our route, banks lined with skeletal branches, gnarled and twisted from years without rain — the perfect ground for an attack. A hand signal from me tightens the formation, rifles sweeping the topography, tracking every possible angle. The air carries the weight of expectation, a stillness thick with unseen threat.

Seconds drag as we cross, steps deliberate, nerves braced for the first crack of gunfire. The silence remains unbroken, but that only makes the situation worse.

A ridgeline rises ahead, jagged rocks lining the crest like the teeth of a waiting predator. The RV sits just beyond, hidden from direct view.

Once again, my raised hand halts movement. The gut tightens. Telltales shift in the wind, and markers placed earlier are now disturbed.

"Hold," I whisper, tension knotting deep in my chest. "Someone's beaten us here."

George sinks into the dirt, rifle shouldered, scope sweeping the approach. "Nothing visual, Steve. Still feels off," he murmurs, voice taut.

A glance confirms readiness. "Simon, go," I signal.

Simon moves, slipping between cover, weapon braced. My turn follows. A slow advance, each step measured, covering arcs of fire, tracking shadows, the weight of expectation pressing down.

"Too quiet," Simon whispers back. "Something's wrong."

An absence of sound clings to the location, unnatural, like something waiting to exhale. Nothing shifts in the trees, yet tension drags thick in the air.

Steps space out, keeping angles covered, and movement is deliberate. The structure in the middle of the RV stands locked, but imprints pressed deep in the ground tell another story.

Splintered timber stretches across the ground, torn and scattered like remnants of something hunted. Nails jut from fractured beams — snapped clean, not weathered. That isn't a collapse, but raw violence, calculated and fast. The table we once gathered around — gone. Structure crushed. Purpose erased.

"This wasn't an accident," George growls in a whisper, eyes narrowing. "This was deliberate."

I glance around the damaged RV. "Agreed. They destroyed everything we used. Purposeful."

Simon steps through the debris, jaw tight. "Whoever did this, left a message."

My grip tightens, voice dropping lower. "And we're here to answer."

Ahead, the old vehicle shed slumps under its own weight. The door is left open, too still. Darkness pools inside. A body sprawls at the threshold — limbs bent wrong, neck twisted beyond recovery.

Blood stains the earth, deep and cracked. The air carries the knowledge of what happened here. Someone came through. The device struck without hesitation.

I step forward. A woman, riddled with bullet holes, lies motionless beside the spring-loaded IED I planted before leaving for the relic.

Pressure plates hold the top board in place, a crude but effective trap. She stepped wrong, shifting the weight just enough to trigger the device, sending a volley of rounds straight up, giving no second chances.

With the RV void of people, we spend some time checking the RV only to find no supplies, equipment, or anything worth salvaging. Just ruins, gutted and abandoned, a message written in fire and force. Whoever did this didn't act on impulse — they followed a plan.

The route to the hide stretches, each step, the distance, expanding, refusing to shrink. Heat presses down, thick, unmoving, swallowing sound, suffocating thought. Unfinished business clings to the moment, trailing behind like a shadow waiting to strike.

We move slow and deliberate. Each boot falls where it did before. There are no new marks, no drag footprints in the dirt, no disruption in the scattered debris. The silence speaks not a word, but it looms close, thick and unsettling.

We proceed with caution, on the lookout for dangers, our hands poised to react at the slightest hint of an ambush. No sounds or movements, yet something lurks. I sense it in my chest. It's a silence poised for detonation.

George and Simon provide cover while I make a slow circuit around the hide to confirm that the traps are still active and in place and verify the location's security.

With the area clear, I move on to the IEDs, confirming that the grenades set before we left for the relic remain live and the tripwires are unbroken.

With a firm grip, I remove each device, replace the safety pins, disarm all devices, and tuck them back into my jacket.

With the traps removed, I call over George and Simon to prepare the vehicles for return to the relic.

Once the Bergens and other equipment are loaded, the engines growl to life, the vibration pulsing through my hands as the ATV hums beneath me.

"OK, let's roll out!" I shout.

"Who do you think you are? A cowboy? you fucking idiot!" George yells back.

"Wrong again, fatboy, Black Mafia," I laugh, wondering if the other two will comprehend what I said.

With our recce troop, aka Simon, leading the convoy, we drive away from the hide. Dirt erupts behind us in dense, swirling clouds as the vehicles lurch forward, cutting a path back toward Lucy and Derek.

A ridgeline tears the sky, jagged and sharp. The Outback sprawls beyond—dust, silence, and heat. Shadows stretch long, warped by the burn of a ruthless sun. Nothing moves without consequence out here. Nothing lives without purpose.

A gust rips through, hurling grit into every seam of gear. My jaw clenches. Smoke hangs low, unmoving, dense with the weight of past fire. The scent bites — charred metal, dried blood, the ghost of something burned hard and fast.

"Eyes on that ridge," I say, over the noise of the engines.

George grunts. "With Sergei, nothing always leads to something."

The mic presses against my lips, "DR, this is S3, approaching from your twenty, over."

Static hisses before Derek's voice punches through. "S3, Roger, all calm here."

Words fade, swallowed by the quiet, yet silence never arrives without a price. Quiet is not peace. It is the moment when predators crouch, when breath is held, when the next move determines survival.

A short drive later, we reach a point close to where Lucy and Derek are held up. Only fools would race straight in. Complacency has no place here.

I need to confirm the site hasn't been compromised, so I stop short. Some idiot might be holding a weapon to Lucy and Derek's heads.

To confirm the location is safe, I call out, "What is the best regiment in the British army?" from about 50 metres away, with my rifle ready to reply to a wrong answer.

"The Royal Green jackets!" Derek yells back.

"Correct!" I shout back.

With the location secure, the approach locks in, tyres grinding over loose earth, the convoy rolling into position. Lucy and Derek brace near the treeline, rifles angled for any unseen threat. The relic remains buried beneath a layer of vegetation, shape broken by careful placement, invisible to a passing glance.

Rough edges grind deep into my palms, the relic's jagged frame pressing like broken promises into raw skin. Weight shifts uneven, dragging with every motion. No wheels move until this bastard settles tight. Each inch fought earns bruises.

The ATV groans. Steel flexes. A screech cuts through the silence like a dying animal. The relic grinds across the hardened tray — loud enough to wake the dead, or worse, Sergei's people. A slip now turns exfil into a dirt-and-blood disaster.

"Hold it steady, you break it, you carry it," I say.

"Touching offer. You volunteering?" comes the reply from Simon.

"Pass. I've got enough on my conscience."

Thick straps wrap around steel. Fibres cut deep. Every tug draws fresh pain. Lucy hauls tight.

"This thing weighs more than Steve's ego."

"Impossible," I grunt.

George plants a foot, testing the binding. "If this jumps loose mid-run, I'm blaming you, Simon."

"If it jumps loose, none of us will be around to hear the complaints," I add.

One final yank — ropes snap into place, tension humming through the frame. Suspension dips. ATV holds.

"Locked?" I ask.

George nods. "Solid as Derek's last marriage."

Derek doesn't flinch. "Still more reliable than your aim, mate."

I test the lines again. Unforgiving. Secure. My grip matches the one on my rifle. Ruthless. Unrelenting.

"Alright," I growl. "If it explodes, at least we won't have to carry it."

No laughs—just smirks. Gallows humour. The kind that keeps soldiers breathing.

A few minutes later, engines roar, vibrations surge through the frame. Simon rides alongside me at the front of the convoy, every twist of the trail already plotted in his mind.

Derek follows second, payload secured behind metal and quiet. George and Lucy trail behind, observing every hill and shadow—nothing overlooked, nothing taken for granted.

Twenty klicks to exfil—each one hard-won. The path cuts through the harsh Outback, dirt hardened and fractured by stones. This land offers no mercy. Neither do we.

The suspension fights every impact, absorbing the relentless pounding of the ground beneath. Dust kicks up in thick waves, swirling into the air, choking the space between us and whatever waits beyond the next rise.

A burst of static punches through the comms, breaking the rhythm of the engines. Derek's voice stays tight with urgency.

"Exfil flight, inbound. Two hours." The window is starting to close fast—no time for any delays.

The convoy shifts, acceleration pressing at the limits of control. The ATVs fight the terrain, built for this kind of hell. Their tyres dig into loose sand, gripping where others would slide.

The world around us stretches into an open kill zone, ridgelines cutting jagged lines against the sky. Shadows stretch below twisted rock formations, shifting with the wind, warping beneath the relentless heat. My gut tightens. This type of quiet never lasts. The next contact might be waiting just ahead.

About half an hour into the journey, a crack splits the air, slicing through the breeze like a blade. Gunfire erupts from the right, a blistering volley tearing into the dirt, carving deep furrows in the sand.

A heartbeat later, bullets hammer into metal, the ATVs rattling under the sudden onslaught. Sparks spit from the frames as rounds ricochet, shrieking off hardened steel.

Simon rips our vehicle into a sharp turn, the violent jolt slamming through the frame. The suspension bucks, tyres biting into the landscape as the convoy veers left. No hesitation.

Engines roar as we push for cover. The machines tear through uneven terrain, swallowing the distance toward a jagged rock formation.

"Send them something to choke on!" Lucy yells from behind, rounds streaking through grit and glare.

A burst of return fire cuts through the chaos, returning the enemy's aggression in a controlled response. Muzzles flash through the dust cloud, fingers tightening around triggers, sending rounds slicing through the air.

The battlefield twists in an instant. A rocky outcropping looms ahead, consuming the convoy into shadow, turning steel into shelter. Boots slam against dirt as our bodies hit the ground, weapons raised, tracking movement through the haze. The moment shifts. Control in our favour returns.

George vanishes into terrain, part of the rock itself. Breath slow, rifle locked. "Target—12 o'clock!" he shouts over incoming fire. "Taking the shot."

Muscles brace, sight calibrated, pressure building along the trigger. A single crack tears through the silence, projectile carving through dead air. The tango stumbles, a violent jerk rips through muscle and bone, momentum broken mid-step.

Motion disrupts the dust as hands strike the ground in a frantic struggle for survival. Scrambling limbs claw for refuge, with retreat driven by necessity rather than strategy. A body crawls across the uneven terrain, urgency etching desperation into movement as the final shelter fades away.

Lucy braces beside George, weapon firing bursts of rounds that rip into the barricades ahead.

Movement flares. Hands claw for the ground, panic replacing tactics.

"They're running," Derek mutters, adjusting position.

Lucy's weapon kicks in rhythm. "Run faster, you bastards."

The sharp percussion carves through the chaos, each shot a hammer blow driving enemies deeper. Muffled shouts mix with the crack of splintering cover, hesitation creeping into their return fire.

A hand signal locks in the next move. Simon veers off to my left, rifle tracking the treeline. Derek stays close, footsteps matching mine, silent and deliberate, cutting through the murk that clings to the battlefield. Derek's posture tightens, shoulders squared, tension coiling beneath fabric streaked with grit. A fractured skyline bleeds into the haze; shapes moving, waiting, compelling a calculated advance.

Broken terrain snakes forward, splintered rock choking the passage, brittle brush bristling in tangled masses. Gnarled limbs jut skyward, stripped bare, frozen in twisted gestures.

Shadows dance across the landscape, shifting with the wind, masking movement where death waits unseen. The enemy stays fixated on the suppressing fire from George and Lucy, ensuring they stay down, unaware of the storm closing in.

A flicker betrays the stillness — an unnatural, almost perceptible, yet sufficient shift. Rifles lift, a cold extension of the intent behind them.

The moment implodes, reflex severing hesitation, aggression responding to aggression. The gap between threat and response closes to nothing, action smashing beyond reason, instinct shaping the split-second choice.

A round snaps past my ear. "Close," I mutter, shifting left.

Bark shears from trees, jagged splinters raining down. I return fire, my shot hitting the man's centre mass, kinetic energy shattering bone, tissue tearing under the unrelenting force.

I return fire. Centre mass. Clean hit. The target stumbles, knees buckling, gravity pulling hard. Crimson coloured blood spreads across the dust, mixing with broken shell casings, the aftermath of violence.

"Dropped one!" I call out.

A push forward forces the engagement. The mind calculates distance, angles, and cover. I squeeze the trigger, the rifle bucks, and the enemy staggers.

Derek's voice crackles through the comms. "Two more pushing your right. Engaging." A burst from Derek shreds the brush to our front.

I shift forward, sights raised. "Simon, cover left flank!"

"Already on it!" Simon shouts, his rifle barking. "They're scrambling."

I squeeze again. Another hit. The form lurches backwards, spine folding. Derek's burst shreds the brush, the blast chewing through leaves and bark.

Simon's rounds punch stone, rattling the rocks. "They're pinned!"

Lead punches through the chaos, controlled bursts shredding barriers, forcing exposure. Fragments scatter, and wood and stone split under pressure. The tempo shifts, desperation surfacing, people twisting out of concealment, movements reckless, ripe for an end.

"They're coming apart!" Derek yells.

Gunpowder clings to the air, thick and unforgiving. Blood cuts through with a sharp edge—metal, smoke, and sweat all twisted into one stench. Heat pushes from the ground, wrapping everything in the weight of what just passed.

Rounds snap past, close, carving through breath and dust. Each step, each trigger squeeze, is part of a rhythm drilled into muscle. No hesitation. Combat flows in patterns—ours controlled, theirs breaking.

"They're folding!" I shout. "Press forward now!"

Our last push crashes forward. Scatter-fire breaks lines. One stumbles, weapon raised. Too slow. I fire once. Head drops like a stone.

"No chances," Derek says, walking past. He fires another round into a twitching form. "Don't care if he's breathing or praying."

The final surge slams into us. Scatter-fire chews the air; our line splinters into jagged gaps. Shots are fired into the heads of the fallen without mercy to ensure we don't have anyone playing possum.

Boots crush collapsed forms. Limbs bend wrong, fingers still clinging to useless steel. The desert swallows the sound—silence steps in—slow, heavy.

That quiet stays too long. The kind that sinks into skin. The kind that warns the next threat monitors from just beyond reach.

Blood seeps into the earth, dark and glistening. Brass cools in the dust. I scan ahead. The fallen remain where they dropped. We don't.

After searching the bodies for anything useful, I radio Lucy, "LK, this is S3, all tangos dispatched. Heading back, over."

"S3, Roger, out," comes the response from Lucy.

Back with the ATVs, engines roar to life, a rumble shaking through the chassis. Dust rises high behind the wheels.

"The primary route's burned. No choice now but to adapt," Simon says, eyes fixed ahead. No map needed—just memory and instinct.

We cut across rough terrain. Rocks crack beneath the tyres, and creek beds twist into the track ahead. Every metre gained pulls us further from certainty. Each turn carries risk. Each bend might end the mission.

A message crackles through the radio's static, cutting through the engine noise. Derek's voice is steady. "All callsigns, exfil flight is 40 minutes out. Out."

A glance at my wristwatch confirms the reality. The diversion holds, but the landing zone remains unseen and unprotected. No doubt that Sergei's men will be moving fast, but what intel did the informer at GSS pass on?

The extraction point remained classified, secured from prying eyes, and only a select few at GSS were aware of its location. A breach within GSS compromised intelligence, but the full extent remains concealed. Any bit of information funnelled into the wrong hands distorts the advantage. A second ambush might be waiting, ready to be sprung when we arrive at the exfil site.

A sun-baked desolation stretches out, wild and unforgiving. Contorted shrubs grasp at the parched ground, the sole indication of life in this barren expanse designed to obliterate footprints, mute all noise, and deter doubt. The stomach clenches.

The exfil stays 10 klicks away. No guarantee of a clean exit. No certainty that the next ridge won't bring another firefight.

A clenched fist signals a halt. Three klicks from the LZ, the convoy pulls off the track, engines dropping to an idle. The ATVs sit among the scrubland, concealed from immediate sight.

I step toward the group, cutting through the silence. "The LZ may be hot when we arrive. So, we split into two groups and approach from different angles. Simon and I take the point. Once clear, the relic moves in," I say.

George, arms crossed, rifle set across two knees, "Find out if the Broome Explorers still want to play their part." The statement lands without weight; a test, a push into uncertain ground.

Simon's expression hardens, breath steady, tone flat. "Who vouches for them?"

The question hangs, waiting for an answer. Betrayal carves deep, leaving behind a ledger of scars that outlive the ones who caused them. Trust carries a cost measured in blood and regret, its currency paid in past mistakes. Certainty remains a luxury no one here can afford.

Lucy doesn't flinch. "GSS ran background checks. They're legit."

"In that case, a fantastic idea, George. Derek, pick up their frequency. Discover if they're close enough to assist. If so, send the LZ coordinates," I say, firing the ATV engine back to life.

Moments later, Derek replies, "I found Nancy on the channel given to us. A message was sent. "

One klick out, the convoy grinds to a halt again, the deep rumble of motors settling into a soft growl. Dust billows in the fading light, curling around the ATVs like a restless spectre.

The radio hisses, a thin layer of static cracking in broken bursts, drowning in the mechanical hum of idling engines. Everyone's breath stalls as the signal struggles through interference. A voice cuts through, sharp and controlled.

"Nancy here. No issue. We are holding the border and will secure your LZ by the time you arrive. So far, no sight of Sergei's men."

A flicker of ease threatens discipline, a fleeting moment crushed beneath the unyielding need to scan for weaknesses. A current tightens across muscle and bone, drawing every fibre to the edge. The unseen might be crouching past the limit of vision, concealed, waiting, patient, unhurried, prepared to strike.

Nancy is calm, lacking gunfire or urgency, and there's no apparent sign of an impending ambush. But silence never guarantees safety. The perimeter stands, but stability means nothing in this game. One push, one misstep, and the balance flips.

Nancy's information sits unconfirmed, intent buried under layers of uncertainty. If this goes south, the exit turns into a blood-soaked retreat, bullets slamming through cover, every step a gamble against unseen rifles.

My hand grips the radio, pressing the transmission. "Acknowledged. Hold position. Moving in now."

The final decision locks in place. No turning back. The next klick decides whether this exfil is clean or ends in blood. The engines growl as the convoy moves forward, slicing through the dust.

A glance at the wristwatch tightens the countdown. Fifteen minutes left—no room for error.

We split at the 500-metre mark. A signal sends Lucy, Derek, and George on a flanking route. The terrain shifts into natural concealment, shadows stretching over the ridgeline.

Derek's steady voice breaks the silence over the radio. "All callsigns, LZ secure. Safe to approach." The words settle, but no step proceeds without caution.

A figure stands dead ahead of me, the lone shape cutting against the track. The throttle eases, the ATV slows, and tension thickens between movement and action. The rifle in the man's hands points our way.

Thirty metres. A final stretch closes the distance. A black jacket marks allegiance. The stance confirms experience, not hired muscle. A silent breath shifts the weight of the moment.

The conversation wastes no time—the exchange is fast and stripped of everything unnecessary. Positions lock in, and every role is defined with precision.

The Broome Explorers cover the perimeter, eyes scanning the ridgelines, weapons ready to cut down anything that moves in the wrong direction.

Nancy grips the radio, posture rigid, unreadable. "The landing zone belongs to us—for now."

The window for exfil shrinks, seconds bleeding into risk, each one an opportunity for unseen rifles to line up their shots.

A flicker of disturbance at two o'clock draws my attention. Shadows break from the scrub, and two ATVs emerge from the dense brush. The team advances in disciplined silence, controlled.

Boots strike hard against the metal as figures pour from the vehicles, bodies slipping into the open like liquid through a crack. The unit operates like a machine with drilled precision without a single wasted motion—precise movement locks the operative into place. AR-15s are raised, ready for contact.

Derek's voice rips through the radio, tone clipped, steady. "Exfil flight, five minutes out." The countdown shrinks, at the edges of time.

A sharp glance moves between the team, the weight of the message pressing in on the moment. The relic sits, strapped down tight, the bulk an anchor tying this assignment to everything that follows. No question of leaving the device behind. The only choice left is what happens going forward.

My fingers tighten around the mic against my lips. "GSS, this is S3. Be advised, relic secured. Requesting confirmation on transport. Over." The transmission cuts through the static, the distant hum of the Osprey's engines filling the silence as the team waits.

A pause stretches across the frequency, the seconds dragging. The mission pivots on what comes next: the relic, the exit, and the risk of carrying it into the remaining phase.

Dave's voice breaks through, clipped, all business. "S3, this is GSS actual. What's the situation with the Broome Explorers? Over."

A glance toward Nancy, standing firm near the ATV, radio still in her hand. "GSS, Broome Explorers secured LZ. Holding perimeter. No hostile presence confirmed. Nancy on site. Requesting guidance on relic and extraction. Over."

The comms crackles again, a burst of static before Dave speaks. "Standby."

The wait drags, every second a calculation. Numerous variables. Too many moving parts. The Osprey is in final approach, rotors chopping through the dust. The countdown closes in.

A sharp breath, then Dave's voice returns. "S3, relic moves with you. Non-negotiable. No risk of compromise. Nancy boards the Osprey under GSS directive. "Green light. Execute. Over." The finality locked inside three clipped words.

The mic clicks in response. "Copy all, GSS. Relic secured. Nancy gets on board. Proceeding to exfil now. Out." The call cuts, sealing the next phase.

Nancy eases forward, breaking the formation, tension carved into a rigid posture. Breath comes measured, a stillness that isn't calm but control.

A question lingers, unspoken. A single head tilt answers it, a silent contract signed in the space between breaths. The final pieces fall into place. The relic stays with us. The subsequent move dictates the outcome. The war doesn't wait.

A quiet vibration rolls through the ground, a distant hum building into a deep, rhythmic pulse. The Osprey emerges over the horizon, the twin rotors carving through the sky, a dark silhouette against the fading light. Dust spirals beneath the approach, the pressure shift sending ripples through the terrain. The aircraft holds steady, banking in a slow arc before transitioning from horizontal to vertical flight.

The ramp lowers as the landing gear compresses on the uneven dirt, a metallic frame that is a lifeline between this battleground and extraction. Heat from the motors distorts the moving air, and the scent of scorched earth mixes with oil and exhaust. The crew inside signals readiness, but no words cut through the roar of spinning blades.

Engines snarl, the vibrations rolling through the steel frames of the ATVs as the convoy surges forward. Tyres bite deep into loose gravel, kicking up thick dust clouds as the Osprey's rear door looms ahead.

Rotors carve through the sky, tearing turbulence and throwing spirals of grit and heat in every direction. The aircraft holds its position, straining against gravity and vibrating with the strain of staying still. Time evaporates fast—exfil windows shrink faster. A minute too long on the deck turns departure into a funeral.

The first ATV lunges into the Osprey, suspension flexing under the sudden incline. The ramp flexes, a metallic creak cutting through the noise as the ATV lurches into the bay. A sharp turn angles the ATVs into their designated stowage location. Lucy swings out of the driver's seat, securing the straps with quick, practised movements, locking the transport in place.

A signal from the crew sends the second ATV forward. The aircraft's frame shudders beneath the stress as the vehicle drives inside, the tyres grasping the metal surface. The suspension compresses as it crosses into the hold, the added burden of the relic pressing deep into the shocks.

The webbing belts holding the ATV groan, but the load stays tight. Derek kills the engine, stepping out, hands moving fast to double-check the security of the relic — no room for error. A single shift in-flight might turn an exfil into a disaster.

Tyres claw at the ramp, traction battling gravity — steel protests as the chassis bucks under the sudden incline. A final burst of acceleration throws the ATV forward, landing hard on reinforced plating. Simon and I move without hesitation, securing restraints with sharp, precise movements.

Weapons remain shouldered, barrels tracking the ridgeline as boots hit the aircraft deck. Nancy steps through the threshold, rigid, jaw tight. Whatever runs through Nancy's mind stays buried beneath a mask of control.

Nancy's stance stiffens, shoulders angled away from the relic, tension wiring through the space separating the two. One enigma contained in human form, the other locked inside an unyielding shell — two dangerous unknowns, both secured in the hold.

A metallic hiss slices through the cargo bay, hydraulics flexing as the ramp rises. Steel clamps bite down, cutting off the outside world. The air thickens with the seal's finality, a metal box of machinery, weapons, and unfinished missions.

The Australian Outback disappears, swallowed by thick layers of reinforced aluminium. A sudden lurch jolts through the airframe as the Osprey breaks from the ground. The engines push against gravity as the aircraft claws toward altitude. The gut pulls tight with the force of ascent, the deck vibrating beneath heavy boots.

Darwin lies ahead. The UK beyond that.

Chapter Twenty-Nine — Debrief

A low vibration hums through the deck, rising from the Osprey's frame like a heartbeat. Twin rotors thrum overhead, steady and unforgiving. The sound drills in, reminding me the mission isn't over until we're on British soil.

The aircraft banks hard. My body shifts with the tilt as the engines rotate, from horizontal to vertical. From the cockpit, instrument lights flicker, casting sharp shadows across the bulkheads.

No one relaxes, because we all know one thing—nothing's safe until we arrive home. And right now, home feels a long way off.

Across the dimly lit bay, bodies slump against harnesses, muscles slack but ready. The team sinks into exhaustion, the kind that settles deep in the bones, beyond repair with a single night's rest.

Sweat clings to skin, the scent of gunpowder and desert heat still woven into gear and fatigues. No one speaks. The silence holds weight, not awkward, not strained—just the aftermath of people who have pushed themselves to the edge and survived.

Leaning back against the bulkhead, I scan the team. Simon's forearms press down, shoulders squared, taking an immovable stance in a shifting world. A breath flows in, steady and forced into even control. The steel beneath the boots carries more than mere movement.

Pressure spreads, silent calculations stacking, and every shift is laden with intent. The air above remains still, yet beneath the surface, decisions sharpen, poised to carve their path into whatever comes.

Metal presses against the back of Derek's head, cool and unforgiving. Muscles stay locked beneath the skin, a quiet war raging where flesh meets instinct. The body craves rest. The mind refuses.

Calloused fingers curl, tracing ridges along worn hands, each groove a reminder of fights that never fade. Scars map across knuckles, reminders of past engagements. The barrel points down, steady, as if pausing for the next threat to step forward.

A rifle lies across Lucy's lap, grip relaxed yet poised, the weight borne by weary muscles. One shoulder shifts slow and heavy. It's not weakness; it's history pushing back, an ache forged in battle. Each shot, every recoil, remains etched beneath the surface. That motion communicates more than words ever can.

A shadow anchors Nancy in place, deeper than fatigue. Silent and unmoving, she appears locked within a calculation no one else follows. Instinct honed by the past shapes the present like a puzzle. Movements flow from recollection, deliberate and exact, built from encounters burned into the bones. Somewhere, the answer exists, waiting, sealed inside scars.

My glance across the team reads exhaustion in every posture, relief in the tension that lingers, but doesn't strangle. The mission edges toward the end, but reality is more substantial than victory. The war doesn't stop because this fight is over. Another one waits, just beyond the edge of vision.

The short flight goes by fast, and soon, the Osprey's rear ramp drops with a metallic clang. A sudden burst of light cuts through the dim interior. The engines hold at a steady whine, vibrations thrumming through the deck.

Outside, floodlights cast long shadows over the expanse of concrete. A towering hangar looms 100 metres away. The massive doors part just enough to reveal the sleek frame of the GSS company jet, waiting under heavy security.

Dust clings to skin, the last remnants of battle trailing as the sprint toward the endex unfolds. Gunfire fades, replaced by the roar of approaching transport. The shift between war and escape never offers clean lines, only a blur of movement and consequence.

One signal from the ground crew triggers the descent, bodies threading down the ramp in seamless synchronisation. Footsteps slap against metal, the impact swallowed by the quiet thrum of engines.

Rifles stay secured but never abandoned, each hand a breath away from action. The relic sits wrapped, a silent force pulsing beneath reinforced fabric, an object far too valuable to trust to chance.

A welcoming glare spills from floodlights, cutting through the hangar's opening. The cool breeze clashes with the lingering heat of the Outback, sending a shiver down sweat-soaked fatigues. Boots scuff on concrete, the weight of exhaustion dragging behind every step.

Inside the hangar, a cavernous expanse stretches ahead. Steel ribs arch high overhead, their skeletal frames crisscrossed with thick support beams. Above, lights blaze in sharp white strips, casting elongated shadows across the floor. The distant hum of a generator thrums through the walls, just about masking the echo of voices bouncing off the ceiling.

Stacks of equipment crates line the perimeter, their surfaces scuffed, marked with faded stencils of serial numbers and unit designations. A workbench sits cluttered with half-empty medical kits, discarded bandages, and red-streaked gauze, the aftermath of hurried treatment.

A woman steps forward, field dressing in hand. Movements are brisk and practised. The eyes of someone who has seen battlefield wounds too often scan the team, calculating injuries before words are exchanged.

A medic crouches beside Derek, hands moving with care as blood-darkened fabric peels away from the torn flesh. The wound gapes, ragged at the edges where shrapnel bit deep. A swab presses against raw skin, the sting sharp.

"Might have been worse," the medic mutters.

Derek grunts, cutting through exhaustion. "Luck's not what got me here." The man doesn't argue, simply pulls the bandage tighter, sealing the gash with firm pressure.

"Stop fucking moaning, anyone would think you've been shot," Simon says, half chuckling to himself.

"Do one, donkey walloper. At least I have damage, unlike that insect bite on your shoulder," Derek replies.

Simon leans against a crate, fingers digging into the wood, grip unsteady yet resolute. Crimson blood seeps through the fabric, a relentless flow. A red stain spreads, slow but steady.

The woman examines the wound, expression inscrutable. "Straight through. No fragments. Messy, but not fatal."

Simon exhales, a breath that lacks relief, just acknowledgement. "Yeah, tell that to my gear! Fucking ruined my best jacket."

A strip of gauze presses firm against the torn flesh. Hands move fast, tightening a field dressing to stop the bleeding.

A glimmer of amusement flickers behind the meticulous motion, the precision of someone who's performed this task countless times.

A second woman approaches with a fresh kit, checking the rest of us. A glance between Lucy and George confirms their injuries are minor — scrapes and bruises, nothing that slows the pair down.

Both sit on metal chairs, letting the medics carry out any necessary treatment without complaint, their eyes scanning the hangar like the fight isn't over.

The sharp tug of alcohol wipes over my bare skin snaps my focus back. The medic working on me doesn't bother easing the sting, scrubbing congealed blood from my knuckles where Viktor's teeth and bone met my fist.

"From the appearance, you lost the scrap, or should I check the other guy?" The medic's words are laced with humour, but the grip remains taught, with the bandage wrapping tight.

A steady pull tightens against split epidermis. Scars vanish beneath a quick pass of gauze, clearing debris from jagged flesh. A thin adhesive strip clamps the wound shut, sealing the tear without ceremony.

Firm and unrelenting pressure follows, ensuring the patch holds. The hands working don't hesitate, don't fumble, just do what's necessary.

"Try not to pick another fight," the man says.

A grunt replaces the answer. No point explaining what happened in that room. The bruises lining my ribs, the swelling along my jaw — Viktor left a mark, but nothing that matters now.

George snorts, arms crossed. "Yeah, wish you luck with that."

The treatment reminds us that this pause is temporary. The relic sits secured in the hold. The war doesn't end here; it just shifts direction.

A moment extends, breaths evening out, thoughts adjusting. The burden of survival embeds in muscle and bone, as the body resists rest while adrenaline persists.

A hum vibrates through the steel floor, the distant engines of the GSS jet starting up beyond the hangar doors. Fluorescent lights cast long, sterile shadows across the concrete, reflecting off discarded gauze, empty water bottles, and bloodstained fatigues. The air carries the sharp tang of fuel, antiseptic, and sweat, mixing into something stale that sticks.

Crates and benches drag into a rough circle, an unspoken agreement that exhaustion wins this round. Backs press against wooden boxes, limbs slack, breaths measured. The kind of fatigue that doesn't fade but anchors into every muscle.

Boots scuff the floor, weapons rest within reach, and silence stretches between us — not awkward, not strained, just the type that follows too many battles and too few words.

The bandage on Simon's shoulder peeks through a torn sleeve, stained dark at the edges; the kind of wound that speaks louder than the man. He breaks the quiet like a squeezed trigger.

"Hell of a trip. Next time, I vote for a job that doesn't involve getting shot," Simon mutters.

Derek braces against a supply case, hands clamped over fresh stitches stretched tight along the bicep. "Yeah? Good luck with that," he says, nodding toward the red-soaked wrap. "That's not the way this game plays out. Never did. Never will. Vegas gives better odds."

Lucy leans back into a crate, grip taut around the sling. Fingers move like they're reading Braille carved into fate. The drone of the engine eats half her words, but the message cuts clean.

"Never does. And won't. Still better than date night with George."

A dry snort drifts from the far side. George rolls his shoulder, a slow breath escaping between clenched teeth. "Date night with me ends the same way — blood, bruises, and nobody calling in the morning."

Simon chuckles through a wince. "Yeah, but at least your meals come hot. MREs don't scream when they're overcooked."

Derek huffs, settling deeper into the case. "We all scream eventually. Just depends who's left to hear it."

A shared silence follows, not heavy, not light—just real; laced with scars and shaped by fire. The kind of silence earned the hard way.

Scar tissue stretches, old damage never forgotten. "Sergei will no doubt be moving in silence, waiting, watching from whatever hole keeps the man breathing. If he finds out the truth of who killed his boss, he will no doubt come looking for Natasha or, even better, us. Need to put this man down!"

George says after sipping on a fresh brew.

Simon adjusts, keeping torn flesh from screaming. "If Sergei's got sense, the man will be running now, full tilt, no stops. If not, he's circling back, and that's worse."

"Won't be long before we have to put that bastard in the dirt," replies George.

Derek exhales through clenched teeth, rubbing grit from an eye. "Everyone's clocked on that we're still knee-deep in this one, right? Save the war stories for the next job; the next bloody mess."

Simon smirks. "Says the green numpty who got clipped first."

"Yeah, at least I didn't take a round like a medieval knight charging a machine gun nest," Derek adds, gesturing toward Simon's shoulder.

Lucy's lips part, voice edged with something close to a smirk, but not quite. A humour carved from experience.

"Must be something in your training. The more rounds flying, the happier you seem. Thrill-seekers, the whole fucking lot of you."

"It's called 'leading from the front,' Spook," Simon huffs.

"That's what happens when you catch bullets instead of dodging them," George replies, a quick grin splitting through the words.

Simon brushes aside concern with an impatient sweep of scarred fingers. "Whatever. Survival counts. Nothing else matters."

"Just about," Lucy replies.

Static clings to the air, sharp as fractured bone, thick between us. No one speaks for a while. Blood crusts on our gear, dried into maps of violence and unfinished business. The kind that sticks long after the fight.

"Viktor deserved worse," Derek mutters, voice slicing through the silence. "One shot, clean through the temple, should've closed this. Natasha stole that from us."

Simon shifts, eyeing Lucy. "Would you have done anything different? Retrieval over revenge?"

"No hesitation," Lucy fires back, cold and sharp. "Hole through bone. Brain scattered. Silence absolute. One trigger. Job done."

I nod, locking eyes with her. "I should've been the one to drop Viktor. No mess. Just clean justice."

George smirks without humour. "Clean justice? That's cute. Thought we left fantasies back in selection."

"Doesn't mean I don't hate that Natasha beat me to it," I say. "Billy deserved better. Viktor earned worse — a slow rot. Something poetic. Maybe a rusty blade and a full week to think about it."

Derek snorts. "Rusty? That's generous. I was thinking dental tools and sandpaper."

"Combat doesn't deal in fairness," I add, low. "It just ends things. No refunds. No closure."

Simon stretches, then winces. "Closure's overrated anyway. Can't spend it, can't drink it. Can't even wipe your arse with it."

George lifts an eyebrow. "Speak for yourself. I'd wipe mine with Viktor's obituary."

Laughter stirs, dry and broken, the kind that comes after too much and never enough.

Simon shifts, wincing from the shoulder wound. "Alright, enough of this emotional bollocks. Let's clamber on that aircraft before someone starts writing poetry."

Derek adjusts the radio. A burst of static punches through the quiet, followed by a clipped voice on the other end.

"GSS jet, exfil in five. Final boarding."

A sharp hiss escapes through gritted teeth, pain flaring underneath bloodied cloth. Simon rises, fresh crimson bandages staining with movement. "At last," Simon growls.

"Think we'll avoid trouble until we reach home soil?" asks George, voice laced with mock hope.

Lucy's lips flatten, tone flat as a firing line. "Safe airborne — for now. Unless Sergei's branching into ground-to-air missiles with a side hustle in skydiving ambushes."

George smirks. "Yeah, but at least we eat for free. Thank fuck for small mercies. Nothing says five-star cuisine like rehydrated beef pretending to be an army chuck-in."

Derek chuckles. "If this is like the last meal, might as well chew dirt and call it dinner. At least dirt doesn't come vacuum-sealed with disappointment."

George shrugs. "Better than eating sand in the Outback. That stuff grits between your teeth and judges your life choices."

Simon sighs, rubbing his temple. "You green numpties have the lowest standards."

A heavy hand slaps Simon's shoulder. Bruised muscle tenses under the load. Derek's grin spreads like a bruise.

"Still rescuing your sorry arse from disaster — some things don't evolve. Like you."

Simon mutters, "One day, I'm going to fake a leg injury and make you carry me."

"Won't be the first time," Derek fires back.

George snorts. "Let's move before more shit finds us — or before Simon starts crying about his knees again."

Minutes later, steps strike the concrete in unison, bodies driven beyond their limits, nerves stretched thin. The relic remains locked inside the aircraft's hold, untouched and undisturbed. A change of location propels the mission forward, the next objective looming closer, heavier than the last.

Onboard, a vibration hums through the cabin, the steady rhythm of the private jet's engines pressing into my bones. The air carries a mix of lavender and the sharp tang of antiseptic from the quick field patch-ups.

As I glance around, exhaustion sinks in deep, dragging at my limbs and pulling at my mind. The fight lingers — always does.

Lucy leans back in the leather seat, boots braced against the chair in front. Across the aisle, Simon slumps, head tilted to one side, a bandaged shoulder's steady rise and fall, counting each breath.

Sprawled out in a seat across the aisle, Derek's expression is blank, eyes shut. To my left, George slouches forward, forehead resting on folded arms, fingers twitching, as though he's still grasping a weapon. I sit in silence, taking everything in, knowing rest is a luxury we seldom find.

Nancy sits up in a rigid posture, pupils unwavering, eyes locked upon images of some documentary that flashes in repeated cycles — fragmented loyalties, shifting battles, warfare remixed in streams across fractured lands.

Lucy lifts a hand, signalling the attendant. "Southern Comfort. Neat, please."

Simon cracks an eye open, smirking. "Starting early?"

Lucy doesn't turn. "Late."

Derek shifts, cracking knuckles. "You spooks have the worst coping mechanisms."

Fingers tighten around the crystal glass, amber liquid catching sharp glints from the overhead lights. Ice rattles against curved walls as the beaker tilts. "Confident words, considering you sleep one breath from rolling clear of an ambush," Lucy replies.

Quiet laughter echoes through gritted teeth, injured shoulder shifting beneath fresh crimson seeping through frayed bandages. Simon's mouth twists, amusement edged with suppressed agony. "Like you fucking lot ever set standards for stable minds."

George's rough fingertips scrape across a tight jawline, stubble rasping under weary pressure. "One hour, that's all, before GSS tries to find another burning wreck to throw us into."

Derek exhales, "Bet you two weeks and we're back in the shit."

Lucy swirls the whisky, knocking the rest back. "Five days."

Simon huffs. "Optimistic. Who says Guardian Security Services will employ us again?"

Nancy breaks her silence, words edged with something unreadable. "Any of you even remember life outside a battlefield?"

"Nope," I reply with a smile. Looking around the aircraft, Nancy receives four more shaking heads.

Outside, connections lock, fuel channels open, and volatile liquid floods into waiting reservoirs. Pilots strap in, their movements sharp and methodical, checking instruments under sterile cabin light. A brief exchange over comms, a switch thrown, permission granted, the beast awake once more.

At the end of the runway, a violent thrust pushes the aircraft into the sky, lifting its wheels free of the ground. Darkness thickens beyond the windows. Another run into the unknown, another fragment of time slips through clenched fists.

After a change of aircraft at a nearby airport, the Osprey drops fast, the landing gear taking the weight with a controlled jolt. The whine of hydraulics follows as the ramp lowers.

The cold British air slices through the cargo bay, thick with the scent of damp ground and jet fuel. Floodlights stretch long shadows across the GSS airstrip, illuminating a waiting vehicle, engine idling, ready to take what we brought back.

A figure stands near the hangar, hands tucked into jacket pockets, watching. A man who understands the job doesn't end with wheels touching down. I spot Dave's gaze sweeping over weary faces, assessing wounds, calculating strategies for actions not yet whispered aloud.

Boots hit the ramp, fatigue dragging at the muscles, but discipline keeping movements sharp. Nancy exits last, shoulders squared, eyes locked forward, carrying the weight that doesn't lift with distance.

Steps crunch as I walk toward Dave. My palm is open, ready to shake hands, in silent acknowledgement of a mission completed.

"How did things go?" Dave asks, voice unhurried, the words more habit than curiosity.

Data streams have cross-secured channels. Raw intel stacks up in Dave's office. The real debrief comes later.

My grip tightens, and voices flatten in mutual understanding. "Messy," I say.

"Always are," Dave replies.

My glance shifts to the transport team already securing the ATVs. The relic disappears beneath reinforced tarps, swallowed by the hangar. 'Someone else's problem now,' I think to myself.

Dave diverts focus to Nancy, tone sharpened with subtle caution hidden behind controlled tones. "What about Nancy? Any issues?"

Quick assessment darts across Nancy's rigid frame, seeking tremors or cracks that threaten.

"Cooperative enough—assisted extraction at the exfil site. Broome Explorers pushing hard to display the relic at their bloody museum," I reply.

"Sounds about right. Debrief in 10," comes Dave's response.

"OK," knowing from experience that debriefing straight away gets the best result and puts an end to any mission, giving you time to relax.

Two women come forward at Dave's silent gesture, boots scraping over gravel-strewn concrete. Nancy moves forward, meeting their approach with calculated certainty. Glances exchanged, unreadable intent crackling between guarded faces.

Harness bites deep, carving a trench through George's shoulder, flesh bruising beneath the tension. Bergen hauls on strained muscle, dragging joints into a punishing alignment.

"If GSS wants us to sort out yet another mess, do you reckon they'll let us have a moment's respite before unloading the next heap of trouble?" A humourless smirk tugs at George's lips as he speaks.

Heading toward the briefing room, without looking back, Lucy throws the order out, already pushing forward, strides eating up the distance. "Shift your arses. Unless the plan is to suffer through another one of Dave's motivational bollocks."

Derek groans, fingers pressing against torn fabric stretched over bruised muscle. "Nah, I think Dave likes us too much for that."

Simon grins. "Or he's worried we'll all die of boredom."

"Don't give Dave fucking ideas," says George, walking inside.

Rhythmic impacts roll through the concrete, the march of bodies recalibrating from combat to protocol. Sweat lingers, adrenaline dulls, but discipline locks movement into precision. A debrief looms, reports wait, and a transition from gunfire to paperwork.

The briefing room hums with the buzz of the overhead fluorescents, their stark light bouncing off white walls and steel fixtures. The air carries the scent of stale coffee. The team settles into their seats, shifting against stiff joints and aching muscles.

Dave enters 10 minutes later and sits at the head of the conference table. A glance passes between us, a silent cue for me to begin.

"Mission objectives achieved," I say, leaning forward, fingertips pressed on the worn surface of the table. "The relic is secured. Viktor eliminated." The words seem hollow on my tongue, stripped of satisfaction, just cold facts marking another bloody line crossed off the list.

Simon exhales, arms locked tight, eyes narrowed. "If you can call one shot to the head 'eliminated'."

Lucy shakes her head, "What, you reckon Viktor's getting back up? Eliminated means eliminated, you fucking idiot."

George scoffs, eyes dark and distant. "Still a waste. The bastard deserved worse."

Derek shifts, jaw clenched, one hand resting on a bandaged arm. "Sergei's still a danger. That's our problem now."

"Natasha?" Dave asks, gaze fixed on me, searching for clarification.

I draw in a slow breath, steadying myself before answering. "Natasha walked. Took out Viktor herself. Said something about Viktor executing her parents." The brief silence that follows hangs heavy. I glance around the room, eyes meeting everyone in turn. "I played the long game with Natasha. Plenty of Russians still nursing grudges would love to settle the score if Natasha becomes an issue. Viktor's old cartel won't stay quiet—not if Natasha decides to pull the strings. A lot of people would pay decent money to find out who ended Viktor."

Dave remains silent, arguments serve no purpose. Judgments are already made, and nothing will change that. A call ripped from reflex, shaped in the instant where instinct collides with consequence. Some decisions lock into place when they're called, unshakable, untouched by doubt or regret.

Silence grips the room again, thicker now, heavy with the bitter, familiar weight of loss. None of us needs to speak the names of those who didn't return from Heinrichsberg. Their ghosts are here, pressing against the walls, settling into the spaces between our breaths.

A rough swallow pushes through Lucy's clenched throat, breath measured, deliberate. "Billy wouldn't have given Viktor the chance to walk."

George shifts forward, hands clasped. "Billy would have wanted to be the one pulling the trigger."

Simon nods once. "We remember. That's what matters."

An unbroken hush keeps the room in place; no shifting limbs and no glances cast aside. Unfinished thoughts press into the silence—unspoken, heavy, something shared yet withheld—waiting for the first to shatter the unrelenting quiet.

Dave breaks the stillness, "Assessment?"

"The operation held. The execution remained tight. A few near misses occurred, but nothing that altered the outcome. Viktor's defences carried gaps, intel sat thinner than expected. Sergei played deeper than forecasted. Heinrichsberg paid for that oversight."

Derek adjusts, rolling one shoulder as if dislodging unseen weight, voice sharp. "Ambush at exfil. Somehow, Sergei read the grid and placed the kill zone in advance. Are you sure you took out the informer?"

Simon's fingers press once against the surface, rhythm absent. Words land without space for doubt: "Strike first. Cut the head before the snake bites."

"So, Sergei remains a loose end," Dave states, gaze locked on the unspoken consequences.

"Yes. Unfinished assignments exact a toll." The comment lingering between steady breaths. "I compiled a mission debrief on the flight, which goes into more depth on everything," I say, sliding the folder over the table to Dave.

Dave's voice stays firm, offering nothing beyond necessity. "Solid work, Steve. The team held and recovered Petrov and the relic. Take whatever rest you need." A quick shift of attention toward the door. "Briefing ends here."

After saying goodbye to Dave, we head to the vehicles in the underground car park. The scent of rubber and exhaust is thick in the enclosed space.

Simon slides into the driver's seat of the first vehicle, fingers drumming on the steering wheel. "Wonder if we will be shot at on the way out. Almost seems wrong not to be."

Derek's smirk lingers, a glint of amusement behind narrowed eyes. "Last thing we need is your mouth summoning trouble, idiot."

A hard swing of the wheel lines up the second, the high beams flooding the abandoned parking area. A sharp turn, tyres scraping over grit, the motor cutting to an idle. Lucy's voice carries over the hum.

"Keep moaning about quiet roads, and I'll make sure bullets start flying."

I exhale through my nose, adjusting my seat. "Let's move."

With Lucy and me in the lead car, Simon George and Derek following, tyres grind over asphalt, the convoy slicing through the daylight. Buildings thin, neon signs swallowed by the dark. No alarms, no last-minute radio calls, no engine growls that don't belong.

The road to the ferry terminal stretches before us, the midday sun glaring off the tarmac. The city hums around us, pedestrians weaving between slow-moving traffic, and the steady rumble of engines fills the air.

The checkpoint appears ahead, a worker in high-vis motioning us forward, clipboard tucked under one arm. The salt tang of the Solent carries on the breeze, cutting through the lingering scent of petrol and hot asphalt as vehicles roll onto the upper deck.

Vans and compact cars squeeze into tight lanes, deckhands waving drivers into position with sharp, practised movements. A deckhand in red overalls directs us to the right, a gloved hand tapping on the side of Simon's car.

Axles grind against the incline, suspension shuddering as the convoy rumbles into the cavernous interior. Underfoot, vibrations pulse through welded beams as the vessel shifts, a reminder of the restless current below the hull.

Lucy eases our vehicle to a halt behind Simon's, fingers loose on the wheel, posture unchanged. Out of habit, I scan the other cars, which reveal nothing out of place—no lingering threats.

Our footsteps clatter up the metal staircase as we move to the passenger lounge. Ten minutes later, the ferry lurches, pulling away from the dock. The mainland shrinks behind us, the buildings blurring into a jagged line of concrete and glass.

Sunlight bounces off the sea, creating a bright glare that slices across the deck's bleached metal railing. Salt clings thick, coating dry lips and stiff fabric. Simon stands motionless, arms crossed over his chest, staring into the endless blue.

"Who's putting money on Sergei coming for round two?"

Derek breathes in, head tilting just enough to dismiss the thought. "No bets. We all recognise the waiting game."

My fingers grip the steel of a flask pulled from inside my jacket, cap turning, the scent of alcohol lingering, sharp against stale air.

"Sergei gets handled when the time comes," I reply.

A family huddles near the bow, their laughter swallowed by the wind. A businessman mutters into a phone, pacing tight circles by the windows. Life carries on, oblivious to the ghosts trailing behind us.

The constant waves crash against the hull. Each movement presses more intense than before, like the ocean trying one's patience. The crossing seems prolonged, time stretched thinner over already frayed nerves.

In the distance, the island emerges from the sea — lush hills, grouped houses, a scene straight out of a postcard. The voice in the ceiling interrupts conversation. It stumbles with static, signalling the imminent arrival on the island.

Once more, vibrations roll through the deck. Doors crash shut, engines cough before surging to life, mechanical growls filling the space. Deckhands make hurried gestures towards drivers as tyres grind against worn metal heading down the ramp, which groans under the weight.

Our two vehicles roll off, wheels crunching over gritted tarmac, thick with exhaust fumes and sea air. The familiar road stretches through winding coastal lanes of the Isle of Wight, sunlight flickering between overhanging branches as we drive to Shanklin.

Back in the park, my home comes into view through the trees ahead, still standing untouched—windows dark, curtains drawn tight, no signs of forced entry or interference. I slow the vehicle and scan the area, looking for even the slightest hint of anything out of place.

After parking, we exit the vehicles. A quick nod to the team, and we split and take different approaches, advancing towards the lodge. Lucy moves around the far side, while Simon and George fan out, checking the shadows at the rear. Derek covers from a slight elevation, alert to threats hidden among the trees.

My boots crunch on the loose gravel path, every step measured. Approaching the front entrance, I glance over the doorway—nothing disturbed, no footprints marring the dirt, no drag marks or unusual patterns in the grass.

A slow sweep confirms nothing moved. Strands of hair rest undisturbed across the threshold, brittle and silent. A slip of paper, folded razor-thin, remains untouched between the hinges, confirming no sign of an entry.

After the perimeter sweeps, we regroup by the steps, forming a loose arc near the door. A final scan finds no threats lurking in the corners. A flick of fingers signals everyone to proceed inside, with muscle memory dictating the angles.

An interior check leaves nothing to chance—rooms are cleared one at a time, and every hiding place is scrutinised. Nothing is disturbed; no signs of intrusion. The lodge is as we left it.

Satisfied, I sling my Bergen onto the spare room bed before returning to the living area, opening heavy curtains and cracking the window open to release the stale air. The rest of the team does the same, boots thumping against wooden floors, kit dumped on beds or chairs, exhaustion evident in their movements.

I glance at the clock—it has been only 20 minutes since we stepped inside. I turn back to face the others, their eyes meeting mine with weary resignation.

"There is no avoiding it. One task remains unfinished. A loose end still dangling," I say.

"Would that be the boozer?" Derek asks, knowing the answer.

"Correct," I reply.

Lucy tosses gear on the couch, stretching out her arms. "We're already late."

George clamps an arm around Simon's shoulder, pulling him toward the exit with a firm yank. "The donkey walloper's buying. Yep. We remember you offered to buy the drinks back in Viktor's command centre."

The pub's warmth hits like a wall, the air thick with the scent of spilt beer and wood smoke. The soft murmur of conversation hums beneath the clatter of glasses, the noise that drowns out memories no one wants to hold onto.

A bar towel twists between fingers, dark smudges spreading across the fabric. Gary's measured glance sweeps the room, settling on me.

"About bloody time you lot showed up."

I tilt my head. "Miss us, did you?"

Leaning against the counter, Gary glances around to ensure no nosey bugger is listening before saying, "I made a few trips to the mainland, and checked in on your kids. They're safe."

A knot deep in the ribs eases, the kind that battle never unwinds. Across the space, a glance—sharp, deliberate—exchanges more than gratitude.

"Cheers, mate, we owe you," I reply.

"Now we have the info, the girls and Hadley are OK, how about some drinks?" Simon says, slapping money down next to Gary.

Gary smirks. "Like you have to ask."

Foam overflows from the rim as glasses thud against the worn wooden counter, the sound softened by the heaviness of the previous mission.

The pub hums with chatter, but the world outside may as well not exist. The first gulp slides down raw throats, carving a path through exhaustion and scouring away the grit of past hours. The flavour is sharp and grounding.

A forearm scrapes dry foam from cracked lips, skin dragging, thirst refusing to settle. The glass drops, striking the table.

"Bloody hell. Either that's a miracle pour, or we've been chewing sand too long," announces Simon.

A gentle twist moves the liquid along the edge of the glass.

"Both," Derek replies in a relaxed voice.

Another swallow alleviates my fatigue, another layer buried beneath the sharpness of bitter hops. The familiar burn settles deep, unwinding something that's been knotted too tight.

"Are we talking about it, or pretending nothing happened?" Derek says, after gulping down a mouthful of beer.

George lifted his drink a few inches above the table's surface, gaze intense and unwavering. With a hint of solemnity in his voice, "To Billy."

A silence falls over us, stretching and painful, punctuated only by the quiet scrape of glasses being raised. Our tribute lands, a muted collision, brief yet enough. Meaning threads through the motion, past unspoken names and unburied grief. It is a ritual, silent but absolute, bound in everything unsaid. The absence remains, carved deep.

Simon exhales, rubbing the left shoulder, fresh stitches pulling taut beneath the shirt. "Might've been worse. At least no one lost a limb. We all held our own. Even the green numpties and the spook."

I shake my head, smirking. "Oh, piss off, donkey walloper."

A slow curve pulls at Lucy's mouth, the kind that doesn't quite reach the eyes. Fingers release the glass, the base tapping against the wood like a silent detonation.

"Funny. You didn't call me that when I dragged your sorry arse out of the dirt."

George leans back, groaning as vertebrae crack like dry twigs. "If you sentimental fuckers start getting misty-eyed, I'm walking straight into the Solent with a rock tied to my bollocks."

Simon waves a lazy hand, eyes half-closed. "Crack on then, mate. I'll write the eulogy: 'Died as he lived—complaining'."

Derek raises his bottle. "To George. More salt than sense."

George lifts his middle finger. "To Derek. More village idiot than brains."

Laughter erupts—sudden, raw, sharp. It cuts through the weight like a bayonet through fabric. The kind of sound that says we're still alive.

The battle still clings—bruises, cuts, haunted flashes buried behind half-lidded eyes. But for now, combat steps aside, replaced by beer, bitter banter, and the wreckage we wear like a badge stitched from hell.

This? This is what survival looks like. Ugly. Loud. Ours.

Derek gestures for another round, eyes flicking to the bar. "Think Gary'll let us sleep here?"

Lucy lifts an eyebrow. "Think Gary's about to kick us out."

Gary looms over the team, arms folded, before saying, "You lot drinking or decorating the bloody furniture?"

Simon grins, "Drinking."

A fresh pour rolls smooth into the glass, the liquid swirling and settling in a deep amber pool. The pint lands firm, fingers releasing without ceremony.

Gary standing close by, head tilting just enough to send the challenge across, "Then down the bloody stuff."

Laughter grates through dry throats, rough voices carving space between the walls. Talk skims the surface — no mention of the next op, no whispers of unfinished business. Just the warmth of the beer, and the brief illusion of normal.

Derek raises a drink. "To Billy."

"To Billy," comes the reply from everyone.

Pints are raised, a silent tribute etched in the lack of sound. The silence conveys its verdict, a truth only to those who have endured combat and emerged injured understand. The impact hums through the surface, a statement heavier than words.

Lucy breaks through, voice unwavering, alcohol lacing but not softening. "Viktor should have suffered and begged for his life."

"No argument from me," replies George.

Simon glances at me, expression unreadable. "Would you have done anything different?"

Thought shoves back, holding the line, forcing restraint. The past waits for no man, never seeks permission to return. "Doesn't matter now," I say, after taking a mouthful of beer.

Derek signals for another round. "Means Sergei's next."

Gary pours without asking. "Sure, the bastard needs killing, and I've not met the man."

The night stretches, drinks pouring, voices rising, tension bleeding out in laughter and curses. The battle lingers in the bruises, aches, and stains not yet washed away. But for now, the combat can wait.

Gary kicks us out at about 11 o'clock, and we stagger back towards my place. Boots scuff across rough pavement through Shanklin High Street, exhaustion hanging off each step. Not long after, the door to the lodge swings shut behind us, locking the night away. Somehow, I even manage to find my pit and lie down next to Lucy.

Bodies hit whatever surface holds them, limbs slack, exhaustion swallowing the last remnants of control. Silence creeps in, broken only by the occasional shift of fabric, the deep, uneven breaths of those too drunk to care.

The following day, a dull ache pounds against the inside of my skull, a reminder of last night's poor decisions. Pushing up from the mattress is like an operation in itself. Every part of my body demands another hour of sleep, but my dry mouth and a splitting headache refuse to let this happen.

Feet hit the floor with more force than intended, the boards creaking under my weight. In the living room, the others remain sprawled in various states of unconsciousness, the room a mess of boots, jackets, and discarded kit bags.

Stepping through the carnage, I move toward the kitchen, keeping each step measured to avoid kicking anything over. The kettle flicks on with a loud, sharp click, the noise cutting through the quiet like a suppressed shot.

A rasp splits the silence—rough, dragged from somewhere deep. Cloth sticks to skin, heat trapped beneath layers soaked in effort. Every pull of muscle acts like hauling dead weight uphill through broken glass.

Arms lift slow, reaching up, joints locking mid-motion. Shoulders refuse to cooperate. Pain settles where strength used to reside. Breath comes thin. Nothing in the lungs wants to move.

"Morning, you ugly bastard. Do you fancy a brew?" The words grind out of my throat, cracked from sleep and worse. Fingers rake through hair. The skull behind it throbs like it took a hit.

Derek slumps forward, elbows to knees, spine curled. "Yes," the voice holds nothing but the echo of too many beers consumed.

Simon shifts, hands pressing hard into temples. A groan spills out, teeth clenched. "And me."

The first sip of coffee cuts through the lingering fog, the bitterness settling something deep in my chest. The house remains quiet, except for the occasional shuffle and the sound of the kettle boiling.

A blanket twists tight over Lucy, her breath steady beneath the fabric's rough weave. An arm drapes over her face, blocking out the morning light. George stirs on the couch, a single eye cracking open, scanning, then shutting again.

The second brew goes down smoother than the first, cutting through the last remnants of whatever hell the previous night left behind. The stomach twists, empty and demanding something solid.

"No food in the house," I say, draining my cup. "The café is not far from here, if anyone fancies breakfast."

A slight shift, just noticeable, strain rippling through shoulders. Silence holds, stretched tight, but no words follow. Simon holds both hands onto the side of his head, muscles twitching under the pressure.

A long, drawn-out breath escapes, voice flat. "Might be the only thing keeping me upright."

Legs drop from the couch, knees clicking as tension unwinds. A grunt, arms dragging toward worn laces. "Got to make an exit before the wife starts planning my funeral," says George, clambering off the sofa.

Simon stands, adjusting a Bergen with slow, careful movements. "Back to the mainland, we can grab some food onboard," muttering, more to himself than anyone else.

George clasps a hand on my shoulder, smirking through the exhaustion. "Try not to miss us."

The heat from another coffee sears down my throat, scorching away remnants of sleep. Stiff joints grind through routine, the promise of breakfast keeping me going.

A door slams hard, the sound cutting through the silence like a gunshot. Lucy steps back into the living room, bare feet brushing over cold flooring, gaze scanning the space. "Others clear out already?"

"Yeah."

The gut argues for rest, leaving the mess untouched, but discipline overrides instinct. A moment hangs sharp between this silence and the next mission's pull.

The time to clean and prepare our kit is now. With that, I pile all our equipment on the table, throwing dirty clothes at Lucy, standing by the washing machine.

By lunchtime, everything is done, and the equipment is repacked and stored in the spare room. I'm sitting down to a brew when the phone rings, cutting through the quiet.

Simon speaks without delay, "Dave called with a green light for more work. Bigger stakes, if we're in." Nothing offered sits untouched for long.

Lucy meets my gaze, expression already knowing. "That didn't take fucking long."

Glossary

Bergen	Backpack
Call Sign GD	George Dog
Call Sign S3	Steve 3(RGJ)
Call Sign TS	Tanky Simon
Chimp	Mind / Anger Management programme used in the treatment of PTSD
Klick	Kilometre
Dhobi Dust	Washing Powder
Donkey Walloper	Tank Driver
Egg Banjo	Egg Sandwich
Escaped Librarian	A term used in the treatment of PTSD
Exfil	Exfiltration/withdrawal
Grunt	Ground Reconnaissance Untrainable
Infill	Infiltration/insertion
LZ	Landing Zone
MRE	Meals Ready to Eat
Merc	Mercenary
Mickey	Cheap Wristwatch
OP	Observation Post
PAYG	Pay As You Go
Pit	Bed
PE4	Plastic Explosive No. 4
Polo Donkey	Horse/Donkey
RV	Rendezvous – Meeting Point
Shanks Pony	Walking
SLR	Self-Loading Rifle
Stag	Sentry Duty
Twenty	Location

For more information about our books and services, please visit

www.greencatbooks.com